The Traveler

The Dead World

By Tyler Kelley

Paperback ISBN: 978-1-7372708-0-5
Hardback ISBN: 978-1-7372708-4-3
Ebook ISBN: 978-1-7372708-1-2

Edited by Brian Paone
Cover by Adrian DKC

Tkelleywriting.com

Acknowledgments:

This project has been a decade in the making and over all of those years I have had the support of dozens of people from family and friends. There are just too many people to name. So many of you helped in both big, obvious ways and small, unnoticeable ways. Both mean so much to me and I wouldn't have gotten to this point without you all, so thank you.

May the Stars watch over you.

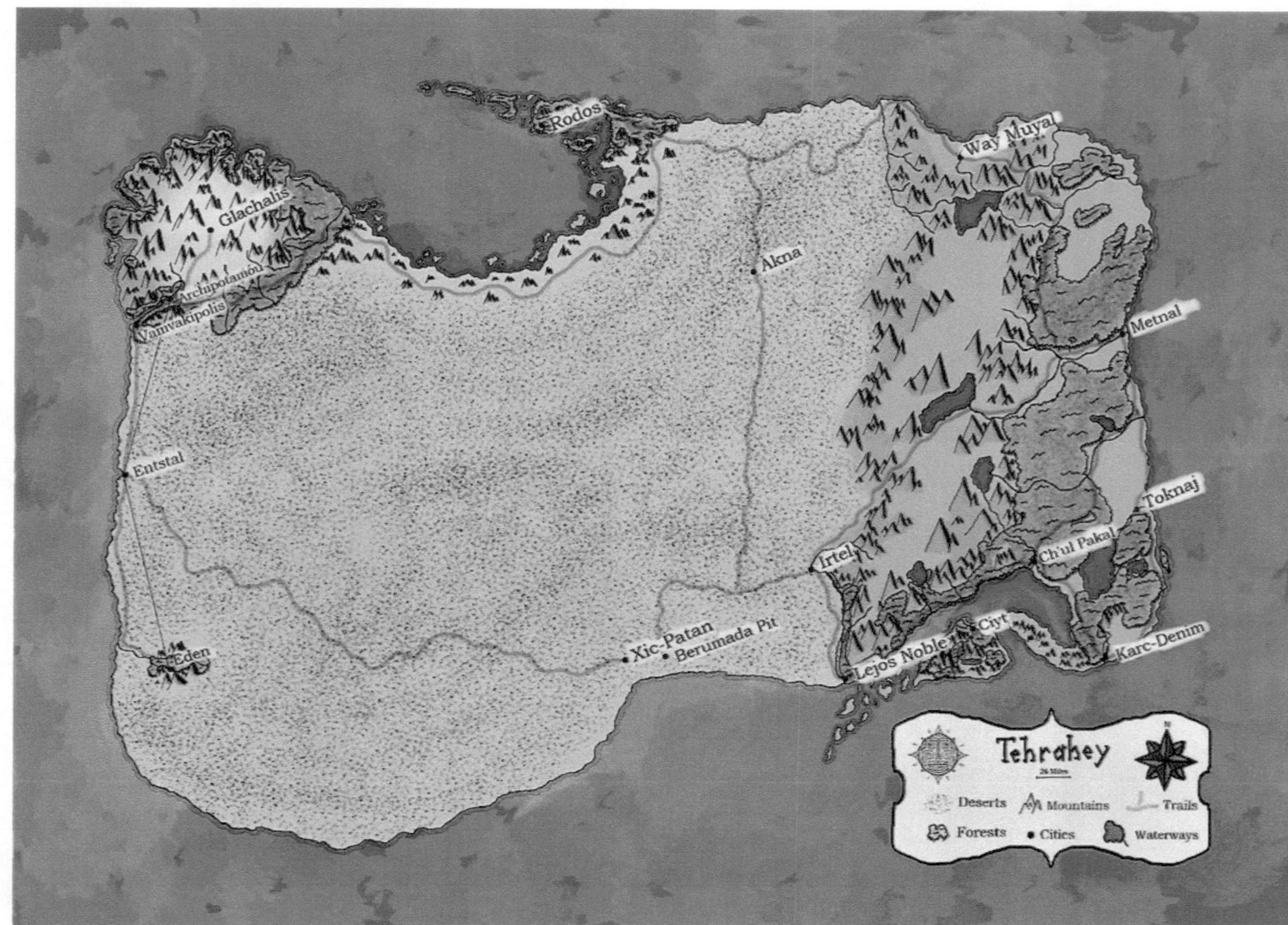

Rodos
Way Muyal
Glachalis
Archipotamou
Vamvakipolis
Akna
Metnal
Entstal
Toknaj
Irtel
Ch'ul Pakal
Xic-Patan
Berumada Pit
Ciyt
Lejos Noble
Karc-Denim
Eden
Tehrahey
26 Miles
Deserts
Mountains
Trails
Forests
Cities
Waterways

Prologue
-A Necessary Goodbye-

May 1, 1893 E.S.T.
2-12.10.19.4.13 T.S.T.
Entstal
Tehrahey

Tehrahey was not a world for precious things. The people of this dimension lacked even the most basic of human decencies taken for granted in other worlds. Tehraheyians did not have families and, therefore, did not care for others. They only looked out for themselves.

The great red sun glared onto the crumbling city of Entstal, capital of Western Tehrahey. Despite the immense heat of the encroaching Erima—a sand-dune desert covering most of the world—a few disheveled people wandered the streets, each person searching for just enough scraps to survive another day. I ignored them, and they ignored me. Sweat beaded and collected on my skin beneath my gray cloak, yet no matter how uncomfortable the fabric became, I refused to remove it and expose the burden I carried to this harsh world.

Lumpy, clay, and mud-brick buildings lined the streets and towered over the road. Large misshapen holes served as windows for each floor and allowed air to pass through the buildings, keeping their inside temperatures just below sweltering. Deteriorating plank shutters hung at odd angles beside the openings. Rickety wooden platforms made from old tree branches protruded beneath each opening. The lower ones appeared to serve as protection from the sun, while the upper ones were used for storage.

Stalls made of weathered wood and aged canvas awnings stood before some of the buildings. Thin, tanned people did their best to make any sort of a living on this baked, dried-up world. Clay pots, leather sandals, and small sheets of dyed cotton were just a few of the things available for purchase. Most items matched the worn, rundown feel of the city and its people. Since the city lacked any natural resources of its own, the items were likely either stolen or imported long ago. I didn't linger to shop. Despite being the capital, Entstal was a slum and offered no promising future to its inhabitants.

The hot, dry air carried the dusty scent of the Erima, along with the smells of sweat and other unpleasant things. I hurried further toward the city's eastern edge, following the sandstone brick pillars of a raised aqueduct. Arches of stone ran down the center of the street and kept the flowing water aloft, well out of anyone's reach. However, people gathered in places here and there with pots and buckets to collect droplets from the elevated waterway. Some formed lines; others clamored over one another. The paving stones beneath those latter groups were usually caked in mud.

The closer I got to the city's border with the Erima, the more rundown and abandoned the buildings became. The street transitioned from one of a bustling city to that of a ghost town. Most tenants in this part of town seemed to have moved on, no doubt to stay closer to the receding shoreline of the nearby ocean. Only the aqueduct and road remained in decent condition. Still, the road had seen better days. In some places, rocks too rough to be considered for use as pavement were placed in the ground as replacements to patch holes almost as plentiful as the bumps. Whoever maintained the road did their best to keep it clear of sand. The tan granules lay in piles here and there. Some of the mounds spilled into the nearby buildings, which no one seemed to mind. No visible efforts existed of removing any of the miniature dunes.

Despite the weight of my burdens, I persisted onward. I could see the end of the aqueduct. The series of archways came to an abrupt halt at the edge of a small plaza. As I passed the final column of the aqueduct, the sound of flowing water emanated from within it, likely flowing into a cistern below the square. Here, all the disheveled buildings surrounding the abandoned square were falling apart. Roofs were caved in, walls lay on their sides or leaned against neighboring structures, and the remnants of an ancient well lingered in the center of the neighborhood. What once provided water to the people had been capped off with stone bricks, preventing anyone nearby from accessing the life-giving liquid.

One building stood out from all the others. Carvings and a faded painting of the sun adorned large, smooth limestone walls. The once red mural situated above the entrance had dulled over time to a unique mix of oranges and pinks. A pair of round, stacked stone brick pillars stood guard on either side of the entryway. They held aloft a large block of limestone where three heads were carved into the outer surface. Two eagle heads with beaks pointed toward the center resided on each end of the block. What may have been the first Maker's scornful face rested in the middle and watched over the abandoned courtyard. The squared carvings were ornate by Tehraheyian standards, but, as they currently stood, they couldn't come close to competing with even the most basic temples back home. The people of Tehrahey simply lacked any real artistic talent.

The grandeur of the building, which only the local polity could maintain, and the presence of the aqueduct meant to provide water for the hundreds of children housed within told me I had arrived at my destination. This was the Child Teaching System, an institution aimed at educating the next generation of Tehraheyians. At least, that was the intent when the Maker created it. As ruler of Tehrahey, the Maker was supposed to provide the people with new technologies from other worlds. The CTS was one such example, and over the centuries, it had become corrupt, focusing less on education and more on control. After all, what kind of system would kidnap children at the age of three in the name of education? Parents rarely saw their children again, and it was easy to see why the people of this world struggled to make any meaningful connections when their families never truly lasted. Very few inhabitants truly knew love here.

Ascending three stone steps brought me into the shaded, door-less entryway of the building. Darkness and gloom filled the bland interior. Not even the sun could force its relentless light inside, if only the same could be said for the blistering heat. My heavy footsteps echoed through the quiet shadows. I removed my cloak's hood, allowing me to better survey the small anteroom. There wasn't much to see. Grains of sand littered the floor and collected in the corners. The room stood barren save for two spear-wielding men who stood guard on either side a pair of large metal doors. Their jet-black clothes concealed them within the shadows, making them invisible until my eyes adjusted.

I approached with caution, unsure of how these lackeys would receive me. The one on the right—the older of the two based off the gray in his facial hair— raised his spear to point at me. "That's close enough, freak."

Heeding his instructions and ignoring the insult at my appearance, I complied with the order before responding in a calm voice, "I wish to speak to a teacher."

I received no response other than the lowering of the spear.

"It's about my child."

"Leave. Your child will not be returned to you," the guard on the left instructed.

I took a deep breath. After this, there would be no going back. Of all the horrible things I had done in my life, this would be the crown jewel. There would never be forgiveness for this deed. "I don't want to remove my child from the system." I opened my cloak to reveal my five-month-old son sleeping peacefully in a sling against my chest. "I want to leave mine with you."

The guards shared a flustered look before the older one gestured with his head toward the doors. The other followed the silent instruction and disappeared into the depths of the building. Moments later, he returned with a young woman no older than twenty. Her thin yet tall form seemed ill-suited for the brown uniform given to all CTS workers. Several knots were tied into the waist of her pants to tighten them, and still they seemed too loose. The pant legs and sleeves were too short, exposing her wrists and ankles. In her arms, she carried a large gourd full of water.

"I haven't done anything wrong," the woman, sounding more like a girl with each second, stated with fear. She turned to face the guards at their post, her chocolate-colored hair hanging halfway down her back swinging to and fro. "I'm not stealing extra rations. I'm just trying to get some water for the mess hall. You can ask Mr. Nadir. He sent me."

"You're not in trouble," the older man snapped, causing the girl to stiffen. "This woman wants to leave her child here. We've chosen you to take care of it. You should be honored."

I recognized the man's lie the moment it left his lips. The only qualification the girl had for this job was they had found her first. Still, she would be the one my son needed. I believed she would be the one to take care of him better than I ever could.

The girl's shoulders dropped, and the water gourd almost slipped from her grasp. She recovered, managing to only spill a few drops. She turned sideways to cast me a disbelieving stare with her brown eyes. After all, what mother would give up her only child, especially at such a young age? Then, facing the guards again, she stammered, "I have to … Mr. Nadir needs me to bring him this water right away. I can't … I mean won't … I won't take a child!" She turned to me and studied my little boy. "Especially not one so young. Besides, shouldn't … shouldn't the omega handle this?"

"Are you questioning the orders given to you by one of the Maker's Guards?"

"No, sir. I would never! I just—"

"You just what?" he asked with a tone which suggested answering would not be in her best interest. She visibly gulped and faced me. Her forlorn expression told me she had no idea what to do.

I gave a pointed glance at what she carried then looked back at her.

She caught my meaning. She placed the object on the ground with a deep breath and stood to stare at me with empty arms. After some hesitation, she took a few cautious steps forward. Her hands rose to accept the baby then jerked back toward herself. Clutching at her shirt, she looked to me for guidance. Under any other circumstances, I might have found it amusing to see someone so big be afraid of something so small.

"I don't know…" Her voice trailed off as she crept forward.

I understood the unfinished question. She was too inexperienced to have any children of her own.

"It's okay. What's your name?"

"Helina."

I offered a reassuring smile while removing my bundled little boy from his sling. "Hold him like this, Helina." I demonstrated.

With shaky yet gentle hands, the girl took my baby from me.

I bit hard on my lower lip, ignoring the copper taste of blood washing over my tongue, as my mouth formed a thin line.

The girl regarded my child in much the same way I had when first holding him. She studied his soft pale face, admired the black hair already sprouting from the top of his head and marveled at his little hands. For a long moment, she couldn't take her eyes off him. Finally, she glanced up at me, a small grin on her face, though it faltered in less than an instant. She held my gaze for an eternity. In her brown eyes, I could see the unspoken question. Why was I doing this? She didn't understand, and never would.

After today, I would not meddle anymore. I had learned my lesson. Whenever I got involved, the people I cared about got hurt. I broke eye contact, choosing instead to stare at the less-accusing ground.

The faintest, sweetest sound came from my waking son held in the arms of another woman.

My body shuddered with a repressed sob.

The girl studied the bundle in her arms with rapt attention. "What's his name?" she asked, her voice soft.

"Kyle." I stepped backward.

She didn't notice. She focused on the son I would never see again.

"He'll need soft foods," I instructed. Tears stung my eyes, and I did my best to blink them away. "When he cries, I sing to him." I locked my mouth shut as another sob tried to escape. "He likes it when I sing," I managed after a moment.

A frown grew on her face, and she tore her gaze from Kyle to tell me, "I don't know how to sing."

"Neither do I," I offered with a hollow laugh.

The girl chewed her lips but nodded before staring at my baby once again.

Unable to stay anymore, I offered my final instruction. "Give him all the love I wish I could."

I fled, and she called after me, as did my crying son, but I left the CTS and the world I abandoned within it.

Chapter 1
-Just Another Fight in the Child Teaching System-

December 21, 2006 E.S.T.
2-12.11.12.17.4 T.S.T.
CTS, Entstal
Tehrahey

The punch collided with my shoulder and sent me stumbling backward toward the edge of the ring. My opponent, a boy just a year older than me, gleamed with delight at managing to land the first blow of this fight. He, like many of my past opponents, seemed to be underestimating me. Sure, I was scrawny, had paler skin than everyone else, and my blue eyes were anything but scary, but I was tough. My arms had muscles. I could see them, and they were bigger than Max's! That's why he liked to tease me and say I didn't have any. He was jealous.

What I lacked in looks, I made up for in endurance. And skill. More importantly, I knew something this jerk of a bully didn't. I *let* him hit me. Doing so ensured all the parental guardians in the room saw him strike first.

I massaged my shoulder as I looked up with a smirk. He would regret ever pushing Andy around or making fun of her appearance. So what if she was paler than everyone else or that her hair was red? Just because everyone else had tan skin and dark hair didn't mean they should pick on her. No one messed with my friends and got away with it.

My smile seemed to catch my opponent off guard. "You really are a freak, aren't you, Kyle?" he mocked.

I sent a warning glare at Andy who stood at the far edge of the crowd beside Jason and Max. She'd given this jerk my name without realizing it. Names were precious in the CTS. Being nameless made hiding from the adults easier.

Andy took a breath through gritted teeth as she brought her chin to her chest. She stared at the ground for a moment before her green eyes pleaded with me through a curtain of red hair.

I could see the apology in her expression. I could also see her begging me not to fight this kid. That wouldn't happen. Jason and I had both agreed; nobody picked on her and got away without a beating.

"You like getting pummeled?" the boy continued.

"No. Who would?" I glanced at a girl near the edge of our ring. "Do you like getting pummeled?"

Without hesitation, she shook her head and backed away, allowing two other kids to take her place.

"I'm smiling," I continued, "thinking about how I've fought third years who hit harder than you." Taunting, just another skill I had to offer when it came to fights. The more teasing remarks I made, the angrier my opponents got, and the worse they fought. This was another thing I had learned from Max, since just being strong like Jason wasn't working for me. He had it so easy when it came to fights. Max and I actually had to work to win ours.

Laughter erupted around us, with Max cackling louder than anyone. He loved to laugh, and he knew laughing at my opponent would only anger him more, thereby helping me out. He and Andy may not always get along, but he was our ally and wanted me to win.

The boy's face reddened as the snickers from our audience continued. "When I'm through with you, you'll see more stars than are in the sky," he threatened through gritted teeth.

I released my shoulder and rolled it experimentally. It still seemed to work. "Not much of a threat, since no one's ever seen a star."

With a growl, he lunged forward, intending to punch my face.

I ducked out of the way, managed to land two jabs on his stomach, then rolled away and scrambled to my feet behind him.

He spun around in time for my fist to collide with his head. He reeled to the side.

Pain coursed through my hand. By the Stars, that hurt! I knew from experience it felt worse for him. Ignoring the throbbing in my hand, I raised my fists, ready for another round.

He shook his head then marched forward. He faked a jab.

I dodged to avoid it, right into his other fist. I quickly returned the favor with my right.

He backed away, clutching at the new bruise.

I hoped he felt that all the way down his arm. With one punch, I had intended to deal more damage than he did in two. For added measure, I socked him in the stomach.

He staggered backward into the wall of kids, who pushed him away. He slumped forward, gasping for breath.

"Tired already?" I teased, needing to keep him angry to keep him stupid. That would give me my best chances of winning.

The following growl, which I assumed to be his favorite response, took a few ticks to escape. He stood upright and glared at me like I'd taken the last good bit of bread from the food counter. He really did not like me.

With a shout, he lunged forward. I expected another swing. Instead, he tackled me.

Trying to recover the lost air in my lungs, I could just decipher Max's chuckling voice through the roar of voices. "You overdid the teasing! Should have tired him out more first."

Okay, so I was still learning how to properly apply Max's techniques; that became clearer with each additional blow. Maybe if I was better at it, I might have prevented all of this pain. Doing a lot of things differently might have prevented this outcome. I could have listened to Andy when she had told me not to fight for her sake. I had chosen to listen to Jason, because this kid really deserved a good beating after picking on her. She had bumped into him in the mess hall, spilling the remains of her breakfast on him. The boy hadn't listened to her many apologies and had pushed my friend to the ground while calling her a freak.

Neither Jason nor I could let that stand. We hated it when bullies made fun of her. Andy was the nicest kid I ever met, and she didn't deserve to get picked on for her looks. I would continue to stand by her and kick the butts of anyone who felt differently.

She could make my job a little easier though if she didn't bump into people. That would be nice.

Punches landed everywhere. My face, my chest, my sides—everything hurt. I tried, in vain, to block some of the blows. Most of the attempts resulted in me hitting myself.

Max shouted something about not hitting myself.

If the Stars were willing, my opponent would tire soon. He'd determine me properly pummeled and move on with his life, let me shuffle away in shame. This should have been an easy fight to win. He was only a year older than me. Jason could have handled this without a problem.

As if to prove my unspoken statement, Jason entered the brawl. With ease, he hefted the bully off me and sent him sprawling to the other side of the ring.

He then offered me a hand with the faintest hint of concern hiding within his usual scowl. "You okay?"

I did my best to ignore the way the world spun. I wanted to prove I was strong. However, when I tried to take a step, I stumbled. Max caught me and straightened me up with a smirk on his thin face. I got the feeling he found my loss entertaining, but only because it meant he had more wins than me. Not that it mattered.

I shrugged him off. "Thanks." I wiped my nose on my forearm, smearing blood all over it. Great. "I'll be fine. Let's just teach this jerk to be nice." I raised my fists and rolled my shoulders, which sent pain shooting down my arms. I flinched and hoped my friends didn't see it.

They did.

Jason shook his head then pointed at Andy. "You're done. I'll take it from here."

"I want to help!"

"You weakened him. I'll finish him. That helps." He faced his rising opponent, trusting I'd heed his order and get out of here. I almost did. Really. I almost let Max drag me away to join Andy at the edge of the crowd, but that stupid kid just had to speak up.

"Where you going, freak? Can't fight your own battles?"

In a gust, I spun to face him.

Jason stuck out an arm to block me, and Max held me back. Of the two people stopping me, Jason's muscled arm proved to be the more intimidating barrier. Max's half-hearted grip on me let me know he'd let me rejoin the fight if I really wanted to.

I held back but didn't hide from the challenge. "What did you call me?"

The bully smirked. "You heard me. You're a freak, just like your little friend over there."

With a growl, I tried to rejoin the fight, but my friends held me back.

"Go!" Jason gave me a sideways glance.

In an instant, I recognized the anger in his voice. So did Max. The time for arguing was over. While him replacing me in this fight frustrated me, it also brought a smile to my face. This kid was doomed.

We backed off, and Jason marched forward without another word. As my friend raised his fists, the sneer on the bully's face shriveled and died once he realized just how intimidating Jason could be. Unlike myself, or even Max, my friend did not taunt or tease his opponents. He didn't like to waste his breath and, instead, focused all his energy on delivering the perfect punch. He knew exactly where and how to hit to cause the most damage to his enemies without hurting himself. He never lost a fight. Combined with his near permanent scowl and short hair, he could make any kid in the CTS run from a fight.

His left fist jabbed forward, catching the bully's left eye.

The jerk's head reeled backward. Once he righted it again, Jason's right hook connected. The blow sent the kid spiraling to the floor. Cheers rose from the crowd. I doubted any of them cared who won; they just enjoyed watching a good fight.

As the kid lay stunned, some kid shouted, "Kick him while he's down!"

Having been on the receiving end of that numerous times, I hated that tactic. Not being able to put up any kind of defense was horrible. Being on the other side didn't feel great either. I had tried it once and stopped almost as quickly as I had started. Doing that just didn't feel right. Jason, on the other hand, didn't have as much of a problem, if he felt the kid deserved it. I recalled a few fights over the year since I met him where parental guardians had to drag him off an unconscious opponent. Andy and I were trying to get him to stop doing that.

I waited to see what he would do, wondering if my arms had enough strength left in them to hold him back. The Stars seemed to decide I wouldn't have to, thankfully.

Jason remained where he stood, glaring at the kid on the ground.

"Get up."

The kid actually listened. He gave Jason a wary look, no longer confident in his victory. Then his face grew even more terrified, which didn't make sense. Jason was scary, yes, but not *that* scary. Only one person in the entire CTS could make someone that scared.

Chapter 2
-The Worst and the Best-

The realization that we were in trouble hit a tick before the slap against the back of my head. I shrunk away from the blow, and Max did the same. We'd both been hit. Another slap echoed through the suddenly silent mess hall.

Jason spun around, ready to face his new opponent, not yet realizing who'd hit him.

I thanked the Stars he didn't swing on instinct. Behind us stood the scariest adult in the CTS, the omega guardian herself, Ms. Hess.

As omega guardian, Ms. Hess ruled over the CTS with a stone fist. Everyone had to listen to her, even the other adults. At first glance, she didn't look like much. Her tall, bony body looked like it could barely hold itself together, yet she knew how to use it to dish out the worst beatings. She hit harder and faster than any other adult. Rage burned in her gray eyes as she stared down through strands of greasy brown hair.

A similar rage burned in Jason's own green eyes, but he kept himself under control. We'd all heard the rumors of what happened to the last kid who attacked a parental guardian, and none of us wanted to disappear.

When the adult growled, Jason was the only one who didn't shrink at the sound. "The first class hasn't even started yet, and you're already fighting."

"He threw the first punch!" I exclaimed, turning to point at the boy, but he was gone, along with the entire crowd. Even Andy had left. I couldn't blame her; getting too close to Ms. Hess only led to pain.

"Quiet, Reject!" She punched me in the gut for added emphasis. As I toppled over and tried to regain my breath, she addressed two of the other parental guardians in the room. "Kass, Janu, I don't have time for these repeat offenders today."

The adults rushed forward because no one kept Ms. Hess waiting.

"Kass, take Snake's Son. Janu, you take Sand Rat."

None of the adults knew our names, and we made sure it stayed that way. Whenever they were around, we stopped using names. They helped identify us, and being picked out of a crowd by any of the parental guardians, let alone Ms. Hess, meant trouble. As it was, Ms. Hess already knew Jason, Max, and me by appearances. I got into a lot of fights over the years but not as many as Jason and Max. Jason definitely had me beat, and he'd only been in the CTS for a year!

We didn't know why she called us what she did, and no one dared ask her. She wasn't someone we could talk to—none of the adults were. All we knew was Jason was Sand Rat, Max was Snake's Son, and I was Reject. My best guess was Jason's name came from him growing up in the Erima and that she thought I didn't have a lot of friends, but I had three, which is a lot in the CTS. I had no idea where Max's name came from.

As the adults divided us and led us from the mess hall in different directions, I had to face the fact Ms. Hess had kept me to herself. This would be fun. Her grip on my upper arm numbed my hand. That got rid of the dull aches from the fight, so I counted it as a win for the time being. Unfortunately, my luck would run out soon enough. It always did with Ms. Hess. She was the worst of the worst, and the rock she kept in her pocket proved it. She loved making kids cry. Her favorite method for doing that was hitting us with her rock. She used a strip of fabric to tie the rock to her hand and punched as hard as she could. She did this to repeat offenders, like my friends and me, all the time. According to rumor, she used the rock against adults too.

The CTS's dim underground hallways had little light to see by. Still, Ms. Hess dragged me along at a rushed pace. The only light down here came from glass-covered openings in the ceiling at intersections. The CTS was a maze of sandstone corridors and matching rooms built below the sands of the Erima desert to help keep it cool. That's what the teachers said anyway. It was only morning and I was already sweating down here, though that probably had to do with the way my morning was going.

Without warning, Ms. Hess stopped in the middle of an intersection. With shocking speed, she spun and slapped me across the face. I tried to reel back, but her grip on my arm kept me locked in place.

"You like to fight, don't you, Reject?" she sneered.

I knew better than to answer her. Speaking would only make things worse. I just had to grit my teeth and take this beating. I had no other options.

"I have more important things than you to deal with today, so I'll make this quick." She released her grasp on me as she pulled the rock from her pocket and fastened it to her hand.

Running crossed my mind for a tick, but I didn't dare move. She'd eventually hunt me down. I had nowhere to run.

Despite her insistence that she didn't have time to deal with me, the omega took her time with the rock's fabric. She fastened it with slow determination. She'd done the action so often she didn't even need to watch her hands to know what she was doing. She took the opportunity to sneer at me.

I, however, remained fixated on the stone. Droplets of sweat formed on my forehead as I prepared for the attack. I hated the CTS.

The beating started with a punch to the gut that took away my breath. As I crumpled forward, she slapped my face again and pushed my shoulders. I stumbled backward a few steps, and she followed me.

She raised her right arm to deal another blow.

My gut told me she was aiming for my head with that rock of hers. I prepared for all the pain that would come from that hit, then a voice shouted from down the hallway.

"Hess!" It was the one nice adult in the whole CTS. Ms. Lahna's black hair hung loosely around her shoulders, and her golden eyes were calm yet worried as she approached.

Ms. Hess yanked me backward. She pulled my arm like she wanted to rip it from its socket. A growl echoed from her throat, as if she were trying to protect her kill from another predator. "Shouldn't you be teaching?"

Ms. Lahna didn't seem fazed by this display. "Yes, but I heard what happened and thought I might offer help."

That statement didn't make any sense to me, and based off the suspicious look on Ms. Hess's face, I wasn't alone in my confusion. "You want to help me beat Reject?"

The teacher shook her head. "I'd never hit a child. However, I know how busy you are today. The records teachers are already running behind schedule without you."

The omega's grip on my arm tightened, which I hadn't thought possible. If she kept this up, I'd lose the arm for sure.

"Those idiots!" she growled, completely unaware of my problem.

My would-be rescuer took a careful step forward and spoke in a calm, quiet voice. "He'll be here any tick, won't he? Do you really want to waste time with this boy?"

It felt weird hearing her call me *boy*. She was the only adult who actually knew my name, and was kind enough not to use it around the other adults. I had no idea what Ms. Hess had planned, but from the way Ms. Lahna spoke, it sounded important.

"Don't fight me on this, Hess. I'm just trying to help. You may not see me as a friend anymore, but I still count you as one of mine." She proffered her hand.

As Ms. Hess weighed her options, I held my breath. I didn't dare move and risk affecting the outcome of this decision in any way.

Finally, after a very long tick, Ms. Hess punched me in the gut once more and shoved me toward my teacher.

Ms. Lahna caught me as the omega stormed off. "Lock him up!"

I stared into the darkness after her, amazed. Ms. Lahna had rescued me a lot over the years, but each attempt usually took more effort than this. I admired Ms. Lahna with awe. "How did you …?"

"She has something more important to do today." With a hand on my back, she guided me from the intersection. "Are you all right?"

My whole body ached from the fight and the beating from Ms. Hess. I thanked the Stars she'd been brief with me. "I'll be fine." I just wanted to sit, and I didn't care if that was in a classroom with noisy kids or a cramped isolation room.

We fell into silence as Ms. Lahna studied me for a moment. She broke that peace with a sigh. "What was it this time?"

I'd been expecting the question but hadn't thought of an answer she would accept. She didn't like it when I got into fights, so I chose to study the stones in the floor and walls instead of answering her.

"Fighting isn't always the answer, Kyle."

"What was I supposed to do?" I snapped. "Let that jerk hurt Andy?" I refused to let anyone harm my friends, and the thought she wanted me to let that happen left a bitter taste in my mouth, worse than a rotten pitahaya.

My teacher grew thoughtful. "So, it was a bully? Andy left that bit out."

I regarded her with hope. Did this mean she wasn't upset with me? "Am I still in trouble?"

She scoffed. "Obviously."

Well, that was disappointing. I kicked a stray pebble and sent it skittering across the floor.

"It's admirable that you want to defend your friends, but starting fights will only bring pain."

"I'm not smart enough to talk my way out of things like you are."

"Everyone has their own way of dealing with things; you just have to find yours. And who says you aren't smart?"

I raised a finger as I counted. "My grades, my teachers, Ms. Hess, and every other adult."

She gave the back of my head a light smack. "I think you're smart."

"Well, you're weird." Saying that to any other adult would have been asking for trouble, but Ms. Lahna was different from all of them for some reason. It was why she was Andy's favorite teacher.

Her amber eyes gave me a hard stare before lightening as she chuckled. "You're a smart boy, Kyle. You should know better than to listen to what Hess says."

She had a point there. "I usually do. I mean, I don't care that she calls me Reject."

Ms. Lahna tensed, and her hand fell from my back.

I watched her, concerned. "Did I say something wrong?"

She shook herself and forced a smile. "No."

For some reason, I didn't believe that. She wasn't very good at lying, like the other adults. "Then what's wrong?"

"It's just …"

I arched an eyebrow as her hand clenched into a fist.

"I just hate that she calls you that."

"Why? It doesn't even make sense." I tried to laugh at the horribleness of the name, but the look on Ms. Lahna's face told me she didn't find it funny at all. A sandstorm brewed in my stomach.

My teacher was quiet for several long ticks. After a while, she said the last thing I expected to hear. "It's because of your mother."

I didn't say anything for a while. What could I? I never met my parents, which wasn't odd. Most kids didn't know their parents. They took us into the CTS at the age of three. My friends were some of the only exceptions. Both Andy and Max had arrived in the CTS at the age of four. They didn't remember much from that extra year with their parents, but they knew their parents loved them. Andy remembered her parents fighting to keep her, and Max could never forget his mother's crying face as she chased after the guards who took him from her. Jason had arrived last year after his father's death. He was thirteen then. Of the four of us, he was the only one to know what it was like to live outside.

Meanwhile, I barely had any memories—one I often suspected to be a dream. In this memory, darkness surrounded me, and I couldn't move. Something glowed faintly of gold in the center of the room, and a woman's voice said she loved me. It was all so faint and faded that I couldn't be sure if it was a memory of something that had actually happened or a figment of my imagination. The other thing I remembered was a song. I didn't know the words, but the tune would still echo through my dreams or surface anytime I was upset. I didn't know why, but it comforted me. Andy said my mother must've sung to me. I didn't know if I believed that, but I hoped she was right.

To hear anything about my mother caught me off guard. At first, I didn't know if I wanted to know more. I'd made it this far in life with nothing; surely, it didn't matter. But it did. Knowing nothing about her meant I wanted to know anything, even if it could be bad. Based off the sideways glances my teacher kept giving me, this would be.

I struggled to find my voice as I asked my next question. "What about her?"

Ms. Lahna took a deep breath and slowly released it. "Are you sure you want to know?"

"I need to."

With reluctance, my teacher told me a story from twelve years ago when a woman arrived at the CTS entrance, begging for help. However, instead of the usual story of a parent begging to get her child back, this woman wanted the guards to take her infant son. She wanted to get rid of him. Worst of all was the boy's description: black hair, blue eyes, and pale skin. Me. I was the reject. My own mother didn't even want me, and every adult knew it.

My eyes stung with tears that threatened to fall at any moment. I fought to suppress them, telling myself this didn't matter. I never knew her, so why should I care that she had given me up?

I didn't feel like talking anymore, so the silence stretched on for what felt like cycles. As we approached Ms. Lahna's classroom, she cleared her throat. "Kyle, I—"

I didn't look over as I cut her off. "Can you just lock me up now?"

Chapter 3
-Looking Back to Move Forward-

2-12.11.12.17.4 T.S.T.
CTS, Entstal
Tehrahey

Any other day, the small and cramped space of an isolation room would have been bothersome. I didn't have enough room to even stretch my legs in front of me. However, today, trapped in the darkness with only a sliver of light coming in from the crack under the door, the room provided shelter. By myself, I could cry, and no one would make fun of me. All this time, I had hoped my first memory wasn't just a dream, but it was. I told myself it didn't matter, but it was a lie. How could my mother have abandoned me? She really didn't love me at all?

Alone in the dark, I hummed to myself. The old, faded tune from some forgotten memory surfaced and did its best to make me feel better. But all it did was remind me my mother had abandoned me.

Unlike other adults, Ms. Lahna didn't keep me locked up all day. She released me in time for my class with Mr. Ethan, so I was only locked up for a few cycles. I headed for my class without a word. I got the feeling she wanted to talk more, but I didn't.

Keeping my head low, I slunk across the front of the room to where Andy sat on the floor. A combination of no one wanting to sit in the front and people not wanting to be near Andy just because she had paler skin than everyone else, green eyes, and red hair, meant she sat alone. At least no one was bothering her today.

She wore a smug grin as I sat next to her. "You're welcome," she said, referencing her sending Ms. Lahna to my rescue.

"Thanks," I mumbled, not trusting my voice to say more without outing me. A part of me wished she'd stayed out of it and just left me to Ms. Hess. What Ms. Lahna had told me hurt worse than any rock punch.

My silence caught Andy's attention. Her face scrunched, disturbing her freckles. "Are you all right?" When I didn't respond a tick later, her mood switched from worry to full-blown panic. "Was she too late? I'm sorry. I got to her as fast as I could!" She grasped the sides of her head and seemed ready to tear out her hair.

Grabbing her shoulders, I forced her to meet my eyes. "I'm fine. Thank you for helping, really."

She dropped her hands into her lap, and her hair fell to its regular position just above her shoulders, only slightly more unkempt than it had been before. Her eyes narrowed as she studied me. I hoped she didn't see through my act. "Well, if you had listened to me in the first place ..."

I refocused on the floor. "I know, I know. You're always right."

She scooted closer to me until her shoulder bumped mine. "Do you want to tell me what's bothering you?"

Of course, she could see right through me, but what could I say? Oh, you know, it's just that my mother didn't love me and abandoned me to the CTS as fast as she could. I didn't want to say that—didn't think I could. The thought alone hurt worse than any punch ever. Besides, she wouldn't understand. Her parents had secretly kept her until she was four. They had fought to keep her. She remembers it took exactly six men to subdue her father as they carried her away.

If Andy had figured out I wouldn't answer that question, she never got a chance to say, because Mr. Ethan entered wearing the standard brown adult uniform. Even the smallest size seemed to be too big for him. He wore it with the sleeves and pant legs rolled up around his wrist and ankles. His eyelids drooped over dark eyes, making it appear as if he had just awoken. His thin brown hair stuck out at random angles.

Behind him came two pairs of parental guardians; thankfully, none of them were the omega. Each pair carried a wooden table covered with strange objects. Not caring if they stepped on anyone, the guardians placed the tables along either side of the room. As quickly as they placed the tables, the extra adults hastily exited the room, glancing over their shoulders as they did. Even in the morning air, beads of sweat formed across their brows. The tables and their random collections couldn't be that heavy. For a brief tick, I thought fear flashed in the adults' eyes, like they were scared of a bully, but that couldn't be, right? Nobody feared Mr. Ethan. He looked like an older version of Max but without any of the fighting experience, or the smiling. He was the kind of person to hide when a fight started, not join it.

The class murmured, everyone wondering what the tables were about. Things weren't usually added to classrooms like this. From behind his desk—the only other bit of furniture in the room—Mr. Ethan glared at the class, silencing most for a brief tick. He then grabbed a piece of chalk and wrote on the board in big, almost unreadable letters: The Travelers.

That caught my attention. Travelers were cool, they were exciting, and most importantly, they could go wherever they wanted. They were the perfect distraction. Most of the time, records classes were boring, teaching about events that happened a long time ago and all the important stuff the Makers did over the years. However, once a year—sometime near the end—the teacher would talk to us about my favorite subject: the Travelers. I waited for this day all year!

"The Travelers," our teacher began, "two of the most famous and *infamous* beings to ever enter Tehrahey. One gave birth to our world, while the other tried to end it. The first Traveler created Tehrahey with the help of *The Book of Time*—" He continued to lecture us, but I tuned him out for a moment, having heard this part of the story before in previous classes. The lesson would only get exciting and new near the end.

The Book of Time belonged to the Traveler. Legends said the book held every bit of knowledge the Traveler had discovered. If someone read *The Book of Time*, they could learn to be a Traveler. I knew Andy would find it the most interesting book ever written, since it even had me interested. If, by some chance, I could find it, read it and become a Traveler, I could save us. I could get Andy, Max, Jason, and myself out of the CTS, maybe even out of Tehrahey, and find a safer place to live. Then no adults could bother us again, but that would never happen. Tehraheyians have searched for *The Book of Time* for thousands of years. People had even tried to steal it from the first Traveler. It happened so many times that he hid it where no one could find it. Soon after that, he disappeared too so no one could ask for his help. He did leave some clues though—a riddle no teacher ever mentioned beyond something about "Destiny's son" and three tablets. Supposedly, if someone managed to find all three of those, they would be shown the location of the book. Even though no one ever saw a tablet, some rumors claimed each Tablet represented a different time: past, present, and future.

Adults were required to spend a few years searching for the Tablets. I didn't know exactly how many years, since they taught that in Tablet Hunter's Prep, and only kids in their thirteenth year of teaching could take the class.

As Mr. Ethan sat at his desk, he spoke in his dull tone, focusing more on his hands than on us. He moved on from the first Traveler to the next, looking as bored as ever. "Three thousand years ago, in four zero nineteen of the First Count, a new Traveler arrived with the promise of returning the Erima into lush jungles."

A desert hadn't always covered Tehrahey. We called the desert the Erima, and it covered everything from one side of Tehrahey to the other. The entire thing consisted of sand dunes and the remains of abandoned cities. Nothing existed out there; the heat burned anyone who set foot in it.

Long before the Erima, trees and bushes covered the land. Animals and crops were plentiful. People could find water everywhere. Cities could be wherever anyone wanted; they didn't have to crowd along the few isolated rivers. Life sounded easier back then. I wished we were born then.

Mr. Ethan continued directing his lecture toward his hands. "Over the next three thousand years, this Traveler brought new ideas, such as aqueducts and our timekeeping devices—alarms. Can anyone tell me some other creations this second Traveler brought us?"

He peered up to see if anyone had raised their hand.

Experience told me none of them would. Only one student responded to his questions, though she never did so in a hurry. After a few ticks, Andy raised her hand, drawing several sighs from kids around us. As far as Jason and I could tell, she always had an answer to a teacher's questions, and they were always right. Kids resented her for knowing more than they did, which could keep her from speaking up, but she felt confident with me by her side.

Mr. Ethan eyed Andy. "Yes, you with the red … hair," he stumbled, still surprised by Andy's hair after teaching us every day for the past year. Probably because he had never bothered to look up. "What else has the Traveler brought us?"

Andy answered but spoke in a hushed tone. "The Traveler brought us steam ships. He is also the reason we have the CTS and every creation inside it."

Mr. Ethan stared at her for a long moment. I doubted he had heard her and expected him to ask her to repeat herself.

"Correct! Near the end of this period, around the end of eleven five eighteen of the Second Count, the new Traveler searched for *The Book of Time*, with the claim that if he found it, he could save Tehrahey. Tehraheyian leaders of that time …"

Ever since the disappearance of the second Traveler, a Maker ruled over Tehrahey. This man examined the relics the Traveler left behind and learned from them to make new technologies. Before the Makers, a king and council ran things. People on the council were highly regarded and thought of as the smartest in Tehrahey. If the Makers never rose to power, I bet Andy would be a part of the king's council. I knew she'd enjoy it a lot; she liked helping people.

Back then, the king tasked four of the council with helping the Traveler find *The Book of Time*—Roger Tal, Samuel Ents, and partners Adam and Eve. Together, they went down in history as the Four Councilmen. Alongside the Traveler, they searched for the three

Tablets that would lead them to *The Book of Time* in order to stop the death of our world.

Then things went wrong.

The Traveler attacked the Four Councilmen, which I didn't understand. The Traveler had helped the world for thousands of years. Why suddenly attack the Four Councilmen before they even found *The Book of Time*? Andy never questioned it, but Jason, Max, and I saw it differently. If the Traveler had been in it for power, like the teachers claimed, he should've waited until they actually found the book. The adults weren't telling us something. With each passing year, Andy agreed with us a little more, largely because each teacher told the story a little differently. None of the stories completely fit together with one another. Some would go into great detail about the attack, while others knew nothing about it; although a few points didn't change.

The Traveler's six powers stayed the same: strategy, stealth, elemental control, swordsmanship, magic, and the ability to Travel between dimensions. The teachers always ended it the same too. The Traveler fled Tehrahey and took Adam and Eve with him. No one saw them again. Roger and Samuel stuck around for a bit before they disappeared too. Their disappearance was weird. How could two important people, two members of the Four Councilmen, just disappear without a trace? At least with Adam and Eve, we knew someone had taken them from Tehrahey.

Mr. Ethan glanced up once more, observing the classroom and several of the kids trying not to fall asleep. Others were sleeping, and a few whispered among themselves. Until this point, only Andy still paid him any real attention.

I faded in an out, waiting for anything new, and from where he had left off, we were caught up with everything I knew.

Mr. Ethan cleared his throat to regain the class's attention. What would come next? "Roger and Samuel spent the rest of their lives searching for their lost friends until they too vanished. In honor of their efforts to continue to find *The Book of Time*, the first Maker founded the city of Entstal as the new capital of Tehrahey."

Mr. Ethan looked like he wished we would all disappear too. He stopped after that, and it became clear he didn't intend to continue.

I grew frustrated that Mr. Ethan never taught for the entire hand cycle. He preferred to teach for ten ticks then sit at his desk, playing with his hands. Could this be how Andy felt, always wanting the teachers to continue with their lessons? I didn't like it. After waiting all year for this lecture, I needed to know what had happened to Roger Tal and Samuel Ents. I needed something to ponder other than what Ms. Lahna had told me.

For the first time ever, I raised my hand. It felt weird and earned me an annoyed look from the man.

"Yes?"

I hesitated for a moment before gathering some courage. "What happened to Roger and Samuel?"

My teacher rubbed his face with his hands, groaning for a long tick. "No one knows for sure. The Makers state they died searching for the Tablets. Some believe the two of them found the Tablets, claimed *The Book of Time* and left Tehrahey. No one truly knows what happened."

That's it? I waited all year to find out no one knows? I crossed my arms and leaned back until my head rested on the floor—stupid class with a stupid teacher.

"Some of you may have noticed two tables were brought in today. On these are some of the many relics the last Traveler left behind. The Maker has graciously let me borrow them to teach you about some of our world's machines. Since these are the Maker's, no one is allowed to touch them." He eyed a group of boys in the back who were the typical troublemakers; they never listened to him, and no one really expected them to start anytime soon. "Take a look at the tables, quietly."

Chapter 4
-Countdown to Another World-

2-12.11.12.17.4 T.S.T.
CTS, Entstal
Tehrahey

Andy and I chose to examine the table closest to us containing several relics, most I didn't recognize. Andy, on the other hand, seemed to know all of them as she mumbled to herself.

I figured by listening to her, I stood a better chance of learning something today.

"Oh, that's a crossbow. It's bigger than I imagined." She noticed me watching her and pointed to the items as she listed them in a low whisper. She enjoyed sharing her knowledge.

My gaze paned between her and the table, amazed but not entirely surprised she could identify so many of the objects.

Knowing to call a hollowed-out wooden stick with holes in it a flute wouldn't exactly help me get through my time in the CTS, but listening made Andy happy, so I did my best to pay attention. Of all the relics, I only recognized one without help. A small alarm for keeping track of time with a strap so it could be worn on a wrist was hidden behind the flute just out of view. I edged around the table to get a better look. Cracks wove their way through the brown hide strap. I imagined if anyone touched it, the thing would turn to dust in their hands. The numbers one through twelve were written in gold around the outer edge of the small circle. The arrows and numbers stood out against the white alarm face. Amazingly, the thing still moved. Ticking away, the arrows circled the face in a steady motion.

Although, they moved in the wrong direction. Instead of counting from one, they descended from twelve.

I grabbed Andy's arm and tugged her over while pointing at the alarm.

She looked at it then back at me, offering a face that said something along the lines of, *Why do you want me to talk about that? You know what an alarm is. You're not that dumb.*

I replied with a face saying, *I'm not dumb. You are.*

She answered that with confusion.

Pointing at the alarm once more, I rotated my finger in the same direction as the hands.

One of Andy's eyebrows rose while she studied me, probably trying to discern how badly I had gotten hit in the head earlier.

My shoulders dropped. I looked at Mr. Ethan.

One of the troublemakers at the other table had earned his attention for the time being.

I turned back to Andy and whispered, "The arrows are moving backward."

She shook her head at me. She must not have heard.

This time I spoke a little louder. "The arrows are moving backward."

She stole a glance at Mr. Ethan before leaning in and whispering. "I heard you the first time."

With Mr. Ethan still focused on the other table, I saw no problem in continuing. "Then why did you shake your head?"

"Because they aren't moving at all." She pointed to the alarm to prove her point. It stopped at twelve.

"I swear they were."

Andy smirked and opened her mouth, mostly likely to tease me, then stopped. Her lips closed as she slowly turned to the alarm with narrowed eyes.

"What?" I asked, shuffling closer until our shoulders brushed.

"Do you hear that?"

A new noise drifted through the room so faint at first I questioned if I heard it at all. The alarm's hands didn't move, but it continued ticking. Each short sound was louder than the last. We turned to Mr. Ethan, but he never took his eyes off the other table.

Andy raised her hand and waited.

I didn't understand our teacher's interest with the others. All the kids were quiet and calm. None of them moved. In fact, none of them even blinked. The same held true for Mr. Ethan.

The ticking persisted.

"Andy, do you notice anything wrong with everyone?"

Her hand lowered as she scanned the room with curious emerald eyes. "No one is moving." She approached a student and tapped the girl's shoulder. No response. "It's as if they're stuck." She stood in front of Mr. Ethan.

His gaze never moved to focus on her.

I joined my friend and waved a hand in front of the adult's face. Nothing. "How do you think this happened?" I could have a lot of fun with this. Maybe get back at Mr. Ethan for his stupid lesson. As I worked on figuring out how to do that, Andy's gaze searched the room.

"I think that's more than just an ordinary alarm." She returned to the table. "Why is it ticking if it isn't moving?"

I hung back a moment, trying to decide what to do with our teacher. Maybe I could draw on his face with chalk, but that wouldn't really work. Maybe I could just stick the chalk up his nose. That would be funny! I reached for the stick on his desk as Andy turned toward me.

"Kyle!" she hissed, stopping me in my tracks. "What are you doing?"

Her tone of voice told me she did not approve of my plan, even if she didn't know what I had in mind.

For less than a tick, I contemplated going through with it, but then I remembered this morning. I hadn't listened and wound up losing a fight. I'd be better off listening to her; she was always right, after all.

I left our teacher at his desk—with the chalk not up his nose where I felt it belonged. The ticking from the little device shook through my bones. I rejoined my friend at the table and found something that made this little alarm stand out from all the others in the CTS. A big arrow helped show the hand cycle, a shorter one showed long ticks, and a thinner one showed the short ticks. However, it also had a tiny, thin arrow for something else.

"It has four arrows," I noted. The fourth arrow appeared to be stuck like the others, though it pointed at two instead of twelve. It twitched with each tick, while the others remained still.

She leaned in closer to the alarm. "I wonder what it's for."

While pondering her question, a thought occurred to me. All of these were relics from the Traveler. What if the Makers hadn't figured out exactly how everything worked? Some of these things could be very different from how we knew them in the CTS. There might even be something magical about this relic! Maybe the Traveler enchanted it with some secret spell!

The desire to touch the relic grew, and my fingers tingled as the thought drifted through my mind.

I reached to grab it, but Andy snagged my wrist.

"What are you doing? We aren't supposed to touch anything!"

After glancing at the unmoving people, I offered her a raised eyebrow. "Who'll see? Mr. Ethan? He's been staring at that table for like five ticks now. Maybe there's a button that can get everybody unstuck." Or maybe even a spell written on it. This had to be some sort of magic the Traveler had left behind. This kind of thing didn't happen every day.

"I guess you can check." She released me and withdrew her hand. "Just be ready to drop it in case Mr. Ethan does get unstuck."

That's why I needed to listen to her more; I hadn't considered that. I plucked the alarm off the table and brought it closer to examine. Surprisingly, the strap didn't disintegrate. After turning the device in my hands a couple times, I offered it to Andy. "I don't see anything useful."

"Let me see it." Once she touched it, the alarm rang.

Already on edge, we startled at the sudden noise. The object fell between us, ringing loudly. Worry brewed in my stomach. I prayed to the Stars our teacher wouldn't get unstuck, otherwise we'd have to explain ourselves, and I didn't think we could.

I tore my gaze away from the alarm on the floor to see if anything had changed in the room, but it was all gone. A dark void surrounded me. My gaze snapped back to my friend, hoping she'd still be there. Thankfully, she was.

Her face paled. Her gaze darted around, searching for anything. She eyed me, and her mouth opened. No sound escaped.

"What?" I tried to ask, but no words left my mouth. My heart raced. We were stuck in darkness, close enough to see each other but unable to speak. The alarm was magic, and with horror, I remembered the second Traveler might actually be a bad person.

We might be in trouble.

As if attempting to confirm that suspicion, something grabbed my waist and pulled me into the darkness. Freeing myself proved to be impossible. Nothing actually wrapped itself around my stomach, but I could still feel it.

Andy clawed at her own waist. As she struggled, her gaze darted to me. At least we weren't alone.

Her fear bothered me more than my own. Not wanting her to be afraid, I did my best to forget my fear and be strong like Jason. At the very least, I could pretend well enough to convince her this didn't scare me. As my face relaxed, Andy's did as well.

She kept her emerald gaze locked on me, never blinking.

A small pale light glowed ahead of us. Each tick it shrunk despite us being pulled toward it. In a gust, the pale light jumped right in front of us, and the feeling on my waist stopped. The darkness gave way to the firelight of several torches and a fireplace illuminating a nearly circular room. It would have been a full circle if flat walls hadn't blocked off one quarter of it. We stood in the direct center of the circle with the intruding square corner directly at our backs. A padded bench sat against the flat wall to our right covered in alarms. Farther to our right was a door, and shortly after that, the flat wall met the curved one.

Bookshelves filled to the brim with books and even more alarms ranging from plain to fancy covered that quarter of the curve and stood behind a large table with six chairs. If our circumstances were different, Andy probably would have raced over to sift through their pages. The shelves stopped at something I'd never seen in a wall before—a window. The large opening looked across a dark world where I couldn't tell what might be out there.

To our left along the other flat wall stood a large wooden cabinet and another single door. Positioned along the curve of this side of the room rested a large bed, bigger than anything I'd ever seen in the CTS. Next came a large stone fireplace, and after that, directly in front of us, was a wooden desk covered with papers. The whole room felt dark and light at the same time. It emanated a mysterious air that worried me but also felt safe and inviting. I couldn't figure out why.

Of all the things that scared me about what had just happened and where we were, the thing that worried me the most was the person sitting hunched over the desk. Long white hair flowed down his back, and I could just make out an equally long beard hanging from the man's chin. The hair spilled over a green robe that looked nothing like the brown uniforms I always saw adults wear. The sleeves stopped halfway down his forearms, and a bit of yellow rope looped once around his waist and was tied in knot on the side.

I noticed all this in an instant, contemplating what we could do. Maybe we could sneak out one of the doors before the adult turned around. Before I could convey this idea to Andy, a rough voice spoke, and it didn't come from the figure at the desk.

Chapter 5
-The Castle Time Lost-

On the bed to our left, where I swear it hadn't been a tick ago, stood a scrawny black cat with pale blue eyes. I'd never seen a real cat before. It resembled the illustrations of ancient jaguars from long ago that Andy showed me from one of her books. Of course, this so-called jaguar was a whole lot smaller. The cat watched us with narrowed eyes as it spoke in an unfamiliar language, but the tone of the voice said enough; we weren't welcome.

Andy and I huddled closer together under the tiny creature's harsh gaze. Animals did not talk, at least not on Tehrahey.

Upon hearing the cat, the man at the desk looked up, first at the cat then at the two of us.

As he rose from his chair, I stepped in front of Andy. If he were to punish either of us, it would be me. I readied for the worst as the man turned but was not prepared for what I saw.

He smiled. His merry brown eyes surveyed us with more excitement than I'd ever seen in an adult before. I couldn't find any hint of cruelty about him.

The three of us stared at one another for several ticks before the old man stepped forward. "Hello, welcome to my home." When neither of us moved, he continued, "I'm Amyntor." He proffered his right hand.

Andy and I jumped backward, expecting him to swing at us.

The cat spoke with its rough voice again, and this time, I understood it. "Tehraheyians don't shake hands. It requires a certain level of civility."

Amyntor's eyes narrowed as he focused on the creature on the bed. He spoke in a soft voice, but I could hear the order in it. "Be nice, Cat."

Andy cleared her throat, earning the attention of our strange new companions. Her hand reached for mine and gripped it so tightly I feared she might break it. "We just want to go back. We didn't mean any trouble."

Amyntor smiled again. "Don't worry. You are not in trouble. You will both be able to return to your home. However, I would like to speak with the two of you first if that is okay."

Andy and I shared a look. Adults never asked children for permission.

Andy eyed Amyntor with caution, searching for any sort of trap or trick in his words.

I couldn't find anything. I also didn't see anything that said I *could* trust him, but I had missed a lot of things in the past. Best to let Andy pass judgment. I watched her, waiting for an answer.

After a few agonizingly long ticks, she offered me a single nod.

I made eye contact with the adult who awaited our response. "I guess that's okay."

"You *guess*?" The cat sneered before the man could respond. "They're Tehraheyians. Why waste your time with them? You made that mistake once before."

It seemed the man grimaced at the cat's words, but it vanished. "Cat, they're children. Be nice."

The cat huffed and circled in the bed before lying down with his back facing us.

Amyntor watched him for a moment. "I must apologize for Cat's behavior. He has seen a lot of terrible things during his lifetime and has a hard time making friends. I hope his behavior has not upset the two of you."

As Amyntor apologized to us, I couldn't believe it. The only adult who had ever apologized to us was Ms. Lahna, and it felt just as weird coming from her. As far as the cat, sure, he scared me and seemed mean, but that was nothing new. He hadn't actually hurt me, so I'd be fine as long as Andy was.

She didn't seem too upset by the little creature. In fact, she perked up and I could see a question forming in her mind. "His name is Cat?"

Apparently, despite appearing to be asleep, the cat was still listening to us, because he groaned.

"Well, that is what you get for not telling anyone your name." The old man chuckled. "Before we continue, what are your names?"

I placed a hand on my chest. "I'm Kyle."

Andy mirrored my action. "And I'm Andy."

"Pleased to meet you, Kyle and Andy." He offered a small bow then straightened up. "Let's take a seat." He motioned toward the bench behind us.

Andy and I complied, and sitting on something other than a stone floor felt amazing. The soft red cushioning provided a level of comfort I'd never experienced before. Not even the cots in the CTS were this nice.

Amyntor pulled over his desk chair. As he sat, a large white bird with black specks flew through the window and perched itself on his chairback.

I leaned away from the animal. It was bigger than his head!

Meanwhile, Andy studied it, her head tilting sideways ever so slightly. "Is that an owl?"

Amyntor nodded, and the owl watched Andy with round, unblinking golden eyes. After a moment, the owl shifted to focus on me. Even though the bird's gaze was warmer than Cat's, I fidgeted under it.

"Luna," Amyntor started, "would you like to say hello?"

I don't know what sound I expected the owl to make, having never seen one before. I definitely didn't expect it to talk too.

"Hello," Luna said in a pleasant voice. "What did I miss?"

"We were just about to send these Tehraheyians on their way, Feathers," Cat said, sitting in front of the window and looking outside.

I leaned left to peer around the corner at the bed to ensure it wasn't a second cat. How had he gotten there without me seeing him move?

Luna's head swiveled in a startling way. I had never seen anyone's head turn that far around. "Don't call me Feathers!" The claws on her feet flexed and scratched at the chair, leaving gouges in the wood.

Cat hissed at her.

Before anything else could be said, Amyntor cleared his throat. Luna's head instantly spun back around. "Sorry. Let's just ignore the furball."

"Good luck with that." Cat said with a chortle.

Luna's claws tore at the wood, but she remained silent.

Amyntor rubbed his chin. "The hard part is deciding where to begin."

He spied some of the alarms, where his gaze lingered for a long time.

As the silence progressed, Cat strolled over. "How about like this?" He used his tail to point to Amyntor. "In the beginning, he created—"

"First and foremost, they would have no idea what I was talking about by starting there! And second, that is not what I wish to explain, and you know it!"

Cat flicked the tip of his tail. "It was only a joke." He returned to the other side of the room where I guessed he jumped back onto the bed.

Amyntor watched him go and sighed. "This is very difficult to explain; although … maybe Cat was on to something. Right idea but wrong place. Kyle, Andy, what do you know about the creation of Tehrahey?"

With that, Andy and I answered questions about how Tehrahey came to be. We played along, but I got the feeling this turn of events confused Andy as much as it did me. I kept waiting for something to go wrong like it always did when adults asked questions. I prepared myself for the inevitable moment when Amyntor would snap over something we said. The longer we talked, the less likely that possibility seemed. Unlike other adults in our lives, instead of getting mad at Andy or me for asking a question, Amyntor smiled.

Each question asked and answered seemed to help Andy push her concern for wherever we were further from her mind. A grin graced her lips and sparkled in her eyes as she spoke with the man. She rarely got the chance to share her knowledge so freely with anyone, so she took advantage of the opportunity. For the moment, she didn't worry about how we would possibly return to where we were supposed to be or how if Ms. Hess ever discovered we somehow managed to sneak out of the CTS, she would definitely kill us. And that was only if we returned. What would happen if we were stuck here? Could this man really be trusted? Sure, he seemed friendly now, but how long would this moment last? Adults were horrible. If I'd learned one thing in the CTS, that fact was it. They were cruel and vicious. We couldn't trust them.

That didn't even consider Cat and Luna. Could talking animals be trusted?

Andy calling my name snapped me from my wondering. "What?" I felt like a teacher had called on me, except this teacher was scarier. Andy could easily be the scariest person in the CTS when she wanted to be. Her red hair could look like it was on fire when she got angry. Despite this fact, she only ever made herself scary to Jason, Max, and me. Luckily, I saw no traces of that expression as she watched me, only disbelief. "Don't give me that look."

"What look?" she asked. As if she didn't know! She gave me the same look every time I stopped paying attention to something she found interesting, like she couldn't understand how I found it boring.

"The one you always give me when you realize I wasn't paying attention."

Still, my friend denied such a look even existed. "I don't have a look for that!"

"Do too!"

In response, she stuck out her tongue at me, and I copied the action. Amyntor and Luna's chuckles reminded us we weren't alone. I snapped my head around to look at him, worried we might have done something wrong. We hadn't.

Amusement twinkled in his eyes. "How long have you been friends?"

"Eight years," I answered.

"That is good. Friends are very important. It's nice to know someone has your back." He remained quiet for a moment, and I wondered if he once had a friend like Andy. He didn't say anything if he had.

As the silence progressed, I took the opportunity to ask a question of my own. "Why do you care so much about the history of Tehrahey and the Travelers?" I had just endured this lesson once and was disappointed. I didn't really appreciate doing it again, so I wanted to know why.

Without a single hint of frustration at the question, he answered, "I just wish to know where I should begin. I do not want to teach you things you already know."

That made sense to me.

Andy continued where we had left off, and this time, I paid more attention. I joined in from time to time as we finished reciting today's Records lesson.

Once we finished, Amyntor straightened in his chair and ran a hand through the gray hairs of his beard. "Very good. That is … everything."

Andy smiled at the praise. She liked being able to answer people's questions.

I didn't share her enthusiasm. Something about how he hesitated stuck out to me; he sounded disappointed.

"However, I am afraid that some of your details were … incorrect."

Andy's smile disappeared. "That's exactly what we were taught in class. I *know* we didn't get anything wrong." She looked to me for confirmation, which I gave with a nod. We told him everything Mr. Ethan had taught us.

Amyntor raised his hands as if he needed to defend himself from us—or more precisely, Andy. Her tone revealed just how much the news of being wrong had upset her. While I had witnessed Jason perform the action a few times whenever he accidentally upset her, I never saw an adult do it toward a kid. "I am sure you told me everything exactly as your teachers taught you. The thing is, you were lied to. While the second Traveler did disappear with Adam and Eve, it was an accident."

"How could you know that?" I asked.

He folded his hands on his lap, his expression emotionless. "I was there."

I figured he might be joking; after all, no one alive today could have been there. I made sure to tell him so. "That all happened five hundred years ago. You couldn't have been there."

"Indeed, it has been a long time since then, but regardless, I was there. Unlike most people, I do not age year by year. For me, it is slower than that." His brown eyes remained calm as he watched us, seemingly waiting for a reaction. "You two are very clever. How is it possible for one man to live thousands of years?"

Andy fell silent as she thought. Her green eyes darted back and forth as if she were reading words on a page that only she could see.

I let my own thoughts wander, trying to decipher what this man meant. Only five people had witnessed the event in question. Of the five, only two had remained in Tehrahey to speak of it. The other three had Traveled out of Tehrahey to someplace else. Maybe he could be Samuel or Roger, but that didn't seem likely. I doubted they ever really left Tehrahey, and that was a thought.

Were we on Tehrahey anymore?

The more I pondered it, the more I realized we couldn't be. It'd been early morning at the CTS, but here day had already given way to night. So, if we weren't on Tehrahey anymore, there were three people to consider. Of the three, only one could live as long as Amyntor claimed. As far as I knew, Adam and Eve were both normal Tehraheyians. I doubted that they would have lived any longer than fifty years, which eliminated both of them.

Upon closer inspection, I realized Amyntor didn't appear to be as old as I had originally thought. His face did not have any wrinkles, and though he had white hair and a long beard, underneath it, he looked like most of the adults in the CTS. He really wasn't aging.

With a gulp, I offered my guess. "You're the Traveler, aren't you?"

Chapter 6
-The Truth about History-

2-12.11.12.17.4 T.S.T.
Time's Keep

A grin spread across Amyntor's face. "Yes, I am the second Traveler from the legend."

We were actually meeting a Traveler! I never thought I'd ever meet someone as amazingly powerful as a Traveler. This man had the ability to go wherever, whenever he wanted. No one could tell him what to do or beat him for not following orders. I envied his ability to avoid places he didn't like. That probably had something to do with why he never returned to Tehrahey. Or maybe it had something to do with whatever had happened with the Four Councilmen. I knew Max preferred to avoid kids after he set them up. It made it harder for them to get revenge.

Andy sat upright and struggled to find her voice. "You-You're really him?"

He offered a single nod. That didn't make things better.

"Why did you attack the people who were helping you?" Andy asked, still caught up in the earlier lesson.

I remained more concerned about our current situation very far from anything we knew. "What are you going to do to us?"

Amyntor stayed calm and did his best to reassure us. "I just want to talk with you. Your story confirmed my suspicions. Roger Tal has been lying about the events of that night so many years ago. He painted himself to be the victim, when in fact, I was."

Amyntor then told us his version of his time spent on Tehrahey.

At first, I was skeptical. With all the amazing powers he possessed, how were we supposed to believe the Four Councilmen had attacked him? No one would be dumb enough to attack a Traveler. A person would have to be crazy to consider attacking a Traveler, and the Four Councilmen were not crazy. They were the smartest minds in Tehrahey. Although, Mr. Ethan had told us people tried to steal *The Book of Time* from the first Traveler. Some of them must have thought they could beat a Traveler; otherwise, why would they try?

Our host only ever stopped his story when Andy or I asked a question. When Andy asked a question, it was to learn more details. When I did, it was to try to trip him up. I figured if I could stump him with the right question, it would prove he had lied to us. The same tactic worked with Max all the time. However, the man managed to answer every question without hesitation. I couldn't detect any signs of obvious hesitation. That didn't mean he wasn't lying, just that he was an adult.

According to Amyntor, the Four Councilmen had drugged him when they got their first big breakthrough in finding the Tablets. With him unconscious, the Four Councilmen had tried, with help from an unknown fifth individual, to transfer Amyntor's powers to Roger Tal. Amyntor had regained consciousness before they could complete the spell and Traveled out of Tehrahey. Adam and Eve had attempted to stop him, but all they managed to do was get pulled along with him. The three of them had ended up someplace new—someplace very green. The whole experience had left Amyntor drained, and it took him days to recover with Adam and Eve's help. During that time, the couple explained how Roger Tal orchestrated the attack against him with help from someone else.

When we asked who the fifth person was, Amyntor shook his head. "They did not know. He only ever spoke to Roger, and the more the two talked, the more bitter and angry Roger became, until he managed to convince the others to turn against me."

"But why?" I could maybe see them attacking him, but why so soon? They had struck after the first clue?

A frown enveloped him as he slowly shook his head. "I did not fully understand it myself at the time, but I intended to find out."

He told us how he had planned on returning to Tehrahey to confront Roger and Samuel. He had offered to bring Adam and Eve back, but they had chosen to stay behind, preferring their new world to their old one. Learning they had abandoned Tehrahey like that came as a shock, but I also couldn't blame them. I wanted to leave Tehrahey and never look back, if I could get Andy, Jason, Max out too. I couldn't leave them behind. I was nothing without them.

When Amyntor attempted Traveling back to Tehrahey, he learned he wasn't as healed as he had thought. He had left the garden of Adam and Eve, but instead of arriving on Tehrahey, he had found himself here, a castle he called Time's Keep. "That was the last time I ever Traveled. I once held out hope that my powers would return but gave up after the first thousand years."

He surprised me by offering a sad smile. That wasn't the thing people normally smiled about. He'd been trapped here. I hoped the same wouldn't be true for us. The thought of staying here caused the hairs on the back of my neck to stand up.

"Where exactly are we?" Andy asked, eyeing the darkness outside the window.

"Take a look for yourselves." He gestured toward the window. He and Luna watched as Andy and I peered outside.

Darkness blanketed the world, but there was just enough of a glow from the empty black sky to discern bits of where we were. Turns out, we were at the top of a very tall stone tower—one of several shorter towers that comprised this castle. The castle appeared to be perched on a cliff edge that dropped into an ocean. I could just make out the moving waves, and, if I listened carefully, I could hear them crashing against the rocks. I couldn't look away. Even though Entstal and the CTS were along the coast, I'd never seen the ocean before.

"I believe," Amyntor continued, "we are in a sort of in-between world. It is called Time's Keep, though I cannot say how I came to know this. I feel as if the world simply told me."

I wanted to ask if he was sure about the world's name, but something stopped me. A mysterious presence, as if the world itself could speak, repeatedly whispered the name back to me in my mind. Time's Keep echoed through my conscious, and I understood what Amyntor meant.

This world was Time's Keep.

We returned to our earlier seats, so he pressed on with the story. "As you may have already guessed, we are not in Tehrahey. However, we are not in the same world where I left Adam and Eve."

Luna stretched her wings before settling down again. "Amyntor once had me search for any sort of land, but there is none. When I fly in a straight line, the castle appears in front of me. I've tried flying in every direction, but I always end up back here. This world consists of nothing but darkness." She sounded so upset, and I understood why;

being trapped someplace with no chance of leaving felt awful, and I dealt with that every day.

Amyntor stroked the owl's chest.

Andy eyed Luna, confused. "I read that owls like the dark."

Luna didn't answer, and Amyntor stopped stroking her feathers. "Under normal circumstances, you would be correct, but it wears you down when it is always night. If it had not been for these two arriving, I have no doubt I would have gone mad."

"How did Cat and Luna get here if we're between worlds?" I asked.

Amyntor regarded Cat with confusion. "Cat found us. I am not exactly sure how. One day, I discovered him wandering around the castle. He has remained ever since. I know he could Travel away if he wanted to. He chooses to stay."

Andy scoffed, "How can he Travel? He's just a cat."

Andy and I jumped to our feet as Cat spoke from directly behind us on the back of the bench. "It's quite simple, really."

I turned from him to the bed where had slept earlier. He was actually a Traveler?

"All cats can Travel." He jumped down out of sight and reappeared from behind an alarm on Amyntor's desk across the room. "It's just most cats don't realize they can." Again, he expertly vanished and reappeared on the table. "The ones that do know how are usually pretty good about hiding it from humans." I couldn't quite be sure since he was a cat, but he looked pretty smug. "Word of advice; just because someone's eyes are closed does not mean they aren't listening." He disappeared behind the alarm and reclaimed his spot on the bed.

I watched him for a moment, waiting to see if he had anymore magic abilities he wanted to show us. If he did, he wasn't sharing.

Amyntor picked the alarm off the floor where we'd dropped it earlier. "After realizing I was trapped here, I tinkered with the many clocks in this castle. The previous inhabitants held a huge fascination with time. I discovered that, while I did not have the power to Travel myself, I could, on occasion, send small objects. I enchanted dozens of watches and sent them to both Tehrahey and my home world over the years. I hoped one would fetch someone to replace me."

What did he mean by that? Did he mean take his place here in the castle or something more?

Before I could ask which he meant, Andy raised her hand. "Did any of the watches bring anyone else to you?"

"This one has come back once before, and two returned from my home world. That is how Luna got here. Never occurred to me the watch would bring me animals." Amyntor hesitated, his face growing sad. "The other brought a young boy. I trained him as best I could, but by then, my world had forgotten about Travelers. They feared him and how he would change their way of life, so they murdered him."

How could people kill someone who wanted to help them? The fact that Tehraheyians had done that didn't entirely surprise me. I knew how mean adults in my world could be. At least I knew how to handle them. I would have no idea how to handle people in any other world. Something told me they would be completely different than anything I was used to, which could be good or bad. One thing I knew for sure, I never wanted to go to Amyntor's home world.

"What happened?" Andy asked.

They must have poisoned him like the Four Councilmen had done to Amyntor. How else could a person gain an advantage over a Traveler? Even then, poison didn't kill Amyntor, so how did someone manage to kill his apprentice? I thought Travelers were immortal.

Amyntor replied in an unsteady voice I recognized; my voice got the same way anytime Ms. Hess made me talk after hitting me. Amyntor cleared his throat. "They just took him away. He did not fight. He knew they were scared. If he struggled, it would only have made things worse."

"How could he make his death worse by fighting?" I didn't believe that. If Amyntor's apprentice had fought back, he might still be alive.

Amyntor looked up from the floor with tears pooling in his eyes. "A true Traveler stands for peace above all else. Fighting would have gone against that." He fell silent. After a few ticks, he took a deep breath and wiped away his tears. "I am sorry. It still is not easy to talk about."

Andy cast me a quick look. Adults never cried in front of us. It felt weird. We didn't know how to react. "We didn't mean to upset you."

The sorrow faded from his features as he shook his head and regained his composure. "No, it is not your fault. Where were we?"

Intent on furthering the learning and knowing Amyntor didn't mind talking to us, Andy got him back on topic. "You were telling us about the alarms."

"Oh, of course." He raised the alarm that had brought us here by its aged strap. "This one has returned on two separate occasions. The first time happened long ago and brought Samuel Ents. He wanted to apologize for his actions. I never expected to see any of my attackers again. I definitely did not expect the conversation to be so civil."

Andy's head bobbed before asking her next question. She understood that fairly well from dealing with Max. Her worst bully becoming something of a friend, at the very least an ally, probably had never occurred to her when we were younger. "What did you do to him?"

"We discussed his cousin, Roger. Samuel was worried about him. He explained their betrayal had been spurred on by the death of Roger's mother. She had not been born on Tehrahey, and he had promised to get her home before she died. He blamed me for failing to fulfill that promise. By the time Samuel arrived here, Roger had overthrown the king and sought to use my stolen powers as the Maker to save Tehrahey in memory of his mother." Amyntor paused and took a deep breath. "I took too long to help. He thought he could do it faster."

That explained the betrayal. If something happened to Andy, Jason, or Max because someone had failed to help us, I'd probably get mad at them too.

Amyntor rose from his chair and walked to the fireplace, gazing into its flickering flames. "Samuel wanted me to return to Tehrahey. I told him that would not be possible but offered some advice for his cousin. Roger needed to be wary of his powers; they were stronger than he could imagine. Without caution, he would destroy everything he touched. Then I sent Samuel home. I don't know what happened to him after that. Several years later, that same watch brought me two people—a young boy and girl. Best friends for eight years living in one of the worst creations Tehrahey has to offer."

Andy and I studied the alarm dangling at his side, realizing one of the Four Councilmen had once held it. How had something that had once belonged to Samuel Ents ended up in the CTS?

Then another thought occurred to me. Amyntor had mentored the first person who had been brought to him, and he had mentioned replacing himself earlier. Did he want to teach us to become Travelers?

Amyntor flipped the watch and held it in his palm. "I am amazed you were both brought here. The watch would only Travel the person who fits the criteria I am looking for, which means you both have the character for the job. The problem is, only one of you can have what I offer."

He *did* want one us to be a Traveler, but only one. I wanted him to pick me. Being a Traveler would be so awesome. Bullies like Ms. Hess could never hurt me or my friends ever again. Plus, I could take the four of us out of the CTS, and even Tehrahey, for good. We'd never have to deal with a horrible world ever again. Maybe I could even find my mother, ask her why she got rid of me.

However, the smart choice would be Andy. She did the best at learning new things, which meant teaching her to be a Traveler would be a lot easier than teaching me. Plus, she had better self-control than I did. She always knew what to do, and her decisions usually ended a whole lot better for her than mine did for me. She'd be a great Traveler.

Either way, we'd get ourselves out of the CTS and find someplace better to live. Whether that ended up being on Tehrahey or another world entirely, I didn't really care, so long as we were together and safe.

My voice shook as I asked my next question, despite my best efforts to steady it. "What are you offering?" No matter how hard I tried, I couldn't prevent the feeling of hope rising through me. If he didn't say one of us could become a Traveler, I'd be crushed.

Amyntor's voice took on a more serious tone as he faced us. "There is no guarantee this may happen, but, if you can complete the task at hand, one of you could become a Traveler."

Could this really be happening? My heart pounded against my chest, and for a moment, it was all I could hear. I glanced at Andy, who wore a nervous expression, but I could see a glimmer of hope in her eyes. A smile grew on my face as I refocused on Amyntor.

"To do this, you will have to find the three Tablets and *The Book of Time*. The book seems to be vital to the success of a Traveler, seeing as how I and my first apprentice didn't fare well without its knowledge. In addition, *The Book of Time* grants its reader the powers of the Traveler. Without that book, neither of you could be a Traveler, and without a Traveler, my world is doomed."

I noticed he only mentioned his world. "What about Tehrahey?"

"Tehrahey will be more complicated. The Four Councilmen and I were cutting it close so long ago. I believe its deterioration has been rapidly accelerating since. It may be beyond saving."

Hearing this proved what most Tehraheyians already believed. Our world was dying. Sooner or later, all the water would dry up, and the food would go with it. That's when some people believed Relyt would begin. Our world would burn, and a new one would rise from the ashes. Some people looked forward to this. Not me. I didn't want to burn. I'd much rather go to a new world. Countless nights I had dreamed of seeing strange, new worlds and leaving behind all the heat, hatred, and suffering of Tehrahey. I never thought those dreams might actually come true someday.

Still, hearing one of my worst fears confirmed didn't exactly put myself at ease. Judging by the dread in her eyes, Andy felt the same.

"So, we can't do anything?" she asked in a quiet voice.

A pained expression consumed Amyntor's face as he glanced between the two of us. "There is no way to know for sure until we've studied *The Book of Time*."

As I thought of a future where we were all safe, I couldn't help but notice the strangeness of it. I had never considered something like that could be possible. By agreeing to help Amyntor, I could help keep my friends safe and give them a future worth having.

"I'll do it," I said.

I never expected to see disbelief on Andy's face; this seemed like such a simple choice, yet we didn't agree. "You can't actually think we can do this. We're just kids."

My shoulders sagged. How could she not want to do this? If one of us became a Traveler, we could escape the CTS for good. We'd never have to deal with cruel adults again. This seemed like the right thing to do, but maybe I was wrong.

When I didn't say anything, Andy continued to explain her point. "Adults have tried to find *The Book of Time* for years. He couldn't even find it!" She pointed at Amyntor.

If this offended him, he didn't show it. He just stood there and watched.

"So, we do nothing?" I asked.

"We could tell one of the adults." She raised her palm as if offering the idea to me. Unfortunately, her idea stunk.

"That's dumb!" How could she think that letting adults handle this would be a good idea? Most of them were horrible people. "I bet we could do better. Besides, would you really want someone like Ms. Hess to get her hands on *The Book of Time*?"

She shook her head so violently that the rest of her body followed suit. "No, that would be terrifying." At least she understood that much. We couldn't trust the adults in the CTS.

"I say it's our turn to give it a shot. At least this way, we'll get out of the CTS, right?" I looked to Amyntor for confirmation, which he gave. "See, we might even get out of Tehrahey completely."

Andy hesitated, her arms wrapping around herself. "But what if this doesn't work?"

"I don't know, but we have to try. We can't count on anyone else to take care of us."

Andy's gaze fell to her lap as her hands toyed with the hem of her shirt. Ticks passed, and the crackling of the fireplace echoed through the room. Finally, she lifted her head to meet my gaze. "You really want to do this?"

I nodded once.

She sighed, and her face grew serious. "Alright then, I'm in too. Someone's got to keep you out of trouble."

Sitting once more, Amyntor studied us with a serious expression. "This quest will not be easy. This adventure could very well be your first, and last. You have to understand that before agreeing."

"I know." I didn't care how tough this would be if it meant getting us out of the CTS.

Andy's earlier concerns seemed to have faded. She spoke with confidence, which she never did before when addressing an adult. "If it were easy, the adults would have done it long ago. We'll do it."

Joy spread across Amyntor's face, but he didn't let it fully consume him. "You are more than I could have ever hoped for. I know you will give this your very best." Amyntor rose. "You will begin your quest soon, however you must first return to Tehrahey. Your absence will not go unnoticed. The last time I saw this"—he held up the alarm—"it was in the possession of Samuel, and it now likely belongs to Roger. He has at least some of my old powers, and I am certain he will notice its disappearance from his world. It is paramount you tell no one you touched the alarm, or that it brought you here. Understood?"

Andy and I nodded. We didn't need to be told not to tell any adults.

"Good. I will contact you later to discuss what must be done."

Andy slowly raised her hand, but it only got as high as her shoulder before she lowered it, realizing she didn't need to do that with Amyntor. "How will you do that?"

"I will send Cat to you with a plan."

A shout came from the bed. "I did not agree to this!" Cat appeared from a black hole on the bench in front of the window. "You can't volunteer me for babysitting!" He hissed.

When did Amyntor say anything about sitting on babies? Why would anyone want to do that? I couldn't believe anyone on Tehrahey being that cruel, not even Ms. Hess. Actually, she would sit on babies.

Cat's anger didn't bother Amyntor. "I know, and I am sorry, but it has to be done."

"I hate the desert. And why should I help them? What's in it for me?" Cat sat and wrapped his tail to cover his paws. The tip continued to twitch.

"You'd be a hero, Cat," Andy said.

Cat turned his pale blue eyes to her. "Hero?" he hissed. "Been there, done that. Let me tell you something. You'd get all the credit, and everyone would forget about the scrawny black cat!" He jumped from the bench and headed for the door with his tail pointed skyward.

Andy stood and took a step after him. "I wouldn't forget about you."

I wasn't the only one caught off guard by the promise. Cat stopped, his tail twitched once, and he exhaled a deep sigh. "Fine, I'll do it." He disappeared into a black hole.

"Now that is settled, it is time to send you back. Cat will meet you later." Amyntor fiddled with a knob on the thin side of the alarm. He twisted it a couple times and pushed it into its original position. "This will take you back and you will find nothing has changed. Put the watch where you found it, and everything will return to normal. Thank you for listening to me. Good luck."

Chapter 7
-The Man of the Desert-

He held out the alarm while Andy took my hand in hers. Once the relic left Amyntor's hand, Time's Keep faded. Ahead of us, a small white light shined, and something latched onto my waist to pull me to it. This time, I didn't struggle. I let the force drag me through the darkness. We were drawn forward until the white light took the shape of the table in our records class. The pulling sensation stopped and the darkness faded to reveal the rest of room.

Just as Amyntor said, nothing had changed. Everyone remained in the same positions as when we had left. Mr. Ethan continued staring at the group of kids standing around the other relics. I put the alarm back where I found it. It began to tick loudly, but soon quieted and stopped.

Andy and I jumped when Mr. Ethan shouted, "I said, no touching!" Relief filled my veins as he headed for the other table to hit a boy in the back of the head. "Next time, listen to me."

"It really is like we were never gone," I whispered. Even though I just Traveled to another dimension and met the second Traveler from legends, I didn't expect everything to be exactly the same. I couldn't believe it worked so well.

Andy scanned the room for a tick and nodded. "It's amazing." She returned to examining the relics on the table as if nothing had ever happened. How she could do that, I would never fully understand. We had learned more from Amyntor than we ever could from Mr. Ethan,

-64-

and she still wanted to look at boring old relics? I doubted any of these were as interesting as that little alarm.

Before I could say anything to her, a blond man strolled into the room shadowed by three other men. Gray eyes in a tight face surveyed the room before focusing on our teacher. Two of the men look almost identical with tanned skin and short dark hair. The third was bald, and sunlight glinted off his skin as he passed beneath a skylight. The blonde man wore an elegant crimson robe with golden edges, while his followers wore all black. The clean, un-frayed edges of the red fabric made it seem like the man had never worn the outfit before today. It dragged across the ground behind him as he moved. The men in black kept their gazes sweeping through the room, as if they suspected one of us might attack at any moment.

I didn't like the look of this group. They wore scowls and a few scars lined the bald man's face.

Andy's shoulder brushed against mine as she shifted closer.

The man in the robe walked with his chest out and chin up just like the boy Andy had bumped into the other day.

Two of the men in black stayed by the door, blocking it. The bald man stayed close to the blond man, but not too close—the same way Max used to follow Jason when had he first arrived. The leader trusted the bald bodyguard, who stopped halfway between the door and Mr. Ethan's desk.

The blond man approached Mr. Ethan and cleared his throat. Our teacher didn't look up from his hands as he spoke. "I thought I told everyone to remain quiet."

The man replied in a harsh and strange voice, resembling Ms. Hess's tone, but with more charm. "You will have to make an exception."

"I most certainly will not!" Mr. Ethan slammed his hands on his desk and stood.

The bald man reached for something hidden within the waist of his pants, but the leader just barely flicked his wrist. The bodyguard stopped but remained ready. It happened so quickly Mr. Ethan didn't even see it.

I saw it because taking my eyes off these men seemed like a terrible idea. The sudden movement caught my attention, and when I studied the lump under the hem of his shirt, I could make out the handle of something small, like a knife.

Once our teacher's gaze landed on the man in front of him, his face paled. With large eyes, he retreated until he bumped into the wall behind him. "I-I apologize, Your Excellency. I didn't realize it was you. I thought you were one of these obnoxious children." He gestured at us with a look of disgust.

I rolled my eyes, because, of course, he tried to blame us.

The man's scowl deepened. "You mistook me for a child?"

The question had no right answer. Any fourth year student would've known not to answer. Remaining silent and still would be the safer option.

Mr. Ethan thought for a tick before slowly nodding.

"Very well." The man sighed. "I'll deal with you later. For the time being, introduce me."

"Right away, sir." Our teacher hastily moved in front of his desk, his hands wringing together. "Class, this-this is His Excellency, rule-

ruler of Tehrahey and creator of every machine in our possession … the Maker."

The class remained silent as the Maker and Mr. Ethan stood before us. As far as I knew, no kid in the CTS had ever seen the Maker before. He didn't appear as scary as I had expected, but that fact didn't stop the worry from gnawing at my stomach. He reminded me of the first time I had seen Ms. Hess. She didn't look like much, but even then, I had known to avoid her. He had all the characteristics of a bully with power and didn't try to hide them.

As the silence dragged on, Mr. Ethan played with his rolled-up sleeves. "I apologize for the students' lack of excitement at your arrival." His face shifted from looking concerned, to angry, and back again in a gust of emotions. He never did anything that fast. "These ingrates, don't understand how important it is to be in your presence."

In that tick, the Maker turned on Mr. Ethan. "As their teacher, that responsibility falls onto you. Take him away from here."

One of the guards by the door stepped forward and tried to remove Mr. Ethan, but the smaller man resisted. The bald guard eyed his cohort by the door and nodded toward our teacher. Short and little, Mr. Ethan didn't stand a chance against the two men. They dragged him from the room kicking, and pleading for another chance.

Our teacher's screams echoed through the halls. "No, please no! I'll do anything! Just give me one more chance!"

When I peeled my gaze from the doorframe to look at the Maker, I expected to find a grimace on his face, that he didn't enjoy listening to screams like that.

His features remained neutral, revealing no clues as to how he felt. "Everyone sit down."

We all sat where we stood; no one dared to move any farther.

The leader of our world studied the board for a moment—far longer than it took to read the two words written on it—then faced us. "Assuming your teacher did his job, you know about the Travelers and the Tablets, correct?"

No one answered his question.

He didn't care.

"The Tablets are the keys to the survival of Tehrahey. If I do not have them, you will die."

Upon hearing those words, fear gnawed at my gut like a starving first year student who just spent a night in isolation.

Other kids in the room shifted and squirmed much in the same way.

The Maker paid us no mind. "Many have tried to find the Tablets over the centuries; all have failed. When the time comes, you'll be the next generation to hunt for the Tablets. Pray to the Stars you don't fail. Time is running out for us all." He strode forward, drawing dangerously close to one group of kids. "On to more pressing matters. I suppose you're wondering why I decided to grace you with my presence." He paused; the air grew heavy with his words.

I tried my best not to squirm and avoided making eye contact with him. I didn't want to draw any attention to myself.

"These relics"—he gestured to the two tables with both arms— "are far too valuable to let some teacher look after. I prefer to keep a close eye on them so I know when one has been touched." Another pause, and more squirming. When he spoke again, his voice held the same level of danger Ms. Hess did when she caught someone. "I know for a fact one of you touched something on these tables. If you do not confess this tick, the entire class will suffer."

Andy glanced at me.

Amyntor had said Roger Tal would notice someone had touched the alarm, and then the Maker accused us of touching one of his relics. Did that mean the Maker was still Roger Tal? That wouldn't be possible. He had lived over five hundred years ago. Then again, he had taken Amyntor's powers, which made that long life possible. How had he managed to keep that a secret?

Even with all his power, he couldn't have known we touched the alarm. Time had stopped before it had happened; no one saw us touch it. No one could rat us out.

"I see," the Maker said, acknowledging the class's silence. He clasped his hands in front of himself. "No one wants to admit to their crime? You leave me no choice. Half rations for a week!" He turned toward the door, and the swift action swept the end of his robe through the air.

Before he could leave, a boy sitting by the other table jumped to his feet. "Wait, he did it. He touched one of the relics!" The kid pointed to the boy Mr. Ethan had hit after our return.

The Maker regarded the accused with a deep frown. "Cylus, grab him and take him to Kin Naltz'am. We have much to discuss, young man."

Cylus nodded and marched toward the kid, who began to spew excuses from his mouth, all of them different and all of them mashed together to create an incomprehensible sound that could only be described as panic. The adult loomed over everyone sitting around our table before he bent forward and latched onto the kid's arm.

The boy yelped as the adult pulled him to his feet.

Meanwhile, the Maker rummaged through Mr. Ethan's desk until he pulled a piece of paper from the drawer. He handed this to Cylus as he returned to the front of the room with the boy in tow. "See to it the mess hall gets these student's numbers so they know which children will only be getting half rations for the next week."

He still wanted to take our food privileges? But he got what he wanted! He knew someone had touched the alarm, and he had a culprit captured. Why carry through with starving us? He probably enjoyed the thought of us going hungry.

The boy who had spoken apparently felt brave. "But I told you who touched the relic."

"Ah, yes." The Maker's smile never faltered, and I didn't trust it. "What is your number so we can mark it on the list?"

I wouldn't have given him my number. Besides our names, our numbers were the only thing adults in the CTS could use to identify us. An adult knowing our number almost rivaled an adult knowing our name. Luckily only Ms. Lahna seemed to care about names.

"Two-five-one-zero-one-five," the boy recited in a rush, as if he expected some sort of reward for the information he gave. I don't think he realized what he had just done.

The Maker smoothed his robe and tugged down his sleeves. "Good to know. Cylus, mark that this boy here gets two weeks of half rations."

Cylus nodded once.

"That is what happens to betrayers." The Maker wagged his finger at the boy. "There'll be no snitches in *my* Tehrahey." He started to leave but hesitated. He turned to the table with the alarm and eyed it suspiciously before studying the table where we sat. He scanned the few kids surrounding our table, including Andy and me, before he and Cylus left.

The pleas of the captive kid didn't echo nearly as much as Mr. Ethan's, but that didn't make me feel any better.

Despite the lack of adult supervision, everyone remained silent.

I couldn't understand what had just happened. Before this morning, I hadn't even known what the Maker looked like. How Jason would talk about the man, I had always expected him to look rough and dirty. He looked like someone who got to bathe every morning and didn't have to wear the same clothes every day. He even had shoes! Very few people had those down here. Beneath his clean appearance hid a cruel bully. I had spent enough time dealing with bullies to feel confident in identifying them.

Class didn't end for another forty-five ticks. I expected Mr. Ethan to return, or at least some other adult, but, as time passed, it became obvious we were on our own. Some more of the Maker's guards entered to collect all the relics into sacks before leaving us alone.

At some point, the boy who had spoken began to cry. No one made any effort to comfort him. He had made the choice to reveal his number.

Once it became apparent no adults were coming for us, kids left the room, probably trying to get lunch early.

When we were the only ones left, I looked to Andy, wondering what she wanted to do.

Her shoulders slumped forward, and her gaze fixed on her lap.

"Andy, it'll be okay." I put a hand on her arm to comfort her.

She shook her head and stood without a word.

"Everything will be fine," I continued, trying my best to soothe her while rising to my own feet. "We won't starve. Jason and Max will share with us."

As her gaze met my own; it became obvious her concern lay elsewhere. "I know they will. Not even Max is that cruel." She pointed toward the door. "Those boys didn't do anything wrong, and they are the ones who will get punished. Amyntor said something like this might happen. The Maker wanted *us*!"

"You don't know for sure." Judging by her raised eyebrow, I wasn't the only one who didn't believe that. The Maker had looked directly at the alarm before he left.

Andy had already figured this out as well. "Do you honestly believe he did all this just because some kid touched a hand iron?"

"What should we do? He's bound to find out that boy isn't who he's looking for."

Andy looked away from the alarm. "We can't do anything until Cat finds us."

A hint of movement caught my attention—not at the door but in the skylight. A strange shadow became visible within the circle of light.

Chapter 8
-Gifts from a Shadow-

2-12.11.12.17.4 T.S.T.
CTS, Entstal
Tehrahey

"What is that?" I moved to stand under the skylight. Nothing ever really moved over the openings. We rarely saw any birds through the glass and never any humans. The mystery of what could be up there beckoned. It could be a chance to see something new, or at the very least, something different. What I found proved to be very new, and I doubted anyone on Tehrahey would ever see anything like it again.

Cat sat perched on the edge of the skylight and looked down with bored, blue eyes.

"Huh, didn't expect that," I mused.

Andy joined me a tick later in staring out the skylight. "Cat."

His bored expression seemed to be waiting for something. I had a guess what that might be.

After scanning the room one last time, I headed for the door and pushed it closed. We were only halfway through this hand cycle. If the Stars were on our side, no one would come to bother us, especially not with the next cycle dedicated to lunch.

I rejoined Andy in the light and called up to Cat. "We're alone."

He backed out of sight, and a tick later, his voice greeted us from behind. "I hate this burning litterbox of a world."

He paced on the floor next to a brown sack and shook out each paw one by one. A grumpy expression covered his face, which didn't surprise me. Something told me he preferred it that way. Once he finished and sat down, he offered us a glare. "Do you know how long

I've been sitting out there?" When neither of us answered, he pressed on with his complaining. "Fifteen minutes. Do you understand what that's like with this fur?"

We shook our heads.

He sighed. "Let's get this over with. The first goal is to get you out of the CTS. You'll need enough food to last you several days in the Erima."

"We're going into the Erima?" Andy squeaked. Her gaze drifted to the ceiling and the world above. The Erima desert would not be pleasant, but it had to be better than staying here and dealing with adults like Ms. Hess.

"That is what I just said, yes. When we leave the CTS, I'll be taking you to Xic-Patan," Cat explained, but it didn't actually explain much. I didn't have any clue as to where Xic-Patan was.

"Where is that?" I asked.

Cat's head dipped forward before focusing on me. "Does it really matter? I don't have all the time in the world here. Someone could walk through that door at any minute."

Oops. We didn't need an adult coming in here and yelling at us for not being in class. Although, in our defense, we were in class. I doubted any adult would actually care. They'd jump at the chance to punish us.

"What do we need to do?" I asked, saving the other questions for later when we weren't on a time limit. I refused to sabotage my only chance of escape.

"Most of your supplies are in Amyntor's old pack." His tail tapped the bag next to him. "Inside are two pairs of sandals, as well as a tent, enchanted canteens—basically everything Amyntor kept with him while on Tehrahey." That flat heap of leather couldn't possibly be holding all of that. The thing appeared to be empty. Cat continued, unconcerned with the current state of the bag. "What it doesn't have is food. The best place to find food will likely be the pantry here in the CTS."

Andy's relaxed state vanished as her body stiffened. "You want us to steal food?"

Cat's head tilted as he addressed her. "Is there a problem with that?"

"No," I replied, attempting to answer for her. Getting food from the storeroom wouldn't be easy, but it also wouldn't be impossible. I knew Max had done it once or twice. Although, he had only ever gotten away with whatever fit in his hands. I didn't know how we'd manage enough to fill the whole bag, even if it did have stuff in it already. Still, if we wanted out of here, we needed to do this. I couldn't let Andy tell Cat we couldn't do this. We should at least try.

Andy crossed her arms. "Yeah, sure. It'll be completely fine. They actually give out food all of the time."

Cat seemed to pick up on her mock acceptance and countered in a pleased voice. "Perfect. Then filling the bag should be a piece of cake."

Andy's gaze narrowed as she watched him but she remained silent. Her lips quivered with unspoken insults and comebacks she decided to keep to herself. I expected to hear them soon enough once Cat left and hoped none of them were directed at me.

"How much time do we have?"

"Less with each passing second. You may want to hurry."

"We can't start until lunch."

"No, you're right, take your time. It's not like the world is counting on you two."

I pointed to the door behind us. "If we walk out that door without an adult accompanying us, we'll get caught and locked in isolation for ditching."

"He's right. Even carrying that bag around will attract unwanted attention. Kids notice me because of my hair all the time. They'll notice that bag, and so will the adults."

Cat tossed back his head with a groan. "Well, then what do you propose?"

"Wait until lunch?" I offered.

Andy agreed with the idea. "The mess hall will be full of kids and parental guardians." However, she didn't stop there. The gears were already turning in her mind, plotting our best option. "There will be plenty of distractions then. However, we'd still need to get *into* the pantry, which won't be easy."

"Alright, so we can get there …" I paused, thinking for a moment. Getting to the room would be the easy part. Entering would be a different story. "But how do we get in? The door will either be locked or guarded, if not both. They don't want anyone stealing food." Every single person in the CTS—child or adult—received a set amount of food each day. While everyone could receive less food as punishment, no one got to have any extra. That's how things were supposed to be, anyway. Sometimes people snuck an extra bite or two.

With a hum, Andy's hand rose to hold her chin. "Didn't Max steal some food when we were younger?"

"He never told me *how* he did it."

"Could he do it again?"

"Well …" I thought for a tick. "Probably."

"We'll need him," Andy said, and I couldn't argue with that, but why stop there?

"Might as well get Jason too. Some extra muscle wouldn't hurt." I knew my friend wouldn't have a problem fighting adults. He had always wanted to fight the parental guardians but held back because he didn't want to get punished and disappear. However, if we could escape punishment by leaving the CTS, he'd have no reason not to go after any adults who might try to stop us.

"His experience outside would be helpful too."

Another good point. We'd want both of our friends with us.

Cat's tail lashed back and forth. "Just what do you think you're doing?"

What an odd question; he knew exactly what we were doing. "Figuring out how to get the food," I replied.

"Just like you wanted." Andy smirked, pleased by his agitated state.

He gave her a hard stare, his tail tip twitching ever so slightly. "You two don't get it. You will have to do this alone. No help from friends."

Well, that didn't seem fair. Andy and I got to help each other; what would be wrong with a little more help? "Why can't we ask them for help?"

"The watch only brought you two, and Amyntor told you not to tell anyone about this quest of yours."

"Yeah, and we won't tell any adults," I said. "These are our friends we're talking about. We're not doing this without them. Besides, the alarm might have brought them too."

"It's bad enough the world is in the hands of two twelve-year-olds, especially with one as scrawny as you." His tail pointed to me—he was one to talk. "Now you want to make it four?"

"Only Max and I are twelve," Andy offered.

I hated it when people assumed I was younger. I stood up straighter as I corrected his mistake. "I'm thirteen! And Jason's fourteen."

The disapproval on his face grew and almost hurt. "All you're doing is cementing my concerns that you're too young to save any world."

Those words actually hurt. But they were no different than anything else I had heard growing up. At this point, I just assumed people didn't believe in me.

Cat's words affected Andy just as much as they did me. The smirk left her face, her shoulders slumped, and her arms hung limp at her sides. We shared a dejected look, then something snapped inside her. With clenched fists, Andy's face hardened, and her hair burst into flames—not real flames, but the red hair definitely gave off the impression that if it touched me, it'd burn.

Due to that fact, I stepped backward.

Luckily, Andy's anger wasn't directed toward me. She faced our tiny friend who, for his part, didn't flinch. Even Jason would have if she had looked at him like that.

Cat's expression did change, but it shifted in a controlled manner, not a panicked one. His ears shifted forward as he focused on Andy scolding him.

"You should have more faith in us! Amyntor thinks we can do this. That should be enough for you. Kyle thinks we can do this, and that's good enough for me."

My face warmed at Andy's words. She thought I thought we could do this. I *didn't* know if we could. I just wanted to try. At the very least, this would get us out of the CTS. I didn't want to lie to her, but I didn't want to stop her either.

Even if her words didn't change Cat's mind, they helped me. This was about more than leaving the CTS. This would help my friends too.

"What does age have to do with it anyway?" she continued, tossing her hands in the air. "If being older meant this would be possible, then an adult would have found *The Book of Time* ages ago. They didn't. Besides, what gives you the right to say we're too young? I've read about cats, and you don't live very long. What makes you think you're older than us?"

Cat's unamused expression never changed as he answered her. "I'm fifty-one, give or take a few years."

Andy faltered, her head dipping forward for a tick before she corrected it. "Fine, so you're older than us. We can still do this. Right, Kyle?"

Two sets of eyes fell onto me—one, questioning blue; the other hopeful green. I couldn't quite believe this. Even though this quest terrified Andy, she had faith that we could do this simply because she thought I did. She needed me. That made my answer obvious, even if it scared me as well. I couldn't let her down.

"We will do this," I answered with the confidence of someone much surer of himself than I currently felt.

Andy beamed at me.

I didn't know if cats could smirk, but it sure did look like one hid under the black fur of Cat's face.

"Alright then. We'll do it your way."

Chapter 9
-Breaking in to Break Out-

2-12.11.12.17.4 T.S.T.
CTS, Entstal
Tehrahey

With the time left in the cycle, Andy, Cat, and I devised a plan. Andy and I would go to lunch, as usual, and meet up with Jason and Max. Cat would follow us from above. We would wait for his shadow at each skylight we past.

Cat didn't like the plan, stating, "I hate being out in that litterbox."

I didn't know what he meant by litterbox, but having him up there would work better than having him follow one of us through the hallways. That would attract too much attention. The bag would be bad enough. We all had so little down here. If one kid had something and other kids found out about it, they would try to steal it. That usually led to a fight, which led to the parental guardians getting involved and confiscating the item. I slipped the bag onto my shoulder under my shirt. This made me look lumpy—which earned a giggle from Andy—but would keep it out of sight of any other kids.

Once the parental guardians shouted to signal the end of class, Andy and I headed for lunch. No one seemed to notice the strange shadow that kept appearing in the skylights.

Andy and I situated ourselves in the dim corridor just outside mess hall the doors to wait for our friends.

Max arrived first, eager to get his next meal and racing ahead of a stampede of kids. However, when he saw us waiting at the doors, he slowed and tilted his head.

"Waiting for me?"

The sandstorm raging in my stomach made it difficult to speak, but I somehow managed. "We need your help with something."

His eyebrows rose as a smirk formed on his face. "Really? You *both* need my help?" He eyed Andy, who formed a defensive barrier by crossing her arms. She chose to remain silent, so Max continued. "Sure, what do you need?"

With Andy refusing to speak to him due to his smugness, the job of answering fell to me. "It's complicated. I'll explain when Jason gets here."

Max leaned against a nearby wall, letting the stones support him as he joined us. "This should be fun." His expression shifted from excitement to boredom. He didn't like to sit still for long unless it meant he got to eat. Waiting with us meant missing lunch.

Other kids rushed past us to get to their next meal, and we stayed close to the wall to avoid getting trampled. Thank the Stars we didn't have to wait long and listen to him whine about it.

A few ticks after Max had propped himself against the wall, Jason emerged from a dark passageway behind a group of kids. They were a few years younger than us and looked terrified by the large shadow behind them. I didn't blame them. With his close-shaved head, wide shoulders, and almost permanent scowl, Jason looked fearsome on most days. His black eye only added to his appearance. It let everyone know the big scary kid knew how to fight. He stopped when he saw us.

"What's wrong?" Concern surfaced in his good eye, as he examined my lumpiness.

This was it. As far as I knew, no kid had ever escaped the CTS before. If one had, he definitely never went on a quest to find the

Tablets and *The Book of Time*. Excitement raced through my body, colliding with my nerves and putting everything on edge, contributing to the growing sandstorm in my stomach. My legs itched to get moving again. "Nothing yet. We need food."

Max hitched a thumb over his shoulder and, in a tone that suggested I had made him wait for nothing, said, "That is what lunch is for."

"We need more than just a meal." I lifted my shirt to reveal the bag. "We need enough for the four of us to last days."

Max's eyebrows drew up, and his mouth parted. Despite his surprise over the size of the task, he recovered quickly. "Even if I could, it won't all fit in the bag."

I had thought the same thing at first, but Cat had assured me this bag would hold every bit of food we needed and then some. Long ago, Amyntor had enchanted it to help him on his journeys through Tehrahey, specifically the Erima. This meant that not only would it hold all our food but it would preserve it as well.

"Trust me, it will," I said. For proof, I removed a pair of leather sandals and handed them to Andy.

She knelt and began fastening them to her feet. Having never done that before, she struggled at first but soon figured it out.

This little display didn't impress Max. "Those don't exactly take up a lot of room."

I readjusted my shirt to conceal the bag. "Just trust me, alright?"

Jason broke his silence with a whisper, a slight grin crossing his face. "Are we getting out?"

I stayed quiet for a moment, too afraid to say the words aloud, which he took as a yes.

"About time." Jason had tried multiple times over the last year to walk out of the CTS, but the guards always sent him back. I had no idea how he found the entrance to this maze in the first place.

Not knowing how to proceed, I repeated Cat's earlier instructions to Jason and Max. "We need food first."

Jason sometimes would tell us about his time up there. A lot of the stories involved going to bed without dinner, because he and his father would run out of food, and as such, he didn't question the need for it. However, he did question our sudden desire to leave. "Definitely. Why now?"

Pointing between Andy and myself, I tried to find the right words. "We made …" I almost said *friend*. That would be the wrong word. Cat didn't count as one, did he? "We met someone."

"In your records class?"

"Not exactly." After all, we weren't technically in our class when we had met Amyntor, Cat, and Luna.

"Seriously?" Max asked, his voice dropping to a whisper as well. "We're breaking out?"

A group of kids passed us, and I didn't answer him until they were out of earshot. "Someone will meet us in the pantry to get us out once we've gotten what we need. Can you get us in there?"

While rubbing his chin, Max scanned the ground, as if looking for his answer there. "It'll be difficult, but if it means getting out of here, you can count on me."

A shout reached us from the mess hall, and Andy whipped her head around toward the noise. Once we confirmed it hadn't been directed at us, she turned around. "So, how do we do this?"

"First time getting your hands dirty?" Max chuckled, already knowing the answer.

Andy shot him a glare.

Jason raised his fist in warning. "Max …"

Max acknowledged the threat by raising his hands in surrender. "I'm just teasing!" When all he got were hard looks from the three of us, he dropped the matter. "Fine. If we want to get into the pantry, the best way to do that is through the back."

Max started walking down a hallway and waved for us to follow.

I pointed after him and Jason and Andy followed the silent instruction. Cat's shadow did as well.

"There's a back entrance?" Andy asked.

"Yep. How do you think they get all the food in there? Have you ever seen them bring in a delivery? It's in the restricted section."

Andy stopped midstride, and I almost bumped into her. "You mean where all the adults hang out?" A gentle push on her back got her moving once again.

The large underground maze of the CTS could be split into two sections. The main area housed the mess hall, classrooms, washrooms, and the sleeping chambers—basically anywhere us kids could go. The other part, referred to as the restricted section, contained the adult's bedrooms, their own mess hall, and the exit from the CTS. Only adults were allowed in this section. Going in there always meant trouble for the kid dumb enough to do it. Still, some kids did from time to time. Max had, Jason too. The idea of going into those hallways didn't sound too great to me either, but I trusted Max. Even if he didn't always make the best decisions, he knew better than anyone how to do this. Plus, none of us wanted to get caught, especially him; it would only ruin his reputation of being the sneakiest of us all.

Max smirked over his shoulder. "Is there any other restricted section in the CTS?" He led us through the hallways until we arrived at the end of the kids' area.

The unmarked hallway resembled every other one down here, but I had learned from experience this one was different. If we ran into any adults down there, they'd beat us and throw us each in our own isolation room.

Max peered around the corner. "No adults in sight," he mumbled.

As I scanned the dim hallway with its patches of sunlight, I wondered if maybe we should have tried to convince Cat to wait until tonight. The darkness would've helped. My gut filled with doubt at our chances of sneaking all the way back to the pantry from this side. The adults didn't like it when kids snuck back here, hated it even more when they tried to steal food.

Andy seemed to have read my mind and voiced my concerns. "I'm not so sure about this."

Max chuckled to himself. "This should be easy, just follow my lead."

Max's confidence did little to sway my nerves, but I knew I should trust him. Nobody could sneak around the adults better than him. He knew what he was doing. Still, with each step, this journey became more and more real. I didn't think could do this. If we actually stole food and got outside, we'd be in the Erima. I wasn't ready for that! I wasn't strong enough to deal with kids in here, how could I hope to handle adults out there?

My mind told me to turn back and go have lunch. We could do this in a few years once I got stronger. But I couldn't go back alone, and Max led us farther into the restricted section, making it harder and harder to walk away from this.

It became clear pretty fast that Max had been back here more than once. He only slowed at intersections to check for adults; he never stopped to wonder where to go next. The farther we got without seeing an adult, the bolder Max grew and spent less time checking corners. As we walked down a hallway, he spun on his heel to look at us with a smug grin as he walked backward. "I told you this would be easy!"

Jason shushed him. "Keep your voice down."

"Why? No one's here."

"There will be if you keep talking!" Andy hissed.

He really should have paid attention to what lay ahead. Then he would have at least seen the next intersection. Jason and I tried to grab him, but he kept going. He stepped into the beam from the skylight, and a gasp rose from one of the hallways. Max stilled in an instant, his expression shifting from carefree to panic in less than a tick.

Without warning, Jason pulled Andy and me backward from the intersection, leaving Max alone to face the rushed footsteps approaching from an unseen hallway. What should we do? We couldn't just leave Max behind, could we? We shouldn't have let him lead. He had gotten cocky, and that had gotten him caught. Would we be next?

"Max, what are you doing back here?" the adult voice asked.

I shook off Jason's hand, thanking the Stars for this luck. Only two adults knew Max, and only one knew his real name.

Sure enough, the adult who joined Max in the light was Ms. Lahna. We weren't in huge trouble.

Andy released a sigh of relief. "Oh, thank the Stars."

This drew the teacher's attention our way. She did a double take before her mouth went slack. In a gust, she ushered Max toward us. "What are you four doing here?" she whispered, bending to our level. "I expect more from you." Though she sounded angry, her golden eyes held concern, like she didn't want us to get into trouble as much as we didn't want to.

None of us answered her question.

Her gaze swept over Andy and me. "You know the Maker is here today. You couldn't have picked a worse day to be sneaking around."

This news shocked Max and caused Jason's eyes to darken. "The Maker was here, in your records class … today?" Jason asked, fists clenched at his sides. His question, as well as his swift change in demeanor, went unnoticed by everyone but me.

Why did simply mentioning the Maker upset him that much? I knew he didn't like him and understood why, but that reaction didn't make sense to me.

"If he or his guards caught you, sitting in isolation for a day would be a blessing. Now tell me why you're back here."

With slumped shoulders, Andy gazed at the ground. "We can't."

Ms. Lahna raised an eyebrow. "Can't, or won't?"

Again, no one answered.

I wondered what she would do. I knew she wouldn't beat us, but would she let us go? How could we get out of this and still get the food? What would Cat do? I could see his shadow pacing in the skylight behind Ms. Lahna.

As the silence progressed, Ms. Lahna scanned our faces.

Max cracked first. "We're just trying to steal some extra food."

Andy's head snapped up with wide eyes. "Max!"

"What?" He shrugged. "She's the nice one, right?" His eyes held a look of, *Shut up, I'm not telling her everything.*

A faint smile covered the teacher's lips at his kind words. However, it vanished instantly. "You can't be stealing food. Come on, I'll take you back to the mess hall." With a hand on Max's shoulder, she began to guide us the way we had come.

With a sigh, Andy turned around.

I didn't follow. We needed to get that food, plus Cat's shadow had left the window. He stood on the other side of the intersection, staring at us with pale blue eyes. We held each other's gaze.

What should I do? This was my chance, what I'd been hoping for since we had entered the restricted section—an escape from this crazy, impossible plan. I could follow our teacher and be returned to where I belonged. I could have lunch and go to classes while pretending this little trip had never happened. I could have an okay dinner, then fight over a cot tonight. It would be the same thing I did every day, but it would be safe. I wouldn't have to go into the Erima and face all the horrors Jason had described.

Did I want that?

I looked over my shoulder at Ms. Lahna. She hadn't noticed I wasn't following yet. I couldn't bring myself to follow her.

Cat studied me with his uncaring expression. I could practically hear him groaning about wasting his time, how he had come here for nothing. But I swore there was something else. He seemed to say, *I knew you couldn't handle this. You can't do anything right.*

In that moment, I knew what I had to do. I couldn't let that stupid, smug black cat be right. "You can't take us back," I said, my voice firm.

"What?" Ms. Lahna finally noticed me, then she spotted Cat standing at the edge of the shadows and gasped. "How did a cat get in?"

"Is that a shadow?" Max asked.

Our teacher's gaze snapped to him like he'd sprouted a second head.

"Ms. Lahna," Andy started in a calm voice, "can I have that item I gave to you back?"

I didn't know what Andy meant by that, but it appeared to mean something to our teacher. She fixed her amber gaze on her favorite student. "You're leaving, aren't you?"

Andy nodded.

Ms. Lahna took a deep breath and covered her face with her hands. She released the air in her lungs and met Andy's gaze. "Of course. It's in my room. You four come with me. I think I've got a better way to get you into the pantry."

Chapter 10
-No Turning Back-

2-12.11.12.17.4 T.S.T.
CTS, Entstal
Tehrahey

Ms. Lahna led us down the hallway at a rapid pace. "The Stars are on your side. The Maker being here has thrown everything into disarray. Everyone, except for Hess who's following him around like his shadow, is doing their best to avoid him. No one wants to end up like Mr. Ethan." She fell silent as she imagined whatever cruel fate awaited him.

Despite her rushed speed, Andy stayed close beside her, so much so that their arms brushed each other several times.

I practically jumped out of my skin when Max's voice spoke beside my ear. "We're going farther from the pantry."

I meant to ignore him. It would have been easy, if not for his next question. "What does she have of Andy's anyway?"

He waited for an answer, but I didn't have one. What did our teacher have? Since when did Andy have anything at all? I couldn't answer that any better than Jason or Max could. "I don't know."

"Really? I thought you two knew everything about one another." A dull thud ended the sentence, followed by a hum of pain from Max as he rubbed his shoulder, glaring at Jason. Something in Max's mud-brown eyes seemed to ask why he'd been punched, but he knew the answer.

I turned to my left and offered Jason an appreciative look.

For just a moment, his mouth twitched into a small grin.

With a huff, Max backed off a step.

This whole time, Cat followed, keeping stride with me despite his size.

Jason kept a wary eye on the creature who chose to remain silent. "Is that a real cat?"

"Yes. He's helping us escape."

They both managed to cast strange looks in my direction. Even Ms. Lahna looked over her shoulder at Cat and me.

I felt as if I'd grown an extra head. "Just trust me …"

My two friends looked from me to each other. Jason shrugged and Max sighed. "Fine, but if you turn out to be crazy and this fails, you owe me lunch for a month."

I didn't bother mentioning that if we failed, we'd probably never eat again. Whether we succeeded or failed, getting fed was not a kindness the adults would give us after today.

We rounded a corner, and Ms. Lahna hurried for a door, pulling a key from her pocket. She opened it to a dark room and ushered us inside. She left the door ajar, allowing some light to spill inside. It became obvious rather quickly the room had not been built to hold four kids, an adult, and a cat. Only a few times bigger than an isolation room, the small space held an adult-sized cot that, while old, looked better than anything I'd slept in before. Next to it stood a single tiny rickety table with a lone candle perched atop a mountain of wax.

Ms. Lahna pushed through us to the table and ripped the candle from its perch. She clawed at the melted wax until she managed to pull something from it and handed the item to Andy. "Sorry about the wax. It was the best I could do to keep it hidden."

Andy wiped off the final bits of wax before clutching the item to her chest. "Thank you," she finally managed, gratitude and joy evident in her voice. However, her face remained serious, and her brows knitted together as she studied the teacher. "Why are you helping us?"

Ms. Lahna took a deep breath and exhaled slowly. "A long time ago, I was told that a day would come when someone I loved would follow a shadow, and I needed to let them." She leaned forward and put a hand on Andy's shoulder. "I'm trusting that that time is now." She pulled Andy into a hug, and my friend hugged back for all she was worth. Tears welled in both of their eyes when they pulled apart.

Sniffling, Andy wiped at her eyes then proffered a hand. "Can I put this in the bag?"

"I guess." I lifted my shirt and held the bag open for her.

She stepped forward, placed a kiss on the palm-sized item, which glinted red from the hallway light, and carefully placed it in the bag. Whatever it was made a noticeable impact in the bottom of the leather. She then ensured the top was sealed tight before allowing me to lower my shirt once again.

"We good to go?" I asked.

She gave a crisp nod.

All attention fell onto Ms. Lahna.

"So, what's this plan of yours?" Max asked, not sounding at *all* bitter about no longer leading. He turned from her as if he didn't actually want to hear her answer.

Ms. Lahna ignored his pouting and focused on explaining her plan. "That shipment of food that just came in, the empty crates for it are still in the pantry. They need to be moved to the front gate, but no one is exactly jumping at the idea of doing the work. No one would question using children to move the boxes as a punishment."

"That'll get us near the pantry?" Andy asked.

Confidence flowed from Ms. Lahna as she replied. "Yes."

"Won't give us much time to grab food," Jason commented with his usual gloominess.

Ms. Lahna maneuvered into the hallway and turned to look at us. To my surprise, she agreed with him. "It won't, but if you were to close the door on me while you're all inside, there'd be nothing I could do but bang on the door and try to get in." She winked to ensure we caught her meaning. She'd let us lock her out, granting us the time we needed to gather our food and escape.

Jason showed his approval with a single, silent nod.

"I think we can work with that," Andy offered.

Max grumbled, "I guess that'll work."

My heartbeat would not slow down. If we succeeded, we'd be in the Erima. What would that be like?

"Of course, if you don't want to try to escape, I could always escort you to the mess hall."

I stepped into the hallway to stand beside her. I didn't want to stay in the CTS any longer. "We're leaving."

"Follow me then." Not even a tick after taking the lead, Ms. Lahna spun on her heel and pointed at Cat sitting on her cot. "How good is that thing at hiding?"

I pointed in the direction we were headed.

Cat hissed then faded into the room's shadows as Andy shut the door. "He'll meet us there."

Ms. Lahna stared at the closed door for a tick or two, probably trying to discern how Cat would escape her room, before guiding us to the pantry.

We ran into very few adults along the way. The ones we did meet, Ms. Lahna fed the planned story to. If anyone questioned her further, she said it was Ms. Hess's idea. That silenced them and sent them on their way in a heartbeat.

Soon enough, we arrived at a room identical to our own mess hall, except this one had tables where far too many adults sat around, eating lunch. Suspicious eyes fell on us from all directions as she guided us through the room. I thanked the Stars none of the eyes belonged to Ms. Hess.

As we proceeded, Ms. Lahna's voice grew tough. "How dare you four sneak back here! If you want to be with the adults, then you'll work like adults!"

While our teacher had never raised her voice at me in the past, how she spoke nearly convinced *me* that we were in big trouble. Andy helped sell the lie by shrinking in on herself. Max smirked. Jason frowned. I avoided eye contact with everyone.

No one bothered us.

She guided us to a door in the back of the room behind the food counter which opened into a kitchen. Grills with embers lined the long wall to the right, capped by two stone ovens at either end. Despite the chimneys above, they filled the room with an unbearable heat. Beads of sweat streaked the faces of the adults working them. Stone counters lined most of the left wall where adults prepped meals. Occasionally, one left their counter space and headed for a large oval basin of water in the center of the room. They'd scoop out some water with whatever utensil they had then return to their work.

Two other doors were in the room besides the one we had entered through. I guessed the one on the wall opposite us led to the kid's mess hall. This proved true when an adult went through the door, and the familiar sounds of chaos rushed in before the closed barrier muted the commotion once more. The other door resided halfway along the left wall, breaking up the counter space. Ms. Lahna headed for that door, but a kitchen worker clutching a knife halted her progress.

"There shouldn't be any kids in here!" he barked.

At the sound of his voice, my heart bashed against my ribs. Thankfully, I wasn't expected to answer, because I didn't trust my voice to remain steady.

Ms. Lahna remained perfectly calm. "Hess's orders, Stavros. They were caught sneaking into the restricted section. Figured we could punish them and get those boxes from the last delivery out of your way at the same time."

The man remained silent. After a moment, he stepped aside with a grumble. "Just make sure they don't steal anything from the pantry. Don't know when the next delivery will be." He resumed his earlier task of slicing meat into strips.

Blood pounded in my ears as she guided us to the pantry door. As we passed under the last skylight, halfway between the door and the water basin, I pointed to it and nodded several times.

The shadow above took note.

Ms. Lahna slid the door latch and held it open for us. No skylights illuminated this room. Ms. Lahna stood at the door, keeping it ajar and letting light inside.

Through the gloom, I noticed shelves and boxes along the walls holding all kinds of foods. We stood amongst the shadows for a moment, letting our eyes adjust.

Our teacher pointed at some crates near the door and spoke with a commanding voice. "You'll carry those boxes out of here!" Then, quieter, she added, "Are you sure about this?"

I scanned our surroundings and found a pair of pale blue eyes watching us from one of the shelves. "We've got this from here."

"Are you sure you won't get into trouble?" Andy asked.

"Don't worry about me, Andy. I'm a big girl; I can take care of myself. Hess can't punish me if I don't work here anymore. I've only stuck around this long to keep an eye on you. Now I can go find the rest of my family. Good luck." Turning to Jason, she added, "I'll buy you as much time as I can, but they'll eventually notice something is wrong and will try to open the door. Don't let them." Ms. Lahna backed out of the room and closed the door behind her, plunging us into darkness. Not a tick later, the handle rattled, as if someone were trying to open it, though no one actually pushed on the door.

Andy's whisper cut through the darkness. "How are we supposed to do anything in the dark?"

Cat's rough yet quiet voice answered, "Self-lighting candle in the bag."

Max struggled to keep his voice down. "Who said that?"

Ignoring his question, I removed the bag from under my shirt and reached inside, thinking of the candle. Sure enough, my hand found something waxy and pulled it out. A small flame burst to life in my hand, filling the room with a warm glow.

Jason leaned against the door to keep it shut, though it didn't look like the attempt to open it was serious. Was it Ms. Lahna pretending?

Andy's gaze went from me to where Cat sat on a shelf near Max's head.

Max tried his best to hide the fact that he very visibly jumped upon seeing Cat. However, we all saw it.

Andy snickered as our friend watched the creature warily.

"Start filling the bag," Jason ordered.

Andy latched onto my arm, pulled me to a crate filled with pitahayas, and we stuffed them inside. The bag grew heavier, though not as much as it should have, with each piece of fruit. The bag didn't get any bigger. It swallowed everything like they were grains of sand.

Max hadn't moved from his spot. His eyes locked on Cat. "This thing is still staring at me."

"Lahna! What's going on there?" Mr. Stavros's gruff voiced bellowed for the kitchen.

Ms. Lahna's much quieter voice mentioned something about being locked out.

A tick later, the rattling at the door increased. Someone pounded on the wood. "Open up!" Mr. Stavros commanded.

"Max!" Jason hissed as the door shook. His muscles tensed.

"On it!" Max rushed to a nearby shelf, scooped an armful of bread, hurried to drop it in the leather sack, and rushed back to get more.

Andy stopped with the pitahayas and scanned the room. "Where are they hiding the meat?"

The door lurched, and a beam of light fell into the room. "Open up!" Stavros shouted. "Lahna, get Hess!"

"Right away," came her less-than-enthusiastic reply.

Jason groaned, struggling to hold back the adult.

I rushed to help him, handing the bag and candle to Andy. I slammed into the door. The blow forced it closed. I shifted to match

Jason's stance. I pushed with everything in me. It didn't feel like it'd be enough. We were only two kids versus one very large adult.

Max pointed to some barrels hiding in the back corner. "Meat's back here packed in salt!"

Andy hurried over. They worked in unison to stuff the bag some more.

"This is getting heavy!"

"Give it!" Max ripped the bag from her hand and slung it over his back. "Keep filling!"

Andy bounced around the room, grabbing foods from this shelf and that, the candlelight zipping around with her.

The door lurched again. We took longer to close it. My vision blurred with the effort. Shadows stretched and shrank before my eyes, and I didn't know if it was from the candle moving or the strain of keeping the door closed.

"Can't keep this up! What's the plan?" Jason barked. He was just starting to feel tired? My arms already shook like a first-year student in their first fight.

The omega's voice pierced through the door. "What's going on in here?"

Stavros explained the situation to her. A moment later, her familiar growl emanated through the wood. The forces fighting against us grew stronger.

"You little brats will be without food for a month!" Ms. Hess hissed.

"Do we have enough?" I shouted.

Hess's growl came through the wood, sounding like she was directly opposite me. "I know that voice."

This did not make me feel better.

"I don't know! Maybe," Andy answered. Maybe was better than no. It would have to do.

"Get them out of here!"

"Pick me up … gently!" Cat instructed Andy. I assumed she listened, because he issued his next order to Max. "Now grab onto her shoulder."

A tick later, the candlelight vanished. Jason and I were alone in the dark.

"What just happened?" Jason asked.

I struggled to form the word to answer him. "Cat … Traveled." My arms were giving out. Just a little bit longer.

"He's a Traveler?"

"You're dead, Reject," Ms. Hess threatened.

Silence fell over us. Sweat dripped from my forehead.

"You hear me? No one will remember you."

Cat, please hurry!

Something smashed against the door. We slid back as it opened.

Blinding light filled the room. Ms. Hess's bony hand reached inside, clawing at my arm. Sharp nails dug into my skin.

I shouted in pain and anger. If only I were strong like Jason. Keeping this door closed would be easy. No matter how hard I pushed, the door wouldn't close.

"I've got you!" The omega gloated, yanking on my arm.

The door opened farther.

We were losing.

From the shadows, two black paws reached up. Claws glinted in the light and latched onto Hess's arm.

She shrieked and retracted her hand.

With a shout, Jason shut the door.

I crumpled to the floor. On my hands and knees, my breath came in ragged gasps.

Cat jumped onto my back. "Touch his shoulder!"

Jason's hand found my shoulder, and the shouting faded.

Something latched onto my waist and pulled me through the darkness. Outside world, here we come!

Chapter 11
-Ghosts and Sand-

2-12.11.12.17.4 T.S.T.
Xic-Patan, Erima
Tehrahey

The tugging sensation on my stomach stopped, and the darkness opened to the outside world. We arrived in an area where the ground beneath me sagged and gave way. Sand. In the CTS, I never stepped on anything other than a stone floor. Cat jumped off my back, and I remained kneeling in hot sand. The warmth quickly seeped through my pants and attempted to burn my skin. I blinked my eyes rapidly, trying to clear them. I gulped down air, hoping my breathing would slow. It was so much lighter than anything I'd breathed before. It still smelled dirty but in a different way than what I'd grown used to. I liked it.

Jason plopped next to me. "That was close." He chuckled as he scooped sand through his fingers.

"Sorry I wasn't more help."

He patted my back. "You did plenty. Couldn't have done it alone." He didn't sound nearly as out of breath as I felt.

I didn't know if I believed him, but I let it be. We were out of the CTS! And. It. Was. Hot!

I groaned and straightened up, keeping to my knees for the time being. We were between two sandstone buildings. Some rundown structures sat at either end of our alleyway, as well as lots and lots of sand. Directly above, the large red sun beat down on the world. The air around me burned, and I scrunched my face at the sensation.

Jason laughed again. "You'll get used to the heat."

"Now you know why I hate this desert." Cat's tail drooped to the ground as he trudged around the side of the building.

Jason followed him, jumping from foot to foot.

One leg at a time, I rose on exhausted legs and immediately understood my friend's odd method of walking. Placing my bare feet on the sand hurt! I needed to get the sandals from the bag. My legs found new energy as they tried to get my feet off the ground.

From the alleyway were at least a dozen structures, all the same tan color. The ruins of more houses, which appeared to have fallen long ago, lay in pieces scattered around the city. A mountainous sand dune had buried some buildings.

I expected someone to question our presence and tell us to go away. No one did. The only sounds were our footsteps and the distant howl of wind.

"Where is everybody?" I asked, breaking the heavy silence. Quiet was something I only ever experienced in the late hours of the night, and even then, there were still sounds to be heard.

"Dead or moved on," Cat answered. He kept close to the edges of buildings, using the slivers of shadows to keep his feet safe. While the method worked for his tiny paws, none of the shade was big enough for us. Thank you, midday sun. "As seas shrank, coastal towns like Xic-Patan were deserted. No one will bother us." He slunk into a building. Inside, the shadows offered some relief from the heat but not much.

Andy paced back and forth across a barren room, her sandals slapping against the floor.

Max rested on the ground, his back against a wall and his bare feet in front of him. A few empty crates and barrels sat in the back corners, their edges rough and jagged.

Relief washed over Andy's face when we entered. "Good, we're all safe."

Cat trudged to the center of the room where he laid down with his paws tucked under him.

The sudden urge to pick him up and squeeze him washed over me, but I refrained. I didn't want to get shredded.

"Cat, are you okay?"

His head moved up and down in slow swings. "Fine, just tired." He yawned, revealing sharp little teeth. "To get started, you'll be heading to a location, which, if Amyntor is right, should be where the first Tablet is located."

"We're hunting for the Tablets?" Jason asked from his position by the door. He kept glancing out every few ticks, as if he didn't trust Cat about this place being abandoned. His lurking in the shadows did not make me feel safer.

"And a magic cat is helping us?" Max added.

Cat hissed, causing Andy to step between the two of them. "I'll explain later. Please continue."

"We believe the Tablet is on an island east of here. With the receding oceans, the island is not likely an island anymore. The clue hinted at a location south of a patch of rough seas called the Berumada Pit."

Jason left the door. "I've heard of the place. Some people think it doesn't exist. The ones who do, say it's in the desert somewhere."

Cat looked like he'd fall asleep at any moment. Why was he so tired? He seemed fine in the CTS. "Maybe you Tehraheyians aren't as dumb as I anticipated, even if you did get the name wrong."

He really didn't have any faith in us, did he? We weren't all smart like Andy, but we could help.

"I didn't say it wrong. That's what it's called," Jason said.

Why, if they had an idea where the Tablet might be, didn't Cat take us there? I asked the question, and he answered.

"I can only Travel to places I've seen before or to precise locations. I've seen Xic-Patan in Amyntor's dreams. I Traveled into the CTS, because the watch gave me its location. I can't get you four any closer than this."

Max snorted. "Well, that's stupid."

Cat's eyes narrowed, and his tail twitched. "Taking you back to the CTS might kill me, but I'll do it."

Max's face paled, and he shook his head.

Cat continued with a final flick of his tail. "The Pit is a good three days east from here. Just follow the rising— Wait, this is Tehrahey. Follow the setting sun and you should be fine. Hopefully, you grabbed enough supplies." He eyed the bag by Max.

I hobbled to the bag on shaky legs and burned feet. Reaching inside, I thought of the sandals. With all the food we put in it, I expected it to be harder to find them. However, they were the first thing I grabbed.

Max grew jealous as I put them on my feet. "Those were in there the whole time?" He scooted across the ground to join me at the bag. "So, we can pull whatever we want out?"

"No," Cat answered. "The bag doesn't create anything, just holds whatever is put inside. Just think about whatever you're looking for as you reach in. The bag will do the rest."

"Wow!" Max's hand dove into the bag, and after a tick of searching, came out empty. "There aren't any more sandals?" He sat back with a flop.

"There were only supposed to be two of you." Cat narrowed his eyes at me, and, for a moment, I expected him to yell. I thanked the Stars he didn't.

Andy either didn't notice the look, or didn't care. "Can you bring us more?"

Jason crossed his arms, making himself look more unmovable than the building's stone walls. "I'm not walking through the Erima barefoot."

Max agreed.

Cat's following sigh sounded like a sob before he agreed to return with more. He then asked for the thing Ms. Lahna had given to Andy.

Andy removed the small object from the bag. Polished metal comprised one side of the circular shape, and a red crystal carved with swirls made up the other. The whole thing fit comfortably in her palm. With care, she placed the object in front of Cat, who placed a paw on it and closed his eyes.

We remained silent, waiting for something to happen, but after several ticks of nothing, some of us grew impatient. Leave it to Max to be incapable of sitting still for more than a tick.

"What are you doing?" he asked.

Cat didn't open his eyes. "Concentrating. This isn't easy in my current state." A few more ticks past, and the red stone on the object shined briefly before fading. "That should do it." He swayed a bit before pushing the object to Andy.

She examined the trinket, rolling it over. "What did you do?"

"I miraged it. If you ever need my help, which I pray you won't, all you must do is think of me and hold the object. I'll feel that I'm needed and will come to help. Please do not need me until after you find the first Tablet."

Andy held the object and ran her finger over the etched crystal. "Thank you, Cat."

"Once it's evening, summon me with that. I'll bring the sandals, and you can begin your journey. Until then, rest." Cat strolled out the door.

Max snuck after him and peaked outside. "He's gone! How did he do that?"

With a humph, Jason joined us on the floor. "He's something."

"You're one to talk," I teased.

"Very funny." He rummaged through the bag and removed some pieces of dried meat and bread.

As we ate, Andy told them what had happened in our records class. From the way she told it, I sounded a whole lot braver than I actually was. I only acted tough to keep Andy safe. I didn't deserve the praise she gave or Jason's pat on the back.

Thanks to the Stars, my suffering came to an end. Jason stretched, lay back on the floor, and instructed us to get some sleep. That sounded like a great idea. My eyes barely managed to stay open as I located the comfiest spot on the stone floor.

Even in the building's shade, closing my eyes didn't block all the sunlight. Some still shone through my eyelids, reddening them. Normally, this might have bothered me, but now, I didn't care.

Unfortunately, Max didn't feel quite the same way. "How are we supposed to sleep like this?" he asked after a long, pleasant stretch of silence.

I opened my eyes to see his arms raised in the air.

"Max," Andy said with a groan from my left. "Just go to sleep. You like sleep."

"I can't with all this light. And why are we walking at night?"

Jason answered, "Too hot during the day."

"How will we see where we're going?"

He pointed to the bag with his thumb. "Candle."

"This sounds dumb."

"*This*,"—Jason lifted his head from the ground to stare at Max, flashing a strange smile—"is how I lived."

Chapter 12
-Desert Bound-

2-12.11.12.17.4 T.S.T.
???
???

We were someplace I never expected to be, someplace where the sands of the Erima met the ocean. How we got there baffled me as much as all the water. How could there be so much here and so little elsewhere? Its salty scent filled the air and reduced the extreme heat. Why did people fight for it when it was much more fun to fight *with* it!

Andy screeched in delight and recoiled as I sent another splash of water her way. "Kyle!"

She retaliated in kind as Max tried and failed to issue a sneak attack on Jason. Our battle raged on for hours until our stomachs rumbled with the setting sun. Once one of us noticed our hunger, so did the rest, and we left the water to eat a small meal, practically finishing off our supplies. Worry gnawed at me as that realization set in, but it didn't last long. After the day we just had, nothing seemed capable of destroying my joy.

As I enjoyed what might have been the sweetest, juiciest pitahaya ever, something tickled my nose. The scent drifted through my nostrils and ruined the fruit's flavor.

Smoke drifted in with the ocean breeze as a pillar of dark clouds formed on the horizon.

Jason rose without a word. He approached the shore, and Max soon followed.

Andy and I exchanged glances before joining our friends.

Together, the four of us stood at the edge of the beach, waves washing across our bare feet. The smoke-scented wind swirled around us then continued up the sand. The sky shifted from its calm blue to a stunning blaze of reds and oranges while the column of smoke climbed higher. Just as the last rays of the sun vanished, a bright golden light appeared from the smoke and rose from the sea, and an island grew beneath it. I couldn't tell if the light pulled up the island or if the island pushed the light.

Having never seen a star before, I assumed that was what they looked like. According to adults, they had all disappeared from the night sky a long time ago. "Must be what a star looks like."

No response came from the others, and when I turned to my right, they were gone. I looked back at the beach, but the sand blew away into nothingness. The island and pillar of smoke faded to black as well. Waves no longer washed against my feet, and no wind stirred. Only the light remained. I tried to move, but my muscles were locked tight. I tried to call for help, but no words escaped my lips.

From the darkness, came a voice. "At last, you have arrived. Beware the soul-consuming sands. The Erima offers no salvation for those who survive here, only death."

"Who are you?" I squeaked out.

In response, something grabbed my waist and pulled me to the light.

My heart pounded as my gut threatened to spill everything held within it. Next, I found myself in an eerily familiar place.

Three figures stood in a CTS hall while evening light seeped in from a distant skylight. The shadowy people were too tall to be kids, and I recognized two of the voices. One would periodically haunt my dreams, while the other I had only just met.

"You disappoint me, Hess." The calm of the Maker's voice hid a sandstorm. I could hear it brewing beneath the surface. "All I asked is that you keep the CTS in complete control, and what did you do?"

Meanwhile, Ms. Hess let her rage be known. "Lahna helped those worthless sand piles escape, I know it!"

The Maker didn't waver; her anger had no effect on him. "And where is she?"

"Gone."

"So, you failed on two fronts today?"

"No!"

He cupped her face. "Hess, you wouldn't lie to me, would you?" He didn't wait for an answer before retracting his hand. "After all, a queen never lies to her king, and you do want to be queen, right?"

There was a pause as the question hung in the air. After a tick, Ms. Hess answered in a small, uncharacteristic voice. "Yes."

His tone shifted in a gust, growing harsh. "Then find this missing teacher." He turned to his silent bodyguard. "Cylus, have my men search the city. If we don't find any of them, your days as omega will be over, Hess. Perhaps I was wrong to trust you."

The two men turned to leave, but the Maker cast one final look over his shoulder toward me.

I remained motionless as his gaze lingered. Did he see me? I don't think so, since he proceeded down the hallway, leaving Ms. Hess alone. As everything faded, I thought I heard a sob.

Air surged into my lungs as I bolted upright. By the Stars, where was I? I scanned the barren room with sand collecting along its edges.

Outside the windows, deep shadows stretched across the foreign landscape in the evening light. I was in Xic-Patan.

Andy lay nearby on the floor, her head resting on a pile of sand.

Max lay on his side against the counter.

Jason sat against a wall, a hand in the bag, but it didn't move. His green eyes were locked on me. "You okay?"

I blinked several times, hoping my mind would catch up with everything. All that water, the CTS hallway, and the darkness that followed must've been a dream. "Yeah… Just some nightmares."

"Hate those," he murmured, resuming his search.

I rose and stretched my arms above me. "What are you doing?"

"Checking our supplies. With rationing, we should make it three days, maybe four. Did you know this was in there?" He removed a small knife. It glinted in a shaft of orange light from a window.

Max rolled onto his side with a yawn. Once his gaze landed on the knife, it lit up, and he sat upright. "Can I have that?" He reached for the object from across the room.

Even with the distance, Jason held it away from him. "No." Jason's tone made it very clear that he would not change his mind on the matter, and I agreed with him.

"That would be a horrible idea," I added.

Max's eyes narrowed as he stood. "What's that supposed to mean?"

Andy stirred and stifled a yawn, answering his question before either of us could. "It means you're irresponsible. We can't trust you with a knife. And do you have to be so loud?"

He stuck out his tongue at her, which she mimicked. "I am responsible!"

Jason rolled his eyes, Andy shook her head, and I scoffed. "You stopped paying attention and almost got us caught!" I explained.

"Can't trust you to keep us safe, can't trust you with a knife," Jason added.

Max's arms went limp, and his head drooped forward. "I can keep you safe," he mumbled.

Andy snorted, which made Max flinch.

"The knife stays with me," Jason said, "We're going to eat, get Cat back here, then leave."

I marveled at how he could take charge of the situation. He saw the argument coming and silenced them both before it could surface. Maybe it was how he said things. His words were never suggestions; they were orders. Why couldn't I do that?

He removed Andy's charm from the bag and tossed it to her.

"Jason!" she screeched as she struggled to catch it and not let it drop to the hard floor.

Our friend apologized as he distributed our meals.

Cat appeared as we ate, two pairs of sandals draped over his back. He didn't stick around, claiming he'd been in the Erima long enough for one lifetime. He answered a few of Jason's questions before disappearing out the door. According to the two of them, we'd be following the setting sun and heading east. He said our best bet was to follow something Tehraheyians used to call the Ha'bih.

I'd never heard of it before, but Andy got excited at its mention. I wondered what this thing was but didn't have to wonder long.

After Cat left, Andy couldn't contain her enthusiasm. "I can't believe we're actually going to walk on the Ha'bih!"

I'd seen her eager before but never like this. She fidgeted as she ate, her eyes bright with the prospects of tonight's adventure. Seeing her like this brought a smile to my face. However, it did not have the same effect on Max.

"I can't believe you know what that is," he commented, earning a punch on his shoulder. He took another bite of dinner and remained quiet.

Since we were finishing with our meal, Jason stood and hefted the bag over his shoulder. "Let's get moving. Hopefully, the Ha'bih hasn't been buried by sand."

I joined him in standing, and Andy did the same.

Max took longer to rise. He finished his meal slowly and refused to make eye contact with any of us. I recognized his pouting for what it was and chose to ignore it. Instead, I decided to encourage Andy's excitement by asking about the Ha'bih.

"Ha'bih is ancient Tehraheyian for Ocean Road. It's one of the oldest roads in Tehrahey, even older than the Megalo Dromos!" Andy exclaimed with a small hop.

I recognized the second road she mentioned as the main route of land travel on the west coast. It ran from Eden in the south, through Entstal and on to Vamvakipolis in the north. Amyntor had helped make it a very long time ago. I couldn't remember ever learning about the Ha'bih. "Why haven't I heard of it then?"

Jason headed to the door. "It's abandoned. Landlocked."

Andy and I followed him. I didn't understand why being stuck on land would make it abandoned. "Aren't roads supposed to be on land?"

"This one used to follow the southern edge of the continent before the oceans dried up. Without any water, the trail is too long and treacherous," Andy explained.

Her explanation didn't do much to make me feel good about our quest. How could this dried-up road be a good thing? "And you're excited about this? You coming, Max?"

He'd yet to get up from the floor. "Yeah, yeah. Right behind you."

"Of course, I'm excited. This road is a piece of history. It's in so many of the old books in the library."

The air outside felt a whole lot better than it had at lunch. The midday heat had weakened from unbearable to just miserable. I hoped things would only get better after sunset. The bottom of the great red sun approached the wavy horizon, igniting the eastern skies. The evening light cast long shadows over the ruins around us. As we wove through the buildings, we popped in and out of the blinding light—a strange experience after living underground for so long. In the CTS, the sun only got in our eyes if we looked skyward.

The sand proved to be an even bigger nuisance. Every step I took, the sand moved on me. On top of that, the grains would slip into my sandals and rub against my feet. I took every chance I got to walk across solid ground.

Andy and Max did the same.

Jason just marched onward.

There were a few moments when Andy, Max, or I would stop after hearing a noise. Each time, it turned out to be the wind whistling through the ruins. Sometimes it even tossed sand in our eyes. None of this bothered Jason. I found myself wishing I could be more like him, unaffected by all the scary things in the world.

At the edge of town, sand covered the buildings. Not just with piles. Entire dunes buried the remains of the deserted city. The powder rose and fell in every direction. Climbing the dunes proved difficult. As we went up, the sand tried to pull us back down. Three of us resorted to using our hands to crawl up the side. Jason remained upright. Our paths left new indents in the already rippled surface of the small hill.

"It's going to be a long night," Max grumbled as we joined Jason at the top.

We sat in the sand and caught our breaths as Jason scanned our surroundings.

Andy's lips parted as she took in the view.

I probably wore the same look. The Erima stretched in all directions; there seemed to be no end. I doubted an ocean even existed. Ahead of us, the dunes were dark, wavy silhouettes before a sinking sun—equal parts breathtaking and terrifying. Behind us, beyond the abandoned village of Xic-Patan, they were a stunning golden-orange covered by a darkening sky. To either side, the dark and light mixed. The two opposites clashed against one another and mingled, finding some amount of peace and calm. Despite everything I *could* see, one thing stood out: we were alone—not one movement or sound from any direction. Nothing stirred, nothing but us and the wind.

A smile tugged at Jason's lips as he pointed to a flat, snakelike, raised stone structure extending from town and weaving through the sands toward the sun—the Ha'bih.

Chapter 13
-What We Lost-

2-12.11.12.17.4 T.S.T.
Ha'bih (Ocean Road), Erima
Tehrahey

The raised road of the Ha'bih kept most of the old path from being buried by sand. I liked how much easier that made walking. It did little to prevent the sand from getting in my sandals—and everywhere else, for that matter. It must've gotten into my clothes while climbing the first dune, and no amount of adjusting the fabric seemed capable of dislodging it. In a few places, a dune managed to build higher than the road and spill its contents across the stones. So far, we were able to avoid climbing the mounds and just skirt around the edges.

As we hiked, the sun set, plunging the desert into darkness and making the isolation feel even worse. The half-moon took its time rising and didn't provide much relief. To help keep us together, Jason removed the candle from the bag and held it up. For the past cycles, I focused on following that tiny flickering light. As long as I could see that light, I wasn't alone.

After cycles of traversing the barren desert, the excitement of being outside dwindled. Quickly. My gaze drifted skyward and found it as empty as always. Not a single star existed. Why had they left us? I wished I had asked Amyntor when we were with him. The stars hadn't been around for thousands of years. Even Amyntor may not have seen them when he had last visited Tehrahey.

As my feet ached, I found myself wishing I were back in the CTS, sound asleep in a cot. Despite the earlier nap, my eyelids grew heavier with each step. I needed to do something to keep me awake. Walking wasn't enough.

Andy marched beside me, her charm held in hand. Every so often, it caught the flickering of Jason's candle.

"Andy, what is that?"

She offered a barely visible smile. "I'm not entirely sure."

"Then why ask Ms. Lahna for it?"

She clutched the item to her chest as if afraid talking about it would cause it to vanish. "It's from my parents."

"Your parents?"

Parents rarely ever gave their kids something before being placed in the CTS. When they did, often the item got stolen. Sometimes other kids took the items, sometimes the adults did. Either way, kids never left the CTS with anything.

"Yes, my mom gave it to me before ..." She took a deep breath and exhaled slowly. "Well, before the Black Guards took me from her. Ms. Lahna took it from me when she arrived at the CTS and promised to keep it safe. Said she didn't want it falling into the wrong hands." She wiped at her eyes. "It's the only thing I have."

This conversation didn't turn out to be the distraction I had hoped for. While I no longer felt tired, a different feeling had taken hold of me, one I liked even less. Of course, Andy's parents loved her. She was awesome. They had fought to keep her. My mother ... didn't. She had gotten rid of me. She didn't care about me. I was worthless.

Andy rubbed her finger over the ridges of the crystal, not seeming to notice my desire for this conversation to end. "For years I've dreamed of holding this again. Maybe after this is all over, I could try to find them."

She looked so hopeful. That made everything worse. I wanted to think she could. If we succeeded, it could be possible, but I also didn't want her to find them. She already had happy memories of her parents; why should she get to find them too?

I quickened my pace to end the talking, but Andy matched me step for step, still focused on her charm and her parents, completely unaware of the discomfort her conversation caused me.

"I like to think they were scientists."

Max snorted and decided to join the conversation. At least that took the pressure off me. "That would explain a lot about you!"

"I'm not smart because of my parents; I'm smart because I study. You should try it." She stuck out her tongue at him, and he copied her. "I think they were scientist because of what I remember of their house."

"You remember their house?" Max asked.

"Only a little. Don't you remember your parents' house?"

"Kind of. I think it was bigger than a classroom. I don't know. I just miss my mom."

"What about your dad?"

"I don't remember him being around much. Mom was fun though," Max said. Even he had better memories about his parents than me! All I could remember was being unable to move in a dark room. Maybe I had heard my mother say she loved me, but after what Ms. Lahna had told me, I think I had just made up that part.

Max spun on his heel and walked backwards. "She used to make these really funny faces, like this!" He smushed his hands against his cheeks and puffed out his lips.

Andy clutched her stomach as she burst out laughing.

He released his face and chuckled back.

I wasn't exactly in a laughing mood.

"We were always playing games together," he continued, the cheer leaving his voice. "That's how I got taken away."

"You were playing a game?" Her voice lost some of its previous happiness.

"We were at a market, and I decided to run away from her. Not far, just enough that she'd have to chase me. I ran straight into the Black Guards."

"That's awful."

"I tried to run from them but wasn't fast enough. Mom wasn't fast enough either." He turned back around, his whole body going slack. "The last time I saw her, she had tripped in the crowd, calling out for me." He sniffled and wiped his face on his arm. Then he laughed, but not for real. It sounded fake. "A pretty standard arrival to the CTS, from what I've heard."

Despite how he tried to act, I knew the story hurt to talk about. I think we all did. However, no one said anything about how upset he was. None of us liked to show any sort of weakness by crying, and this wasn't the sort of thing friends teased each other about.

We were all prepared to let the subject drop, but Max had other ideas.

The lack of sleep must have inspired his next question. "What about you, Jason?"

"Max!" Andy and I exclaimed, somehow managing to find the energy to shout.

Jason paused, and I expected him to hit Max, hard. He deserved it, for asking that question.

Jason clenched a fist, but the blow never came. He moved again, and when he finally spoke, pain echoed through in his voice. "Fine. My mother died giving birth to me. Spent my whole life moving, exploring the southern coast. We were looking for the Berumada Pit. Father wanted to prove it existed. His father claimed to have found it years ago—"

"Did they find each other after leaving the CTS?" Andy asked.

I worried Andy's interruption might cause Jason to stop talking. He had never said this much about his past before, and I wanted to know more. I think we all did.

"Most people don't go to a CTS because The Maker doesn't rule all of Tehrahey. My grandfather was born in Metnal—"

Andy interrupted him again; sometimes her thirst for knowledge could be really annoying. "Where's Metnal?"

If her questions upset him, he didn't show it. "On the east coast. It's the true capital of Tehrahey." Jason explained how his grandfather had followed the southern coast all the way to Eden, a town south of Entstal. During the journey, his grandfather claimed to have found the Berumada Pit. Sometime later, the family took a ship back to Metnal after his father's birth to avoid the CTS. He explained how his parents met in the eastern capital and decided to search for the Pit together when they grew up. "I came into the world, and my mother left it. My father didn't quit. Spent most of my childhood in Lejos Noble on the eastern edge of the Erima. There, my father taught me how to survive. About two months before he—" Jason's voice became strangled. He closed his eyes and took a deep breath. "Two months before I met you guys, we started another walk along the coast from Lejos Noble to Eden. When we finally made it, my father was in a terrible mood. We failed to find the Pit again, and people taunted him for it. Never saw him so mad. First night in Eden, he got in a fight with a bald man. The man slit my father's throat right in front of me." Jason's fists clenched tighter. "No one helped, just stepped around him. I …" Jason sobbed once.

It sounded so strange coming from him I must have heard it wrong. He couldn't be crying; Jason never cried! However, a quick look at my other friends and their stunned expressions confirmed it had really happened.

Andy put a hand on his shoulder. "Jason—"

He stormed away from her and spun around. He didn't look at any of us; he fixated on the ground. "I tried to fight back but was too weak. He hit me once, and I blacked out. Woke up on a wagon headed for the CTS." He started walking again.

Jason didn't like to discuss his father's murder, and none of us really wanted to know more about it. We tended to avoid the subject whenever it came up. For the first time ever, he had told us the whole thing. Back in the CTS, we had all avoided the subject of our parents like they were parental guardians. One night out here and I had heard about all their parents. At least they could remember theirs. At least their parents had cared about them. Not one of their stories involved a parent giving them up.

The silence after Jason's story lasted all of eight ticks before Max glanced at me. "And you?"

"I don't remember anything."

"That's a lie," Andy countered. "You're even humming the song right now."

I hadn't even realized I was, but sure enough, I'd started at some point. Once aware of the noise, I stopped, but the damage had been done.

Andy's tone was soft as she continued. "We all shared. Now it's your turn."

I really didn't want to do this, but I didn't have a choice. "I don't remember much. I was in a dark room. It was cold. I couldn't move. Something golden glowed in the dark. I think my mother told me she loved me, but I'm pretty sure I imagined that. I don't know where the song came from."

"It probably came from your mother. See, that wasn't so bad, and I'm sure she cared about you," Andy said.

"There's more."

"Wait, really? And you didn't tell me?"

"I didn't know until this morning. Apparently, the reason Ms. Hess calls me Reject is because my mother gave me to the CTS when I was a baby. She had to beg the guards to take me."

"That can't be true! Who told you something like that?"

"Ms. Lahna."

Any response Andy might have had prepared died in her throat.

"Still think my mother loved me?" I asked.

Andy didn't try to meet my gaze anymore, and Max and Jason kept their heads fixed forward. No one felt like talking after that.

The night dragged on in silence. We kept following the path. The moon descended toward the horizon. Its pale light created just enough shadows along the dunes to play tricks on my eyes. Coupled with my increasing exhaustion, I struggled to trust anything they saw. I tried to keep them fixed on Jason's candle, but they still swore to see things move at the edges of my vision. No matter how many times I checked, we were alone, and the sand dunes were never ending. We wove around one and found hundreds more. Even after dreaming about an ocean, I couldn't imagine an end to the sea of sand.

Andy stumbled for maybe the hundredth time. She rubbed her eyes and hesitated.

Up ahead, Max yawned, and his pace slowed some more. If we kept up like this, we wouldn't make it to the island.

Jason had yet to stumble or show any signs of fatigue. He only slowed to match our declining speed.

I parted my lips, and inhaled a lungful of the still warm, dry air. I worked the stiffness from my jaw as I used it for the first time in cycles. "Jason, I think we should stop for the night." I licked my lips, trying to wet them again. I needed another drink of water.

Jason looked over his shoulder at us. "We'll camp on the north side of this dune." He veered off the Ha'bih and trudged through the sands.

At the mention of rest, Andy, Max and I found some more energy and quickened our pace.

Jason set the bag down to remove the tent. First came a large roll of white fabric about as long as Jason and I if I stood on his shoulders. I didn't know how that fit in there. Next came a few coils of rope. The wooden posts came next, all much larger than should have been capable of fitting within the leather sack. Last came some wooden stakes. Jason kept going until he extracted an empty hand.

I studied everything once he had laid it out before him. "How does this all go together?" I asked, unsure of how to proceed.

"Easy. I'll show you." He set to work putting things together and showing us.

Andy grasped the tent's design first and correctly guessed how things went together.

Max and I just followed their instructions until we stood before a small tent with a square body and a triangular top that stood just a bit taller than us. Ropes extended from each corner and two spots in the middle on either side and were tied off to stakes in the sand. On the front and back, the fabric separated to let us in and out. Crossbeams reached from post to post and worked with other beams to support the ceiling. They meant we'd have to crouch while inside, but I didn't mind if it meant shelter from the sun. Speaking of which, the sun had brightened the skies along the western horizon.

Jason and I admired our handiwork. "That tent's magic," he commented. "Went up easier than it should have."

"Are you complaining?" I teased. The night's previous emotions faded as the prospect of rest drew closer.

Andy poked her head out from the fabric. "It'll be tight, but there should be enough room for all of us to lie down in here."

Jason shrugged. "It'll do."

Max trudged around from the back and forced his way passed Andy. "I call that side." He plopped in the sand, and a soft snore escaped his lips a tick later.

"You can't be asleep already," Andy said, withdrawing her head.

Max snored in response.

Jason and I shared a laugh.

"Well?" I asked.

"One night down. A lot more to go." He stooped inside, and I followed.

Andy and Jason collected piles of sand to rest their heads on, and that seemed like a good idea.

Jason chose to lie next to Max, probably to keep him away from Andy. We didn't need them fighting during the day.

Andy positioned herself next to Jason, and I lay next to her. She yawned and closed her eyes. "Good morning, Kyle."

"Good morning."

Chapter 14
-We Aren't Alone-

2-12.11.12.17.5 T.S.T.
Ha'bih (Ocean Road), Erima
Tehrahey

I woke up several times that day, each time due to either the heat or the sunlight piercing through our fabric construction. Occasionally, a breeze would push aside the fabric doors and allow direct sunlight to attempt to burn off our feet. Many of the times I woke up, I noticed Jason tossing and turning. He must not have liked sleeping in the day either.

Thankfully, the dune blocked the early and late sunlight, which helped. I managed to fall into a deep enough sleep to find myself dreaming of the island again. A voice called out to me once more, saying to join him.

Andy shook me. "Come on, the sun is setting. Jason says it's time to get moving." She exited the tent, and I followed.

Even with the sun sinking into the sand and a distant dune casting its shadow on us, the air in the Erima burned. I recalled last night and realized that, even with the sun gone, the desert stayed warm.

Andy shook herself out, trying to rid the sand that had collected in her clothes. As the itchy, scratchy bits rolled through my own clothes, I figured shaking out would be a good idea. I joined her, she giggled.

Max snickered from the side of the tent. He and Jason sat on the ground with the bag between them.

I stopped moving, and my stomach growled. I was ready for breakfast, or was it dinner? Unfortunately for me, Jason wanted to tear down the tent before we ate. My stomach and I groaned, but taking the tent apart proved to be easier than putting it together. We had it done in half the time.

Then we got to sit and tear into a meal. It felt amazing to get off my feet, which, along with my legs, ached from last night's walk. I did not look forward to having to start moving again. Jason kept the meal light but was pleased none of the food had spoiled during the day. The canteen was passed my way, and I gulped down several mouthfuls of water. Despite that, the container remained as filled as ever. As I wiped some sweat from my forehead and studied the area where the tent once stood, I felt thankful to have met Amyntor. Without his magic supplies, being outside would be a whole lot worse than it already was. Trekking across the Ha'bih would be impossible without the ability to carry large amounts of water. The four of us would have easily finished this canteen after one hand cycle.

With the meal over, Jason returned the canteen to the bag and stood. As he loomed over us, his head exited the shadow of a dune and became illuminated in the golden evening light. "Let's get moving."

The rest of us stood, and our leader guided us across the sand to the Ha'bih. Once on the road, we turned into the sunlight and aimed for the distant horizon where the sun sank into the waves of sand.

<^>

This night dragged on longer than the night before. By the time the moon started to sink into the sand, we were all stumbling. I expected my legs to fall off at any moment. There was no end to this sand. I understood why Jason hated the Erima and why he wanted to leave Tehrahey more than any of us.

Max yawned and halted. "Can we stop? We have the tent."

Jason called over his shoulder. "One more cycle."

Max groaned. "You said that two cycles ago! Once this adventure is over, I am never walking anywhere."

Andy tripped once more. "Maybe you'll stop talking too."

Jason and I laughed.

Max scowled. "Yeah, sure. When she does it, it's okay. If I say one mean thing to her, I get punched."

"You tormented me for seven years; I have some catching up to do."

Jason and I laughed harder. It felt good to laugh after the cycles of silent walking. It distracted me from my legs.

Max threw his hands in the air. "I apologized for that!"

Andy nodded. "And I accepted. Now I'm just getting even while Kyle and Jason will still let me."

We probably should have stopped her from picking on Max like we did when he picked on her. Of course, she didn't make him cry. I figured, for the time, we'd let it be.

Max looked at me pleadingly. "Please make her stop talking."

I snorted. "You should know by now that even I can't make Andy do anything."

Jason and Andy continued laughing.

Max growled and quickened his pace to take the lead, putting some distance between him and us. He rounded a bend and disappeared behind a tall dune. We found him standing perfectly still when we came to the turn. He snapped around and blew out the candle in Jason's hand.

"What was that for?" I asked.

Down the road, shadowy figures held torches as others set up tents.

"We aren't alone," he stated.

Without a word, Jason instructed us to sneak up the dune.

Max and I understood; Andy did not. She remained motionless as we climbed.

"Andy!" I hissed.

She snapped out of it and followed.

Max and Jason poked their heads over the top of the dune. Based off the gasp from Max, and the growl from Jason, these tents were not a good sign. Sure enough, they weren't.

It wasn't just a few tents; it looked like a whole city. More people than I had ever seen in the CTS walked through the cloth buildings. Their voices carried across the tops of the sand, along with the clanking of metal and the thudding of wood. What were all these people doing out here?

Fear gripped at Andy's voice as she asked, "What is that?"

In the dim light, I could still see Jason shake his head. He kept it facing forward, locked on the tents. "Don't know. There shouldn't be anything out here. Not enough water."

"Should we go through?" Andy asked.

With a grunt, he replied. "I see a lot of armor and weapons … It's an army."

An army? We were in the middle of the Erima! "What's an army doing in the middle of nowhere? There are no cities to attack."

Jason walked to our right. "Don't know. Don't want to find out. We'll sneak around."

Andy peered over her shoulder. "Jason, it's almost sunrise."

He didn't stop. "Then we hurry. A half-blind cat could see us in the middle of the day. No more talking."

The three of us rushed after him. He kept us several dunes from the tents and every few ticks, he'd check them out. We were making progress but not fast enough. I glanced at the horizon to our left. The last part of the moon crept behind the sand as the sky changed from gray to white. The top of the sun peeked out of the sand to the west.

I hurried to Jason's side and whispered. "We're out of time."

"We keep moving."

I didn't like this. If these adults were anything like Ms. Hess or the Maker, we would be in huge trouble. Ms. Hess could only hit us; these people had swords and guns and weapons, many of which I'd never seen before. Every time Jason paused to study them, I did too. I didn't like what I saw. They'd definitely kill us if we gave them a chance. Even Jason looked nervous, which terrified me more than anything. I knew he'd never admit it, but I could tell. He startled every time some metal clanked. That didn't say much; we all startled. The sun crept into the sky for its daily cycle of burning the desert. Sweat rolled down my back, but the sounds from the tents dwindled. Just like us, they wanted to sleep during the day.

Maybe we would make it around the camp.

A cry from the tents, followed by rapidly clanking metal, grabbed our attention. We stopped moving.

I searched the temporary city for the source of the sound. Movement caught my eye.

A man franticly waved and kicked at an object. His shouts carried across the desert. "You worthless pile of sand, I ought to leave you out here to rust. Let you be somebody else's problem." He succeeded in knocking over the object and walked away from it, right in our direction. He stopped in his tracks.

"Can he see us?" Andy asked.

"Entstal spies!" the man shouted and ran into the tent city, his arms waving.

He could see us.

"Run!" Jason sped off, with Max right behind him.

Andy didn't move.

"Go, Andy!" I pushed her, and she sprinted after the others.

The man's shouts continued as others joined his.

We sprinted around a dune, and the camp vanished, but the shouts followed us.

"What's the plan, Jason?" Andy huffed, though that didn't stop her from talking, just slowed her. "We can't outrun them, and there's nowhere to hide."

Jason didn't answer for a tick. "Keep running."

"You didn't have an escape plan?" she asked, casting me a shocked look—one I matched.

He didn't answer.

A roar of cheers replaced the waning shouts.

Max stopped running and looked back.

We couldn't see anyone, so why were they cheering? They hadn't caught us. "Are they giving up?"

"Just keep moving," Jason instructed.

A new sound rose over the cheering. We were being followed. I looked over my shoulder to see someone riding a large black creature round the dune behind us. It charged past us in less than a tick and circled in front of Jason. The animal reared on its hind legs; metal glinted as it wildly kicked its front feet and released a shrill screech.

Jason fell backward to avoid them and knocked the rest of us to the ground.

The animal slammed down and circled us. It towered over us on four thin yet tall legs. Two red eyes rested on opposite sides of a long head; pointy ears rested at the top. Long dark hair ran down the back of its neck to an elongated body. A tail made entirely of hair protruded from its back and almost reached the ground.

The looks the others gave the creature told me they'd never seen anything like this before either.

The woman riding on its back had long black hair that hung well past her shoulders, much like the creature. Her chalk-white skin shined in the morning sunlight. Her pale eyes and lips held the same sinister sneer Ms. Hess liked to use. However, on her, it looked worse. She bent forward and patted the creature's neck, eying us. "Well, well … What do we have here, Taraxippus?"

Chapter 15
-The King of the Other Side-

2-12.11.12.17.6 T.S.T.
Ha'bih, Erima
Tehrahey

None of us moved. We couldn't with the strange creature and the woman towering over us. The large nostrils at the tip of the creature's nose flared as it breathed heavily. The air filled with its strange scent. The woman straightened upright but remained silent. She held herself the way the Maker did. That didn't bode well for us.

When nothing happened, she spoke. "Well? Rise!" When none of us moved, she reinforced her command. "Now!"

The four of us jumped to our feet.

The woman's smile darkened. "Follow me."

The animal headed to the camp.

Jason didn't follow, so neither did we. "I think we can—"

"I wouldn't try anything. Taraxippus is the fastest horse in all of Tehrahey. *Nothing* can outrun him," she said.

Jason, being his stubborn self, didn't budge. This woman gave all the signs of being as bad as Ms. Hess, if not worse. I didn't want to anger her or find out how dangerous this Taraxippus thing could be.

I took the lead and followed her.

Andy and Max kept right behind me and, with a faint growl, Jason brought up the rear.

A huge crowd of men, with no signs of any women, gathered at the edge of the tents. Most were clean shaven, which exposed scars on many of their menacing faces. They sneered and hollered as we approached while thrusting their fists into the air. Some were empty;

others contained weapons. I identified swords, axes, spears, and crossbows—even a few guns. Several others, I failed to recognize. All seemed as violent as the men who carried them. There were as many styles of weapons as there were people in Tehrahey. Were they really necessary? There couldn't be that many ways to kill someone, could there?

Someone in the crowd shouted, "Queen Melinoe has captured the spies!"

The cheers grew in volume.

The four of us squeezed even closer together. They thought we were spies? That couldn't be good.

Andy's hands latched onto my arm.

I almost jumped at the contact, and then again at how tight she squeezed.

The crowd parted as Queen Melinoe approached. All eyes focused on us. None of the faces held an inviting look. A neutral look would have been nice, but no. Every single adult here hated us.

"Entstal scum!" one man said and kicked sand toward us.

Taraxippus turned on the man, and he fell backward from the horse, reinforcing my fear of the creature. If the adults feared the horse, we should too.

Melinoe patted the creature's neck before regarding the man sitting in the sand. "Leave them be; they are children. It is not likely they're spies for the Maker, but I cannot be sure. Cizin will be the judge of them, not any of you." Her voice grew louder for the next part. "Have I made myself clear?"

The man gulped and scooted backward across the sand with a bowed head. "Yes, Your Highness."

The rest of the crowd echoed his answer.

"Then finish your duties and get some rest!"

The crowd dispersed like dust in the wind. In just a few ticks, things returned to how they had been when we first spied the camp.

Taraxippus resumed walking and guided us deeper into the intricate labyrinth of canvas shelters. Each tent was twice the size of our own, at least. Many were even bigger. All were fancier as well. They had green borders with evenly spaced gold squares running along the edges. The fabric walls rustled with each slight breeze, causing movement where there shouldn't have been any. Groans and gruff voices drifted on the wind, along with several unpleasant scents. At one point, we passed a pit of mud that reeked like a CTS washroom. I knew exactly what the mud was made of and kept my distance.

Most soldiers disappeared inside their shelters; a few transported crates from tent to tent or worked on weapons. The remaining few munched on pitahayas and loaves of bread.

My stomach grumbled at the sight of the food, letting me know exactly what time it was.

Andy leaned closer to me and whispered in my ear, her voice shaking, "She didn't say Cizin, did she?"

Jason answered her before I could. "Yes."

"Who's that?" I asked. The name didn't sound familiar; I couldn't recall ever hearing it in the CTS.

"Cizin is a man who claims to be the true ruler of Tehrahey," Andy said.

"According to the books in the library." Jason believed the books in the library were filled with lies all supporting the Maker.

Andy disagreed with him—or at least she had until she met the Maker in person. I think she was starting to believe Jason more than the books.

"He's the King of Eastern Tehrahey. Remember me mentioning the east and west are always at war? Cizin is making the first move this time."

"Cizin will do more than strike first," Melinoe commented over her shoulder. "He'll destroy the Maker, level the slum that is Entstal, and bring peace to Tehrahey."

"By killing hundreds of people," Andy muttered.

Andy's comment didn't affect Melinoe. "A small price to pay for total liberation of Tehrahey."

How could someone see hundreds of lives as a small price to pay? While I understood the need to fight, did it have to lead to death?

Taraxippus stopped in front of the biggest tent yet, and Melinoe dismounted. She patted the creature's neck and spoke to it. "Do as you wish, but keep an eye out for these four. They are not permitted to leave without an escort." Taraxippus snorted and bobbed his head up and down.

Melinoe approached the entrance of the tent but did not enter. She held her hands behind her back and cleared her throat. "My lord, I have the trespassers."

"Bring them in," a deep voice replied.

Melinoe peeled back the door flap and ushered us inside.

The interior of the tent contrasted with the bright world outside; my eyes took some time to adjust to the darkness.

Only two cots, a trunk for each bed, a large table with a map, and two chairs occupied the tent's enormous space. It had more furniture than a teacher owned in the CTS and yet still felt empty. The objects took up so little space. The cots rested in opposite corners on the back wall. An assortment of furs and pillows covered one. The other cot reminded me of what we had back in the CTS—only a thin black sheet. Melinoe and Cizin must share the tent. They were partners.

A man sat on the far side of the table resting in the center of the space. Short black hair sprouted from the top of his round head. He wore tan clothes capable of hiding him in the sands of Erima. He held his hands in the shape of a triangle in front of his angular nose. He didn't sit straight like the Maker and Melinoe. He sat relaxed in his chair and remained motionless as he studied us.

Melinoe walked around the table to stand on Cizin's left. "These are the trespassers, my lord. I caught them myself."

He grabbed her hand and touched his lips to her knuckles. "Ah, my queen, you have done well in capturing these four. Surely, after seeing them for yourself, you can agree with me that they are not spies sent here by the Maker."

Melinoe's mouth dropped open, and her head jerked back to look at him. "But, sir, how can you be sure?" She gestured at our chests. "They even wear the golden eagle and red sun. They are from Entstal."

Cizin chuckled. "This is why women are not fit to rule." Too preoccupied with his own thoughts, he didn't notice Melinoe's gaze darken, though I recognized the look in an instant. She wanted to hurt him. "You women become set on an idea and will miss the simplest of clues that would tell any *man* he was wrong. I know for certain these four are not spies. Would you like to know how I know?"

Melinoe toned down her look and her mouth formed a thin line before speaking. "Yes, sir. Please, enlighten me." Her voice held no enthusiasm in it. She sounded like Max when Andy would try to explain something to him.

Cizin either failed to notice or didn't care. He stood and took his time to walk around the table to us. "I know these four are not spies because the Maker would have to expect us to be up to something, which I know he does not."

Before she could stop herself, Andy spoke up. "But isn't that the point of spying, to find out what you don't know?" When both Cizin's and Melinoe's attention turned to her, she shrunk under their gazes. Her grip on my arm strengthened. If it got any tighter, she'd crush the bone.

"No, you stupid girl," Cizin started.

Andy flinched at the insult.

"One spies to confirm one's suspicions of the enemy. The Maker would have to suspect our attack to send spies. And, even if he did suspect an attack, he wouldn't expect it to come from the Erima. No one uses the Ha'bih for travel anymore. The desert has claimed the old road as its own. That is how I know you are not spies."

Melinoe didn't appear convinced; she appeared agitated. She glared at the four of us harder than before. "How can you know for certain the Maker does not—"

Cizin swiveled on one foot to face her. "Are you suggesting we have a traitor in my army? No man here would even think of doing what you are accusing them of. They fear the consequences of such an act of treason."

"But, my lord—"

"No! Not a single man out there would dare defy my orders. Only you dare challenge me, and, if it were not for your beauty, I would have you killed."

These two were not what I expected of paired adults. I thought partners were supposed to support each other, or at least get along. Even Ms. Lahna and Mr. Ethan would have gotten along better than these two.

Melinoe rolled her eyes at Cizin. A kid doing that to an adult would earn themselves a beating. After what Cizin had just said, I feared for Melinoe, but Cizin seemed to miss the act entirely.

He walked past her to the cot with the all the blankets and pillows. "Send them on their way. We have no need of them, and they're no threat to us."

Would he really just let us go? Adults always found a reason to punish us.

Melinoe frowned and brushed some hair behind her ear. "Sir, why not keep them? I'm sure we could use some more slave labor."

Slaves? I'd really been hoping they were a myth some of the adults told to scare us.

At the mention of the word, Jason glanced at the entrance to the tent. I followed his gaze and saw Taraxippus's shadow on the tent wall. I doubted we could outrun the creature if we needed to. We were trapped in here. Great.

Cizin didn't turn to answer Melinoe directly. He tossed the shirt he wore onto the trunk at the foot of his bed. "We do not need any extra slaves. We do not have the food nor water for four more mouths. We brought exactly what we needed into the Erima—no more, no less."

Melinoe looked indignant as she crossed her arms. "There is no need to feed all our slaves."

"No. We do not need them; they are only children. We wouldn't get enough decent work from them before the succumbed to the heat. Escort them to the perimeter and send them on their way."

It became increasingly obvious Cizin was the nicer of the two. Lucky for us, he did seem to be the one in charge of the partnership.

Cizin laid down and wrapped himself in all the furs and blankets, which I struggled to believe would be comfortable. How could he stand that kind of heat? Just thinking about it caused sweat to pour down my back.

Melinoe eyed us a tick. "If I may, sir, let me search their bag before I escort them away. It would allow me to sleep peacefully knowing you were completely correct in your assessment of these four."

A sandstorm burst to life in my stomach. We couldn't let her search the bag. She'd find all sorts of stuff that shouldn't be in there and know it was magic. Then she'd probably keep it for herself and hurt us because … well, because adults were mean like that. They didn't really need a reason to hurt kids, but a kid having a magic bag would be reason enough.

Cizin sighed. "Very well. If it will help you sleep, you may search their bags. A woman does need her beauty sleep. Wouldn't want to have an ugly queen, would we?" He chuckled but said nothing more— and missed the glare from Melinoe once again.

She snapped her fingers and pointed to the table without taking her gaze from Cizin. "Bag on the table."

Jason met my eyes.

What should we do? Taraxippus still paced outside, and even without him, I doubted we could escape through the camp. Offering the smallest shrug I could muster, I gestured to the table with my eyes.

He stepped forward and proffered the bag.

Melinoe ripped it from his hands and spilled its contents on the table.

What came out surprised me. Only a few bits of pitahaya and bread rolled across the table, along with our canteen and candle, which was shockingly unlit. Nothing else came tumbling out—not even Andy's charm. The magical container must have a few tricks hidden within it. Thank you, Amyntor.

The adult studied the contents with clear disappointment. "That's it?"

Cizin taunted from his bed. "Found nothing of interest?"

Melinoe's fists clenched at her sides, and her scowl grew. With him in bed, she no longer had to hide it. "No," she grumbled through her teeth.

"They are not spies. Pack their things and get them out of here."

Melinoe huffed, before returning the items to the bag. After the queen returned all our things, we left Cizin's tent. Alongside Taraxippus, she escorted us to the southern edge of camp where she had found us.

The place had calmed down while we were inside. Everyone hid in their shelters to escape the great red sun burning the Erima.

She bid us farewell with a single word. "Leave."

We didn't question her. Jason took the lead and guided us across the sand, away from the army.

Melinoe watched us until we were out of sight.

Once free from her view, we turned left and followed our original plan of skirting the camp. Sweat drenched my body, and it darkened the fabric of my friends' clothes as well, but we didn't stop—not until we were back on the Ha'bih and half a cycle from the camp.

We set up our tent as quickly as possible. It went much easier this time, with everyone knowing how to assemble it. We followed this up with a light meal then quickly hid within our shelter to sleep away the day.

Chapter 16
-The Great Metal Bird-

2-12.11.12.17.7 T.S.T.
Ha'bih, Erima
Tehrahey

"Time to get moving." Jason's voice woke me. He grabbed the bag and left the tent.

Andy and Max stirred. Their eyes looked as heavy as mine felt.

Stepping outside, my legs shook uncontrollably and made it difficult to move. I'd never walked farther than the CTS library before, and it only took so long because I couldn't find it. I wanted to crawl back into the tent, actually sleep at night, and then maybe I'd be ready to walk again.

Jason sat in the shade of the tent, eating a pitahaya.

My stomach complained that food was more important than sleep, so I sat next to him.

Without a word, he passed one to me.

As I split open the fruit with practiced ease, I surveyed our quiet group. "Am I the only one whose legs hurt?"

"Mine do," Andy said. She accepted her meal and peeled it. Her stomach rumbled in approval as she swallowed her first bite.

Max lay on his back and flopped a hand toward our leader.

Jason ignored the outstretched hand and placed a pitahaya on his stomach.

Max almost took a bite out of it before he realized what he held in his hand. "Blegh!" He tried to pass it back to Jason.

"It's that or nothing, Max," Jason said.

"Then I'll take nothing."

I almost couldn't believe Max would be this childish, then I remembered that's what he was good at.

Jason stared at the pitahaya then at Max. "Eat that, or I'll shove it down your throat!"

Max noticed the glare aimed at him. "Fine, I'll eat the stupid thing." It took him a few ticks to muster enough courage to take a bite. He swallowed quickly and shook. It stayed down, and he kept quiet.

Andy finished her piece of fruit and looked to Jason. "What about your legs?"

He stretched his legs on the sand and massaged them. "I've been worse. Haven't had to move this much in over a year. It's painful, but manageable."

"I don't know how far we can walk tonight," I said.

Jason finished his portion and reached into the bag. "We'll be slower tonight."

We quieted as Max, Andy, and I finished our pitahayas. Then Jason handed us some bread and meat. He finished his dinner with a long drink of water. He passed the canteen to me, and I did the same. As the rest of us finished, he stood and disassembled the tent. I tried to help but dropped to the ground in less than a tick of getting up. Standing hurt more than crawling.

Jason watched me with actual sympathy. "I've got it." He finished and packed it away and stood over us— "If the Stars are on our side, we'll find the Berumada Pit by tomorrow morning."

"Then from there we head south until we find an island—or what's left of an island," Andy said.

Max sat upright and looked at her. "How are we supposed to know if we found it?"

"If we really need help, we could always ask Cat," I said. He had miraged Andy's charm so he could help. He did tell us not to need his help, but I didn't understand why. We'd need his help at some point.

With a glance at the sinking sun, Jason hoisted the bag over his shoulder. "We need to get moving."

Andy, Max, and I all groaned.

"I know it's tough, but the longer we sit here, the harder it'll be to get up. Let's get going."

Jason donned a clearly fake smile. He meant well but had a hard time pretending to be happy. "Let's get this over with." With that, he led us toward the setting sun.

As we passed the halfway point of the night and the moon sunk toward the horizon, we came to an upsetting realization; the Ha'bih had turned. We weren't heading due east anymore. We were angling north. Andy said it was to follow the old coast. If we wanted to find the Berumada Pit, we needed to leave the Ocean Road behind and walk across the dunes.

I didn't like that idea for two reasons: one, I hated walking on sand—the grains got everywhere and didn't sit still—two, if we left the road, we would truly be on our own. How would we know where to go? What if we got lost? I didn't like the idea of spending the rest of my life in this infernal desert with itchy feet.

Maybe our impending doom would be a good enough reason to call Cat?

We were told to head east, and, after much debating, Jason guided us into the desert. Cycles passed. The night came and went. There were no signs of the Pit. As a group, we decided to keep going. We had to be close!

Max asked the question lingering at the back of all our minds. "Are we sure we're going in the right direction?"

The first glimpse of the sun rose from the sand behind us, and the world grew hotter each tick. None of us were in the best mood. A silence similar to the one from the other night after the talk about our parents hung over us. Aching limbs and mounting heat weren't helping.

"Cat told us to follow the setting sun," Jason stated. "We're going the right way. Our pace slowed, and we didn't get as far as we should have." He stopped and removed some strips of dried meat. He handed them out. "This will be breakfast for now. We'll eat more when we call it a day."

I took a bite and headed toward where I had last see the moon. "Alright then, let's keep moving."

The others fell in line behind me. With any luck, we'd find our goal soon.

Several hand cycles later and that hadn't happened. The Sun hovered halfway between the western horizon and the top of the sky. We didn't seem to be any closer to the Berumada Pit, and things were getting worse with each tick. Tempers rose with the heat. Simple questions received harsh answers. Beaded sweat dripped on bare skin. Faces were red, eyes narrowed. We should have stopped for the day, but we didn't.

We had to be close.

"Why does it have to be so hot?" Max grumbled.

"I don't know!" I snapped. We had never learned about stuff like this at the CTS.

Jason's stomach growled for the hundredth time, which made his following complaint even more annoying. "By the Stars, I'm hungry!"

Why did he have to remind me about my own hunger? My stomach wouldn't let me forget; I didn't need him reminding me every five ticks. I wished we had more to eat for breakfast. We should stop, but just one more dune. We had to be close.

"Will you please stop talking about food?" Andy shouted.

I kept us moving. Even though my legs were killing me, I didn't want to stop and lose progress.

Jason and the others kept moving, and he kept complaining too. "I'll stop talking about it when I get food."

I stopped halfway up the sand dune and peered into his squinted eyes.

Andy and I kept our grumblings to ourselves. Jason and Max felt the need to share.

The idea of hitting Jason sounded great. I shared that. "Jason, if you don't stop talking about food this instant, I swear by the Stars, I'll punch you."

Jason laughed. "You'll punch me? You're joking right? You'd never—"

I socked him in the face.

His head jerked right; he lost his footing, and rolled past Andy and Max to the bottom of the hill, losing the bag in the process. A cascade of sand followed him and created a rumble which echoed across the desert.

The Erima growling at me drained the fight in me—or maybe it was my friend lying motionless at the ground.

"Jason? Jason are you okay?"

No response.

What if I'd really hurt him?

Andy and Max panned between the two of us.

In silence, Jason tried to stand but fell. He sat in the sand and glared at me.

I stopped moving, possibly even breathing. I couldn't move with that glare focused on me. It had never been focused on me before.

Andy stepped between us and shielded me from his eyes. "Jason … he didn't mean it. It was the heat. Let's just all take a deep breath and try to calm down."

We'd all seen him this angry before. It never ended well for his target. I took a step back up the dune.

Andy's words weren't working; Jason screamed and launched forward.

I turned and climbed the dune as fast as possible. I couldn't run very fast with the sand and my tired legs holding me back.

"Guys, stop!" Andy shouted.

Jason wouldn't listen, so I didn't. I crested the top of the dune with Jason right behind me. He tackled me, and we rolled down the opposite side. When I stopped, I tried to sit upright, but found it difficult when *up* kept moving. I laid there. Golden dunes spun around me.

Andy's voice came from my left—or had it been my right? I couldn't tell. "Are you two all right?"

"I'm okay."

"You won't be once the world stops spinning. You'll regret punching me!"

Too late for that. I covered my face with my hands, willing the world to stop spinning. It actually worked after a tick or two. Everything stayed still like it should.

I sat upright. I needed to act fast. "Jason, I'm sorry. I let the heat get to me." I realized he hadn't landed where I thought he had. "Where are you?"

His reply came from behind me. "Over here. Why did I tackle you at the top?" He lay face up in the sand, his eyes watching the sky.

I rose on very unsteady legs. "I'd help you, but I don't know if you still want to kill me."

"Get me on my feet, and I won't kill you." The anger had left his voice. His eyes shut as I drew near.

"Sounds like a deal. Give me your hand."

He reached out, and I pulled him to his feet. Between his weight and my tired knees, we almost fell back to the ground.

"There."

He opened his eyes for a tick before slamming them shut. "Bad idea!"

"It'll stop soon. Try again."

He opened his eyes, the relief evident on his face, until he frowned. "What?"

He pointed over my shoulder. "That's not supposed to be there."

I looked to where he pointed. Something flat and shiny poked over the top of the adjacent dune. "What is that?"

Andy and Max joined us. Andy took turns punching Jason and me in the shoulder. I didn't bother asking why. I knew.

Max gestured to the shiny thing. "Do we know what that is?"

Still rubbing my arm, I popped the *P* of my next word. "Nope."

"Didn't think so." Max readjusted the bag on his shoulder. "We going to check it out?"

Jason and I glanced at each other. "Probably," I answered.

With that, we climbed the dune. I expected the thing to be small, but I couldn't have been more wrong. More of the object hid on the other side of the sand pile, and it was big!

It resembled a giant metal bird—a large, long, almost cylindrical body with two massive wings, one of which was what we had seen from the other side. The back of the object had a flat triangular structure, similar to the so-called wings rising from the top and pointing skyward. Near the base of this structure were two smaller wings. The whole thing gleamed bright silver in the sunlight.

"What is it?" Andy asked.

"You're the smart one," I said. "Don't you know what it is?"

She rolled her eyes at me. "I don't know everything." She tilted her head as she examined the object. "I've never seen anything like this in a book—at least not anything made of metal."

"That's a first," Max said. Andy looked like she might retaliate when metal scraped against metal.

Jason had opened a door on the side of the machine. He looked inside before looking at us. "It's empty, and there are seats. I say we sleep in here."

Nothing else needed to be said. Max hurried over and pushed past Jason to be the first inside.

Andy climbed in after him. "Must you always be the first to lie down and sleep?"

Max snored in response.

Jason climbed in, and I followed him.

Were we close to the Berumada Pit?

Chapter 17
-Asking Questions and Having More Afterward-

The day ended too quickly. I felt like it had only been half a cycle since I laid down when Jason shook me awake. Sleeping in this machine had been one of the most comfortable rests I'd had since we left the CTS. The thing had a lot of room inside, enough for an adult to stand. There were seats for nearly twenty people. A row of seats ran along one side, then a walkway, and then two more rows of seats on the other side.

We'd each chosen two seats to sleep on. Combined, two seats weren't long enough for any of us, but they were comfortable. They weren't damaged much. It seemed the Erima struggled getting inside.

I went to wake Andy, but Jason stopped me. I tried to ask why, and he put a finger to his lips. He pointed to the door, and I followed him outside, staying quiet until he shut the door. "Why aren't we waking them?"

"If we keep this pace up any longer, the four of us won't be able to walk anymore."

"But we need to find the Tablets."

"And, if we kill ourselves trying, it'd be a waste. We need to take a break to rest—not the whole night but part of it. Besides, we're almost to the Berumada Pit." He had the faintest trace of smile.

"How do you know we're close?"

He pointed at the metal machine where our friends slept. "This. None of us have ever seen anything like it. One of the rumors about the Pit is there are strange machines in it."

I raised an eyebrow. He based this on a rumor? "Okay … so then we're close to the Pit?"

Jason beheld our surroundings while running a hand over the top of his head. "I wish we knew how much farther. I hate being unsure of where we're going."

I agreed. Being told a direction to walk and just going bothered me. That's how I got lost in the CTS. The restricted sections weren't exactly marked, but the adults didn't care if we wandered in there on accident.

"I'm going back to sleep. I'll wake everyone later. Wanted to run this by you first." He opened the door and climbed in with me right behind him.

I resumed laying on my seats, and he did the same. I closed my eyes, but sleep did not come. My mind churned, worrying about everything.

Andy's charm! I could use it to ask Cat if we were going the right way. I rummaged through the bag by Jason's seat to find the charm and went outside, careful not to wake anyone. Once outside, I stared at the object in my hand. Cat had said we must hold it and think of him. I wondered if he'd really know we needed him. It didn't seem possible.

"You better have the first Tablet."

I startled and turned around.

He sat on top of the machine, his pale blue eyes shimmering in the weak moonlight. He looked better than the last time I'd seen him. His eyes were wide and alert.

"We don't have the Tablet yet."

His tail twitched. "I thought I told you to only need me if you had the first Tablet."

"I wanted to make sure we're headed in the right direction. We've hiked for three nights now, and we haven't reached the Berumada Pit."

Cat's tail twitched even more. "What are you talking about? You may not have found the center of the Pit, but you're close. This plane should have told you that." He stretched and stood as he surveyed the machine.

Plane? I'd never heard of such a thing. I'm sure I looked confused, because Cat sighed.

"This thing I'm standing on is a plane."

I took a deep breath. "I got that. What is it used for? None of us have seen anything like it."

"It is an old vehicle from my world. Humans fly these to get from one place to another."

This thing could fly! Could we use it? Judging by the broken bits of the wing near the body and the sand piled on the front, that seemed unlikely.

"Then how did it get here?"

"I only have a theory. Dimensions and worlds are more connected than anyone realizes. It is entirely possible there is a hole from my world to here, and this plane, along with the others, fell into it and landed here. But I have no solid proof to back it up."

I had never heard of anything like that before. Wait. "What others?"

Cat pointed his tail eastward. "The other craft I can make out. If I'm right, it's a big hole."

"I don't see anything."

"It's there. If that is all, I'd like to go home. I hate it here."

When I spoke with Cat, the more questions he answered, the less I knew.

Cat bowed and disappeared.

Could I see the other machines from the top of the plane too? Trying to be quiet, I climbed from the buried front and stared across the desert—nothing but sand dunes all the way to the horizon. The sand glowed light gray from the moonlight, and the sky remained as black as always. The two colors met in smooth waves all along the horizon. Wait, no they didn't. In one spot, jagged lines replaced the smoothly curved dunes rising from the sand. The Pit! It had to be. We were closer than we had realized!

I slid off the plane and dropped to the sand. I didn't land gracefully, but no one saw. "Wake up, wake up, wake up!" I ran inside.

Jason jumped from his seats, Andy bolted up right, and I could see Max glaring at me through the cracks in the rows. He didn't even try to get up.

Jason scanned the entire plane for anything wrong before his eyes stopped on me. "I thought we agreed." He yawned.

"I spoke with Cat, and we're almost to the Pit. I think I can see it from the top of the plane." My explanation only added to their confusion.

"You talked to Cat?" Jason asked.

"And you could see the Berumada Pit from the top of what?" Andy asked, scooting to the edge of her seat.

"I could see the Pit from the top of this thing; it's called a plane. It's from Cat's world. He thinks it was meant to land in the Pit, but it crashed here."

Everyone stayed quiet for a moment.

With a groan, Jason grabbed the bag. "Well, since we're all up"—he shambled the door—"might as well get on our way."

"I don't want to get up," Max complained.

Andy and I shook our heads as we headed outside.

Jason leaned against the side of the plane. When we joined him, he tossed us each a pitahaya. When we were almost finished, he gave us each a handful of dried meat strips. With a knock on the side of the plane, he asked, "Max, do you want dinner?"

The inside of the plane rumbled. Max shot out the door and fell face first into the sand. "Are we having something other than pitahaya?"

Andy laughed as Jason held a fruit and meat out for him.

Max grumbled as he crawled next to me and sat. "You enjoy it when I get tormented, don't you?"

Andy shrugged as her smile faded. "You enjoyed tormenting me."

Not that again. I'd really hoped we'd gotten past this. "Maybe we should just eat quietly," I suggested.

Jason nodded enthusiastically before taking a drink of water. The quiet lasted about eight ticks.

"I said I was sorry!" Max shouted.

Andy continued to eat in silence.

"I apologized for being mean!"

I hoped Max would drop the conversation. I doubted Andy enjoyed it.

As if to prove my thought, she stood and started down the dune. "Are you coming or not?"

Jason and I followed without question.

"I'm still eating!" Max complained. He shouldn't have upset her if he wanted to eat in peace.

She waited for us then swept her arm around her. "Alright, Kyle, where do you think the Pit is?"

"It's this way." I led the others toward the Pit with Max running to keep up.

<^>

After cycles of walking, a silhouette grew on the horizon. Something loomed in the night sky. At some point, Jason took the lead again, and that didn't bother me. Leading scared me. If we got lost, it'd be my fault. I followed him, with Andy behind me, and Max in back.

A tension existed—one not brought on by being alone in the middle of the Erima. We all knew the earlier conversation upset Andy. We were doing our best to not make her angrier.

I fell in alongside her.

She didn't say anything.

"Are you okay?" I knew she wasn't, but that's how these conversations always started.

She turned her head away from me.

After several ticks, she answered me in a low voice. "I don't want to talk about it." She quickened her pace to try to get away from me, but I matched it.

"Why not?"

She didn't answer.

"Come on, I'm your best friend."

Still nothing.

"Andy, talk to me. I don't like seeing you upset."

"I'm not upset. What makes you think that?" She still didn't look at me.

"Do you really think I can't tell when you're upset?"

Her head drooped. "No."

"So?"

Andy spied Max to see if he might be listening.

He paid us no attention.

"It's what Max said earlier."

I replayed the conversation in my head. He hadn't said anything that I or Jason considered cruel. If he had, he would've been punched. "But he didn't say anything mean."

"He didn't. He just said I like tormenting him." Her gaze dropped to the ground.

I didn't see the problem with that.

Her voice shook as she continued. "I don't want to be like that!" She stopped in place. "He tormented me for seven years. Then Jason comes along and gets him to apologize for everything. I thought it was just another one of his tricks, but he was serious. Now I'm doing what he did to me."

All progress stopped. Nobody moved or said anything.

Andy finally broke the silence, and when she did, she did so with a whisper. "I can't be that kind of a person." She fell to her knees.

Jason led Max away while I knelt in the sand next to her. "You aren't turning into Max."

"I tease him just like he used to tease me! I'm exactly like him."

"You have not turned into Max. You tease him like a friend."

She grabbed up a handful of sand and let the grains run through her fingers. "If that were true, he wouldn't say I torment him."

"Andy, he was kidding!"

"It's still true. I do torment him and hate myself for it." She slammed her empty hand into the sand.

Max joined us, despite Jason's pleas to not. "I feel the same way about what I did to you. I hate that I used to be such a bully. The only excuse I can offer is that I was stupid, but even that isn't much. I'm sorry."

Andy wiped her eyes and smiled at him. "Thank you, Max. I have forgiven you. It's just … I can't handle doing the same to you, knowing how it feels."

Max laughed, taking us by surprise. "You don't really think you're as bad as me, do you? Your so-called insults are weak. If you're really that upset, just do what I do. If you say something bad, have Jason sock your shoulder."

We all laughed as Jason joined us. "Yes, like you choose to have me constantly punch you."

Max glared at him for a tick before refocusing to Andy. "If it means that much to you, I forgive you for every mean thing you've ever done to me."

Andy released a deep breath and stood. "Thank you."

"You're welcome. Just don't start expecting this from me."

"Don't worry, we won't." Jason clapped his hand on Max's shoulder, making him flinch.

"Yes, it was weird." Andy smirked at him, and he grinned back.

"Come on, guys. I'd like to get to the Pit before morning," I said.

Jason, Andy, and Max fell in line behind me. Come dawn, we'd be at the Berumada Pit.

Chapter 18
-The Hole Between Worlds-

The sky brightened as we finally arrived at the Berumada Pit. After hearing the name so many times, I expected a large hole in the ground. I didn't expect it to be so big and visible from a distance. I could hear it too. A grumbling roar filled the air and shifted with each gust of wind. Wrecked vehicles littered the sand. Some resembled a drawing Andy once showed me, and I assumed they were of Tehraheyian origins. Others were like the plane we found.

The largest thing here was one of several wooden ships. Four masts reached into the sky from the largest. On all of them, the sails were torn and the wood worn and jagged. The ship groaned and creaked. Ropes dangled from masts, bits of metal held in their grasp. Every gust of wind sent the ropes into motion, and the metal bits thudded into the wood and clanged against one another. Meanwhile, the shreds of sails snapped and fluttered. Carved into the prow of the biggest ship rested the upper half of a skeleton. Even in the pre-dawn light, I swore the skeletal eye sockets watched us as we passed. It did little to help ease the discomfort growing in my stomach.

Andy voiced her concerns with nothing more than a whisper. "I don't like this place." She locked eyes with me, and I agreed with a simple nod.

We wove through the shadowy graveyard of ships and planes, aiming for the hole in the ground. The wind couldn't settle here. It howled nonstop and carried a damp scent. The heat lessened from burn-our-faces-off to almost nice the closer we got to the Pit, and the roaring wind seemed to come from within. The sand dunes gave way to solid ground around the rim, which dropped away into dark cliffs.

Stopping at the edge, Jason, Max, and I peered into the depths. Andy kept her distance. The Pit looked like a giant version of one of Cat's eyes, with the two points aimed north and south. Far below us, farther than the light could reach, bubbled up a continuous roar. Some vessels balanced precariously on the edge. Less fortunate ones—what was left of them anyway—were caught on the side of the precipice below.

Jason beheld the whole area, a smile tugging at his features. "It *is* real," he whispered.

Max preoccupied himself with tossing a stone over the edge. It disappeared into the darkness with echoing clatters until they faded into the never-ending roar. "Neat."

At least they were enjoying themselves. Despite the amazing view into an abyss, this place bothered me. It did not feel like the rest of the Erima. While the entire desert felt harsh and unforgiving, this forgotten field of wreckage seemed otherworldly. I wanted to believe the stranded machines caused this sensation but no. Something else was here—something other than these ancient relics. I didn't like the sensation it caused in my stomach. Some invisible force pulled at and twisted my insides, as if trying to rearrange or take them for itself, like the Pit wanted to Travel out of Tehrahey.

I didn't dwell on it for long. As the sun rose, getting out of the light became a priority. We needed to set up camp.

"Preferably away from the cliffs," Andy stated.

Jason and I agreed.

However, Max wanted to explore. "You guys set up the tent, I'll check that out." He pointed toward the large wooden ship.

Before any of us could argue with him, he dashed behind a wrecked plane. I don't know where he found the energy. He'd been complaining about being tired before we arrived. I considered going after him. The idea of any of us being alone here didn't sit right with me. However, he didn't make it far before he shrieked and scrambled back around the corner.

"Are you okay?" I asked.

He patted himself down, trying to get rid of the sand clinging to his clothes. "Fine. Never better." He glanced over his shoulder like a scared kid meeting Ms. Hess for the first time.

Jason paused from unloading the tent from the bag. "What did you find?"

Max opened his mouth to say something then stopped. His eyes darted to Andy. "Nothing."

With a hard stare, Jason rose and followed Max's tracks around the plane. He returned almost instantly, his brows furrowed. "We're not sleeping here."

He packed up the tent and took us away from the plane, toward the southside of the Pit.

I fell in line next to Jason. "What did you see?"

He glanced back at Max and Andy. "You really want to know?" he asked, his voice low.

I grimaced, already not liking whatever he saw. "Probably not but tell me anyway."

"A body, what's left of one. Didn't want Andy or you to see. Bad enough Max saw."

"Will he be okay?" I looked over my shoulder to study our friend.

Max's head jerked from side to side, searching for something. It made me nervous.

The grim expression on his face lightened a little as he offered a heavy nod. "With time, yes. Seeing a dead body isn't easy."

I gave another sympathetic look over my shoulder at Max. He didn't see it, still watching our surroundings with a wary eye. At least he'd be all right. If anything, the scare would probably keep him sticking close to us and not trying to run off to explore. Still, I didn't envy them for seeing that. "What about you?" I asked. They'd both seen the body after all. Why wasn't Jason acting like Max?

Jason gave a half laugh. "I've seen worse."

I knew that. It amazed me he smiled as much as he did, which wasn't very often. "You know, it isn't a good thing you've seen worse."

"Yeah, but life doesn't always give you good. Our world is dying, and this may be our only chance to escape, but can we really do that?"

He didn't say it, but I knew he meant how could we do what countless generations of adults couldn't? They'd never found the Tablets or *The Book of time*. What hope did we have?

A counter thought occurred to me, one I knew Jason would appreciate. "No one could find the Berumada Pit either."

He became thoughtful as a grin spread across his face.

We found a more agreeable place to set up the tent—one free of any dead bodies. Once our shelter was up, we ate breakfast in uncomfortable silence. Max's obvious agitation and the surrounding wrecked ships put all of us on edge. We finished eating in a hurry and went inside to sleep. Well, some of us did.

Max lay almost motionless, staring at the ceiling. His earlier discovery sent the four of us drifting through an uneasy sleep.

<^>

I awoke to Jason stating it was dinnertime. I groaned as I stood; my legs did not like that they needed to move again. I shook Andy's shoulder.

She opened one eye. "Do I have to get up?"

I didn't blame her. "You don't have to get up. We'll just leave you here."

Andy opened her other eye to glare at me. "It would be horrible if you guys left me by myself."

"We'd never do that to you. Max maybe, but you? Never."

"As annoying as he is, I don't think I could leave him behind. It wouldn't feel right."

I tried not to imagine how horrible it would be to get left out here by myself. The CTS was bad, the Erima worse, but I had my friends to help make the experiences better. If I had tried to do this alone, I would've died my first night.

"Yes, but we'd never do that to each other. We stick together."

"Obviously." Andy laughed. She sat upright and ran a hand through her hair, taming it a little and dislodging a lot of sand. "We tell them we're leaving to wander the Erima and they want to come with."

Did that make them crazy or noble? Perhaps both. "When you say it like that, you make it sound like we're all crazy." The more I thought about it, we probably were. Who else would follow directions from a cat?

Andy shrugged. "Everyone is crazy." She passed me and walked outside.

We joined Jason and Max sitting in the sand for dinner. Max's eyes were droopy, and every tick or so, he'd glance in the direction of the body. Even out of sight, it scared him.

Andy passed me my meal, and we fell into silence as we ate.

Max kept looking into the distance. This little action affected everyone and put us on edge. Jason watched Max worriedly, while Andy tried her best not to ignore him. However, I knew my friend. The longer this carried on, the more her curiosity would nag at her.

Sure enough, she joined Max in glancing over her shoulder. She huffed and dropped her hands in her lap. "Would you stop looking over there? You're making me nervous." She paused. "Do I want to know?"

We all shook our heads, Max more vigorously than Jason and me. It was easy to forget he was only twelve. It only made him a year younger, and he liked to act tough, ready for anything, but that wasn't always the case. In this moment, he looked absolutely terrified.

While we hadn't been in the best of moods the past few nights, I knew this would be worse. I needed to snap them out of it before it could take hold. I moved to block Max's view. "Stop staring at it! None of us needs to be worrying about that. It's behind us; we only need to worry about what's ahead." I pointed southward. "Finish eating so we can get moving." I finished my meal and disassembled the tent. By the time it was back in the bag, the others were done with their meals. "Come on, we have an island to find." I tossed the bag over my shoulder and headed south.

My friends quickly fell in line behind me.

After only half a cycle, we left the Berumada Pit behind. The last traces of it were jagged bumps on the horizon. Its secret were nothing more than a memory.

<^>

We spent most of the walk in silence, and by the time we were halfway through the night, we'd wandered across large expanses of sand.

"How will we know when we found the island if it isn't surrounded by water anymore?" Max asked.

I looked over my shoulder to the one person who had every answer. "Any ideas?"

Andy's head tilted toward the dark sky as she thought. "Well, islands are landmasses that float on the water. If the ocean levels dropped fast enough, the island could've been left behind on the mainland, like a boat or fish. If that's the case, it'll probably be more rock than sand. It should stand out in this landscape." She gestured around us.

"Why do rocks sink when islands float?" Jason asked.

I had asked the same question back in my lands class. My teacher didn't like me questioning him and insisted that's how islands worked.

"If you get enough rocks together and spread them out just right, their weight is spread equally across the water, making it easier to hold up. It's like if all four of us carried something at the same time, we could hold it higher," Andy explained.

We continued in silence, walking up and down the smaller dunes and skirting around the larger ones. Every time we reached the top of one, another lay beyond it and another beyond the next one. I doubted anything other than sand existed in this world.

Jason broke the silence of the night. "Did anyone see that?"

Everyone stopped and looked at him. He pointed toward the horizon.

I searched the border between the land and sky. "I don't see anything."

"See what?" Andy asked.

"Yeah, I didn't see anything," Max said. Three to one said nothing was on the horizon.

Jason rubbed his eyes before his hands dropped to his sides. "Guess I'm seeing things."

A cycle past and still no sign of any strange rock formations. I wondered how long it would take for us to find the island. Cat had only said we would find it south of the Berumada Pit; he never told us how far. It could take us nights to find what we were looking for. With my aching legs, that didn't exactly sound fun.

I stopped. No footsteps sounded behind me. Did I lose them? No, they were still there.

Andy stood still, sniffing the air while Max and Jason watched. "Do you guys smell that?" she asked.

I couldn't smell anything other than desert, which I never realized had a smell. It smelled like dirt. Dry, hot dirt. Even at night, I could still feel the heat from the ground. "Nothing."

"You must be going crazy," Max said.

Jason punched his shoulder and placed a hand on Andy's.

"I'm losing it too. I keep seeing things on the horizon. Maybe we should call it a night." If he suggested stopping before night's end, something must really be bothering him.

I almost agreed, but Andy shrugged his hand off her shoulder and stepped forward. "I can smell something different; I just don't know what." Her hand shot out and pointed toward the horizon as she bounced up and down. "I saw something!"

We rushed to her side. Just like when Jason had said he saw something, I didn't see anything other than sand.

When Jason spoke, he sounded hopeful. "What did you see?"

"It was light. Something flickered way out there somewhere."

"That's what I've been seeing."

Max saw an opening for the insult, and he took it. "Or you're both losing your minds." He rubbed his shoulder after getting punched again and gave our friend a hard look.

Jason shrugged it off. "Not like you didn't know that was coming." The truth of the comment didn't stop Max's glaring.

The four of us remained quiet as we watched the horizon, waiting for the light to reappear and find out if Jason and Andy were crazy. After several ticks of darkness nothing happened.

"I still don't see anything." I turned around in time to see all three of them jump.

"Great, now I'm going crazy too!" Max said.

I searched the horizon, desperate to find what they had seen. I couldn't be the only one who had missed it. However, there was only sand to be seen. I watched Andy tilt her head.

"You didn't see it?" Despite Andy's earlier excitement, a sad smile tugged at her lips. When I didn't answer, she continued in an encouraging tone. "Well, the light keeps coming from up ahead. You'll see it soon." She pushed me to get moving again.

Before that point, the walk had been annoying, the same way it always was hiking across the sand. With the appearance of the lights, it got worse. Not only did I still have to walk on tired legs over sand dune after sand dune, every few ticks, Andy, Jason, or Max would make a noise signaling they saw the light again. The sounds were annoying. They weren't evenly spaced out. Sometimes they would happen less than a tick apart, and other times, five ticks would pass before another came. The appearances of the light were completely random. I just happened to be the one unfortunate enough to miss all of them.

Then Max made a noise, and I stopped in my tracks. I finally saw it—a small flash of white light on the horizon. If I had blinked a tick earlier, I would've missed it again.

Andy placed a hand on my shoulder. "You saw that last one, didn't you?"

"Yes." I looked back at her. "Do you know what it is?"

"I don't have a single idea what it could be. I've never heard of anything like that happening before." The fact Andy didn't know what the light might have been worried me. She had read every book in the library, some multiple times, especially the ones about Councilmen Adam and Eve Good. I had found her rereading those books more than once. Every time, I'd ask her why she read them again, but she could never give me an answer other than *"I like them"*. Something about Adam and Eve captured her attention, and she wouldn't let them go.

Jason sighed and took a deep breath. His eyes shot open, and he sniffed the air. "Do you smell that?"

Nope, just sand, same as always. Though maybe something smelled a bit different.

Jason slapped his forehead. "I'm sorry, Andy, I forgot. You are always right."

Max groaned. "Not this again."

Jason ignored him. "It's water." A smile crept onto Jason's face. "We must be close to the sea."

The sea? We were actually getting close to the ocean! I remembered the dream from Xic-Patan—the four of us playing in the water. Could the dream have been a prediction? It couldn't have been, could it? Dreams were just dreams, not predictions of the future.

I glanced at the thin sliver of a moon sinking in the sky. If we could smell it, we had to be close, right? "I'd like to be there before the sun comes up." I resumed walking, and the others fell in line behind me.

"Why do we keep seeing lights on the ocean?" Andy asked.

In a surprising twist, Andy had asked a question, and Jason answered it. Usually, it was the other way around. "The lights are fish. I remember one spot where the fish shone at night. My father called them starfish. They're what stars looked like."

"I've never heard of fish doing that before."

Jason shrugged. "They only do it along one spot on the coast. The Maker probably doesn't want anyone to know about them."

"Surprise, surprise," Max muttered, echoing my own thoughts.

The flashing lights occurred more often and spread across the horizon. After only half a cycle, the ocean became easy to see.

Chaotic, ever-changing waves of water rippled across the horizon, replacing the gentle slopes of sand we'd seen since leaving Xic-Patan. The smell became more obvious as well. It wasn't clean and clear, like water in the CTS. It smelled different, a good different. I had never experienced anything like it before. The air here became less warm as well, and I knew the water caused it.

The crashing of waves filled the air. It felt strange to be so close to water. I had grown used to the sands of the Erima and the concrete of the CTS. I knew the CTS was in Entstal, on the coast, but I had never seen the ocean before. At least not on Tehrahey. The idea of being visibly close to so much water excited me. It had been so much fun in my dream.

I took a step and found firm ground beneath my feet instead of sand.

"I knew it." Jason examined the rock with his feet before continuing onward.

Max excitedly dropped to his stomach on the rocky ground. "Solid land!"

Even though I didn't join him, I felt the same way.

He sat upright and patted it. Andy and I laughed as he truly worshiped the ground he sat on, holding rocks to the sky and thanking the Stars for their existence.

Jason continued walking for little bit. "You guys should see this."

Andy and I joined him. "What did you want us to see …?" We stood on the edge of an enormous cliff. I took a few steps backward, Andy took several.

Jason remained right on the ledge.

He peeked over, and I did the same. The ground dropped a long way into darkness—not as much as the Berumada Pit but still a whole lot farther than I was comfortable with. To our left, a canyon divided the cliffs. While this canyon may have once been as tall as the rest of the rock formations here, sand had filled it in, leaving an easy slope to get down from above. That made getting down a lot easier. Although, we had a new problem; where was the island? Had we missed it?

"I remember these cliffs. We passed them on the way to Eden." Though he didn't say it, I knew he meant his trip with his father. Thankfully, Andy and Max got it as well. He pointed eastward along the cliffs. "They're called K'aktun. Lejos Noble is two week's that way."

Andy's gaze followed his finger, and she stood on her toes, trying to catch a glimpse of the city.

I doubted we could see it from here.

Max continued to enjoy the ground without paying much attention to the rest of us.

Jason pointed toward the brightening sky in the west. "Sun's almost up."

For once, it looked like we'd get to set up camp before sunrise. I looked forward to the end of the night and the extra bit of sleep. Plus, a day by the water would be nice. "Alright, let's get moving. Come on Max." With caution, I slid down the sandy canyon.

Andy and Jason followed.

Max rushed after us. "Wait for me! Hey, where did these cliffs come from?"

"Good job listening, Max," Andy said.

He mimicked her in a high-pitched voice.

She ignored him.

We maneuvered our way to the bottom of K'aktun, and the sky brightened from black to gray. The ground leveled out, and we were still within the confines of the two cliff faces. Jason decided it would be the best place to camp for the day. Their shade would be very welcome. We assembled the tent and ate our breakfast in a hurry, eager to get to sleep before the sun woke up.

My legs were exhausted, but I forced them to work in a hurry. The sooner the tent was up, the sooner I could rest. With that thought in mind, I slumped into the tent after everyone else. My stomach felt nice and happy after our meal.

Jason had given us a bit more than usual, I think in celebration of finding the ocean.

We all laid in the sand, and not a tick later, Max snored.

Andy looked dumbfounded. "How does he do that?"

Jason closed his eyes. "Tunes the world out or empties his mind."

Andy's eyes shut, and her voice grew heavy. "It's probably the *empty the mind* thing. I don't think there's much in there to clear out."

I gave her arm a light punch. "Be nice."

Andy waved dismissively. "At least I said something was in there." She opened an eye to look at me then frowned when she didn't see me smiling. "It was just a joke." She closed her eye. "Goodnight, you guys."

"I think you mean good morning," I said. If she responded, I didn't hear it.

Chapter 19
-Water is Fun, and Troublesome-

2-12.11.12.17.9 T.S.T.
K'aktun, Erima
Tehrahey

"Kyle," a voice called to me. "Kyle, wake up."

I awoke to find Andy staring down at me.

"It's about time!"

I sat upright, stretched my arms, and rolled my head. Dim daylight seeped through the fabric roof, and I groaned. Just because we had gone to sleep early didn't mean we had to get up early! How could Jason do this to us? Wait, where were Jason and Max? Andy and I were the only ones in the tent. Our friends were laughing in the distance.

"Come on, I want to go play in the water!" She grabbed my arm and pulled me from the tent into the shade of the canyon.

To my surprise, the sunlight came from the east and was already fading into the golden oranges of sunset. I didn't wake up once all day! Was I finally getting used to this new sleep schedule, or was I just too tired to care?

Outside the tent, a breeze drifted through the air. This helped prevent the beach from getting too hot. I already liked the beach a lot more than the Erima. Max and Jason stood next to the best part: the water. Waves splashed against their legs, sending droplets into the air. That looked nice.

In the light of day, I noticed the sand on the canyon floor—as well as a narrow strip leading to the water—was whiter than the other bits of sand. It looked nothing like the harsh, golden ground we had traversed the last few days. This looked softer and, somehow, more inviting.

Andy removed her sandals and placed them with the two pairs already next to the tent. "I'll race you to the water!"

I liked the sound of that and copied her. Once my bare feet touched the sand, I took off running down the beach. My legs hated that, but I didn't care. The sand felt great between my toes without the confines of the sandals, and thanks to the ocean air, it wasn't too hot either.

Andy shouted after me, "Cheater!" She never managed to catch up, and I reached the water's edge first. She bent over and rested her hands on her knees. Once her breathing steadied, she pointed at me. "You cheated."

I pointed back. "And you wouldn't do the same thing?"

She straightened upright and placed a hand over her heart. "I would never cheat in a race between friends." A staring contest followed. I almost apologized, but then she caved. "Okay fine, I thought of doing it, but you"—she renewed her pointing—"actually did. I'm innocent!"

Without warning, I found myself on my butt in the water as a wave crashed over me.

When the water cleared, Andy stood over me. "That's for cheating." She reached out and helped me to my feet.

I wiped the water off my face. "I deserved that." I did cheat, and the punishment wasn't too bad. Having the heat washed away felt wonderful.

Andy faced the ocean as the others joined us. "Now what?" Her shoulders slumped as she gazed across the water. "We were supposed to go south until we found the island."

How were we supposed to continue? We didn't have a boat and had no way of getting one. Maybe Jason had a plan or knew of a place to get a boat. "Jason?"

"You know how to swim?" he asked. He received three separate head shakes from each of us. "Then there's nothing left for us to do. Not without help anyway." His gaze drifted left toward the setting sun.

There had to be a way. We couldn't have walked all of this way for nothing. Wait a tick, help! We needed help, and I knew just who to ask. "Andy, where's your charm? Maybe Cat can help."

Andy hesitated. "He said not to bother him, and you already did that once."

She had a point, but the few times I'd met Cat, he'd never been in a good mood. I had a feeling he didn't even know how to be happy. "I don't think it matters. We'll always be a problem to Cat."

"You may be right about that." She headed back to the tent. She disappeared inside the fabric walls, and less than a tick later, she shrieked. Red light illuminated the inside of the tent as she scrambled outside. As the entrance flapped closed, I noticed the red light came from her charm, which rested in the sand next to the leather sack.

Jason recovered first and pulled Andy to her feet.

"Are you okay?"

She nodded, her eyes fixed on our shelter.

"What's in there?" Max asked, rejoining our group.

I'd been so focused on Andy, I didn't see him run away. Nobody answered, and no one moved to find out.

Jason remained steadfast in front of Andy, who chewed her bottom lip.

Max's gaze darted between the red light and any possible escape routes.

My heartbeat raced, and blood roared in my ears as the ticks past. I took a deep breath to calm my nerves and stepped closer.

Andy's voice broke the quite that had fallen over us. "Kyle, be careful."

I offered her a smirk for reassurance as I crept forward. Hopefully, it showed more confidence than I felt. Peeking inside, I saw the crystal remained perfectly still. It looked like it normally did, except for the light shining from the crystal. "That's strange." I grabbed it and brought it to the group. "I'm guessing it isn't supposed to do this."

Andy took her charm to examine it properly. "It's never done this before." She brought it closer to herself, and the light dimmed. "Interesting." She stepped closer to me, and the light brightened. It lit up when it got near me? That was definitely new. She scanned the canyon, not seeming to think I was the special cause of the light. "It must have something to do with where we are."

Stepping toward the ocean brightened the light. Walking to the back of the canyon dimmed it.

"It gets brighter the closer you get to the water," Jason said.

We followed her to the water and stopped out of its reach while Andy stood with it splashing around her ankles. Her prized possession shone like the setting sun. Both light sources cast stunning yet terrifying crimson light across the water. That, combined with the orange sky, made it seem as if the entire ocean were on fire.

Andy's eyes, the only bit of green in the entire blaze of color around her, fixated on the charm. She rolled it over, observing every side. "I've never read about anything like this before." She scratched her head and turned to us. "Have you guys?"

She looked mainly at Jason, which didn't bother me. I had no clue. I had no idea how a rock could glow. I doubted Max had any ideas either. Given Jason's experience in the real world, he might have come across something like this.

Jason's forehead wrinkled as thought. "No, I haven't."

They were supposed to have the answers for everything, and yet this strange little charm stumped both of them. That worried me a bit, but it also meant something. The only possible solution for the weirdness was something so old that no one alive had ever experienced it.

"If you haven't read about it, it has to be from the Traveler," I said. If I was right and the object really did come from the Traveler, the fact that it glowed as we tried to get to the first Tablet could be a very good sign. "We must be on the right track."

Andy smiled and bounced a little. "That's wonderful!"

Jason, being the not-so-happy person we knew him to be, crushed her excitement. "If we're right." He inhaled, and confusion spread across his face. "Do you smell that?"

Max's hands shot into the air, and he stepped away from Jason. "It wasn't me."

Andy looked between all three of us, appalled. "You boys are disgusting." She insulted me. I didn't fart that much. Why did I have to be included?

Jason frowned at Max. "Not like that. Do you smell something burning?"

I gulped; this had happened in my dream too. The scent of smoke drifted on the sea breeze. An island would appear next if my dream truly had predicted this, but it couldn't have. The thought that I may have seen the future terrified and excited me. How could I possibly have that ability? I had never glimpsed the future before—a power like that would have helped me out with surprise tests in the CTS. A teacher never would have caught me off guard, and my scores would've rivaled Andy's. However, they didn't, which meant I could not predict the future. I must have just been lucky; although luck had never been on my side before. Were the Stars actually out there, watching me? If so, why?

Not trusting my friends to stay put, I stepped back, keeping them and the horizon in sight. Sure enough, smoke rose from the water. For a moment, no one noticed it; they were too busy scanning the coast. I pointed toward the column of ash-colored clouds. "Look."

"Is that a steam ship?" Andy's gaze followed my outstretched arm.

"A lot of smoke for one ship," Jason said.

The smoke climbed higher, the sun sank lower, and soon, the shapeless pillar reached higher in the sky than the sun. Max lost interest and sat in the sand out of the water's reach. When the sun vanished completely beneath the ocean, lights appeared all over the water. At first, I thought they were related to the smoke, but a few burst out of the water and the starfish were easy to recognize. They looked like any other fish except they glowed in varying shades of blue and white. Many of them seemed to be moving away from the bizarre scene before us.

Most of the lights fled, putting quite a bit of distance between them and the disturbance. However, one light appeared in the base of the ash cloud. Instead of moving away across the water, like the fish did, it rose above the ocean. An island rose from the sea beneath it. My heart thudded in my ears, and my mind raced, trying to understand how I had seen this days ago. Everything about this moment made my stomach churn. Collapsing into the sand next to Max sounded like a good idea, so I did it. I glanced at my friend and found him studying me.

I hoped he wouldn't ask any questions, because the answers I had didn't make sense to me. How could I even begin to explain this to the rest of them? Would they believe me, or would they think I'd lost my mind in the Erima? Maybe that was what had happened. The heat had gotten to me. Would they want to keep me around if that were the case?

A small sense of relief washed over me as Max finally tore his gaze from me to resume watching the strange sight.

"What's that?" Andy asked, not taking her gaze off the island.

"Is that how islands are formed?" Max asked.

Andy's head tilted to the side as she searched her mind for an answer. "It's said the Stars helped the Traveler create Tehrahey, but that was ages ago, and I thought they had all left us."

The Traveler and the Stars, this was their doing. All of it. I couldn't have really seen the future. "This looks like magic to me," I announced with a shaky voice. Thankfully, they didn't seem to notice that little detail.

Max faced me with the look Andy usually gave him—*You're stupid.*

I groaned and took a deep breath, trying to calm myself. If my voice sounded weird, they'd ask questions, which is something I wanted to avoid. In a much sturdier voice, I said. "It's probably related to whatever is making Andy's charm glow." I pointed to the object for extra emphasis.

"My charm has something to do with that?"

"I'm not sure." The words hung in air, practically echoing around us, which couldn't be possible with all the noise. But there wasn't any noise. Only silence. There was no roar of the ocean or whistle of the wind against the cliffs. The ocean sat motionless, completely flat, like a pane of glass. Starfish swam through the darkness, and a few jumped from the water, shattering the smooth surface for a tick before it calmed. The golden rays of twilight hung in the air and bounced off the surface, leaving streaks of color atop the bleak ocean.

The only place where water moved could be found beneath Andy's feet. She stood in a small circle of sand surrounded by water. The site of the water avoiding her proved my point. "Come to think of it, yes I do think it has something to do with your charm." I pointed to her feet.

She looked down and jumped from the circle. Well, she tried to; it just followed her. She landed where water should have been, but there was no splash. "Amazing," she mumbled to herself. She experimented with moving around, and the water avoided her. She turned over the charm in her hands and caused another miracle. When the red light touched the water, it moved away, revealing another circle of damp, white sand. She looked up from her studies, the beginnings of an idea evident on her face, but she stayed quiet a little longer. Her attention shifted to the beach and the canyon beyond. Then she looked over her shoulder at the island.

The canyon, the strip of white sand, the island, and even the Pit all lined up. How did they all connect?

Andy's gaze met mine. I could see the same question plaguing her.

Max rose to his feet and trudged to her with his arm outstretched. "Let me see it!"

Andy pulled her charm to her chest and backed away. She would not be letting it go any time soon, not when it had become so interesting. Max would need to use force.

Jason and I both prepared ourselves to break this up. Turns out, we didn't have to.

Max never got the chance to try and steal her charm. He tripped and fell face first into the water with a nice splash. He rested on his stomach but lifted his head above the water. "That hurt." He followed up the obvious statement by spitting out sand.

I tried my best not to laugh like Andy did. This wasn't the time to make fun of him. I managed only a few giggles. "What happened?"

He surveyed his feet still submerged beneath the water. "I tripped."

Andy pointed her light at his feet, and the water retreated, revealing a tiny pillar of cloudy white rock the same color as the sand around us. She went to investigate and the light brightened. A circular indentation resided atop the little pillar.

Max lifted himself from the water. "What's so special about this dumb rock?"

None of us had an answer.

Andy knelt and felt the stone. "I wonder …" She placed her charm light side up on the stone. Nothing. She frowned and scratched her head. "It seemed like a good match."

Maybe it had been put in the wrong way; both sides were the same shape. "Try the other way," I said.

Andy flipped her charm so the light shined against the rock. Without the sunlight or the charm, the beach darkened before the stone glowed red.

She clapped her hands together, excitement lighting up her eyes. "It's a crystal!"

2-12.11.12.17.9 T.S.T.
K'aktun, Erima
Tehrahey

I thought crystals were just pretty rocks. What did it matter that we found one?

Andy returned to examining the small pillar as she explained. "Supposedly, they can store magical energies. It's rumored the Tablets are made from crystals. I bet the Traveler left it here to help us get to the island."

"Look!" Jason gestured toward the island; a stripe of water glowed the same red as Andy's charm. Even the white sand around us tried to mimic the color.

She slowly stood, her hand moving to cover her mouth. "By the Stars …"

The ground shook, and we braced ourselves. None of us knew what we were witnessing. The bubbles quickly grew into waves. The waves surged away from the light. The water did its best to flee from the crimson glow. Cloudy red and white crystals climbed from the sea and the damp parts of the beach. Their sharp heads pointed skyward like spears. The crystals reached the height of the beach, and the red glow faded from their tops. The rocks grew taller and cracks formed. The unlit points shattered and rained shards into the sea. Water droplets flew in every direction. As the last shards fell away, the water stilled. A flat crystal bridge extended to the island.

The four of us let out a group *whoa*. I understood why the crystal excited Andy.

"It looks like we're walking after all." I started for the bridge. "We'll leave the charm here. We don't know what will happen if we take it with us." When the light had faded from the crystals as they grew, they shattered. I did not want that happening while on top of them. I stepped onto the bridge and almost fell flat on my face. The water on the smooth surface made it slippery. I regained my balance and studied the new structure. I'd never seen anything more amazing.

Jason and Max followed and had their own share of trouble with the slick surface.

Andy stayed put with her arms crossed. "I can't just leave my charm here."

Knowing my friend and how much the charm meant to her, I realized changing her mind would be impossible. If she wanted to stay, fine. But I wouldn't let her stay by herself. Luckily, one of us wouldn't mind waiting. "Okay. You and Max will stay here. Jason and I'll go to the island to get the Tablet." I waited for a complaint, but it never came.

Andy brushed a strand of hair behind her ear, a determined gleam in her eyes. "I'll keep an eye on my charm and make sure nothing happens to it."

Max ungracefully jumped off the bridge, walked up the beach well out of the water's reach, then plopped down. "And I'll take a nap."

I didn't criticize him; he just needed to keep Andy safe. Despite their constant bickering, I knew he could do it.

"Jason and I will come back as soon as we have the Tablet." I paused. "If we aren't back in a day, come find us."

Max didn't look so happy to be staying behind anymore, and Andy gulped before putting on her brave face—the one she used to wear when Max picked on her.

I flashed a reassuring smile before walking toward the island with Jason alongside me.

Once we were out of earshot Jason spoke up. "Neither of them complained about being alone together?"

"You don't think they might actually like each other, do you?"

"The day they like each other will be the day it rains."

It took half a cycle to reach the island. An amazing sight greeted us. Small specks of golden lights hovered at varying heights along the beach, casting more than enough light to see. They illuminated numerous plants with large leaves bordering a narrow strip of sandy beach. I had never seen this many plants before—never any this big. The only plants I had ever seen were small, sickly yellow, and attempting to grow in stone pots. They didn't live long. The plants on the island though looked like they were doing just fine by themselves. They were an amazing shade of green, almost like Andy and Jason's eyes.

"Have you ever seen anything like this?" I asked.

Jason shook his head as he walked up the beach. He stared at the plants in wonder, much like I did. "I saw a lot of plants while in Ciyt and Lejos Noble but not like this. Andy will be jealous."

Andy would've loved this. However, we needed to focus on finding the Tablet hidden on this island. "If you were a magical Tablet, where would you hide?"

He thought for a tick. "On a magical floating island."

I did my best impersonation of Andy when Max would ask a stupid question. I must've done a good job, because Jason recognized the look. "I know what you meant. The island is a good enough hiding spot. I bet the Tablet is at the bright light on top of the mountain."

A part of me agreed. The other part of me knew things were never that easy. "Wouldn't that be too obvious?"

The two of us spun around and fell on our butts when a new voice answered, "Not when you think about it, really. The island spends most of its time underwater and only rises when the key is nearby."

A girl our age stood a few steps from us. She had some of the messiest brown hair ever—not greasy like most adults, just messy like she hadn't taken care of it in a while. Bits of sand clung to her. The girl's hair reached past her shoulders. Bright blue eyes stood out, capturing my attention.

I had never met any other human with blue eyes. I assumed no one else had them. Apparently, that was wrong.

The girl wore what might have once been CTS shorts, but the gray fabric was torn in several places; her brown shirt didn't seem to be in much better condition.

Jason studied her intently, but the girl either didn't notice or didn't care. "Who are you?"

"My name is Jenny, and you are?"

Jason looked confused—the kind of confused when he didn't know the answer to a question a teacher asked.

I raised an eyebrow at him before answering the question. "He's Jason, and I'm Kyle. How did you get here?"

"I walked, same as you." She said it like anyone could walk to the island at any time, like crystal bridges rose from the water every day. "Are you two looking for the Tablet?"

I looked at the bridge behind us and then at her. "How did you walk here? We didn't see anyone else."

Jason still seemed to be having trouble with his words. He mumbled something, but I didn't understand him.

Jenny rightfully ignored him. "I got here before you. The Tablet is this way." She turned and waved for us to follow.

Something didn't feel right about this. I looked at Jason, who didn't trust anyone.

His unblinking gaze followed her down the beach.

"Don't you think this is a little weird?"

Jason shook his head, as if recovering from being punched into a daze. "Did you say something?"

I stared at him as I repeated, "Don't you think something seems strange about Jenny? She claims she walked here too."

He shrugged. "I don't see the problem."

Where was my friend? What had happened to him on the short walk here? "You're kidding, right?"

Jenny called from farther down the beach. "Do you want to find the Tablet or not?"

"We're coming!" Jason called back.

This didn't feel right, but he didn't have a problem with it. I glared, which surprised him.

"Don't you want to find the Tablet? She knows where it is."

"So she says."

Jason ignored me and hurried after Jenny.

I wanted to scream. How did he trust this stranger? He had never acted like this before. Was it because she wasn't an adult? By the Stars, what had happened to him? I rushed to catch up as they walked side by side—or, at least, Jason tried to walk beside her. She kept changing her pace.

She turned to look at me over her shoulder. "While you were right about the Tablet's location, reaching it is not so easy. You cannot simply walk to the top. There is a path covered in traps."

I gazed up the steep forested peak then scanned the jungle. It didn't look so bad, just dark under the leaves. "Why use the path then? We could create our own." Why waste time with things that could hurt us?

"You are welcome to try, but if you walk into the jungle, you will just come out by the start of the trail. The whole place is enchanted to make sure you follow the path."

"Great, so we're forced to follow a path that's trying to kill us." I turned to Jason, who still stared at Jenny with that strange look. He had to have an opinion about the path trying to kill us. He always had opinions, especially about bad things. "What do you think about that?"

Jason smiled at Jenny. "Jenny seems confident. With her help, we can handle it."

Her cheeks grew red at his words. Was she sick? Were they both sick? He never smiled!

She tucked some hair behind her ear before trying to straighten the rest of it a bit—a task that seemed to be too little, too late, but she tried nonetheless. "You are too kind." Something in her voice had changed.

Her confidence had faltered. Her hands grabbed one another. However, they soon separated and returned to her sides.

I must've imagined her doubt. I couldn't read her like Jason.

He'd been fine until Jenny arrived. Maybe she had cast a spell on him, but she'd have to be a Traveler to do that. She did have access to one of the Tablets. Maybe she had found the other two, but why would she offer to help us?

"The trail starts here." Jenny stopped and gestured to a spot between two large rock pillars supporting a third stone to form a sort of door into the jungle. A trail continued into the foliage, illuminated by more floating lights. A message was carved into the top stone with ancient symbols we didn't use anymore. One meant path. Another could mean one of two things: either ten or death.

Based of Jenny's earlier description, I felt safe in assuming which word it meant. Another strange symbol caught my attention. Three curves crossed over one another, forming what looked like a cluster of three cat eyes. I recognized the symbol but couldn't remember why or what it meant. The writing didn't make me feel any better about this trail.

Jason studied the doorway and its path for less than a tick. He didn't even try to read the message. "Doesn't look so bad." He puffed out his chest, managing to make it even larger than it already was, as he stepped through.

In a gust, I rushed to stop him. "What are you doing?"

He looked at me, confused again. "Trying to get to the Tablet. Move."

He tried stepping around me, but I blocked him once more. "Weren't you listening? The path is covered with traps. We can't just go walking down it like a hallway in the CTS."

"Well, what do you suggest we do?"

I pointed to Jenny. "She seems to know a lot. Why not let her lead?" The idea sounded fair to me. Jenny knew about the path and the traps; she should lead.

Jason, however, regarded me as if I'd lost my mind. "We can't do that! What if she gets hurt?"

"She knows about the traps, so she can probably get past them."

He gave her a worried look. "Can you get us to the Tablet safely?"

"My father and I have solved nine of the traps."

Oh great, an adult was hiding up there somewhere, along with one more trap.

"So, there's no problem then?" Jason asked.

Jenny shook her head, and her face grew serious. "Not if he"—she pointed at me—"does not trust me."

This revelation surprised him. "You don't trust her?"

He normally had more sense than this. I couldn't figure out what had happened to him, but he needed to snap out of this. I needed my friend back. "Of course, I don't. Her story doesn't make sense! We watched the only path rise from the sea. No one but us was on it. I thought you had a brain up there." I pointed at his forehead, and he frowned. "She is trying to trick us. I know she is."

I hoped he'd listen to me. He always tried to hear what I had to say about anything, but this time was different. I found no trace of understanding on his face.

"Leave her alone, Kyle." He clenched his fists. He didn't normally get upset this quickly.

"I'm right, and you know it. At least you would if you were acting like yourself. Use your head and think!"

I had the urge to poke his forehead, but I didn't. I didn't want to start a fight I couldn't win. That didn't mean I wouldn't try my best to get through to him, but he wouldn't listen. All he seemed to hear was I didn't like Jenny. Why did that bother him so much?

"Knock it off, Kyle, or else."

He threatened me! I hadn't done anything but try to talk to him, and he threatened me. "Or what, Jason? What will you do, hit me? I'm not afraid of you."

That was a lie. He could beat me into a pile of sand, but he wouldn't do that to me. We were friends, and we weren't distracted by heat and rage. Why would I be afraid of a friend?

I realized how thoroughly this girl had enchanted Jason. I narrowly missed his first swing at me. I stepped backward as he swung again and again. Lucky for me, he was beyond mad and blinded by rage. It made his punches easier to avoid.

Jenny shouted at us to stop, but for the first time since he met her, Jason didn't listen.

I couldn't stop until he did, unless I wanted a matching black eye. I backpedaled up the trail, avoiding Jason's blows, until I felt the ground beneath my foot sink away. I would've fallen if Jenny hadn't pushed past Jason and grabbed my shirt. Beneath me, a pit opened, and wooden spikes rose from the bottom. Wedged between some rested the corpse of a person who hadn't had someone to catch them.

Jenny's face paled at the sight. She pulled me from the edge and faced Jason. "I told you there were traps!" She then glared at me. "Now will you trust me?" She poked me dead center in the chest.

I didn't take my gaze off the pit as I nodded. Maybe I had more to be afraid of after all.

The dirt came alive and covered the pit once more. If I hadn't seen it happen, I wouldn't have even known the pit existed. I took a deep breath and calmed myself. "Thank you for catching me."

"You are welcome."

"How do we get past this?" I asked.

"You see the leaves on the ground? Step on them, and the dirt will not drop away. Follow me and be careful." Jenny stepped across the leaves with ease.

Jason brushed past me to follow behind.

I chose to ignore him and focused on getting to the Tablet alive.

Chapter 21
-An Extra Trap on the Trail of Death-

2-12.11.12.17.9 T.S.T.
Island of Destiny, Erima
Tehrahey

Jenny proved she knew the trail's dangers. She led us by trap after trap, all of which were very unique ways to kill someone. We passed sand that swallowed people, trees that came alive and strangled their victims, rocks that fell from nowhere to crush their targets, and several variations of sharp things. She led us through the first eight without a scratch.

Jason refused to speak to me and followed Jenny like her shadow. Luckily for me, I didn't want to talk to him either. He had almost gotten me killed! If we wanted to get out of this alive, he would have to listen to me at some point. Jenny didn't have any trouble getting him to listen. Whenever she spoke, Jason hung onto her every word. He did whatever she said right away. He never listened this well to anyone before. By the Stars, he didn't even heed his own advice that well. For the time being, I stopped trying to understand what she'd done to my friend. If she wanted to kill us, I would be at the bottom of that first spike pit.

Jenny stopped and pointed to the next section of the trail. "This is trap nine, and it is fairly simple. Just avoid the moonlight." She wove through the shadows, avoiding the patches of light.

Jason waited until she reached the other side before he spanned the trap.

Once he joined her, I took my turn navigating the shadows.

As I crossed, Jason asked Jenny about this current hazard. "What would happen if Kyle stepped into the light?"

I took a deep breath and tried to ignore them. I did not want to hear that conversation right now.

Neither of them seemed too concerned how I felt about their discussion. Jenny pointed to the patches of light. "Do you see the small plants in the light? If shadow falls on them, they remove what cast it. Large leaves are hidden at the edge of the path." She pointed into the shadows where large, dark shapes loomed. She continued in a voice which reminded me a lot of Andy when she shared some piece of information she found interesting. "They grab whatever blocks the light and pull them into the jungle."

With this latest bit of information, my heart raced as I crossed. Just knowing the trap could kill me freaked me out. Knowing exactly how made it worse. I made that clear when I reached safety next to them. "Thanks, for telling me that once I was on it."

Jenny apologized.

Jason looked away, causing Jenny to raise an eyebrow at him. Even she picked up on his weirdness.

She bent down and snatched a rock from the ground. "Watch this."

She threw it toward the beams of light.

Two large leaves exploded from the edge of the jungle and snapped shut around the stone. They disappeared back into the trees.

Jenny walked up the trail and out of sight around a bend.

Jason went to follow her, but I stepped in front of him. "You have no right to be mad at me, you know? You almost killed me."

Jason glared at a tree to his left.

"Ignore me all you want, but you know I'm right. Let's just get the Tablet and get off this island before either of us gets hurt."

"Fine." He shouldered past me up the trail.

I followed him around the corner where we stopped in place.

Four men stood between us and Jenny. Each had more facial hair than I'd ever witnessed in the CTS. Their faded clothes were in worse shape than Jenny's. They had been torn more times than I could count. It amazed me the pieces of fabric stayed together at all.

One wore a black triangular hat with a gold feather sticking from it. He smiled, exposing cracked and chipped yellowed teeth through his black beard.

"Lookee, here boys. It seems the girl was good for sometin' after all. They may not be the men I'd have been expecting, but a thank ye, Jenny, for bringing 'em here safely. Get 'em!"

The other three men rushed forward and grabbed us. One held both my hands behind my back; it took both of the other men to restrain Jason.

"I told you we shouldn't trust her." I scowled at Jason.

He never noticed. He focused on trying to break free from the two men, which didn't get him anywhere.

I focused on the man in charge. "What do you want with us?"

He leaned in and stopped, his face only a hands length from mine. His breath smelled like the all-too-familiar scent of rotten fish. "It be simple, really. It cost me most of me crew to get here, and, as ye can imagine, I do not want to waste anymore on this accursed trail. The two of ye will help us get to the top and that Tablet."

"And why would we do that?"

The man stood upright, the smile never leaving his face. "If ye refuse, I'll be forced to send ye back to the Locker from whence ye came!"

Locker? Did he mean the CTS? The way he tapped the handle of the sword hanging from his hip, I got the feeling he meant something much worse. That caused my mouth to go dry.

Jenny cowered up the trail away from the commotion. I expected her to look happy or pleased; she'd successfully tricked us. Instead, she looked horrible. She looked exactly like Andy had when she had tricked Max into fighting in front of Ms. Hess. Jenny mouthed one word to me: *Help*.

She needed us? As much as my mind said it was a trick, something told me she really needed us. We couldn't leave her with these men. I doubted they were any nicer than they appeared. With a sigh, I resigned myself to our fate. "Fine, we'll help you."

Jason stopped struggling. "You can't be serious."

Apparently, he had started listening to me again.

I looked at him and used my eyes to point to Jenny.

He didn't look at her; I'd been too subtle.

I growled in frustration. "We don't have a choice."

"That be true. Now, ye," the leader pointed to me, "ye be wise to accept. He will show us the way."

The man restraining me shoved me up the trail toward Jenny.

"Captain Jones?" Jenny asked, trying to be brave, but I saw through the act. I think Captain Jones did too. "Where is my father? You promised you would let him go if I helped you."

The wicked smile returned to the captain's face, exposing his yellowed teeth once more. "Aye, I did. I let him go farther up. He didn't make it far."

Jenny's eyes widened, and even from my distance, I could see the tears forming. "You cruel monster!" Her voice shook as she shouted at the wicked man.

"Life is cruel!" he retorted.

When Jenny began to cry, Jones slapped her, the force of the blow sending her to the ground.

Jason growled and struggled again but couldn't break free.

Jones noticed Jason's renewed attempts and looked between him and Jenny. The man's eyes shone with evil. "Ah, it seems one of our captives fancies Miss Jenny. Young man, if ye try anything, me sword will find a home in poor Miss Jenny's heart."

I didn't understand what Jones meant by Jason fancying Jenny, but I think Jason did. The threat I understood.

Jason scowled at the captain, and when he said nothing, Jones smiled. "I thought so. Take ahold of her. I wish to keep her close."

The man who had held me, pulled Jenny to her feet.

Before I knew what courage had come over me, I spoke. "Wait! I need her help."

"No, ye don't. Just keep walking until we reach the top or meet yer end. Once ye die, yer friend be next."

It was a bad idea, but I kept arguing. Andy had rubbed off on me. I had a plan—at least part of a plan. "That's a great idea, and once Jason and I are both dead, then what? You going to sit here and wait for someone else? Together, Jenny and I can get you to the top."

Jones stroked his beard for several ticks. "If ye step out of line, I will kill all of ye."

He signaled to the man holding Jenny, who pushed her away and she tripped.

She brushed herself off and marched past me. "We do not want to keep Jones waiting."

I followed her, and we took our time to ensure no traps were present before we stepped. I'd never been more nervous in my life. It had been bad enough when Jenny led us. This time, she had as much knowledge as I did.

I studied Jenny. The wet path of a tear streaked her scraped-up face. She hunched forward, keeping her arms either at her sides or crossed over her chest. Her blue eyes darted from side to side. She jumped at the slightest noise. She looked like any kid who grew up in the CTS. She just wanted to survive.

"My father was the only thing keeping me safe from Captain Jones and his men. I hope he is all right."

The men behind us were all the types I would have avoided in the CTS if kids had a lot of muscle and hair. I understood needing a protector from the likes of them. I hoped Jenny's father was still alive too. We could all use some protection.

We continued in silence for several ticks before I noticed Jones and his men had fallen behind. "Why are they walking so slowly?"

"They are afraid we will miss something." She looked up from the ground. "Whoever hid this Tablet did not want anyone to find it."

I grabbed Jenny's arm to force her to look at me.

The group behind us stilled.

"You don't know who hid the Tablet?"

She shook her head.

"Do you know what it does?"

Again, she shook her head.

How could she not know? Everyone in Tehrahey knew the story of the Traveler and the Tablets. "Does Jones know then?"

"I don't think he does. He is being paid to bring it back to some rich man who lives in the Locker."

She used that term too? "What do you mean by the Locker?"

Jenny raised an eyebrow at me. "How do you not know about Davy Jones's Locker? It is where we are."

That didn't make any sense. "The island?" Jones had threatened to send us *back* to the Locker. Why would he threaten to send us where we were?

"Not the island. I meant everything here. The whole world is the Locker. Jones created it to punish his dead enemies, and only he and his ship can leave this place alive."

I shook my head. That couldn't be right. Jones couldn't be the creator of Tehrahey. The first Traveler had been nice, and besides, if Jones were the Traveler, he'd know how to get to the Tablet. "This world is called Tehrahey, and Jones didn't create it. The man who created it hid this Tablet. Whoever gets their hands on it is a step closer to great power. It's why Jason and I are here, to keep it out of the wrong hands."

Jenny stared at me. "What kind of power?" She sounded curious, like Andy wanting to learn.

"Enough power to reshape Tehrahey. If an adult like Jones gets his hands on this Tablet, we're in trouble."

She stood next to me and put her hands on her hips. "And here I thought this was about gold."

Something dawned on me. "You aren't from Tehrahey, are you?"

She shook her head. "My father and I never really had a home. We traveled from port to port in the Caribbean. He did whatever work he could to make sure I got a meal."

I had no experience with parents, but Jenny's father didn't sound too bad. "He sounds like he was a good person."

"He is the best."

"What about Jones, how did you end up with him?"

Jenny scowled at the ground. "He is a pirate." She kept us moving and told me everything about her life in some place called Caribbean. Jenny and her father were sailing when Jones attacked their ship. He killed everyone but the two of them. He kept them prisoners because her father promised they could be useful. They'd been trapped ever since. She stopped her story and pointed to a small puddle on the ground. "There is blood on the ground."

The walls of the CTS had plenty of blood stains, so I knew the difference between old and new blood. "That's fresh."

Jenny's eyes widened. "Father!" When she tried to run up the trail, I wrapped my arms around her in a gust. She almost sent the two of us falling toward the blood puddle.

"We have to figure out this trap before you run off!"

She fought with me, but I held firm until she calmed down. Her eyes met mine, and her face reddened. She straightened up and gently pushed me away. "Right. What can we find that might help us?"

We couldn't edge around the path like we had for one of the earlier traps, because large trees bordered the walkway on either side. We might have to climb along the sides of the trees. They were covered with small holes that we could grab. It'd be difficult, but not impossible. The blood formed a pool in the bottom of a round depression as wide as a person. There were several of these indents for forty steps up the trail. The ground in the circles didn't look like the rest of the path; it looked like they were filled with sand.

"Those indents, what about them?"

"They could be something. Hand me a rock," Jenny said.

I did as instructed.

She leaned over and dropped it in an indent. The sand swallowed it whole.

"They are sinkholes. If we avoid them, we should be okay."

I stopped her from taking a step. "I'll go first." Of the two of us, she knew more about the traps, meaning she would be better equipped to deal with things if I didn't make it. It made sense to me, and I stepped forward before she could argue. As I neared the puddle of blood, I stopped. "Jenny, why is there blood?" Sinkholes weren't the sort of thing to make you bleed.

Her voice grew squeaky as she answered me. "We missed something! Come back! We can figure this out where you are safe."

Jones stomped up to her before I could do that. "I've been trapped on this island fer too damned long. Get across or die!"

Jones grabbed Jenny and threw her toward me.

She landed and skidded to a halt a few steps away.

A thud and a scream shattered the silence of the jungle. The captain howled and clutched at his thigh where a thorn larger than my fingers stuck out.

Behind him, one of the men holding Jason lay face first on the ground.

Another man turned over the body to find a long thorn protruding from his eye.

I looked anywhere but at the body. It freaked me out.

Jones bellowed as he removed the thorn, blood trickling down his leg. A storm of words erupted from him, and while I didn't understand most of them, their meanings as curses were pretty clear.

Even from a distance, Jones terrified Jenny. She scanned the trail in a panic, unable to figure out where the thorns had come from.

With reflexes I didn't think the old man had, Jones grabbed Jason and drew a dagger from his belt. "One of ye best figure this out quick or I shall end this boy's life!"

Jones placed the knife against Jason's throat.

Jenny's panic grew while fear for my friend filled my stomach. I looked around, trying to take in all the information I could. What had triggered this trap?

Chapter 22
-I am Worthy of Nothing-

2-12.11.12.17.9 T.S.T.
Island of Destiny, Erima
Tehrahey

Something on the ground had activated all previous traps. If I stepped on a certain part of the path, it would disappear, a plant would come alive, spikes would shoot from nowhere, or a rock would crush me. Nothing on the ground here, other than the indents, stood out. They couldn't be what had set it off, because I never touched them.

Maybe we were blocking some moonlight. No, the canopy above us prevented any moonlight from reaching the trail. Some thin branches reached low enough to be touched but were too high for even my head to brush them. One of the branches still swayed above Jenny.

"Did you hit a branch when Jones threw you over here?" I asked.

She looked up then back at me. "Maybe. I was far more preoccupied with not landing in a sinkhole."

"I think the branches might be the trigger."

"They can't be." She pulled a hand through her hair as she thought. "All the other traps were activated by something on the ground."

"Exactly! No one would expect it, plus it explains why I didn't set it off." For once, being a kid seemed to be paying off. I stepped closer to her and lowered my voice to a whisper. "This could be our chance. We can run through. Jones and his crew will have to slow down. We just need to get Jason free."

In an effort to rush us, the captain shook Jason and pressed the knife harder to his throat.

I expected to see fear on Jason's face, but he showed none. He looked relaxed, which calmed my stomach. Maybe he'd experienced this sort of thing before.

"You okay?" I asked, loud enough for him to hear.

"Fine."

Jones shook him again, but it didn't faze Jason.

I hadn't known my friend as long as I'd known Andy, but I'd seen him in plenty of fights. I knew the difference between him losing and him being in control. He felt in control. I heard it in his voice. All I had to do was say the word, and he'd break free. Unfortunately, Jason didn't understand subtle. I couldn't say anything he would understand as *Get away from Jones*.

"Get ready to run," I whispered.

Jenny's incredulous look told me what she thought of this plan, but she nodded anyway. No going back.

"Jason, let's go!"

He smiled. Before Jones could react, Jason kicked the captain's injured leg.

The man wailed in pain, and his arms dropped away enough for my friend break free.

He grabbed a rock from the ground, and smashed it against the side of Jones's head.

The man stumbled backward while his two followers stared.

"Grab his sword!" Jenny shouted.

The other men snapped out of their shock and charged forward to help.

Jason nabbed Jones's sword from his belt and ran.

"Stay low and avoid the holes!" Jenny instructed.

I hurried farther across the trap, with Jason and Jenny right behind me. We kept our heads down. We weren't taking any chances.

"After them!" Jones shouted.

I reached a point where the sinkholes stopped and moonlight fell onto the path.

Jones's men began crossing the hazard, avoiding it as well as we had. It didn't slow them as much as I'd hoped.

"It won't take them long to cross that."

"This will help!" Jenny grabbed a shoe off her foot and threw it at the low-hanging vines. "Run!"

She didn't have to tell me twice. I had no intentions of being anywhere near this trap when it went off. We ran up the trail as fast as we could, Jones's roar chasing us. There weren't any sounds of pursuit, but I didn't plan on stopping. I had no idea if Jones and his men were dead or not. At the time, I didn't care. My friends and I were alive for the moment and that's what mattered. I knew the best way to stay alive would be to put as much distance between us and them as possible.

The trail grew steeper until actual steps appeared. The trees became sparse until they stopped, leaving nothing but brown and black rocks. I led the way as Jenny stuck close to Jason.

"Are you all right?" she asked, probably noticing the small cut on his neck. He'd suffered worse.

"I'm fine. Shouldn't you be looking out for traps?"

"I don't think we need to," I commented between breaths. "Those symbols at the start of the trail, one of them was the symbol for death."

"I wonder why?" Jason asked, though he knew the answer. He sounded more like his usual self. The fight must've snapped him back to his senses.

I came to a conclusion—probably not the safest one but it meant keeping distance between our enemies. "That symbol can also mean ten." If I was right about that, there wouldn't be any more traps. That last one was the tenth one. I couldn't tell if it was fear or something else that allowed me to make that assumption.

"You sure you're not Andy?" he teased.

I wished. If I was her, I'd feel more confident about where my feet were running. I refused to stop looking for any subtle changes in the trail as the barren, rocky slope of the mountain loomed above us while a black, empty sky surrounded us. Not a single star existed to watch over us. The floating balls of light lit the path for us, and the thin crescent moon tried to help.

As we continued, Jenny told us about how she had gotten here. Their ship had come from Caribbean through the Berumada Pit. It was still there, the one with the skeleton carved onto the front. The crew had walked to the ocean, where they had met a man who gave Captain Jones the key to the island. The key was Andy's charm. It had to be; she described it perfectly. A portion of the crew had crossed the bridge, found the trail and lost a lot of men to the traps, even with Jenny's father deciphering them.

We stopped to catch our breaths. The trail was getting steeper. When we resumed walking, Jenny resumed her story. Jason and I listened to every word.

The crew had stopped where we had found them, and they had sent Jenny back for more crewmembers. She told us how she had reached the beach and avoided the traps by walking off the trail. I mentioned that would be a good escape option if the need arose. Jason and Jenny agreed.

As Jenny had approached the bridge, the light had faded from the crystals, and they had shattered. Then the island had sunk with her still on it. A barrier had kept the water out, and she had passed out soon after. The next thing she had known, the island had surfaced, and we had been there.

Neither Jason nor I dared to mention to her this all must have happened a long time ago, since there were no signs people had been on that beach—not to mention Andy's charm had been in the CTS for the last few years. We didn't say any of that. But I think she knew. Her voice shook, and she wiped at her eyes to hide her tears.

The stairs grew taller and circled around the mountain. Our pace slowed; we had moved faster when we were in the Erima. Jason, Jenny, and I were out of breath. Sweat coated my skin and caused my shirt to cling to me. We stopped once to catch our breaths.

The stairs took a sharp turn and led straight up the mountainside. The steps became tall and awkward. The climb became even more of a struggle. The path cut through the rocks to the peak. Above that, the trail must flatten out.

"I can see the top, guys," I said.

"Thank the Lord!" Jenny exclaimed.

"Who?" Jason asked.

I peered over my shoulder, expecting an answer.

She raised an eyebrow at him and shook her head. "You Locker people are crazy." She never bothered to explain what she meant by *the Lord.*

At the top, the path leveled and stretched across a large chasm where it stopped in the center. Sitting at the end on a rock pillar rested a book-sized Tablet that glowed yellow, too bright to look at. The warm light from the relic fell onto the narrow walkway. My heart raced at the sight of the ancient object. We were so close; I don't think anyone had been that close to a Tablet since the Traveler himself had hid them.

I stepped onto the path. A red glow filtered up from far below in the mountain's hollow center.

Jenny and Jason stepped next to me and peered over the side.

"A volcano," Jenny said.

I thought of asking what she meant, but there would be time for questions later, and I had a growing list of questions. Right now, though, we needed to grab the Tablet and run. I wanted off this cursed island. I walked across the thin path, doing my best not to look down. The light from our goal drew me forward.

Jason and Jenny followed close behind with just enough room to walk side by side. Heat rose from the chasm.

The closer we got, the more confidence I had. We actually found a Tablet of Time and were one step closer to finding the Book. We could do this.

"Do not touch that Tablet!" Jones shouted.

We spun around to see him standing at the top of the stairs. Blood from wounds all over his body soaked through his clothes. A spike remained lodged in his left shoulder. With a hiss of pain, he ripped it out and threw it over the edge. "Ye three may have killed me men, but I'll be damned if I let ye take that Tablet. The Maker promised me mountains of gold for that shining relic. Now, get out of me way!" He stepped farther onto the path.

The Maker had sent him? Was that the man Jenny had said they had met on the beach? Of course, it was. It made perfect sense. This was the Tablet Amyntor and the Four Councilmen were going to get when they turned on him. Roger Tal had become the Maker. He knew it was hidden here; but couldn't get to it, not without the key.

"Jason, give me the sword." Jenny reached for him, but he didn't relinquish the weapon.

"I can do this." He puffed out his chest and clumsily extended the blade. He looked as awkward as Max did when answering a question he didn't know the answer to. I doubted he could do much.

"Hardly. Give it here." She didn't wait for him to release it. She ripped it from his grasp, swirled it and pointed it at Jones. "My father knew if we lived in the Caribbean, we needed to know how to wield swords. This blade belonged to Father. And now, I will slay you with it."

Her face hardened, but I saw right through the look. I saw it for what it was—a scared kid trying to stand up to an adult. I wore the same expression anytime I attempted to stand up to Ms. Hess. I knew the captain terrified Jenny. She did her best to cover it up. I hoped he couldn't see through her act.

"Ye'll receive no mercy from me!" Jones growled. He raised his own weapon, probably taken from one of his men. The gold handle and guard almost glowed in the Tablet's light. Fresh blood ran down the weapon's length as he pointed it at her.

"I didn't ask for any." Jenny lunged forward.

The Captain blocked and countered with a longer reach.

Jenny lost ground.

The two stared at each other for several ticks, sizing up their opponent. At once, they lunged again. Swords met with a clang.

Jones swung at Jenny.

She deflected and countered. Her sword slashed through the air; a tear appeared on his shirt. She stepped forward and drove him back toward the stairs.

His foot slipped. He growled and swiped wildly.

Jenny retreated. She couldn't reach him. Swords glinted in the darkness, lit by the light of the Tablet.

The Tablet! I ran to the relic. I could use its light to blind our enemy and give Jenny the advantage she needed. The metallic clangs of clashing swords echoed all around. The hollow mountain made the noises louder. The sounds bounced through my head as my heart thudded in my chest. I grabbed the Tablet. White light flashed across my vision, and a strange sensation rushed over me. A cry of pain tore into my heart. My eyes snapped open.

I turned, and Jenny fell to her knees clutching her stomach.

Jones stood over her with a smirk—the same smirk all adults wore. He pressed the tip of his sword to her throat, forcing her to look at him. "Prepare to see yer father again, Miss Jenny." He raised the blade.

Jason roared and launched himself at the man. He shoved the captain from Jenny and grabbed both of his wrists. The two struggled against one another—Jones trying to break his sword hand free, Jason doing everything in his power to keep that from happening. All the training my friend had done, all the fights he had gotten into, had prepared him for this. He kicked Jones's injured leg and forced him farther backward.

I watched the light from Tablet in my hands fade. Dread filled my stomach. My plan wouldn't work if the relic didn't shine.

"Point the Tablet and think light."

I didn't question who said those words as I pointed the Tablet at the fight, and light erupted from the relic in my hands. It collided with Jones's eyes.

He shouted in pain. The sword fell from his hands as he tried to shield his eyes. Jason saw his chance. With the captain distracted, Jason landed blow after blow. He turned and pulled his opponent toward the edge.

I followed the movement, keeping the beam of light focused on our enemy's face.

Jason released the adult's hands, which flew up to shield his eyes. Jason's right shoulder dropped back as he readied his fist, then hit his target's wounded shoulder. The arm instantly pulled back and repeated the action a second time. Jason pulled his arm back once more—farther than the other two times—and fired it forward, a roar erupting from him. The blow landed in the center of the man's chest.

Captain Jones stumbled backward and fell from the walkway. His screams faded into the pit below.

I lowered the Tablet, and the light dimmed to a soft golden glow.

Jason stood at the edge of the path; his fists clenched, and his shoulders rising and falling at a rapid pace. Sweat dripped from his forehead. He stared into the darkness. He took a deep breath, turned from the edge and approached Jenny. To my surprise, he didn't hurry.

I'd seen a lot of bad injuries growing up, but she looked worse. Blood oozed from between her fingers, which didn't do much to stop the flow. It ran across her legs and formed a puddle around her.

Jason knelt beside her. "Are you okay?"

Jenny coughed, and some blood dripped down her chin. "I'm fine. I've been cut by a sword before."

Jason wiped away the blood away with his hand; I didn't miss how it shook as he did so.

She smiled at him. She tried to sound tough, like he had earlier, but her voice failed to hold the strength. "Thank you … for saving me."

"Don't thank me yet."

She tilted her hands away from her stomach for a tick to examine the wound before slowly replacing them. The action didn't help the dread I felt in the pit of my stomach. Even with the fight over, and the Tablet in my hands, I didn't feel right.

"He did get me pretty well, but you! You killed Davy Jones! You'd be a legend back home. There is not a sailor alive who did not fear the captain. Then you come along and fight him bare handed. You are spectacular, Jason."

I stood there in silence. A new feeling joined my dread—discomfort. I felt out of place. I wanted to leave them alone, let them be together, but they blocked my only escape.

Jason shifted from kneeling to sitting, and the two of them stared at one another.

Then she did something neither of us expected. She leaned forward and kissed him.

Jason looked shocked for a tick before she pulled back, and they both smiled.

I'd never been kissed before, let alone seen someone kiss. I had no idea why they both smiled like that.

"I am feeling tired. I think I shall lay down for a bit."

"Jenny don't. You need to stay awake," Jason said.

She ignored him and turned around at a slow pace, and I didn't miss the hiss of pain she made. Then she laid down, her head resting in Jason's lap.

She sighed. "That's better." She looked up and frowned. "Where are all the stars? Back home there are so many of them."

Jason and I followed her gaze to the lonely moon sinking in the empty sky.

"The stars left our world long before any of us were born," Jason said.

"That's too bad. I wish I could go home. I miss it terribly."

"We'll get you back home … if you come with us."

Jenny smiled. "That would be nice. What do you think about that, Father?"

I looked around. We were alone. "Jenny, your father—"

Jason silenced me with a miserable look. He'd only ever looked this sad when he mentioned his own father, and I finally got it.

I understood the dread gnawing at my insides, why my stomach wouldn't settle. It saw what my mind refused to admit; there was too much blood on the ground.

Jenny kept talking like she never heard me. I don't think she did. "Father says he already knows how to get home."

Jason nodded. "He probably does."

His voice broke. He sniffled, and she looked up to him.

"Why are you crying?"

He didn't answer, but she smiled.

"I shall miss you too, Jason." She looked from him to the sky again before closing her eyes. "Farewell, you two."

"Bye," Jason whispered.

Chapter 23
-Green and Blue-

Red light glowed around us as we crossed the crystal bridge. The book-sized Tablet remained tucked safely under my arm. It was made of a polished yellow crystal. The bright light it emitted earlier had dulled to a warm glow. Despite succeeding in the first step of our mission, I felt no joy.

Jason carried Jenny in his arms; she was gone.

I'd never seen anyone die until tonight. To just stand there and watch the life fade from someone's eyes, to see them stare at nothing, felt horrible. We were the same age. Worst of all, she didn't belong in Tehrahey; Davy Jones had dragged her here. Because of him, she had died.

Our return to the beach took twice as long as our original trip. Jason kept stopping to rest. He refused to leave Jenny behind, said she deserved to be free of it.

I couldn't argue. I offered to help carry her, but he wanted to do it alone.

When we reached the beach, Andy ran to greet us. She stopped short when she saw Jenny. Her excitement at our return vanished as fear and concern covered her face. "What- What happened?" She wrapped her arms around herself, trying to form a shield from the news we brought.

Jason ignored her and marched toward the cliffs.

Max joined Andy. The two of them watched our friend before turning to me for an answer.

I didn't give one—couldn't bring myself to say it. I walked to where Andy's charm sat on the small pedestal and removed it. The light faded from the crystals, and the bridge crumbled within ticks. No barrier formed as the island lurched and tilted sideways into the sea. The whole thing crumbled and disappeared into the water. The waves returned and settled into a rhythmic pattern, making it appear as if tonight had never happened.

I wished it hadn't.

I studied the object resting in my palm. The Maker had given this to Jones years ago. How had it ended up in Andy's possession? Knowing it once belonged to a dangerous person, I didn't want to return it to her. If she got hurt because of this thing, by the Stars, I'd never forgive myself. However, this relic had been safe so far. Cat would have sensed any evil enchantments on it back in Xic-Patan, wouldn't he? Maybe it was safe.

My friend's hand twitched when I didn't immediately offer up her charm. She wanted it back.

I took a deep breath and returned it to its latest owner.

She took it with a hesitant hand and studied me for a long moment in the crimson light. "What happened over there?"

I glanced at Jason, watched his silhouette lay Jenny on the sand beneath the cliffs, watched him prepare himself to bury a kid like us. "We made a friend."

"Who was Jason carrying?" Max asked.

"The friend."

Jason remained kneeling next to Jenny, his head hung. He stood and went to the cliffs.

I led Andy and Max over.

Jenny's eyes were closed, and she almost looked peaceful.

"She's pretty," Andy said.

"I don't know—" Max began.

Jason, returning with an armful of rocks, interrupted him. "Finish that sentence, Max, and I'll bury you next to her."

Max closed his mouth in a gust as Jason placed the rocks around her body with an unsteady hand.

"What was her name?" Andy asked.

"Je-Jenny," Jason said. A tear streaked his face, and it reminded me too much of blood in the crimson light of the charm.

Andy knelt next to him. She placed her charm in the sand, put one hand on Jason's shoulder and used the other to grab the rock he held.

He wouldn't let it go.

"Let me help," she whispered.

Jason took a shaky breath and released the stone.

Andy placed it at the edge of Jenny's body. The two of them began to outline her. They didn't have enough, so Max and I got more.

I don't know how long it took us to bury Jenny. It seemed like only a few ticks, but it felt like it took a lot longer. The crescent moon still hung in the air while the skies grayed along the western horizon. Dawn would arrive soon. The four of us stood in silence around the finished tomb.

Max moved first. He left us, and after a tick, I heard something shattering.

Andy and I turned to see him on his knees in the water, taking a rock to the small crystal pillar. We watched in silence as he broke the gem free. He brought it over and placed the little pillar on top the mound of rocks.

Jason raised his head long enough to say thanks before he returned to staring at the sand.

Max glanced at Andy and me. "What do we do now?" he asked, calling a final end to the silence.

I startled as Cat's voice spoke from behind us. "Now it's time to move on, find the next Tablet."

Did he really have to sneak up on us like that? I turned to see him sitting in the sand behind Andy. I didn't know how long he'd been there.

He walked over and jumped onto the grave. "You four did find the Tablet this time, right?"

Jason clenched his fists. "Get off!"

Cat sat down and wrapped his tail around his paws. "Why should I?"

My friend took a step forward.

I feared I might have to try to hold him back—something I didn't think I could do on a good day. I feared he might kill our guide.

"It's a grave; show some respect!"

"Why? I did not know this person."

"I did. Now get off!" The sentence bounced around the cliff; even the ocean waves couldn't drown it out.

"Interesting." Cat jumped onto the sand. "How long did you know her?"

"How did you—"

"Know she was a girl? Your reaction. You obviously loved whoever you buried."

Three sets of eyes fell on Jason as we studied him in shock. He loved her?

Jason's fists unclenched and he stepped backward from the dark creature. "Only a few cycles—"

Cat's tail gave a quick flick. "You only knew her for a couple hours?"

Jason scowled, and his hands balled once more. "Is there something wrong with that?"

"No. People like you are the reason for the saying *love at first sight*. You fall hard and fast, don't easily fall out of it. I have no doubt the watch would have brought you to the castle as well. Do you know where this girl came from?"

Jason shrugged. "Jenny mentioned a place called Caribbean."

"The Caribbean?" His tail swished. "She was from my world." He looked puzzled more than anything. His pale blue gaze studied the four of us.

Our heads hung low, and either our hands were holding themselves or our arms were shielding our bodies. None of us were excited at finding the first Tablet.

His gaze rested on Andy the longest. He sighed. "Would you like me to say a few words?"

No one said anything.

"Very well." He focused on the grave. "Jenny, the Lord is your shepherd; you shall not want. He makes you lie in green pastures; He leads you beside the still waters. He restores your soul; He leads you in the paths of righteousness for His name's sake. Yea, though you walk through the valley of the shadow of death, you will fear no evil, for He is with you."

Andy looked up from the ground. "That was very pretty, Cat. What does it mean?" It felt good to hear her trying to learn something new. It almost made things feel normal.

After hearing something like that, I expected Cat to have a meaningful reason. He didn't. "It's meant to help the living feel better about the dead. Nothing more. Now, the Tablet?"

I looked up from the ground. I didn't feel like moving. My legs were tired, and my feet ached. I'd seen and done enough for one night.

Cat watched me, waiting for an answer.

"I put it by our tent." I walked away.

Everyone but Jason followed. He remained by Jenny.

Andy knelt and grabbed her charm before regarding him. "Are you coming?"

"In a tick." He never followed.

I snatched the Tablet from the bag. Its warm, golden glow did little to make me feel better. In fact, I felt even worse. A voice inside screamed I had caused Jenny's death. If I had acted quicker, if I had moved faster, I could've saved her.

"The Tablet of the Present, you actually got it."

I didn't say anything, didn't have the energy to complain about his lack of faith in us.

"How did you know what Tablet it was? Is that what those symbols mean?" Andy asked.

Even though the Tablet was the size of a book, it only donned two symbols carved into the top center on one side. We didn't know what they meant. According to Andy, they were ancient.

"No, *sak balam* means white jaguar, if I'm not mistaken." He turned from the relic and focused on Andy. "I knew the Tablet by the power it emanates. Surely, you can feel it."

I didn't feel any power coursing through me. If anything, I felt powerless. I wanted to go to sleep and forget everything I saw, but I knew my dreams would haunt me. I shook my head; Andy and Max did the same.

"I don't believe that. What are you feeling right now?" Cat asked.

Andy answered first while glancing over her shoulder at our friend. "I'm worried about Jason."

"Sad." Max gulped. "Scared, what did we get ourselves into?" He scanned the three of us before all eyes turned to me for an answer.

"Empty, like nothing we're doing is worth doing."

Cat nodded then washed his face. "That about sums up the emotions you would be feeling right now, in the present. The Tablet is amplifying those emotions. Since it's mostly blank, put it back in the bag. That should help."

I did as Cat suggested, and my grief diminished, but my doubt lingered. I still felt like I had caused Jenny's death.

"Did you find anything on the island that could've been a clue? Something to point us to the next Tablet?" He regarded all of us, until Andy and Max eyed me.

"I don't think so."

Cat blinked twice and sat down. "Tell me everything you saw."

We formed a circle in the sand as I told him everything that had happened tonight. He paid close attention to the details of the captain. I told them everything except how I had heard a voice when I grabbed the Tablet. Hearing voices was never a good sign. There were stories of people who spent too much time in the desert and believed invisible people spoke to them. They all ended up locked away, or worse.

"You say you saw white when you grabbed the Tablet?" Cat asked.

"Yes."

"Did you see only white, or was something there?"

I recalled when I'd grabbed the Tablet, my heart pounding, my mind racing. I heard Jenny's scream as Jones's sword found its mark. It all blurred past in a couple of pain-filled ticks. A bright flash, but I could see details hidden within the light. "It was white everywhere. Pieces even fell from the sky. I saw a blue cave …" I noticed something else, but I couldn't put my finger on it, so I studied the scene again. My eyes shot open as I noticed the final detail. "It wasn't hot!"

"It was cold." Cat stood up. "I think you're trying to describe snow. This is good; along with those symbols, it's a clue. Let me confer with Amyntor and gather the right memory from him." Cat disappeared.

Over the course of the story, Andy's arms wrapped around herself. That was her first time hearing what had happened on the island. "That's so horrible. I'm glad you're okay."

I didn't care about what happened to me, only what happened to my friends. I hadn't known her long, but Jenny was like us, even if she came from a different world. We could have been great friends, but she was gone.

"It's a good thing Jenny was there," Max added.

My body tensed, ready to tackle him to the floor. How could he be so thoughtless?

Andy turned on him before I could. "Max! She died."

Max recoiled and raised his hands in defense. "I know, I saw her grave. It's sad, but, if it weren't for her, we'd all be dead. They would have died on the trail, and we would have gone looking for them." He gazed into the darkness, thinking for a moment. "She's a hero."

My shoulders slumped. I wouldn't have to beat him up after all. While what he had said helped, it also made things so much worse. We owed Jenny a lot. I took a deep breath and rose on aching legs. A steady breeze blew in from the water. It carried the salty scent of the ocean and mist to me, removing any final traces of heat.

Jason didn't answer as I joined him at Jenny's grave. We stood in silence. I knew my friend well enough to know that if he didn't want me there, he'd tell me to leave. After several ticks, he spoke. "I keep thinking what could've happened if I had kept the sword."

I couldn't tell if he spoke to me or himself but answered anyway. "You'd be dead." Against Jones, I knew he would've died in a sword fight.

"But she'd be alive."

"It's not your fault, Jason—"

"Yes, it is!" He said it so suddenly, with so much force. He'd been thinking about it for a while. I couldn't believe him. He had done everything possible to save her. He had reacted, fought even. Meanwhile, I'd hesitated.

"No, it's mine."

Jason looked up from her grave.

In the early light of daybreak, I could see the trails of tears on his face. I had never seen him this broken before. How could someone so strong be undone and broken so easily? What did that mean for me?

"I wasn't quick enough," I mumbled.

He remained silent.

"If I had gotten to the Tablet sooner, I could have stopped Jones before he killed her. Max should have gone. He's faster than me."

"He wouldn't have grabbed the Tablet." Jason refocused on the grave.

I clenched my fists and turned from the mound of rocks. It tore me up to think I could've saved her. I had failed her. "He would've done something! He wouldn't have sat there and watched someone get killed."

"You didn't stand there. You reacted, just not fast enough. Neither of us were fast enough."

Cat appeared from the darkness in front of me. "But you were fast enough to save yourselves. You two are still grieving?"

Jason turned around. "It's our fault she died." He sounded calmer, like his normal self again, the version that locked away all sad emotions.

Cat's head tilted, and his tail lashed back and forth. "Really? As I recall, Davy Jones killed her. Not the two of you."

"But—"

"*Jones* killed her, *not* you. From what I heard, you did everything you could. Now, you can either stay here and mourn or learn from it and move on."

Jason and I remained quiet.

"Let's get your things. We know the location of the next Tablet." Cat stalked to the crevice, his tail pointed skyward.

Jason placed a hand on one of the rocks before he followed.

I faced the grave once more. It still hurt to look, but I made myself. I stared at the Tehraheyian tomb for a girl not of our world. When I couldn't take it anymore, I glared at the sky and made a promise. Never again would I fail someone. "Goodbye, Jenny. May the Stars watch over you." I walked away and didn't look back.

I found Andy talking with Cat as I entered the cave. She and Max had torn down the tent and were ready to put as much distance between them and this beach as we could. Getting out of here sounded like a great idea.

"Where are we going?" Andy asked.

"You're going to the coldest place in Tehrahey, the only location to always have snow—Glachalis," Cat said.

"The mountain range up north? Will it be nice?" Andy sounded hopeful, and I didn't blame her. Hopefully, Glachalis would be better than the Erima.

Jason leaned against the rock wall, keeping his gaze on Jenny. "I've heard of it." He uncrossed his arms. "It's a city north of Entstal."

Cat's tail flicked back and forth as he looked us up and down. "I'll need to get you outfitted properly before you go searching for the next Tablet. Let's get going. The sooner I help, the sooner I can leave."

He walked to Andy, and she picked him up.

Max placed a hand on her shoulder, and darkness swallowed the three of them.

Cat returned ticks later.

I knelt and lifted him up.

Jason placed a hand on my shoulder. The cliffs, the smell of the ocean, and the sound of the waves all faded away. A long, dark tunnel lay ahead of us, and a flickering light beckoned at the end.

2-12.11.12.17.10 T.S.T.
Glachalis
Tehrahey

My stomach tingled as the sensation of being pulled by an invisible force faded, and we arrived in a dark room. The only bit of light came from the candle Andy held. Their shadows stretched and danced through this new room in a haunting way. I half expected something to lash out from the shadows, but nothing stirred.

Max huddled right next to her, his hands outstretched toward the tiny flame. He muttered something about not liking the cold, but I disagreed. This place wasn't hot, and I liked that a lot. It was even cooler than the beach! Looking for a Tablet in the cold would be much easier than looking for one in the burning sands of the Erima.

"Where are we?" Andy asked.

Cat yawned before answering. "This is Amyntor's house in Glachalis. It should provide you with what you need." He detailed the washroom's location, where to find firewood for the hearth in the center, which cabinets were enchanted to preserve food, and the magic wardrobe that could provide us with clothes. He mentioned not trying to get to another world through there, but I didn't understand why. Did people climb through wardrobes to Travel?

Cat and Jason went upstairs, because apparently, we were underground. Again. Hurray. They disappeared through a slanted door at the top of the stairs. We were told to keep it closed at all times to keep the heat downstairs. I'd never seen a door not be straight up and down. The thing looked like it had fallen backward, and Amyntor had decided to keep it that way. Jason grabbed some firewood from up there, and Cat ensured the door—which Amyntor had enchanted, like everything else here—would let the four of us back in once we left. Jason returned downstairs. Cat didn't. He left without saying goodbye. Shocking.

We ate breakfast as Jason started the fire, which couldn't be done fast enough. I understood why Max didn't like the cold; it quickly became unbearable, just like the Erima's heat. When the flames finally took to the logs, collective sighs of relief came from everyone. The smoke drifted to the stone ceiling and through a hole into a shed above ground that Cat had told us was for smoking meats.

With new light and warmth spreading through the room, we explored and searched for the things Cat had told us about and anything else of interest. Knowing who had once lived here, I expected a lot of clutter, like in Time's Keep, but that wasn't the case. The room was a decent size—about as big as a classroom in the CTS—and carved from gray stone. The raised circular hearth burned in the center of the room. Carved into the side of this resided a scene of twelve people fighting various monsters. Wooden cabinets with a pale stone countertop lined the front half of the left wall. Each little door had a crystal handle. A table and chairs rested in the back left corner.

A good-sized wooden bed resided in the back right. Max plopped onto it and sighed in delight. It'd be big enough for at least two of us, though it didn't look like he planned on sharing. A floor-to-ceiling wooden wardrobe with multicolored crystals embedded in the wood stood guard at the foot of the bed while a trunk sat nearby. Bookshelves covered the rest of the right wall, which immediately grabbed Andy's attention. Unfortunately for her, they weren't written in Tehraheyian. The stairs to the surface jutted out from the center of the front wall. In the wall next to the staircase, a door lead to the washroom.

Along the floor, various smooth crystal trails led from the washroom to the firepit, then to different items in the room, such as the wardrobe and cabinets. A few trails even led up the walls to small candles, which had ignited on their own once Jason had lit the fire. On more than one occasion, I thought I saw a pulse of light follow the trails from the fireplace to the other items.

We were all happy to see a washroom again. It would be so much nicer than relieving ourselves in a hole in the sand. It was even better when we learned the receptacle emptied itself. There was no smell, and none of us would have to clean it! Yet another plus, the room had a fountain of hot water that filled a bath on its own and shut off the water flow once it filled. The water spilled from a carving of a woman tipping over a clay pot. Around the carving, more assorted crystals shimmered.

Andy examined the books, hoping to find one she could read.

Max snored from the bed in the corner, his feet dangling off the edge.

If only I had thought of doing that first. Instead, Jason and I had decided to head up and out, just to look. We had no idea where to get started. Cat, in his caring way, had told us to follow my vision, which wasn't useful at all.

Upstairs, the smooth stone walls and floor gave way to patchworked stones of various shapes cemented together. This room was a lot smaller than the other but still bigger than an isolation room.

A large pile of wood sat stacked along a wall to our left. In front of us stood the door to the outside.

I had no idea what to expect out there. Even after my vision, I hadn't expected a world of pure white. Just outside the house was a small stone platform covered by the wooden roof. A soft, white mass covered everything in sight. When I touched the stuff, my fingers cooled and grew wet.

"I guess this is snow?" I asked Jason.

He shrugged at me. "Never seen it before."

With caution, I set my foot on the white fluff. It gave way, and my foot sank until the top layer of fluff stopped at my knee. The snow chilled my leg's bare skin, and I ripped it back to stand on solid ground once more. A quick shake sent droplets flying but did little to warm it again. Cat's earlier comments of finding warmer clothes made a lot more sense.

Another small, stone building with a wood roof stood across from us. Lines of similarly built buildings stretched in both directions for a good way off. If there was a road, it was buried under the snow. Behind each structure, including Amyntor's, was a small shed. A few other buildings seemed to comprise this town, but that was it. Beyond, the white rose into mountains that disappeared into the sky where ever-shifting shades of gray blocked the sun. This was more clouds than I'd ever seen. I couldn't believe a place like this existed in Tehrahey.

After the shock of this new world wore off, something stuck out to me, just like in Xic-Patan. We were alone. I couldn't see anyone other than Jason. As the cold became too much, we went inside and reported our findings to Andy.

Together, the three of us who were awake concluded we'd wait until later in the day to explore. This wasn't just so we could sleep. We hoped it would be warmer.

Jason found some furs and blankets in the trunk by the bed and handed them out.

We laid around the fire, and despite the stone floor, this was the comfiest I'd been in a long time.

My tired eyes closed as the crackling of the fire lulled me to sleep.

I found myself in a strange place. Bits and pieces of my surroundings flashed across my vision, but nothing stuck long enough to make any sense. The few things that did stay had remained blurry streaks of tan, brown, and red. Hot air rushed and roared like a sandstorm. The force swirled around me and knocked me about like a First Year in a crowd. I closed my eyes and covered my ears, but I couldn't block the voice hidden within the wind; it came from everywhere.

"Of course, Jones failed, Samuel!" Anger spewed from the voice.

With each word, the wind became more violent and tried to shove me to the ground. Standing against it became harder every tick. My legs struggled to stay upright, and my eyes burned.

The name echoed through my mind. *Samuel*. It was important. Why? Only one Samuel came to mind—the one from Records: Samuel Ents. But he was dead, right? Roger wasn't, so maybe he wasn't either?

The voice continued, not caring what I thought. "You came up with the idea to use him. You failed us! Now someone else has one of the Tablets; I can feel it." Footsteps echoed through an empty room—first away, then back, then away again. "I'll have to increase my efforts in Ozmerald. It's time I broke through there. I'll have Cylus bring me a list of the prisoners. If those aren't enough, he can always round up some more. Someone has to be strong enough to get through eventually."

Another familiar name—the Maker's bodyguard. The longer I listened, the more the angry voice sounded familiar.

"The last one still eludes me." The voice lost some of its anger as he thought out loud. "How can something be forgotten yet guarded?" Silence for a tick, followed by an approving hum. "You are right; perhaps I should arrange another expedition to Akna. Finding the K'ubih will be difficult, but we've found the road before. We can do it again."

"Wait …" The storm billowing around me died, and the stillness in the air became unbearable. It pressed in on me, and I struggled to breathe. I opened my eyes and found only darkness. No burning fireplace, no furs, and no friends. Where was this place? I could remember Glachalis, but where did I go from there?

"This is strange, but I can feel him within my mind," the voice continued, growing more menacing with each spoken word. "He's here, listening." A red beam of light arose from the darkness and searched in long, sweeping arcs. "Where are you?"

I had never left Glachalis. I laid down and went to sleep. "I'm dreaming!" I whispered to myself.

The light hesitated its search, then made a straight line toward me. "This may be a dream for you, little sand pile"—venom oozed from the voice—"but I am very much awake. Do you know what happens to people who get in my way?"

The blood-red shaft approached and I dove out of the way. I landed hard, and, for a tick, everything went black. I wanted out of this nightmare and almost welcomed the idea of passing out. However, something important was here. I needed this information. I rose as the light searched through my dark surroundings.

"You can't hope to find *The Book of Time* on your own. Bring the Tablet to me and all will be forgiven."

My tired brain finally made the connection. That was the Maker. That's what I needed to hear. He was on to us! The light vanished, and I fell into darkness.

I landed in a new dream, climbing the steps of a strange structure towering over a vast jungle. Four more stepped pyramids stood in a circle nearby. Three were identical to this one, with a small room at the top. The last one, larger than the others, had two giant stone pillars standing on top. Many smaller structures were scattered below amongst the pyramids, but no one stirred. A hot wind blew through ruins, creating ghostly howls and haunting, shrill whistles. A dull mixture of regret, sadness, and anger swarmed within me. Until recently, I wouldn't have recognized the sensation. Jenny's death had changed that. Someone had died.

I'd never seen this place before, yet my body walked through it without hesitation, seemingly knowing where it wanted to go. When I reached the top, I found a stairway in the tiny room and descended deeper into the structure until all daylight faded. My right hand rose on its own, and a small golden fire burst to life in the air above the palm. Firelight danced across the stone stairway as I marveled at how the flame could burn like that. Was this magic?

Down and down and down I went. With each step, my fear grew, but something kept suppressing it. Some small voice told me not to worry. I had nothing to fear in Akna. This only caused more confusion because I had no idea what or where Akna was. The Maker had mentioned it too, which didn't make me feel all that better about being here. Still, the quiet voice—more of a feeling, really—insisted everything was fine.

At the base of the stairwell, I met a large stone wall adorned with a painted red sun. On either side rested two unlit torches, which quickly became lit as two bits of fire separated from the flame in my hand and ignited them. I waved my left arm in front of the wall. The grinding sound of stone sliding against stone filled the space as the wall moved aside to reveal another room.

As my left hand returned to my side, I realized it was not my own. I was not in my body. That explained how I had known where to go, probably explained the small voice too. Some part of this other person was talking to me and was pleased I'd figured this out. With the way this person kept performing magic, I couldn't help but wonder if I had found myself in the first Traveler's body.

When I entered into this new room, the flame in my hand shot out and ignited torches around the spacious, empty room before it vanished. Piles of items littered the corners of the room, most I didn't recognize. Some glittered in the flickering light while something filled the room with sweet scents. What captured my attention the most was the stone altar in the center of the room. Carvings of storm clouds, winds, and lightning adorned its sides. On the altar itself rested a body wrapped tight in cotton donning a gold mask with red, blue, and green jewels.

I knelt on the floor before the final resting place of someone who'd been very important to this other person. A sigh echoed through the room, and a voice spoke from me, but it wasn't mine. I recognized the voice from my dream of the island and the one that had told me how to use the Tablet. "Not a day goes by that I don't miss your company, Mali. You were a friend when I needed one most." He paused and fought back a sob. "I've been busy this last year …" He detailed his past exploits and mentioned different preparations he had made for hiding *The Book of Time* but never with enough detail to be helpful, which was frustrating.

Why show me this if he didn't want to give me a clue?

He grew silent for a moment before mentioning a subject that made him—and by extension, me—uneasy. "I hunted down your killers."

Silence filled the chamber, the only sound the faint flickering of the torches. Their light glistened off all the sparkling treasure in the room.

With a shaky breath, I—*he*—continued. "It didn't help. Neither did wishing for things to have been different. I know now I could not have done anything. *They* made the choice to kill you, not me. They killed you, not my failures."

With all the powers the Traveler and his Book possessed, I found that hard to believe.

"Admitting that helps, but what makes me truly feel better is remembering you as you were and reminding myself that you are in a better place now. I hope you were born again in a world other than Tehrahey, one where water and life are plentiful—a place free from the struggles of Tehrahey. And I have hope that I will meet you there. It will take time, but I know I will find my way back to you, no matter what world you now call home. Until we meet again, my beloved."

I rose from the floor, and the feeling this would be the last time he spoke to her shimmered through my mind. He would leave to hide *The Book of Time* and would never return.

Chapter 25
-May We Come Inside?-

2-12.11.12.17.10 T.S.T.
Glachalis
Tehrahey

I snapped awake, tossing aside the suffocating fur blankets. Andy still slept on the floor, a smile on her face. Max snored from the bed, and Jason sat on the edge of the firepit. He poked at a log with a metal prod. His gaze lifted from the flames to study me and I saw dark spots under his eyes, but figured they were shadows caused by the flickering light.

"Bad dream?" he asked.

"No, no. I …" I started to lie. He'd think I was insane if I told him about my dream, or any of the odd ones I'd had since escaping the CTS. What if he, and everyone else, thought I'd gone sun-crazy while walking through the Erima? The weird kids in the CTS were always left to fend for themselves. What if my friends did the same to me? What if they wanted nothing to do with me? How could I survive without their help?

But, if it was real—which my gut said it was—this involved them too. The Maker would be coming for all of us, not just me. I had to share this news with them, no matter the consequences. They deserved to know.

I stood and stared at the fire. "Actually, yes." As he raised an eyebrow at my sudden change of answer, I told him about my dreams—all of them since our escape.

Andy and Max awoke during my story. I filled them in on everything. In the end, they remained silent for a while; I prepared for the worst.

"That's crazy." Max's comment made me flinch. "But not surprising after everything we've seen."

The others quickly agreed.

I released a breath I hadn't realized I had been holding. "You don't think I'm crazy?"

With a smile, Andy placed a hand on each of my shoulders and looked me in the eyes. "Of course, we do." She let me panic for a tick. "I told you back in the Pit we all are."

"You're like the rest of us," Jason confirmed.

I wanted to believe him, but a lot of things made me different from them—and not in better ways. Still, it was nice to know they wouldn't be abandoning me anytime soon. I'd always have them by my side.

Jason stood and stretched. "Worrying about the Maker won't fix anything; let's get moving."

Before heading out again, we checked the wardrobe Cat had showed us earlier. Whenever one of us opened it, we found a new outfit inside, despite it being emptied a moment before by the previous person. Each set of clothes it created would perfectly fit whoever opened it. There were boots, pants, and a jacket. Each item was made from brown leather and fluffy white fur with faint gray spots. The items were thicker and heavier than our CTS uniforms. They would have been uncomfortable, if not for how warm they were. With these on, venturing out didn't seem like such a cold idea anymore. So, we did just that.

Outside, the air was just as freezing as I remembered. At least with the furs I could bear it. They kept most of my body nice and warm. The hood kept the back and sides of my head warm but left my face exposed to the bitter wind. The tip of my nose stung, and the inside froze with each inhale. Since we were last out here, snow fell from the sky in little floaty bits.

Jason led us into what could have been the street. With his new jacket, he practically disappeared into our white surroundings.

I kept close to avoid losing him. We trudged through the snow, which felt more difficult than wading through water. We left a trench behind us. Unlike the water, the snow didn't fill in our path right away.

The similarities of each house became more apparent the farther we walked. Every remaining building mirrored Amyntor's. Had he built these houses as well? With each step, it became obvious the town was abandoned. Doors hung open on most buildings, letting snow inside.

The longer we went without seeing anyone, the bolder Jason and Max became, wanting to enter one of the houses.

Andy and I didn't like the idea but didn't get much of a say when they paired off and disappeared within the shadows of a building. We followed them, knowing if left alone together, they could get into trouble.

As we set foot indoors, Max bounded up the stairs from below. "Too dark down there. I'm going to get that candle."

Andy tried to stop him, but he ignored her and jumped from the steps into the snow, to head back to Amyntor's house. He didn't make it very far before he stopped, looking off through the increasing snowfall.

A large creature with a white fur body and a brown head lumbered up the road, clutching a long item in one hand and dragging something else behind it.

"Jason!" I hissed down the stairs.

At the sound of my voice, he rushed to join us on the porch. "What?"

I pointed up the road to Max and the creature. "We aren't alone."

As it drew closer, its appearance became more humanlike and I realized it wore an outfit like our own. At least it wasn't a monster, but that didn't make me feel all that better. Adults hadn't exactly been kind to us since … well, ever.

The person stopped when it saw Max. "What are you doin' here?" he barked.

Max, in Max-like fashion, turned and ran to us without a word. He didn't worry about leading the person to us, only about getting away from him.

The man gave pursuit, and, as he drew closer, I realized he clasped a large axe in his hands.

"Get back!" Jason took position in front of us and drew a knife.

I hadn't seen him take it from the bag, but there it was. I guess he had kept it with him, and I understood why. Maybe if he had it on the island, things would have gone differently; Jenny might still be alive.

The man slowed to a halt when he saw Jason and his knife. Unfortunately, the little blade didn't make me feel better about our situation; the man looked massive. He towered over us, more than any other adult. His arms were as thick as Jason's head, and they lifted the axe over his shoulder like it was nothing. His mountain of a body practically blended with our surroundings, thanks to the white furs.

Scruffy brown hair fell from the top of his head to his shoulders, while a matching beard sprouted from his chin. Only the smallest bits of red skin were visible on his face. Brown eyes studied the four of us.

"Easy now …" He raised his empty hand in a disarming way. I might have appreciated the gesture more if he wasn't armed. "No one needs to get hurt."

"Get back!" Jason snarled while slashing with the knife.

"Alright, alright. I just want to talk." The man stepped backward. "Where did you come from, and where are your parents?" He scanned our surroundings before refocusing on us.

Jason remained silent and made no signs of lowering the weapon.

Andy and Max both hid within the house, peering out from either side of the doorframe.

No one else jumped at the idea of answering that question, and I didn't get the impression this man would leave us alone if we kept quiet. Fighting wouldn't be a great option either. This man, unarmed, could probably take Jason with his reach alone. Add the axe, and Jason's little knife didn't mean anything. Even if all four of us attacked at once, I doubted our chances. Our best bet would be to keep him in a good mood. That meant no threatening or fighting—basically everything Jason did.

Even if I didn't trust this man, I needed to speak with him before Jason made things worse. I took a position beside my friend. "How do we know we can trust you?"

"You have my word."

I raised my eyebrows and looked toward the axe.

He caught my meaning. "Sorry." He coughed and lowered the weapon. "Don't get many visitors." He fell silent and pointed over his shoulder with his thumb. "This snow will only get worse. Why don't we head to my place? Helina ought to be gettin' dinner ready. Would you like to join us?"

Max stepped out from hiding, nodding so much it looked like his head might fling off if he kept it up. With hunger came bravery as Andy followed behind him, more reserved but equally excited based off the way she licked her lips. Maybe I imagined it, but it sounded like Jason's stomach rumbled at the thought of getting a warm meal. My own mouth drooled. We hadn't had a real meal in days, and a fresh-cooked meal was rare and was worth facing Ms. Hess for.

The man saw the answers to his question on our faces and smiled. "Alright then, I'll just grab the sled."

As we walked, he asked for our names. After we told him, he told us his—Alvis. He grabbed a piece of rope tied to a small platform mounted on two long pieces of metal. The sled slid atop the snow and would have been big enough to carry the four of us if it weren't currently holding a neatly stacked pile of split wood and a few other tools. That explained the axe. He guided us down the road and into another house. Inside the small upper room hung a vast assortment of tools on the right-side wall.

Alvis headed straight for the slanted door that led to the main room. He opened it and called inside, "Helina, we've got company!"

A large woman appeared at the base of the stairway. Her face lit up when she saw us. "Come in, come in!" Her excited beckoning to come down were hard to ignore, especially combined with her giant grin.

The four of us went downstairs while Alvis unloaded the firewood.

Like her partner, Helina towered over us. This wasn't uncommon for adults, but they were the tallest people I had ever seen. While larger than most women, she wasn't as large as Alvis. Most of her size came from her height. Once we were at the same level as her—at least ground-wise—she studied us with excited curiosity.

We fidgeted as her gaze swept over us. She got to me last, and I swore she lingered on me longer than the others. Sure, I didn't like it when adults looked at or noticed me in anyway, but this felt different. Whatever bothered her, she didn't say.

She asked for our names and definitely tensed when I told her mine, but, just as quickly as it happened, the moment passed, and she moved on. After that, she ushered us toward the warmth of the fire and then headed to the cabinets on the left wall.

The room resembled Amyntor's, though not as clean or fancy. As far as I could tell, no crystals were here, and the scent of dust hung heavy in the air. I fought off the urge to sneeze. Their table was smaller, with only two chairs. Instead of bookshelves on the right wall, three different types of furs were hung. The white ones were the biggest of the three, had gray spots, and were fluffier than Cat. The brown furs were smaller in size and hair length, but were still big enough to wrap around someone. Some brown furs were used as rugs to cover patches of the smooth stone floor and looked far worse for wear than their companions on the walls. The gray furs were much smaller, barely bigger than my head, and were just as fluffy as the white ones. Helina's dress was mostly made from the brown furs with bits of the gray as trim.

Aside from dust, another scent permeated the air, accompanied by the sizzling of meat cooking on a grill above the central fireplace.

Helina worked by the cabinets, doing I don't know what. She spoke with us as she did so, and soon enough, the conversation had engrossed all of us. Sometimes she asked questions, sometimes she told us about herself, how she went to the CTS years ago and had even taught there a few years before any of us had arrived. From there, she told us about meeting Alvis in a city south of the Glachalian Mountains called Archipotamou.

Alvis soon joined the conversation, sitting by the fire and tending to the meat on the grill. He explained how he traveled there twice a year to sell furs and buy things he might need back here. The loud, happy man made the conversation livelier as he told how his family had lived in Glachalis for generations before the town froze over.

From there, the conversation shifted from the adults and toward us as my friends each took turns telling them about themselves. Andy spoke of her love of books, of course, and how she took some advanced classes.

Helina mentioned she had a book or two that Andy could borrow if she wanted. The woman took a break from cooking and led Andy to a cabinet where two books resided.

Andy cherished the chosen book carefully as Helina returned to her previous task.

Max told stories about some of the best pranks he had pulled on bullies. Many had Alvis doubling over in laughter, and he joked if Max didn't stop with his stories, we'd all be eating burnt food. Still Max continued, doing his best to make the man laugh until at one point, the man shot water from his nose while taking a drink. This, combined with Max's little celebration, only caused more laughter from us boys.

Helina smiled at Andy before rolling her eyes, as if to say *Boys are dumb*, to which Andy silently agreed with by nodding.

Jason shared a happier version of his walk along the southern coast of Tehrahey. Instead of focusing on the negative parts of the trip, like the sand and heat, he described the adventure and how he had bonded with his father. The story only grew sad when it reached its inevitable end as he and his father had arrived in Eden. He struggled to talk about the murder, but Alvis silenced him by placing a hand on his shoulder.

"You don't have to say it, son," Alvis said.

The conversation in the room waned after that. No one knew what to say next.

Helina kept peering my way, as if waiting for me to talk about myself, but I didn't. There wasn't much to say. I didn't do well in my classes, I didn't have any funny stories that Max hadn't already told better than I could ever hope to, and I hadn't been on any adventures worth sharing. I didn't count the one we were currently on, because I didn't think it would be a good idea to tell them why we were here.

With a cough, Alvis resumed tending to the meat and talked about cooking. When it came out that none of us knew how to cook, the adults shared a look. From that moment on, they walked us all through each step. Helina showed us how she prepped the meat, while Alvis showed us how to cook it. The pair were so friendly it became easy to forget we had just met them.

As we sat to eat, Andy asked why the town was so empty, and Alvis explained how everyone else had either died or had gone somewhere warmer. He and Helina were the only two left in town. That was why they had been so surprised and excited to see us.

Helina mentioned how she always wanted to be a mother and how she almost enjoyed working in the CTS, if not for the cruelty. Again, her eyes fell to me.

Max paused in stuffing his face. "Why don't you have kids, then?"

The pair stiffened and grew silent before Alvis explained they'd had a daughter once named Kirsten. She didn't survive her first year.

Max offered a muffled apology and resumed shoveling food into his mouth at a slower pace.

When she finished glaring at Max, Andy explained to the adults how we were staying in a house down the street and that none of us had any parents.

The adults didn't voice any response to the news, just kept eating, but I noticed pleased smiles forming on their faces.

After the meal, we helped them cleanup.

Alvis offered to walk us home, while Helina invited us for breakfast the next morning, if we helped them with some chores afterward.

The four of us exchanged looks. With a silent conversation, we all agreed to that deal. We couldn't refuse a real meal, and they seemed safe so far.

Helina jumped for joy as we accepted the offer.

Alvis guided us up the stairs and into the cold while Helina planned tomorrow's meal out loud, trying to make us hungry all over again.

Chapter 26
-The Legend of the Living Snow-

2-12.11.12.17.11 T.S.T.
Glachalis
Tehrahey

The next morning, no one complained when we woke up. We were eager for our next fresh-cooked meal and hurried to Alvis and Helina's. As with the night before, we helped them cook breakfast. As we worked, Helina hummed. In the CTS, most people didn't hum, which was why I kept my humming to myself and Andy. A few teachers would do it from time to time, but Ms. Lahna liked to do it a lot. Each adult seemed to have a preferred tune they always resorted to. Helina's was unique, and yet, it felt familiar. The simple song resounded inside me, and I found myself predicting the notes before they arrived. How did I know her song? I kept pondering it as we sat down the fire to eat.

Alvis distracted me from my thoughts with a story passed down through his family since the city first froze. A monster called Living Snow hunted even the most skilled of hunters who wandered too far north of town. Everyone in Alvis's family had respected and feared the monster. Starting today, I feared it too. Who wouldn't fear a monster who could stand within arm's length of a person and never even be seen?

Once we were done eating and had cleaned the dishes, Alvis led Jason, Max, and me up the stairs and outside to finish cutting up a tree with him.

Meanwhile, Andy would stay with Helina to help her clean the house.

Of the two tasks, I would've preferred to stay at the house, especially after Alvis's earlier story. However, he wanted our help, and I did need to get out there to try to find that cave.

Alvis led us to the tools hanging on the wall, turned, and focused on Jason. "Now, Jason, your father taught you how to hunt?"

"Yes, sir." Since yesterday morning, his mood had improved. He actually sounded excited and hung onto Alvis's every word.

"Good." Alvis pulled a long gun off the wall and held it out for Jason. "You take this."

Max and I exchanged gazes as our friend took the rifle. He wanted a kid to carry a weapon!

Jason examined the weapon with care and a calm demeanor. Once satisfied with his study, he eyed our host. "Are you sure?"

"Aye, long as you know how to use it."

Jason's mouth set into a straight line before he replied with a simple, "I do."

"Good." Alvis then handed over two small bags. "Here's your powder and your shot. We may not need it, but out here, you can never be too careful."

Alvis grabbed another rifle for himself then gave me a dagger. He started to give one to Max, to which both Jason and I made noises; that still felt like a bad idea.

Max glared at us as Alvis hesitated.

"Max, can you be trusted with this?"

"Yes!" he snapped and reached for the blade.

Alvis pulled it back as Jason and I made more unsure noises through grit teeth. He eyed us both before fixing a hard stare on Max and holding up the dagger. "This is not a toy. This is a tool meant only to be used for protection. Carrying it is a big responsibility. Can you be trusted with it?"

This time, Max took longer to reply. "I don't know …" His eyes lit up as Alvis handed him the blade. He took it with caution and hung it from a loop in his coat, just like Alvis had showed me.

Our guide removed some tools from the wall and loaded his sled with them. Once he finished, we followed him into the bitter cold of the frozen world.

The wind roared around us. Max pulled up his hood, and I kept mine up for a while too, but it made scanning our surroundings difficult. After a while, I pushed it down and did my best to tuck my head into my shoulders to keep warm. Our surroundings were comprised of varying shades of white. I couldn't find any trees and wondered where we'd find them.

Alvis led us north from the forgotten town and up the valley in which Glachalis rested. On either side, mountain ranges rose skyward until they disappeared into chaotic, gray clouds. The valley floor rose and fell, twisted and turned. We followed the basin for what felt like a cycle. I couldn't be sure without the sun to tell time. As we marched, I watched for anything that reminded me of what the Tablet of the Present had shown. I also kept a look out for Living Snow, even though Alvis told us it was indistinguishable from snow. I figured it didn't hurt to stay diligent.

After walking for a while, we saw trees growing on the distant horizon. Their dark green leaves stood out against the plain white snow that covered the landscape. These were different from the ones on the island. These were almost triangular with long needlelike leaves. Snow covered the treetops and consumed ground beneath them until the canopy became so intertwined that no snow and very little light broke through.

Once that happened, Alvis stopped, grabbed the axe from the sled, tossed it over his shoulder, and instructed Max and me to carry a saw that was taller than either of us. "We'll leave this here. The tree we're lookin' for is just a ways in."

Max slumped at the prospect of walking farther. His hand swept outward, gesturing at our surroundings. "Why not cut one of these?"

I wasn't thrilled at the idea myself, we'd done enough walking, but I kept that to myself. Complaining to adults was never a good idea in my experience.

"Too close to the edge of the forest. Their replacements would struggle to regrow." He led us further into the depths of the forest. "The forest once grew next to town, but, as the cold lasted, the townsfolk cut down the trees faster than they could regrow. Everyone waited for them to grow back in a spring that never came." Our guide checked his surroundings with long, sweeping movements of his head. "Keep your eyes open. Don't want anythin' sneakin' up on us."

He and Jason kept scanning our surroundings. They made me nervous.

"What's out there?" I asked.

"Livin' Snow, leopards."

He hadn't mentioned that the Living Snow were leopards. Knowing made them a little less terrifying. I'd heard of leopards in the CTS but had never seen one. I figured they would be bigger versions of Cat. "What do they look like?"

"Big cats that look like us. We're wearin' their fur." He halted and swept his head from side to side. "I told you earlier, these mountains belong to them." He lowered his axe. "We're here."

A tree lay on its side nearby with all its branches removed and placed in a pile. Snow drifted through an opening in the canopy to cover the base of the fallen tree. Max and I were tasked with cutting the log into smaller pieces. Alvis would split the pieces, and Jason would carry them to the sled.

For the next few cycles, we worked as Alvis instructed. We cut half the tree into pieces. Jason had finished filling the sled a while ago and piled the rest of the wood in the clearing.

In one expert swing, Alvis split another log in half. He made it look easy, but after watching Jason try it once, I knew it wasn't. Alvis straightened up and wiped his brow. "Alright, boys, we've done enough for today."

"Yes!" Max exclaimed and released the saw mid-cut to raise his hands in joy, which meant disaster for me.

Without his help, the saw stopped, and my stomach rammed into the handle. I crumpled to my knees. Why did getting hit in the stomach have to hurt so much?

Max's arms dropped to his sides. "Sorry, Kyle. I forgot."

"I'm just going to sit for a tick." I crawled to a tree and sat against it. I'd be fine, eventually. Sadly, Max hitting me in the stomach was nothing new, though in the past, he used his fists.

"Good job, Max," Jason said as he stacked the last few bits of wood.

Max glared at him. "I said I was sorry!"

Alvis strode to us, his axe swung over his shoulder. He looked calm but very intimidating. "Jason, leave him alone. It was an accident."

Max stuck his tongue out at Jason, until Alvis turned to him.

"And, Max, you need to pay attention to what you're doing." He spoke with a voice similar to that of a teacher but without any of the wickedness I'd come to expect from adults.

Max solemnly bowed his head.

"Let's get the tools on the sled, boys. Come along, Kyle."

The three of them gathered the tools and walked to the sled, leaving me in peace for a moment. I did not want to get up yet and figured giving them a few ticks head start wouldn't be the worst thing ever. Silence felt strange to me. I had spent my entire life in a place filled with noise. At this moment, all I could hear was my breathing. I observed the snow falling through the gap in the trees and collecting around the stump. A chill ran down my back. It didn't feel the same as the cold from the wind and snow. I felt eyes watching me.

Something cracked.

I looked in the direction of the sound, opposite of where the others went. Unless they managed to sneak around me somehow, the sound hadn't come from them.

I rose and drew my knife.

Something white lurked in the shade of the trees.

I froze, and my heart pounded. There shouldn't be snow under the trees. I watched as it moved through the forest.

It circled around me before stopping behind the stump. It stared at me with large white cat eyes.

I pointed my knife at it, the tip shaking in my unsteady hands.

The leopard remained motionless, not even its long tail twitched. Its eyes never blinked. The beast focused on the knife and shook its head.

I stared at it curiously. Had I imagined that? Cat said all cats were Travelers, so I decided to trust him and lowered the knife.

The leopard flicked its head behind it, as if beckoning for me to follow. It turned and took a couple steps before staring at me again. It moved its mouth, and a strange sound came out. It paused then tried again, and this time, I understood. "Come."

A part of me tried to tell myself I had imagined it speaking. But Cat could talk. "Did you just say, 'Come'?"

The creature nodded before walking away. Alvis had said leopards were dangerous but talking animals implied magic. Maybe it knew where to find the Tablet.

The leopard looked back at me again from farther away. "Come, Traveler."

That wiped away any last bits of reservations. This had to be about the next Tablet. I kept a safe distance between us, just in case.

The cat was bigger than me and made slow, deliberate steps. It never tripped or stumbled, and never backstepped. Its tail swung lazily behind it. The ears remained perked and swiveled from side to side, listening to sounds I never heard. My guide led me up the side of the valley on an unseen winding trail.

With each step I took, the distance between myself and my friends grew. Everything looked the same; I didn't know if I'd be able to find my way back. "Where are we going?"

It kept walking without offering an answer. The trees became scarce, and snow covered the ground. At least it wasn't falling. The leopard stepped lightly, barely leaving a trail behind. Its coat blended with the surroundings. If it stopped moving, it vanished. It could've been watching us the entire time.

I didn't feel too safe anymore, but I followed closer just to ensure I didn't lose it. If I wanted to, I could have reached out and touched its fluffy fur. Instead, I kept my hands to myself and the fluff of my own coat. They were warmer and safer there.

The leopard led me along the side of the mountain.

"I can't go too far."

The leopard twitched its ear but remained silent.

Maybe I should turn back, but could I? Would this thing let me go? As I pondered that, we rounded the side of the mountain, and I saw jagged ridges running up and down the center of the valley. It looked like snow had filled the whole valley to at least half the height of the tallest mountain. The ridges were cracks in the snow. Some were shallow and only showed varying shades of white. Others reached deeper and exposed sky-blue scars. My thoughts of retreating vanished. "What is that?"

"Ice." As the leopard continued to speak, it became obvious that it struggled with each word. "It … cover … valley. Protect … secret."

"What secret?"

The leopard regarded me with its large, calm white eyes and remained silent.

My mind flashed to the cave again. The same pale blue material covering the valley formed the cave—an ice cave. "The Tablet is down there?"

The leopard nodded. Its ear twitched, and the creature spun around. A snarl erupted from its throat as it faced the unseen threat. It fled, and two explosions rang out. The leopard fell on its side in a soft crunch.

I ran to it, watching its side rise and fall in time with each fast, shallow breath. Wide eyes scanned our surroundings for danger.

Blood poured from two wounds in its side no bigger than a fingernail. I'd never seen anything so small bleed so much. The beautiful white fur reddened, and the snow beneath us turned crimson. The frantic eyes fell on me. They looked so scared, so terrified.

I wanted to help, but how? "What do I need to do?" I asked, panic gripping my voice.

It gasped for breath, its side rising and falling at a rapid rate. Its legs tried feebly to run. The eyes begged for help.

I didn't know what to do.

Its mouth opened and closed repeatedly as it tried to speak. The legs jerked to a stop, and the chest shuddered. The eyes gazed past me into the cold wilderness.

I dropped to my knees next to the cat. Red snow rested all around me. I could see it soaking into my clothes, staining them the way it had the leopard's coat.

Snow crunched behind me.

I turned, knife at the ready.

Alvis approached with his rifle pointed at the leopard and Jason and Max in tow.

I didn't understand guns. They weren't sharp like swords or axes, and the way Alvis and Jason held them, I had no idea how they could possibly do any damage.

Alvis didn't take his eyes off the leopard. "Are you hurt?"

"I'm fine."

"Did you know the leopard was there?"

"Of course, I did!" I stood and pointed at the body. "I was standing right next to it. Did you see what killed it?"

Alvis glanced at the leopard before he lowered the rifle. "It was a good shot if I do say so myself. Hard to hit a moving target." He slapped a hand on Jason's shoulder.

I didn't understand what he'd meant. He hadn't been anywhere near the leopard when it fell. "What are you talking about?" I shifted my eyes between the two of them.

Jason removed the rifle from his shoulder, pride consuming the last traces of worry on his face. "We shot it."

That's what guns did? They never told us that in the CTS. "You …" I staggered backward. "*You* killed it?"

"Eh, saved your life." Alvis wagged a finger at me. "Next time, don't go wanderin'. I was halfway through showing them how to track a deer before I noticed you were gone." He looked stern but happy. They had killed the leopard without even knowing if they needed to or not.

They killed it! "How could you?"

His expression changed. "What?"

"It was helping me!"

Max wouldn't look at me, preferring to look over his shoulder.

Jason stared me down.

Alvis's face grew stern. "Leopards kill!" He'd told us as much this morning.

A lot of Glachalians, his ancestors, had been killed by the Living Snow over the years for wandering too far from town. I think I figured out why. They were protecting the Tablet, and, for some reason, this one deemed me worthy of finding it. Why would it do that?

As I studied the lifeless body, I couldn't help but think it should've chosen someone else. If it had, it would still be alive. "It wouldn't have killed me," I muttered, walking away from all of them.

Chapter 27
-The Valley of Ice-

2-12.11.12.17.11 T.S.T.
Glachalis
Tehrahey

Once we returned to the house, we hung the tools and rifles in their corner and piled the wood in another.

Alvis avoided my gaze since the incident. He set his rifle on its hook and glanced at the floor before studying the three of us. He probably noticed Jason glaring at me or felt the tension in the air between us.

Max clearly felt it; he fidgeted where he stood.

"I'll just go in and let the girls know we're all right. I'm sure they've got a warm meal ready for us." Alvis opened the door and headed downstairs, ensuring to close the door behind him.

Jason stood in front of me, the veins in his neck bulging. "What was that about?"

What did he mean? They had murdered something. I pointed at the guns on the wall. "You killed the leopard."

"Yeah"—Jason poked the center of my chest—"to save you!"

"We thought it would hurt you, or worse," Max offered as he fiddled with his knife. He stayed near the corner of the room, away from the two of us, like a Second Year watching the older kids fight for the first time. He probably wanted to follow Alvis downstairs, but Jason and I blocked his escape route.

"Well, it wasn't going to." I focused on Jason again. "It showed me where the Tablet is hidden."

I thought that would change Jason's attitude. It didn't. He stepped closer to me and threw his arms in the air. "We were trying to protect you!"

How helpful was it to kill something? Killing was violent and painful and cruel … and it was wrong. "You could've helped without killing the leopard." I stepped forward as well.

"How?" He crossed his arms and raised an eyebrow.

"I don't know." I tossed up my hands and let them drop to my sides before I paced the room. He could have done all sorts of other things, I knew it, but nothing came to mind. After a tick, I faced him once more. "It wasn't necessary."

"This time." He didn't say more, but I knew what he meant. He thought there would be times where killing someone would be the right thing to do. He was wrong. He had to be.

"No, Jason. It is never okay to kill something."

Jason's clenched his fists, but he didn't make a move toward me. Not yet anyway. "Really? You said I had to kill Jones to save Jenny. You were right. I had to. Wish I did it sooner." He stepped forward, placing his face right in front of mine. I could see the fury in his eyes. He pointed at the door to the outside. "I wish I'd killed all those men! Jenny would still be here. They deserved to die!"

I knew he was right. If he had somehow managed to kill those men sooner, Jenny wouldn't have died, but he couldn't be right. I refused to accept that. I studied the boy before me. He seemed so much more grown up. Was he really only a year older than me? I recognized a look in him, one I had seen in countless adults before. I could never quite name it—and I still couldn't—but it was there. It scared me. Like it or not, Jason was becoming an adult. Soon, he could be like every other one I'd ever met. What did that mean for our friendship and for me? Was I doomed to follow his path? I could try going my own way, but could I even survive without him by my side? I didn't like my chances.

"People deserve to live, Jason." I spoke softly, unable to believe I needed to say this.

Max remained hidden in the corner. He probably wondered who would throw the first punch and whose side he'd be on. Even I wondered.

Jason stepped backward, rage still lingering beneath the surface of his voice. "What about the Maker?"

I hadn't considered him.

"Doesn't he deserve to die?"

Before we had started this adventure, I would've agreed with him. The Maker was awful. However, the last few days had changed my mind. Jenny's death had brought me to a conclusion that surprised me. I would never kill someone. "I could never kill another person. Everyone deserves a chance at life."

"Not everyone."

I felt my own gaze harden as I studied him. How could he be like this? Tired of arguing, I left, ignoring the cold outside. I planned to return to Amyntor's house, but then snow crunched behind me. I didn't turn around before shouting, "Go away!"

"No."

I turned to face the last person I had expected. "Max?"

He flashed a sly smile as he joined me. "You were expecting Ms. Hess?" He tried to make light of the situation. It didn't make me feel better.

I stormed off, hoping he wouldn't follow.

He did.

I growled and kicked at the snow, sending small pieces into the air. I wanted to hit something, anything. Only one thing was within striking distance. "If you don't leave, I'll punch you." I thought the threat would scare him off. Should've known better. My threats never worked on him.

He laughed at it, same as always. "You couldn't catch me if you tried."

I decided to ignore him. Maybe that would get him to leave me alone.

We walked in silence for a while. It didn't last long. Max saw right through my attempts to get him to leave. "Is this the part where you ignore me and hope I go away?"

"Would you just leave me alone?" I snapped. I faced him and scowled at his positioning.

He stood several steps back from me and even looked ready to run if necessary. He crossed his arms and actually looked powerful. The fur clothes made his arms look bigger than they really were. "No, you need to talk about what happened, and the person you'd normally go to is inside dealing with Jason. I'm not about to send her out in the cold just to calm you down."

For a tick, I forgot my anger. Had I heard that right? Did Max just admit he had done something nice for Andy?

His tough appearance faltered as the silence grew, and he seemed to realize what he had said. He pointed at me. "Don't tell her." His hand cut through the air. "I'd never hear the end of it."

It reassured me to know he felt concern for Andy, even if he buried it under a dune of sand.

"Were you serious about trusting the leopard, even after Alvis's story?"

I nodded.

He shifted from one foot to the other, the way he always did before he ran. "Then what are we waiting for? Let's go get ourselves a Tablet!" He rushed past me up the street. His sudden desire to do something amazed me.

"What about the others?" I asked, standing my ground.

He faced me, a goofy grin on his face and excitement gleaming in his brown eyes as snow collected in his hair. "We'll make it quick." He awaited my response, bouncing in place.

I didn't know about this. Leaving without telling anyone seemed like a really bad idea. We'd be disappearing on them, no matter how fast Max thought we'd be. Jason wouldn't even let us relieve ourselves in the Erima without telling everyone first. He told us he didn't want anyone to get separated. At the time, it just felt embarrassing to have to announce that to everyone. After a while, I realized it wasn't so bad. It meant I wouldn't get left behind.

We should probably head back and tell Andy and Jason. Although, I didn't want to talk to him or bring him along. He'd probably want to kill more things on the way.

"Don't worry, we'll be fine on our own. We don't need Jason," Max stated with confidence.

Max's confidence was rubbing off on me and so I agreed with him. We didn't need Jason to take care of us. I had survived before without Jason, I could do it again. We could do this!

With that, we retraced our steps to the forest and the valley of ice. My legs cried about walking too much all over again. At least this was different than walking through the Erima. We weren't burning to death, though I knew freezing to death was also an option. Alvis had warned us about it earlier.

Still, we pressed on, following the faded trail up the hill to the edge of the valley where the leopard's body lay. The snow beneath it had faded from crimson to varying shades of mud-brown. Its eyes still stared at nothing. Across the valley, the ice cut through the mountains all the way to the horizon. There, whites, blues, and grays all collided.

Max studied the leopard, his expression different from earlier. Then he regarded it like a terrifying parental guardian. This time, it was closer to how he had looked at Jenny. His eyes held both respect and sorrow. He took a small breath. After another tick, he tried again. "So, we need to go out there?" Something caught his attention across the valley, and he pointed at it. "Was that there a tick ago?"

Following his outstretched finger, I saw something unexpected. A column of clouds spun on top of the ice much closer than the clouds on the horizon. They hadn't been there a moment ago. Stranger still, they seemed to be rising from a crack in the ice. "No, it wasn't." I remembered the first time I had seen this place. They hadn't been there then, so why were they here this time?

Max looked between me and the clouds. "What do you think is happening?"

"I don't know, maybe—" A bit of snow floated past my face, interrupting me. More flakes quickly followed. It was snowing again. Something finally snapped into place in my mind. Cat had said this was the only place in Tehrahey where it always snowed and a Tablet was hidden somewhere under that ice. It made perfect sense—the only place in Tehrahey where it snowed constantly and it also happened to be one of three places where the Traveler had hid a Tablet. That couldn't be a coincidence. The cold and snow made Glachalis so dangerous that most of the inhabitants had deserted the town. That made Glachalis the perfect place to hide a Tablet. It was a trap, just like the island. I explained this to him.

He pulled his coat tighter around him as a cold wind buffeted us. "This whole magic business makes the most unusual stuff normal."

I agreed; between sinking islands, growing crystals, talking animals, and snow, we'd seen a lot of strange stuff since we began looking for the Tablets. Anything seemed possible at this point. "If the Tablet is causing this, those clouds are where we need to go." It was only a guess, but it was the best one we had. It's not like Max had offered any suggestions, and we couldn't ask Andy.

"Of course, they are. You lead then. If we get lost, it's on you." He gestured for me to lead the way.

I started toward the ice, and he fell in behind me. "Thanks for the confidence," I said over my shoulder.

We quickly learned how difficult walking across the ice was. In some places, snow squished under our feet. In others, ice was hard and slippery. Then there were the crevices. The white ones weren't so bad. We could slip in and out of them with no problem. The blue ones were terrifying. If either of us fell in, there'd be no getting out. I didn't want to think about being stuck on this ice forever.

Worst of all, the place sounded alive. The whole valley echoed with moans and creaks. It sounded worse than the time a CTS window had broken during a sandstorm. I thought that had been scary, but at least I'd known for sure the wind had made the noise. At times, the ice would be completely still, and a tick later, it would shudder and shake, as if it were cold as well. In those moments, we dropped to our knees and prayed to the Stars a new crack wouldn't appear beneath our feet.

The weather did not help. The snow made the ice patches slipperier. It took the two of us nearly half a cycle to learn to walk on it without sending our feet in opposite directions, which hurt a great deal. On top of that, the wind stirred. Sometimes it came from behind us, other times, from in front. Whenever it decided to change on us, Max and I would fall—usually on our faces, occasionally on our butts. It knocked us around like we were First Years in a crowd. It even howled like crowd of kids shouting insults at one another. We had more bruises from the ice than any one fight in the CTS.

The clouds rose from the ice ahead of us. The wind changed yet again, and I fell forward. Somehow, I managed to catch myself without using my head.

Max got up first and waited for me to stand. He didn't complain, just stayed quiet. He shivered, and snow stuck to his hair. I couldn't tell if hitting his face repeatedly on the ice or the cold had caused it to redden.

I rubbed my nose, hoping the burning sensation would go away. It did, for a tick.

The longer we walked, the more I regretted what we were doing. We had wandered off on our own, in a storm, across terrain that wanted to kill us. And we didn't tell anyone! What happened if we didn't make it back? The others would worry. Could they find us without knowing where we had gone?

"Maybe we should go back," I suggested.

Max shook his head—actually, he shook his whole body. He did his best to talk while his teeth moved on their own. This cold was miserable. "No, we're closer to our goal than to the house."

So, we pushed on. The ice sloped up toward the clouds, making our walk harder. As we neared the top, a weird sensation came over me. I felt like I'd seen this place before. "Max, stop."

He crossed his arms. It was hard to sound determined when his teeth were clattering, but he managed to do so. "We're not going back."

"I know." I pointed to a crevice on our left. It was shallow here but got deeper closer to the clouds. "I think we should go down there."

He frowned at the crevice. "Why?"

"I just have this feeling." It felt like when I'd get lost in the CTS. I'd know when I found someplace familiar, even if it all looked the same. Surprisingly, Max didn't argue.

We descended into the crevice, and the walls grew around us. The farther we went, the bluer they became. At least down here, the wind couldn't bother us. The snow and ice beneath our feet became dirtier. Dark streaks ran along the floor of the natural hallway. Tufts of fur and bones littered the ground. The hair at the back of my neck rose, and I couldn't tell if it was from the cold or the scattered remains. My eyes darted about, scouting for anything that might decide we were a meal.

We reached a spot where the walls above joined one another to form a ceiling. I knew where we were. We had found the cave. "This is it."

Chapter 28
-Ancient Guardians Still Live-

2-12.11.12.17.11 T.S.T.
Glachalis
Tehrahey

We found ourselves in a small cave about twice the size of a CTS classroom. Ice formed every aspect of this structure. The sides I could see, due to the light that trickled in from the opening behind us, looked to be frozen images of ocean waves. Swirls were etched into all the almost-translucent, blue walls. For just a moment, I imagined I could smell the saltwater. The roaring wind outside could easily be mistaken as the breaking of waves upon the shore. The floor seemed level enough, though there were some uneven surfaces. This would be fun to walk on, especially as we went deeper.

While I could see fine in the front of the cave, shadows shrouded the back wall. I couldn't tell exactly how far the cave went, but, if it went any farther, we'd be walking in total darkness. The only upside was the cold seemed to vanish in here, maybe because we were out of the wind. Though that didn't seem right; we were surrounded by ice.

"So?" Max's question hung in the air and mixed with the faint sounds of dripping water as I studied the dark spots at the far end.

While I knew we were where we needed to be, I didn't like the shadows. I couldn't explain it, but something in the back of my mind told me we were in danger. I glanced over my shoulder at Max, and his face grew serious. A small, quick sound spewed out from the shadows, snapping our attention to the source.

I saw nothing but snow and ice. With dread, I realized the snow saw me as well.

Two large white eyes stared at me from across the cavern. We weren't alone.

I remained motionless.

So did the leopard. It kept its body low to the ground and watched us with unblinking eyes.

A whispered question wafted over my shoulder. "What do we do?"

I didn't know. On one hand, the last leopard had sent us here. On the other, Alvis didn't trust them. He had said they were killers. Could I trust that this large cat would be as kind as the last one, or had that simply been luck granted to me by the Stars? Could I have that kind of luck again? I hated that I could only come up with one plan to find out.

"If things go wrong, run," I answered without looking back.

His response was a single muttered word. "Great." Judging by his tone, he knew he couldn't outrun the creature. That was why I counted on keeping its full attention on me. I wanted one of us to get away.

I studied the animal a little bit longer before taking a deep breath. By the Stars, I hoped this worked. I took a hesitant step forward and tried to speak in as calm a voice as possible. "Hi."

A hiss answered me.

The sound sent my heart pounding, and the rapid thudding echoed in my ears. For just a tick, I saw sharp teeth and did my best to not imagine what they would feel like tearing through my skin. "We're uh … We're looking for a Tablet. Another leopard sent us here." I stood in place, hoping it understood my words

The eyes blinked once, and a single, barely understandable word came from the creature. "Where?"

Well, we got a word. That was something. Unfortunately, I didn't understand the question. "Where, what?"

"Where leopard? Where he?"

My heart stopped as the question sank in. My blood froze in my veins with the realization that we'd have to tell this leopard that its friend was dead. Worse yet, our friends had killed it. I doubted it would take the news well. I tried to speak but struggled with the task.

Before an answer could form in my mind, the same small sound from earlier cried out again. The noise didn't come from the leopard but from something it hid. Something wiggled beneath its belly fur. The large cat's head turned to focus on the movement, a growl emitting from its throat. However, the wiggling continued until a small head popped out. It only looked small compared to the larger version next to it. It was probably as big, if not slightly bigger than Cat. The baby leopard watched me with its own set of tiny white eyes until it focused on the larger cat. A short wail was accompanied by another muffled cry. A second head emerged from underneath the leopard and joined its sibling in whining.

My breath caught in my throat at the sight before me.

"Babies," Max stated with more than a hint of awe in his voice. "She must be their mother." He stepped closer but remained behind me; I wanted to remain between him and the large cat. Max took another step seeming to forget about the possible danger for a moment. "Look at the way she's hovering over them. She's protecting her kids!" The corners of his mouth twitched into smile. "That's what good moms do. It's what my mom tried to do."

I didn't miss the way his voice caught in his throat. I cast him a concerned glance, and he frowned at me.

"Shut up, I'm fine," he replied with a little too much anger to allow me to believe that lie.

Tears stung my eyes as I studied the family before us. "You realize who the other leopard was then, right?"

The sudden breath he took was my answer. They were waiting for their father to return. "If Jason ever finds out about this—"

I cut him off. "He won't." We both knew how Jason would take learning he had killed someone's father.

The mother tore her gaze from her babies to stare at us. Her ears perked forward, awaiting an answer.

I couldn't bring myself to meet her gaze. I looked everywhere but those pale, snow-white orbs.

She correctly translated my avoidance as her answer. Her ears flattened back against her head as teeth became visible. Her next words were more strained as she struggled to speak through her anger. "What. Happened?"

The two cubs resumed hiding beneath her belly.

I tensed at the display but remained where I stood. I couldn't leave without explaining, even if it got me killed. I knew what it was like to be left without answers, to have so many questions to ask and no one to provide me with answers. Why'd my mom give me up? Why did she hate me?

I hung my head. "He showed me where to go, and … then our friends, they shot him." I looked up to see so many emotions playing across the supposed monster's face—anger, loss, pain, disbelief, hatred. They were all looks I knew from my friends' faces when we discussed our own losses. I recognized and understood every single one. All of them were there in the creature's eyes, and we were the cause.

The hatred lasted the longest, and I couldn't blame her. We were the monsters here. "I'm so sorry."

The leopard roared and launched forward.

Guilt and fear kept me rooted to the spot. I hoped Max ran. I shut my eyes, listened to the nearly silent paws thud against the icy floor, and waited for the inevitable. However, no pain came. Neither claws tore through my clothes nor teeth bit into my flesh.

I opened my eyes to find the leopard standing just out of reach, teeth bared in a silent snarl, and ears still pinned against her head. My heart hammered, and blood roared in my ears. My legs shook; I thought they'd give out at any moment.

After a tick, her look faded, and her head drooped to the ground. "He made good choice," she lamented before returning to the corner where her cubs remained, still whining.

I watched her walk away, confused.

A hiss of breath escaped behind me, and I glanced back to see Max perfectly motionless. A hand covered his mouth, and his gaze jumped from me to the leopard and back again. He hadn't run like I'd told him to. He did it all the time when he got scared, but this time, he didn't. I'd have to yell at him for it later.

I focused on the retreating animal. "You're not going to hurt us?"

She lay down in the corner, and her babies pestered her again. The two little ones didn't seem at all concerned by our presence, only their mother did. "You won't hurt them?" she asked, eyeing the bundle of furs now wrestling with one another in front of her.

I followed up my swift head shake with a single word. "Never."

"Then take secret. We protect it long enough." She pointed with her tail to the darkest point at the back of the cave. "What you hunt, through there."

I hesitated for a moment, and Max nudged my shoulder.

He followed it up with the best reassuring look he could muster. It wasn't much, but it helped knowing he had my back.

My heart raced at the thought of strolling past a mother leopard and her kids just to walk through a pitch-black ice cave.

I began a very cautious trek across the cavern. After making it almost halfway, a patch of uneven ice proved to be extra slippery. I stumbled but managed not to fall.

The sudden movement caught the attention of the two cubs. They stared at us, as if noticing our presence for the first time.

Under the scrutiny of all three sets of white eyes, I froze.

One cub rose from its position of chewing on its sibling's tail to approach us.

The mother watched intently as her child drew nearer, sniffing at my feet.

I swallowed the breath lodged in my throat and studied the little thing. I noted the faint gray spots mingled amongst it mostly colorless fur. "Hello there," I whispered.

I expected a response, but it didn't come from the kitten. "No talk yet. Not till older."

We watched the baby sniff at my fur coat, and I realized how we must look to them. We were the monsters. The cub lost interest and returned to mercilessly attacking its sibling. The two squeaked at one another as the fight continued.

"There were many, long ago," the mother began. "Now there only us. It be nice no longer serve, be free from ice." She glanced at us with an almost pleading expression. Did she want us to take the Tablet?

I straightened up, the question in my mind helping me temporarily forget my fear. "What do you mean, serve?"

"We were created one purpose. Leopards protect secret." She rose and stretched her paws in front of her. Claws flexed outward into the ice to leave gouges. "We made stronger, deadlier. Leopards kill any man who seek power but never harm innocent." She passed us as she headed for the entrance. The wind ruffled her fur. "I fear trapped like him, but now free." She made a soft noise that gained the cubs' attention.

They joined her, and the group set out into the storm.

Chapter 29
-Getting in Was the Easy Part-

Max and I remained motionless as we watched the empty exit. The leopards had been put here to protect the secret, which I assumed to be the Tablet. The Traveler had created them to be guardians. From the way Alvis spoke, it sounded like they did a very good job of keeping people away.

Max exhaled a long, slow breath. "That did not go the way I expected."

I rubbed my chin as I agreed with him. "Expecting more blood and anger too?"

"It's what I would have done if someone hurt my family."

My hand dropped to my side as I raised an eyebrow in his direction. "Even Andy?"

He hit my shoulder then pointed an accusing finger as he headed to the back of the cavern. "No one picks on her but the three of us, right?"

He really did see Andy as a part of his family, even though they tended to bicker more than they got along. The image of the two cubs wrestling with one another crossed my mind. Sure, they looked like they were fighting, but it was just a game to them. They didn't mean any real harm by it. Could that be what Max and Andy's relationship was like?

Max stood in the shadows, barely visible. "The tunnel goes deeper into the ice." A narrow passageway stretched before us, just wide enough for one person. "This should be fun," Max mumbled, echoing my earlier thoughts; if only we had brought the candle with us. He perked up and looked at me, a question apparent in his eyes. "What do you think she meant by 'stuck like him'?"

I hadn't given the sentence much thought at the time. The fact she had just up and left confused me more than anything else. Had someone else once tried to get the Tablet and wound up trapped down there? The idea of possibly getting stranded in a dark ice tunnel didn't sound appealing. "Stay close."

Max responded by placing a hand on my shoulder.

For a while, I could still see in shaded color, but it eventually faded, far too quickly in my opinion. I found myself leading us through darkness on a slick and uneven surface. I tripped multiple times.

Each instance caused Max to stumble too, but he never complained. The only sound he made was his breathing. It was quiet, but in the soundless darkness, it was all I could hear. It brought some calm to my rapidly beating heart.

My shoulder brushed against a wall, and I reached to place a hand on it. This helped my balance. I stumbled less but soon lost feeling in my fingers. There was a lot of time to think in the darkness, plus it helped distract from the increasingly painful cold pricking at my fingers.

Unfortunately, the sight of the mother leopard had conjured thoughts of my own mother. I ignored the questions burning through my mind, which only triggered something worse. I flinched as my earliest memory gusted through my mind—dark, cold, and very little light; perhaps a promise of love, but I doubted it. I pushed the thought to the depths of my mind where it belonged. I had more important things to worry about, like how my hand felt like it would fall off at any moment; still, that song surfaced in my mind, and I fought the urge to hum it. Max would probably just make fun of me.

I changed which hand touched the wall and leaned toward the other side with arm outstretched. This gave my left hand a break while my right one guided me onward, gradually freezing like the other.

A tick later, a gust of hot air rolled through the tunnel. I stopped, confused. I hadn't experienced air that hot since we left the Erima. I actually stopped shivering for a moment.

Max's voice spoke from beside my ear. "That was weird."

As I pondered the strange shift in temperature, water trickled over my hand and rolled down the wall. When I moved my foot, I could hear the distinct sound of moving water. That slight movement caused me to stumble on the suddenly slipperier surface. I needed to be careful.

"The warm air melts the ice. That must be how the tunnel is here," I said to Max. It made sense to me. The fire at Alvis and Helina's house had done the same thing. Cold things didn't like hot things. Snow melted when exposed to fire. If that blast of hot air kept rolling through often enough, the tunnel would stay forever.

I took another step, attempting to use my hand to steady myself, but my foot found nothing to step on. I fell forward into the darkness. My chest slammed into the ice, and Max fell on top of me.

We slid faster and faster. Cold air blasted my face. I reached for the sides of the tunnel, desperate to stop us. The ice burned like the sand in the Erima when I touched it. I retracted my hands; they weren't doing anything but getting scraped. I had no idea how far we slid, but

I guessed a very long way from the start of the cave. Some moments felt like we were slowing, but then our speed increased again.

When we finally stopped, Max jumped off me. "Sorry, Kyle."

"It's okay." I stood and tried to look at my hands. They stung like they were burned, but I couldn't see anything in this cave. I closed them into fists and hissed in pain.

"What's wrong?"

"I tried to slow us down. My hands got scrapped pretty bad." When Max stayed silent for a few ticks, I panicked. "You still there?" Had he left? I'd never been afraid of the dark before, but this felt different. Most nights, the moon offered some light, some hope, but this cave held none of that.

"I'm still here. Just thinking of what to do for your hands. We don't have any of our usual supplies." By supplies, he meant water and some torn pieces of fabric. Neither did much to help with pain, just kept it from getting worse a few days later.

"I'll be fine." I'd hurt my hands before, though never both at once; the situation didn't feel entirely new to me. I'd be all right. I wished we'd told someone our plan, or at least had thought of bringing some supplies. Panic coursed through me. How would we climb back out?

Max's hand stopped me from voicing these concerns. It palmed my face before he apologized. "Sorry." His voice shook. So did his hand as it gripped my shoulder. He was afraid, and he needed me.

I had to act tough, for his sake.

"Let's get moving."

We stumbled around in the dark as we tried to get our bearings. The tunnel was still narrow, and one way sloped up. We went the other way.

I don't know how long we walked. With each passing tick, it felt like the darkness worsened and my heart quickened its pace. Its beat pounded in my ears and throbbed in my hands. My shoulder grazed the wall as the tunnel turned, and I could finally see something.

"I see light ahead!"

Blue light illuminated the tunnel. It got brighter with each step. The sounds of wind and dripping water echoed from farther ahead. As my heart slowed, my pace increased. I wanted out of this darkness.

"What do you think it is?" Max's hand left my shoulder as he followed me.

"Only one way to find out." I continued toward the light, unsure of what we'd find.

The light flashed, and a wave of warm air rushed past. The gust staggered us for a moment, but we kept going. Whatever lay ahead of us created the hot air.

As the light brightened, the tunnel became wide enough for Max and me to walk side by side. Soon enough, the tunnel stopped, and we entered a large cavern. High above us, clouds formed from thin air. They spiraled skyward from the opening in the cavern roof. The blue light came from the center of the room, from something I hadn't expected to see.

Max saw it and stopped. "Kyle ..."

"I see him."

Someone sat in the center of the room, their bare back turned to us. Whoever it was, they had long black hair. For a tick, I feared it might be Melinoe, but this person's skin was too dark to be her.

"Hello?" I called out. No response greeted us. I edged closer and tried again. "Hello?"

Still nothing. I circled around the stranger.

He had a red sun painted on his forehead. His eyes were shut, his legs crossed, and his arms held a book-sized Tablet of translucent blue crystal. He remained perfectly still, didn't even breathe.

"I think he's dead." I stepped closer and very slowly tapped his shoulder, ready to jump away at a moment's notice. Nothing. Was this the *him* the leopard had mentioned? I placed my hand on his shoulder and quickly pulled it away.

Max nearly ran out of the cavern. "What happened?"

I showed him my bloody and raw hands; touching the man's shoulder had hurt.

"Right," He approached me to inspect them. "Those are pretty bad."

I pulled them to my chest and carefully closed them. They couldn't quite decide if they wanted to sting or burn and kept switching between both feelings. "I'll be fine."

Max gave me a silent skeptical look, but didn't say anything more.

I swallowed and touched the body's shoulder again, this time using the back of my hand. The man's skin felt as cold as the ice around us. "Dead." I quickly removed my hand from his shoulder. The thought of touching a dead man freaked me out.

Max kept his distance as he stepped around to the front of the body. "He's only wearing pants?"

I turned away from the body. "Doesn't matter. We just need the Tablet."

"Well, then take it."

Glaring at Max, I held up my palms.

"Right." He stared at the body for several ticks but made no move to take the Tablet. Finally, he looked to me with sad eyes. "I-I can't." He fell quiet for several ticks as he stared at the ground. "I know you're hurt, but … can you do it? I can't go near the body. I just can't."

Never had I heard Max sound so defeated. I looked warily at the man. I was sure he was dead, but this felt too easy. Walking through the cold had been difficult, but much easier than walking along the path at the island. That was deadlier than this. What if, when I tried to grab the Tablet, the man grabbed me? Maybe moving Tablet would bring him back to life.

With a deep breath, I stepped toward the body, pulled my sleeves over my palms for padding and grabbed the Tablet. Warmth flowed from it, despite the cold surroundings and the sleeves separating my hands from it. I pulled on the relic, but it didn't move. It slid from my grasp. "I can't get a good grip with the fur."

I glanced at my friend for help, but Max just stared at the ground. I sighed and extended my hands from their sleeves and carefully placed them on the Tablet. The contact didn't hurt like I had expected. I pulled harder, and it budged a bit. With a lot of effort, I pulled the relic free.

The Tablet flashed blue, and a warmer wave of heat rushed over us. The walls and floors groaned. Clouds stopped forming, faded and revealed darkening sapphire-colored skies above.

I dropped the Tablet.

Max jumped away, ready to run. "Are you okay?"

"Yeah, yeah … I'm fine. It just startled me."

He edged closer, still keeping his distance. His gaze darted around the room, searching for any signs of trouble.

I knelt to grab the Tablet and stopped. "Max …" I offered up my palms for him to see.

He stopped his restless searching and studied them. "They aren't scraped anymore. Did the Tablet do that?" he asked, inspecting his own hands.

"It must've." I lifted it. Still emitting heat, it left a Tablet-shaped indentation, along with two more old symbols, in the ice floor. "Two down, one to go."

"Good, let's get back; that body scares me." Max gestured at the slumped, shirtless corpse with his head. He turned to leave. "Do you feel warmer?"

I did and thought the feeling was due to holding the Tablet. Was that another of the Tablet's special powers—that and healing those who touched it?

We took two steps before a sound stopped us in our tracks. A crack echoed through the cavern, and the ice groaned.

Max asked his next question with an unsteady voice. "What was that?"

The ground shook, and we fell to our knees. Max gasped at something behind.

I followed his gaze, ready to see a walking corpse headed our way. Where the body rested, a hole opened in the floor and swallowed the man. The roar of rushing water filled the distant darkness. The ice was melting. "We have to get out!"

"And how do we do that?"

Ahead of us, large chunks of ice blocked the tunnel we had entered through. The cavern groaned louder. A split appeared in the wall.

I scrambled to my feet and studied our surroundings. My stomach felt like I'd swallowed rocks. I understood the trap. The hard part wasn't getting to this Tablet, it was leaving alive. This couldn't be happening! There had to be a way out.

No such luck. Unless the Tablet let us fly, we were stuck.

"Where do we go?" My head swung back and forth in a desperate search for any kind opening, a solution to our problem, any way to escape this death trap.

"I don't know!"

Another ear-splitting crack echoed through the chasm. The ice floor collapsed beneath us. We were plunged into the water. Freezing liquid surged into my lungs, choking me. I surfaced and saw sky for a tick before the water dragged me into darkness. Sunlight disappeared in an instant.

A sapphire-colored glow emanated from up ahead. The Tablet! I reached for it. Ice crashed onto it, pushing it away. The fur clothes weighed me down and pulled me under again. I struggled upward and inhaled air. The water slammed me into ice. I grasped at it, but it slipped. The current pulled me farther into the dark.

Max gasped behind me. Blue flashed far in front. I reached for the Tablet, but it lurched to the right. I hit more ice but managed to grab hold. Water roared all around and tried to dislodge me, tried to drown me.

There had to be a way out!

Something knocked me from my perch. From beneath the waves, I saw blue. I swam forward. A shoe kicked my face. I surfaced again.

"Max!" I choked it out. Water replaced the air in my mouth.

"Kyle!" Max's hand grabbed my face. He pulled me to a rock. We clung to it as everything surged past us. "You— all right?" he said with a gasp. His teeth clattered together.

Mine did too. I found it hard to breathe. "Yes—" I coughed. "Tablet?"

"Don't know." We needed that Tablet. We couldn't let it get away.

"Have to get it." Scanning the darkness didn't help.

"How?"

"Don't know. Have to try." I hated my idea.

"I'm scared."

Didn't blame him, I was too. I found his arm, held it firmly while trying to sound confident. "Stay close." I really hated my idea. I pushed off the rock.

Max splashed into the water. Panicked hands found my shoulders. The water gained speed. We slammed into every rock and struggled to stay afloat. Blue light gleamed in the distance.

We hit another rock. I pushed off with everything I had left.

Max's triumphant shout rose above the crashing water. "Got it!"

Chapter 30
-Alive but Dead, and It's My Fault-

2-12.11.12.17.11 T.S.T.
Glachalis
Tehrahey

The water carried us farther into the dark and tossed us against rock after rock in a constant attempt to drown us. I never once in my life thought I might die by drowning in our dried-up world. I didn't like that, and the Stars seemed to be on my side. The water dumped us into a cavern with a large pool of spiraling warm water. In its center stood a large golden crystal radiating just enough light to be visible but not illuminate the whole cave. More light came from the dim blue Tablet in Max's hands, which danced off the water through a layer of steam and along the cave walls. Light and shadow wavered in unison.

The heat in the water was shocking but not unwelcomed. As the water carried us in a circle, it became obvious that the heat came from the large gemstone. Somehow it heated the whole pool, despite all the cold water flooding in from the rapids.

A straight cave branched off and was shallow enough for us to stand on, with the water around our knees. Here, the walls became perfectly flat with carved columns spaced equally along each side. They were a stark contrast to the naturally rugged and rough walls surrounding the pool. We caught our breaths and rested for a moment before following it farther. Water lapped at my knees. The soaked leopard fur weighed me down and tried to hold me back. Max struggled as well. Our sloshing footsteps echoed through the cavern. Someone obviously had dug the tunnel, which I figured meant it must lead somewhere. Unfortunately, it did not. It ended in deeper water where the current tugged at us, threatening to pull us into submerged darkness.

Max and I decided we didn't want to go that way. We'd like to learn to swim before trying that path. After all, our first attempts at swimming hadn't gone so well. But at least we were still alive.

We returned the way we had come and studied the walls around the swirling pool. I hoped we'd find another way to go, but there was nothing. We were trapped.

Max asked the question already running through my mind. "Now what?" He clutched the Tablet to his chest as he awaited my solution, which I didn't have.

How could I know where to go? I'd never been here before, and, from what I could tell, our options were trying to swim into the end of the tunnel, which was impossible, since neither of us knew how to breathe under water, see in the dark, or swim. We were lucky to have survived the rapids—which was our other option, try to swim back up them. That seemed impossible.

We were stuck.

I avoided meeting his eyes, which left me scanning our surroundings once more. There just had to be some way out of this tunnel. How else could someone have carved it? A more thorough investigation only caused more frustrations. The walls between the columns were perfectly smooth, except in one spot. The creator of this place had done the truly horrible thing of carving what looked like a door into the stone just above the top of the water. The etching was faint but unmistakably a door, with even a circle for where the nonexistent handle would be. Why would someone do that?

We were trapped down here, and some cruel person had thought it would be funny to leave a carving of a door in the wall? With my back against the opposite wall, I slumped into the water in defeat. There was no way out. We were stuck. Why didn't we tell anyone what we were doing? Cat was the only one who could help us, and he had no way of finding us. Tears formed in my eyes as I stared at the door. Of all the things that could have killed us, this was it?

Max sank into the water next to me, a blank expression on his face. He sat with his knees pressed to his chest and his arms wrapped around them. "I guess I should have let you leave that note."

With that simple statement, I broke down completely. I cried, and, for the first time ever, I didn't care if anyone, even Max, saw. It didn't matter anymore. It wasn't even just the fact that we were trapped. Andy and Jason didn't know where we were. We had left without telling them. They wouldn't know where we went, and even if they decided to look for the Tablets without us, it wouldn't matter. Thanks to us, one of the Tablets of Time was stuck in some lost, underground cavern. With one stupid decision, I had doomed not only us, but my friends as well. Worst of all, I knew whose fault this mess was.

Mine.

Max may have convinced me to leave, but I could have said no. I knew better than to let him lead me or to leave without a word, yet I had done it anyway. With time, my tears dried up, and my sobs turned to hiccups.

Max sobbed into his knees.

Seeing him cry hurt as much as seeing Andy do the same thing. I wanted to fix it. "This is all my fault," I mumbled.

He looked up with a sniffle. "What?"

"I should have at least left a note." I sat up straight and looked past the carving of the door. "I definitely should have grabbed our bag of supplies. I knew better."

He opened his mouth to say something, probably argue with me, but I didn't let him. "Do you remember our last fight before Jason arrived?" I asked. If I couldn't fix this situation, I could at least distract him from it.

We sat and talked for a long time. We discussed old fights, terrible teachers, and rumors from the CTS. Every time the conversation stopped, I started it up right away again. I don't know how many times I changed the subject. All I knew was I needed to keep Max's mind from the situation. It didn't hurt that it kept me preoccupied too.

As silence fell over our conversation once again, and I struggled to come up with something else to talk about, the unexpected happened. The carving of the stone door opened. Bright firelight flooded the steam-filled cavern, blinding us after so much time in the Tablet's dim blue light. On the other side of the door was a carving of a woman tipping over a clay pot. The tiny figure of Cat stood in the doorway; behind him was the washroom in Amyntor's house.

His head cocked to the side as he studied us. "What are you doing in here?"

I looked from him to Max. We weren't going to die!

True to himself, Max bolted from the tunnel, through the washroom and into the main room, cheering all the way.

Cat hissed after Max as water splashed in his wake.

I grabbed the Tablet Max had left behind as I rose.

Cat and I locked gazes as I tried to figure out what to say. My mouth opened to say something, anything, but no words came out.

"Get out of the water," he ordered.

And I obeyed.

Meanwhile, he grumbled about our fur clothes stinking up the whole place. I turned and watched Cat close the so-called door by pressing his paw against one of the crystals surrounding the carved mural. The woman with the pot returned to spilling water into the tub once again.

"How did you find us?"

"The cistern is magically sealed and the last place anyone would look, so I checked it first." Cat strode out the room with his tail pointed skyward.

I followed him as Andy began to yell.

In the other room, Max cowered by the fire as Andy berated him. Normally, he'd be annoyed by her doing such a thing, but this time, he struggled to conceal a grin.

When I entered the room, Andy turned to me. So many emotions played across her face as she crept toward me. She stopped just in front of me, a smile encompassing her face. In a gust, it changed into a scowl as she pummeled my left arm with a barrage of fists.

I dropped the Tablet while trying to defend myself.

She shouted at me the whole time about how dumb I was, how worried they were, and to never do anything like that again.

I apologized and agreed with her until she finally relented and hugged me, despite my soaked clothes. Even though she seemed to have forgotten her anger, it felt like she wanted to crush me to death. The thought of dying this way didn't scare me as much.

She glared at me as she released me. "Stay here and dry off."

That was not an order I planned on disobeying.

"I'll let Helina know we found you." She tightened her coat as she ascended the stairs.

Meanwhile, Max and I shed our fur clothes, leaving us in our CTS uniforms. We laid the clothes on the floor around the fire. I collected the discarded Tablet and propped it against the stone ring of the firepit.

At some point during Andy's assault on me, Cat had situated himself on the bed. He watched us dry off in silence until Andy returned with food from Helina. Jason would be back just as soon as he and Alvis returned from their search for us.

Chapter 31
-They Want to Quit?!-

2-12.11.12.17.11 T.S.T.
Glachalis
Tehrahey

Eventually, Jason returned from his search with Alvis. Snow clung to his furs and fell from his boots as he stomped down the stairs. I hoped it was cold and not anger that caused his face to be so red. I had already taken one beating from Andy; I didn't want another from him. Glancing at Max and seeing his eyes dart around the room for possible escape routes or hiding places told me he wouldn't be volunteering to take it for me.

Jason halted at the bottom of the stairs.

I swallowed the lump in my throat. Silence filled the air and drowned out the crackling of the fire.

My friend studied everything in the room before his gaze rested on his target—the plate of food we had set aside for him next to the Tablet. He aimed for that and sat without a word. He tore into his meal as I tore into myself, trying to figure out how to begin apologizing to him. How long had he been out in the snow looking for us? We had been gone for cycles.

As the silence progressed, I focused on the fire. Knowing Jason, he'd say something. Eventually.

Eventually arrived after he finished his meal and shed his frozen fur clothes. "Glad you're all right, but how could you be so stupid?"

So I explained it to him. I started out apologetic. But, as I continued and he kept scowling and giving his best disapproving adult stare, all the anger from earlier returned. Then I said something along the lines of 'we didn't need his dumb help to do everything.' Then we started fighting all over again.

And this time, it was worse.

We went from arguing about how dumb the other was, to what we were doing on this adventure. It started out as just me and Jason, but soon Andy and Max got involved as well.

"You could've died!" Andy shouted.

Max sounded offended as he retorted, "You think we don't know that?"

"We were trying to help," I argued.

"You tried to show off," Jason countered.

"Did not!"

"Did too!"

On and on went the shouting and bickering until our voices became hoarse. Older and older grudges got unearthed. More and more, Andy referenced Max's bullying. She even called him Poop-Head. Not a terrible name—we had come up with it years ago when he was just a nameless bully to us—but it hurt him. She hadn't used it in a very long time, and when it came from her lips, Max visibly recoiled. After that, he started revisiting old taunts. I didn't stop him.

The whole time, Cat watched in silence. He never said a word and never picked a side.

Meanwhile, the squabble had drawn a line between our group. On one side of the fireplace stood Max and me. Jason and Andy stood on the other. Throughout the argument, we had all said a lot of mean things. Some of them, I realized too late I didn't mean but didn't know how to take them back. Judging by the hurt and remorse on my friends' faces, they felt the same way. A hush fell over all of us as the argument died, at least for the moment.

Cat rose and stretched. His yawn broke the silence. "Got that out of your systems?"

No one answered him. Teary gazes drifted around the room, too afraid to make eye contact with anyone else.

He strolled over and situated himself on the floor between our two sides. He focused first on Max and me. "What you boneheads did was incredibly stupid. You should be dead."

We flinched in unison at Cat's words.

He turned his ice-blue gaze to Andy and Jason. "You were rightfully worried, but they aren't dead. It's in the past. Let's move on and figure out where we're going next." Cat focused on me and the Tablet resting against the side of the firepit.

However, before he could say anything, Jason spoke a single word. "Why?"

Cat's tail twitched. "What?"

"Why keep looking?" Jason stood up straighter as everyone stared at him.

His question didn't make sense to me. He knew we had to find *The Book of Time* if we wanted to escape Tehrahey. We needed to find the last Tablet so we could locate the Book. Yes, what we were doing was dangerous—Jenny's death had proved that—but wasn't the end goal worth it? We'd leave this world and the ever-growing Erima behind for someplace better; preferably one without horrible adults who beat and abandoned children on a daily basis.

"If we keep going, one of us will die," he continued, holding Cat's gaze.

In theory, that would be an easy thing to do, but not in practice. Cat's cold blue eyes were hard to look into. Even from his tiny height, he seemed to stare down at me and make me feel incapable of doing anything. Still, Jason's green eyes locked onto Cat's and didn't back down.

Something else hid behind the determination in his damp eyes and echoed within his voice. It dawned on me how rough these past cycles must've been on him. If he got so upset over losing a new friend like Jenny, possibly losing both Max and me must have been too much of a blow, even for him.

By the Stars, how could I have done this to him?

Our guide decided to humor our friend for a moment, but I didn't miss how his tail lashed from side to side. "And what would you prefer to do?"

"Stay here where it is safe."

Max scoffed. "You call this cold safe?"

"It is when you listen to Alvis," Jason snapped. He wasn't acting like this because he was too afraid to continue with the quest; he was too afraid to lose any of us. I knew that, and maybe Andy did as well, judging by the way she looked from him to us. After all, she must've been with him when they had learned we were gone. She had seen how he had reacted and how he had really felt about this.

We all fell silent again except for Cat. He chuckled. It wasn't really a laugh, more of a rasping wheeze. That said, hearing it didn't make any of us happy or excited. With a shake of his furry little head, he asked, "So, you faced death a few times, and now you're ready to quit?"

Andy rubbed her arm. "It's more than that. We started this to find a new home, and now we have. We don't need the Book anymore." She finished with a shrug.

Did the two of them really want to stay here for the rest of their lives rather than leave this world completely? We'd had dozens of conversations about escaping over the past year, and more so over the last week. I thought we all wanted this. Had I been wrong, or had the last few days shaken them? How couldn't they? We'd lost someone. We may not have known her long, but Jenny had been a friend. None of us wanted to be next, and really, Glachalis wasn't that bad. Alvis and Helina were nice enough. Maybe with time, we could get used to living here, and Andy would be right like always, but I wasn't ready to admit that yet. Alvis and Helina really were great, but I still couldn't bring myself to fully trust them. I didn't even fully trust Ms. Lahna, and she had helped us escape the CTS! She'd been so kind, and yet I couldn't shake the feeling that she'd hidden something from us. Adults always had an ulterior motive. They would always play nice and then strike when least expected.

I didn't even want to think about what Amyntor might be hiding from us. I just hoped adults not from Tehrahey were better than the ones I had grown up around.

Cat didn't seem to like the idea of us staying. His eyes darkened as he shook his head. "You know nothing about death."

What more was there to know about death? I hated seeing it. It made me feel horrible. What could Cat have seen that was worse than what we had seen?

Cat's eyes became unfocused as he stared past us. I followed his gaze but saw nothing except the stone wall. I looked back at him; he seemed so small.

"No. You've seen nothing. A man falling from a cliff, a girl bleeding to death …" He shuddered, and his fur puffed out. "I have watched as children's souls were ripped from their bodies. It's painful for all who are near." His hollow voice bounced off the stone surfaces around us until it filled the room. His claws scraped against the stone floor. The Tablet's blue light lost its warmth and, with each passing tick, resembled Cat's eyes.

I shivered and stepped closer to the fire. It didn't seem to be emanating much warmth anymore.

"The kids screamed and screamed, and the monster, she-she smiled at their agony. She laughed as their bodies twitched and trembled … as they lost their souls. It's a slow death. You get to watch as your very essence leaves you. And when you aren't in your own body, there's no one to control it. No one to tell it to give up. To die."

Andy closed her eyes and covered her ears.

Max covered his ears as well.

Jason remained unfazed, though he almost seemed to be completely ignoring the conversation. He didn't even look at Cat.

I wanted to do the same, to block out his voice, but I couldn't.

Cat didn't notice the distress he caused and continued with his hypnotic voice. "The body desperately clings to life though it has none. After an eternity, the body loses hope. It stills, and the eyes close, then your soul sees your lifeless corpse."

I wanted him to end the story. "Cat, stop."

All the warmth in the room had vanished. The few dark shadows in the room grew and slunk toward us. They seemed to be reaching for our guide, trying to drag him into darkness.

He didn't hear me. "This was what the monster waited for." He shrunk as he cowered against the ground. His ears flattened against his head. "Now she can eat, and she lets you watch. She—"

Ice crept from the relic by the fire, coating the stone figures.

I realized what the Tablet was doing; it was manifesting Cat's old memories. It had to be the Tablet of the Past! "Cat, stop!" I ripped the Tablet from the ice, and it burned my hands as I quickly tossed it into our bag, hoping that would block its powers, like it had the Tablet of the Present's.

The chill in the air vanished in a gust. The shadows retreated to the edges of the room as everything returned to normal.

Cat blinked as he snapped from his trance. He stood and studied us. Sorrow filled his eyes as stared at Andy.

I don't think he planned on sharing that story with us, and I wished he hadn't. Whatever monster he had faced, I prayed to the Stars I would never meet it. I didn't want to die or lose my soul. Worst of all, it was just another monster out there that could kill us. Whether or not it existed on Tehrahey didn't matter. This was just more proof for Jason that we weren't capable of dealing with the dangers out there.

My hand on Andy's shoulders let her know the story was over.

As she and Max uncovered their ears, Cat's next words were spoken slowly and as if he hadn't fallen into that trance. "The CTS, Glachalis, it doesn't matter where you are. Tehrahey is dead. One day, and likely soon, this world will cease to exist and take every one of you with it."

He spoke the truth. I knew it, and so did my friends. They had to. The adults in the CTS had said similar things all the time. Our world was coming to an end, and from what we had seen in the Erima—from the lack of life to the fact that war was on the way—that end felt a whole lot closer than it ever had, hidden underground in the CTS.

When his words had no effect on our friends, Cat turned to Max and me. "And what do you two want? Do you want to stay or to finish this?"

He was asking if Max and I wanted to go at this alone, which neither of us did. Not after our last quest. Aside from that, the thought of leaving Andy and Jason behind terrified me. They were my friends! I couldn't just leave them, not even to find a book that could make one of us a Traveler and get us out of here. I didn't want to do this alone. We had started this as a team, and we'd finish it as one, whether we finished it or not.

I offered Cat a slow shake of my head as my gut twisted into a knot. "We're sticking together."

He sighed. "It's your funeral." He walked around the firepit and was gone; he didn't even take the Tablets with him.

Andy broke the long, awkward silence that followed, saying Helina and Alvis were expecting us for dinner in a few cycles. With that said, we all silently agreed that what we wanted to do was rest. It had been a long day. We did that until it was time to head to the only other inhabited house in the city.

Once we arrived for dinner, Helina scolded Max and me for running off before hugging us each. That was the last anyone mentioned our running away. From there, the subject moved on to us staying in Glachalis for a while. The adults loved that as much as Andy and Jason did.

Max and I remained quiet.

Chapter 32
-Two Very Different Talks-

That night after dinner, we returned to our house with higher spirits than when we initially had left it. The dinner and company provided by our neighbors had helped us put the day's misadventure behind us. At least, that was what I thought as I went to sleep. As it turned out, the Stars had other plans. My dreams took me to a hazy room. I could swear I spied flashes of bookshelves, a bed, a map-covered table, and a large window overlooking a city through the murk. However, none of the images stayed long enough for me to study clearly and remained fuzzy at best.

What did stay was heat and a constant red glow that grew with each passing tick. Both intensified until a furious voice echoed from the darkness all around me. "How could you have found another Tablet?" the Maker fumed, and the air around me stirred. "I've spent lifetimes searching for those cursed relics, and now you have two?" His growl shook the ground. The wind increased to a full-blown storm and the temperature rose until sweat formed on my brow. I didn't miss the heat of the Erima.

Unlike our last encounter, I recognized this for what it was—a dream. "This isn't real!"

The wind calmed, but it just made the air unbreathable. "This may only be happening in your mind, but I can assure you it is very much real."

A beam of red light shined down on me. For just a tick, I hoped it would reveal some of my surroundings; however, nothing existed beyond the edges of the crimson glow.

"You have captured my attention, boy. Tell me, how is it you managed to find two Tablets?"

"Who said I did?" Only my friends, Cat, and I knew we had acquired the Tablets. There was no way the Maker could actually know about any of this.

"I can see them in your mind."

My heart stopped. I hoped he couldn't actually see in my head, then I remembered that was exactly where we were. Why couldn't I wake up?

"The first one is made of topaz and emits a golden light." He paused, then a small gasp escaped him. "Oh, that poor girl. Jenny was it? She didn't deserve to die, but Jones was never one for talking." He stopped for a tick, and memories swarmed around me.

Swords clashed through the dim light, their clangs sharp and painful in my ears. I flinched each time they met. Worst of all, I heard Jenny howl in agony once more. Blood oozed from the darkness and pooled at my feet. I screamed and fell back in terror. The crimson liquid splashed around me and soaked into my uniform.

"I warned you that you weren't ready for this. It's a shame you couldn't save her," the voice echoed, both around me and from within my head.

I brought my hands to my ears in a desperate attempt to block the sinister thoughts.

"Now you have blood on your hands, boy. Look what you've done trying to do a man's job. Only I can find all the Tablets. If I had been there, the girl would have lived."

Jenny's scream rang out again. No matter how hard I tried, I couldn't prevent the sound from reaching me. It echoed within my head. Tears stung at the corners of my eyes. I'd failed her. I could have saved her if I had just moved faster. "I'm sorry, Jenny," I said with a sob.

The Maker sneered, and the world around me rumbled, sending sickening ripples through the pool of thick red liquid. "The girl is dead because she had to depend on you instead of a real savior."

I wanted to ignore him, but I couldn't. He was right.

"I am destined to save Tehrahey. Only I can do this. Bring the Tablets to me in Entstal before any of your remaining friends suffer a similar fate."

The screams of Andy, Jason, and Max filled my head as the Maker's voice faded. The blood around me rose faster. I tried to stay above the rising liquid but soon found myself choking on it, all the while the screams continued.

I jolted awake and sat upright on my makeshift bed on the floor. No one else was up. The fire had simmered to a few coals and would be out soon. I rose to add another log. In the faint red glow, I glanced at my friends sleeping peacefully and found myself wishing Jenny were here with us. If only we could have kept our promise to help her get home.

As I placed the new log on the fire and returned to my bed, I imagined what things would've been like had our new friend lived.

The next few days passed at an agonizingly slow pace. Most of our time was spent helping Alvis and Helina with chores. In return, they taught us everything they knew and provided us with good food. Jason and Andy loved it. Even Max and I warmed up to our neighbors. According to my friends, this was what having a family felt like, and admittedly, it was nice. Knowing someone cared about us and worried over us was incredible. Yet, something didn't sit right with me.

At first, I figured it was the lack of sleep. Every night, the Maker tormented my dreams by reminding me of all my failures. He would even mention my mother and how she had abandoned me. Sleep became difficult, and so I took over the job of keeping the fire going all night. It meant less sleep, but I was okay with that. Jason didn't put up too much of a fight to give me the job.

With each passing day, my reflection looked more like Jason's. I frowned, grimaced, and watched our frozen new home with dark, baggy eyes. According to Max, I was no longer any fun. Meanwhile, my hair stuck out at whatever angle it wanted. One strand of black hair went this way, another went that way, and several other went whichever way they felt like going that day. Maybe that was why Jason kept his hair so short.

On the fourth day, Jason, Max, and Alvis went hunting; something I wanted no part of. Luckily, no one objected to my staying behind with Andy and Helina. The two fell into an easy routine of washing dishes and discussed what to make for lunch. I wanted to help but couldn't even find the energy to get off the floor. Neither said anything to me, but Andy did cast a worried glance in my direction. She kept asking if I was all right, and I always said yes.

Sitting by the fire, I began to doze. My head drooped forward as warmth washed over me. I don't think I was out long, but when I woke up, I was hot, sweaty, and in an underground room. Was I in Glachalis or the CTS? Did it make a difference? Both involved hiding in a hole in the ground.

I jumped to my feet and backed away from the fire while shedding my fur clothes. I tripped over them in the process, revealing the CTS uniform underneath. Had I ever really left? My panicked gaze darted around the room, only stopping once I found Andy. She stood next to Helina, and the two watched me with startled expressions.

Andy's cautious voice didn't help me calm down. "Are you okay?"

I couldn't do this anymore, sitting in a hole in the ground pretending everything would be all right when we knew that each day the world above us died a little more. We couldn't stay here forever. I wanted to leave to go find the last Tablet, but I couldn't do it on my own. Getting the last one proved I should not be the leader. I had made too many mistakes.

As I opened my mouth to answer Andy with some made up story—because I was too afraid to admit the truth to her—she interrupted me. "Are you about to lie to me again?"

My mouth snapped shut, and I shook my head. So, she hadn't believed me all those times. With a sigh, I started, "I can't sleep."

She rolled her eyes but stayed quiet.

"The Maker keeps telling me it's my fault Jenny died, and he's right. And how do I make up for that mistake? By practically leading Max and I to our deaths! My mother was right to give me up."

Helina remained motionless at the cabinets, studying me like I might turn into a sandstorm at any moment.

The thought that I might have revealed too much to her came to mind, but I didn't care. "My mother didn't care about me. She must've known I was a failure even back then."

"That's not true!" Andy looked ready to fight me on the matter.

"It isn't," Helina's soft voice echoed.

I wanted to believe her, but what other reason could there be for getting rid of me?

She must've noticed I didn't believe her, because she continued. "I don't know why your mother gave you up, but she didn't do it willingly."

I raised an eyebrow and prepared to tell her she didn't know that, but she didn't let me speak.

She pulled up a chair to join us at the fire and told us a story from when she had still worked in the CTS. A blackguard had taken her to the entrance where a woman wanted to place her infant into the CTS. Helina had reluctantly taken me from my mother and had done her best to take care of me those first few years when, try as I might, I could not remember. She said my mother had told her I liked singing, and so she would sing to me whenever I cried. For proof, she sang her familiar tune. "*Hush little one, dry your tears. I know you're scared. So am I. I don't know what I'm doing, but I will try to keep you safe, fed, and in my arms. Please stop crying, trust me. Whatever you need, I will provide. Just hear my voice and know you are loved.*"

As Helina sang, my body relaxed, and my frown gave way to a grin. The memory of the words to my song may have left me long ago, but I knew them as she sang. They came back to me like friends I hadn't seen in a long time. As she finished, a tear escaped down my cheek.

"That's the song." I stood there unable to move. I never expected anything like this; it seemed so unreal. I glanced at Andy, unsure of what had just happened.

Her eyes sparkled as she nodded at me. She had heard it too.

Facing forward, Helina held my gaze. She opened her arms, and I felt drawn forward. Her arms wrapped around me and I buried my face in her shoulder. For the first time in a very long time, I felt safe. I held onto her for all I was worth, and she didn't complain once.

With a deep breath, I unwound my arms from around her and backed away. She allowed me to step back a little but kept her hands on my arms as she looked into my eyes. "I'm won't leave you again. From now on, you'll always have me, do you understand?"

I wiped at my eyes as I nodded.

"You're stuck with me too, by the way," Andy added.

My chest swelled as I looked between them. It didn't matter if I wasn't the best at something, they still cared about me.

Helina released my shoulders as she stood. "You should get some rest."

"Wait! What did she look like?"

Helina didn't hesitate as she answered, like the memory was more recent than it actually was. "You have her eyes, the same incredibly deep shade of blue. However, your hair must come from your father because your mother's was white as snow. She was short, compared to me anyways," she said with a chuckle. "She wore a gray cloak over a sparkling white dress. Overall, she looked rather odd for Entstal. By the Stars, she wasn't even dirty!"

For the first time ever in my life, I could imagine my mother. I never thought that would be possible. I sniffled, and Andy placed a hand on my shoulder. "Thank you, Helina," I said after a moment. "I just wish we knew why she did what she did."

The adult grew thoughtful. "I don't know why your mother gave you up. Maybe she did it to protect you. I did everything I could to protect Kirsten. If it meant saving her, I would have even given her to the CTS." She shut her eyes tight and took a shaky breath. "Your life has been filled with challenges, but you are here. You are alive and are a lot stronger and smarter than you give yourself credit for. I see it."

"Me too," Andy added.

"You're doing fine, mistakes and all. Relax and get some sleep." She pointed to the bed in the corner.

I smirked at Andy as she mirrored the adult's gesture. There'd be no arguing this, and I really didn't want to, so I did as instructed. I fell asleep with a smile on my face.

Chapter 33
-It's All Right to Feel Lost-

2-12.11.12.17.15 T.S.T.
???
???

"Yaluk, how did everything go at the Rim?" A woman I didn't recognize asked. Bright green eyes shined from behind a few stray strands of black hair as she peered up from her work at the counter.

As I studied her, a name floated through my mind: Mali. His partner. She was alive! Based off the way the other person, Yaluk, reacted to her, this wasn't new. This particular memory must be before her death.

"Good," I said in a voice that wasn't mine but I recognized. This was another dream from him. "I found the hole and plugged it."

"Hopefully, this time it will last longer."

I—or Yaluk—hummed in agreement while sitting on the floor of a simple clay-brick hut. Exhaustion coursed through my—his—body, along with so many thoughts and emotions in a great, big sandstorm of confusion. I couldn't make much sense of any of it. A fire crackled and burned in a fireplace, staving off the darkness that tried to creep in through the windows. I didn't recognize any of this, but I didn't feel afraid. This was home, for Yaluk anyway. The fire offered warmth, while a cool night breeze drifted in one window and out another, keeping things pleasant.

The sweet scent of whatever meal Mali worked on made my mouth water and my stomach rumble. I wanted the dinner, even if it wasn't ready for me. His eyes closed, and he focused on the sounds of the fire, the rustling of leaves in the wind, and the steady movements of the woman behind him. I got the sensation that, for a moment, all was right in his world.

"What did you use?" she asked, genuinely curious.

Without opening his eyes, he answered, "Granite. Should hold for a few more centuries."

I wanted to know what it was they were talking about, but Yaluk wasn't sharing that particular bit of information. How kind. I guessed he didn't like to share things directly.

"Is there perhaps a better way to hold the water, other than building higher mounds of dirt?"

"Truthfully …" He opened his eyes and glanced over his shoulder.

She stopped and held his gaze with innocent curiosity.

"I don't know. I have no clue what I'm doing. Tehrahey was never my plan." He resumed watching the flames swirl up from the burning wood. "I'm sure the others had their plans for this world, but they never got the chance to share them with me."

Others? Did Yaluk mean he didn't create Tehrahey alone? Were there other Travelers with him? Could there be more than one Traveler at a time? As these new questions raced through my mind, he didn't answer any of them.

"They didn't put anything in the Book?"

My eyes darted to the spine of a brown leather book sitting flat on a shelf above the fire. *The Book of Time*! If only this wasn't a dream, I could just grab it and be done with the adventure.

"Nothing."

"What about other worlds?"

"Too risky. Tehrahey is not my home. If I were to leave, who knows when I would come back. By then, it may be too late." The sweet scent in the air became impossible to ignore any longer. He rose and faced Mali. "No, if there is an answer to saving Tehrahey, it will have to come from me."

After joining Mali at the counter, he helped her finish preparing our night's dinner. Apparently, Yaluk knew as much about cooking as I did.

She laughed as he stumbled through the preparations. "You may not know what you're doing, but you are trying."

A smile enveloped his face. "And that is what matters."

The hut and Mali faded into an all-too-familiar darkness as a single shaft of red light shone down from above. The final words of Yaluk and Mali's conversation repeated through my mind. Yaluk had no idea what he was doing back then, but he kept trying to keep Tehrahey going as long as he could. He was more like me than I realized.

The Maker's calm yet terrifying voice echoed from the darkness. "Getting tired already? Bring me the Tablets and I will let you sleep again. Unless, of course, you prefer to continually relive your failures, like me."

On cue, the swords dueled once again. The clanging of metal was just as painful as I remembered it. They ended with Jenny's scream, and blood pooled around me. I hated every bit of this, and it made me shake to my core.

"It's a shame you couldn't save her," the voice echoed. "If I had been there, the girl would have lived."

Jenny's scream rang out once again. No matter how hard I tried, I couldn't prevent the sound from getting to me. The sound echoed within my head. I couldn't stand to hear it anymore, yet it lingered. I hoped for a day when her memory wouldn't haunt me, but that day felt very far away.

The image of kneeling before Mali's body flashed through my mind. The red light around me flickered for a moment. Yaluk had shown me that during my first sleep after Jenny's death. He wanted to help, not to find the Tablets or the Book, but to move on from the guilt. He had mentioned blaming himself for his partner's death and having to admit it wasn't his fault. Perhaps that was true for Jenny too?

As the thought crossed my mind, the clanging of the swords weakened to little more than a whisper.

Jones had killed Jenny. Not me.

Her scream faded.

I had done what I could to help her. Maybe Jenny was in a better place, one far away from Tehrahey and with her father. I smiled as I imagined the two of them sailing on a ship over blue waters, a cool ocean breeze running through her hair. She smiled and waved at me. I waved back.

"What are you doing?" the Maker shouted, shattering the vision. He was responsible for her death.

I growled. "You sent Jones after the Tablet."

"Now, now. There's no need to get upset. I did no such thing."

The puddle of blood around me shrank. "You're lying. Jones said the Maker promised him gold for the Tablet. Jenny's death is on you, not me."

"There have been many Makers over the millennia. The Maker you are angry with no longer exists."

"Not according to Amyntor. You've failed to save Tehrahey, Roger, and because of that, we have to struggle to survive." I took a deep breath.

The red light intensified and the air around me stirred anew. "So, that is how you've done so well! Where is he?"

I ignored the wind. This wasn't real; it was all in my head. With that thought, the wind vanished, and the air became more bearable. "I won't listen to your lies and manipulation anymore."

A growl echoed out, but nothing stirred, which only seemed to anger the Maker further. He was no longer in control here. Even his crimson light flickered. "You'll regret that. Relyt is coming, and I'm the only one who can save you or your friends. Give me the Tablets, and I may still spare you."

Was that a threat? It felt like one. He wanted me to hand over the most important relics in history, or he would let us die. A sandstorm brewed in my stomach. That was the last grain of sand. No one threatened my friends like that. Not bullies in the CTS, nor him. My friends were all I had. I had failed to act fast enough to save Jenny. I promised I wouldn't do that again. That meant I couldn't hide from the Maker. If I wanted to keep my friends safe, I couldn't hide underground. I needed to finish our quest and get the last Tablet.

"I will do whatever it takes to protect them, especially from people like you. You will never get the Tablets from me."

A tick later, something flashed across my vision. Two people stood atop a tall tower encased in darkness.

"Amyntor didn't kill your mother. You know he did everything he could to help us," one said carefully.

The second shouted at the first. I couldn't decipher the words, but the tone spoke volumes, and I recognized the voice as the Maker's. Once he stopped spewing harsh words, the first man offered garbled apologies. The two remained still for a moment.

"You speak with him, and suddenly, you don't want to help anymore?" the Maker muttered; his voice sounded broken and so unlike I'd ever heard it. "I never expected you to betray me."

A sandstorm burst to life over the top of the tower. It came without warning and caught them both off guard. I had witnessed enough storms from beneath the Erima to know that was not natural and remembered what Amyntor had said about the Maker needing to be careful with his powers or he'd destroy something.

The two men struggled to stay on their feet. The other man backed up, trying to get away from the Roger, and fell from the tower.

A cry of anguish rang through the darkness. "Samuel!"

The light surrounding me shimmered and disappeared as the Maker howled in pain. The sound quickly vanished as the darkness swarmed around me once more.

Chapter 34
-There's Only One Left-

2-12.11.12.17.15 T.S.T.
Glachalis
Tehrahey

I shot up in bed, startling everyone else in the room. Max sat by the fire while Alvis's and Jason's voices drifted down from the shack above. They said they wouldn't be back until well after lunch. I'd been asleep for several cycles.

My gaze landed on Andy, who had probably been in the process of helping Helina finish lunch. My eyes met her emerald-colored ones. They went from startled by my sudden movement to sad. We needed to leave, and I think she knew that. She nodded, then raised a single finger as she glanced at Helina. She wanted a little more time. I figured we could give her until the end of the day.

I rose from the bed and stretched, feeling more refreshed than I had in days. I moved to join Max, and, as I made myself comfortable next to him, he leaned over and asked, "What's the plan?"

I looked at him shocked for a moment. "I'm piecing it together. You in?"

His brown eyes offered a look that said, *You have to ask?*

Two down, one to go. Jason's voice intermittently drifted down from the hole in the ceiling above the fire along with Alvis's. I must've been staring up there for a while, because Max elbowed my side. "He'll be tough, but I have an idea. Let's wait until after dinner."

I didn't know how to feel about Max having a plan, but I did like his idea of waiting until after our friend had a full stomach. Hopefully then, he'd be in a more agreeable mood. So that's what we did. We spent the rest of the evening with Alvis and Helina. We ate dinner, laughed at jokes and old stories, and had a good time.

I tried to enjoy myself, but I couldn't stop worrying. I didn't know what scared me more, the thought of trying to convince Jason or heading to our next destination, wherever that was, and angering the Maker even more.

Once we cleaned up after the meal, we headed back to our house.

As Jason stoked up the fire, I stood behind him, though well out of striking distance. "Jason," I started, "we have to find the last Tablet."

He stood and faced me. "We decided we were done."

"You did, but I didn't. We can't let our fear hold us back from trying."

Jason's chest puffed out as he tried to make himself even taller than me. "We don't know what we're doing."

I shrugged. "Neither did Yaluk." I told them about my dream and how not even Yaluk, a Traveler, knew what he was doing, but he kept trying anyway.

If there had been any doubt that Andy would follow me, this new information changed that. Determination filled her eyes.

Still, Jason looked unconvinced, and he refused to hold anyone's gaze. I studied him, looking passed the anger and exhaustion in his eyes. Deep beneath all that, was fear. It had been hiding there all this time. I searched my memories and saw fear in every single one of his looks. Even when he laughed, he felt afraid. My gaze drifted down, just a little, to the dark spots under his eyes. They were like mine, caused by never-ending nightmares that refused to give me even a tick of peaceful rest.

The world came crashing down around me as everything fell into place. Every time we slept, Jason would toss and turn and would be the first to wake. I assumed the heat caused his discomfort, or that he was just being a leader, but it was something so much worse. He would get angry with adults so easily, because they had taken something from him, something Alvis almost replaced. No wonder he hated the idea of leaving.

Jason was strong. We all said it and believed it with every fiber of our beings, but he didn't. How could he? The one moment he needed his strength most, the moment his father needed *his* help, he could do nothing but watch. He witnessed his father's murder, and I could see in his eyes that he saw it every single night.

A deep breath shook my body, rattling my very core, as I stared at my friend in a new light. I saw in him the same scared kid that hid inside all of us. While ours would all sneak out from time to time, he never let his show, because he had to be strong. And he was tired of being strong.

He needed someone else to take on that role, and while in the past I wouldn't have chosen myself, deep down, I knew it had to be me. Going after the last Tablet was my idea. I would be the leader for this part of the journey, which meant, whatever happened, it would be because of me. Keeping everyone safe had to be my top priority.

In a steady voice that surprised myself, I did my best to comfort my friend. "Jason, we won't lose anyone else. I promise."

With a shake of his head, he whispered, "You can't guarantee that."

"Maybe, but know I'll be doing everything I can to keep you all safe. You can count on me."

He looked like he might argue, but Max intervened and revealed his plan. "Jenny died for this, Jason."

Our sneaky, young friend had a point. A very good one. Jenny had died helping us get the Tablet of the Present. If we didn't find the last one, then she had died for nothing.

Jason's final reserves crumbled. "Alright, we'll go."

"Where are we going?" Max asked.

Andy grabbed our bag off the table and pulled her charm from it. "The last Tablet is in Ozmerald. It has to be."

I'd never heard of the place, and when she explained it was a temple built by the first Traveler, Yaluk, and covered in crystals just outside of Entstal, I wondered why. The CTS should have taught us about something built by a Traveler, especially something so close to us. We came from the CTS in Entstal, and now we'd be heading back.

According to Andy, Ozmerald held the only Tablet the Maker knew of. When asked how she knew this, she responded with the obvious answer. "I read it a long time ago. I tried to reread it recently, but someone had removed it from the CTS library."

With all the time she spent reading, she had probably reread the whole library a few times over. If anyone were to notice a missing book, it would be her.

"Roger probably removed it," Cat commented as he bounded down the stairs.

We watched him, not entirely surprised by his sudden appearance.

The gaze from his pale eyes landed on me. "Finally come to your senses?"

"We're going to Ozmerald to get the last Tablet."

I expected him to be surprised to know where we were going. However, he didn't let me have that satisfaction. "I figured as much. Anything else?"

"We need to be back by morning," Andy added. "I don't want Alvis and Helina to worry."

I agreed. "We get the Tablet and can keep it away from the Maker by bringing it to Glachalis."

"That's what you call a plan?" Cat asked in his usual, unimpressed fashion. Could anything impress him?

"It's the best we can do with what we've got," I answered. That was the truth. We'd figure things out as we went. It was what we'd been doing since we had left the CTS, and that's how Yaluk had taken care of Tehrahey for all of those years. Why couldn't it work for us?

"Besides, we don't have time to plan," Andy interrupted. "Ozmerald's gate opens with the moon. If we want to beat the Maker to the Tablet, we need to leave now."

With that, we discarded our fur clothes. With Entstal and Ozmerald being in the Erima, we wouldn't need the extra warmth. While we ate most of our meals with Alvis and Helina, they insisted we store some food in our own house. So, we packed some in our bag just in case we didn't make it back before morning. I refused to get stuck anywhere without supplies again. Once we were ready, Cat Traveled us from Glachalis and onto the next leg of our journey.

Chapter 35
-Playing Nice, For Now-

2-12.11.12.17.15 T.S.T.
Ozmerald, Entstal
Tehrahey

Max and Jason went first, followed by Andy and me. The shock from the jump in temperature helped distract from the churning in my stomach caused by the strange sensation of Traveling. Would I ever get used to it? Did Cat feel nauseated after Traveling too? He only ever looked tired.

Cat jumped from Andy's hands and nearly disappeared into the surrounding darkness. I had to strain to see my friends and couldn't see anything of our guide except for his ice-blue eyes glowing in the crescent moon's faint light. A moment later, flickering light spilled out around us as Andy removed the candle from Amyntor's bag. With this new light, our surroundings were made clear.

We stood on a sandstone platform before a large stone gate. In the center of the platform, the builders had carved an intricate sun. Four large points were at the top, bottom, and sides of the circle. Between each of those were four smaller points, and between every point a broken ray shot out. Within the circle, chaotic lines bent and swirled around one another in a never-ending pattern. Though they were carved in stone, the lines almost seemed to move. They stretched out and wove through each other, then snapped back into place.

The gate and the towers that stood aside it were taller than those at Time's Keep. They looked like they touched the sky. After the towers, the walls of Ozmerald curved out into the desert to encircle the whole structure.

Having never seen anything close to this size of building, Max marveled at the walls. "This temple is huge."

Cat remained unimpressed. "Those are only the outer walls."

I looked to him for guidance, but he kept his gaze fixated on the Erima behind us and the flickering lights in the distance. The sight of Entstal caused a lump in my throat. I didn't want to be this close to that city and the CTS ever again.

Cat's ears twitched, and he darted off, vanishing into the shadows.

Before I could ask what he was doing, an all-too-familiar voice greeted us. "Well, it certainly took you long enough to get here." He held his head high as he stepped from the darkness and into our small circle of light. His ornate red robe felt out of place here in the Erima, but he didn't seem to care.

My blood ran cold; Cat had abandoned us. I wished we'd had some time to make a plan. My friends and I retreated into a small huddle in the presence of the self-proclaimed ruler of Tehrahey. Andy stood behind me, her free hand latched onto my arm. Max stood beside her, and Jason stood behind them. For just a moment, I thought we might be able to handle him on his own, but then two more people joined him.

First came Cylus in his all-black outfit. He held a knife in one hand with several more strapped to his waist. His other hand held the end of a rope. Behind him came Mr. Ethan, led by the rope with his hands bound together.

I didn't miss the low growl from Jason when the pair appeared and wasn't sure who it was directed at.

When our teacher saw us, he grew ecstatic. "You came to save me!"

Everyone ignored the absurd thought except for Cylus, who yanked on the rope, pulling the prisoner to his knees.

The Maker's lip curled as he regarded us. "You are the four who've stolen my Tablets?"

I met the man's gaze and held it as best as I could. "They aren't your Tablets."

"Didn't see your name on them," Max said with a laugh. I didn't know if this was the best time to be upsetting the Maker, but it felt nice to know they were still there.

Cat's voice spoke from somewhere behind me. "Leave the kids alone."

The adults glanced past us to the gate.

I chanced a look for just a tick and saw Cat's eyes staring from the darkness. He hadn't abandoned us; he just wanted the shadows to try and scare off the adults. The candlelight reflecting in his eyes, combined with the fact they were cat eyes, gave them a sinister, monstrous appearance.

Cylus reacted first by throwing a knife at the shadowy creature. If our guide had been human, the attack probably would have hit square in the chest; however, it just clattered harmlessly into the shadows. Cat didn't even blink. The three adults wore shocked expressions. Mr. Ethan even backed up until the rope pulled tight.

The Maker watched the eyes warily. "You have a monster with you. Explains how you've been so lucky."

Knowing Cat still had our back and that the adults were afraid of him gave me the courage to speak up. "He's our guide, and we're getting that last Tablet."

"And how could you possibly hope to achieve that?"

"We already got two." I intended to stop there, but the Max in me gave me one last taunt. "Last I checked, that's more than you have."

The Maker's jaw clenched. "I warned you about getting in my way. I warned you that you would get hurt. Your friend died, and now I'll have to kill you too."

"No, you can't!" Andy released my arm and held the bag above her head. "This bag is from Amyntor. It's enchanted, and only we can remove stuff from it. You kill us, and our two Tablets are lost forever."

It was a lie, a brilliant one, but a lie all the same. The bag would work for anyone, but the Maker didn't know that. So long as he thought he needed us to get the Tablets, he couldn't kill us.

The Maker let out a long, slow breath. "Then perhaps we can come to an agreement."

Jason snorted. "Unlikely."

Our enemy frowned at us, and he seemed to strain to keep his voice under control. "I will not let you insolent little brats have my Tablets." A breeze picked up, kicking sand into the air. His shoulders were rigid as his hands opened and closed into fists.

We were angering him, and far too quickly for my liking. If we upset him too much, too soon, it wouldn't end well for us. It wasn't the time to fight.

I stepped forward with hands raised. "We don't need to fight. We're all trying to save Tehrahey, right?" Didn't he want that? If we could work together, we might be able to fix things.

The Maker's body relaxed as he studied me. "At least one of you can see sense. We all seek the same prize."

I didn't believe him for a second. According to Andy, he had known this Tablet was here, and yet, word never got out. I couldn't trust him, but the way I saw it, we weren't getting into the temple without him leaving us alone. If that were the case, the best thing to do would be to keep him were we could see him. I didn't want to leave him here just so he could show up when we had the Tablet in our grasp. I made that mistake with Jones; I wouldn't make it again.

"We'll work together to get the Tablet," I stated.

Cries of disagreement erupted from my friends, and I silenced them with a look. I wanted them to know I hated this as much as they did, but we didn't have a choice. I met each of my friends' gazes, hoping they understood.

The Maker remained silent for a long moment. "Very well."

Cat spoke from the shadows, his voice low and not leaving any room for arguing. "The kids will go first. You will remain several paces behind."

"Fine." The word was forced through gritted teeth.

"Good," Cat purred. "Let's get started then, and remember, Roger, even when you can't see me, I'm watching you." Cat's eyes disappeared into the darkness.

I trusted that he was close by but liked it better when we could see him. I kept searching the shadows for any sight of him.

We started toward the gate with Andy and Max in the lead while Jason and I brought up the rear. As we crossed the threshold of the gate, Max tripped and fell, startling the rest of us. That never happened to him.

Andy helped him to his feet as fast as possible.

"I'm fine," he said, shrugging her off and moving to swap places with me. "I'll keep an eye on them," he whispered, indicating the adults who were starting to follow us. "You two think of something."

Andy and I put our heads together and kept our voices low as we tried to concoct an escape from this, because my plan of get the Tablet and get away was not good enough. We needed more, but our options were limited. We didn't know what we were walking into and had no idea what we faced with the adults. In the end, after a lot of arguing, we settled on an escape plan for Andy. Since she had the bag and the Tablets, she needed to keep away from the adults. If we got the other Tablet, I would get it to her somehow. If the Maker tried anything, she needed to find Cat and Travel back to Glachalis. We trusted that Cat heard the plan or would know to act if the time came. The rest of us would stall the adults.

The interior grounds encircled by the wall differed from the Erima outside. Beyond the wall, only sand existed. Inside, numerous sharp, jagged rocks rested on solid ground. The small light of our candle created long, frightening shadows that moved with each step Andy took. The rocks themselves looked sharp enough to cut anything they touched.

"Why is it so different inside the wall?" I asked.

Cat answered from somewhere close by, which helped calm my nerves even more. "It's the Tablet of the Future enchanting the land around the temple to represent the future of Tehrahey."

"What do the rocks mean?" I asked. Rocks were strong and dependable; could this landscape be a good thing? The unease churning in my stomach I got when looking at them, told me otherwise.

Cat confirmed my fears. "Nothing good. This place was green and alive the last time Amyntor visited. I wonder why that changed. Any ideas, Roger?" He said the last bit loud enough for the other group to hear.

The adults did not reply, and Cat's chuckle faded into the shadows.

Andy chewed her lip and occasionally glanced back to the adults. After a while, Andy passed the candle to me and shifted the bag on her shoulder so it rested against her stomach.

"What are you doing?" I asked.

"I want to try something." She removed just the top portion of the Tablet of the Past from the bag and kept it close to her chest where the adults wouldn't see.

For a tick, I thought she had lost her mind. When the feelings from the past surfaced in my mind, I understood her plan. The Tablet would affect everyone, even the Maker.

Cat's voice whispered close by from the shadows to our left, "Let it be known that I hate your plan." He didn't try to stop us, so we went ahead with it.

We waited a few ticks, letting the relic work its magic.

Andy looked over her shoulder at the adults and broke the silence. "Why did you hide the locations of the Tablets from people?"

While I knew the Tablet might make him more open to sharing his past, a part of me didn't expect it to work. He was probably too far away.

In the flickering light, I watched him consider Andy for a moment, then he answered, "I can't trust anyone. You have to do something yourself if you want it done right. Jones's failure proves that."

"That's why you need friends," Andy countered. "Maybe if you were a little nicer to people …"

"I've been on both sides, and everyone will betray you in the end," His voice lowered as he continued, "Even if they didn't mean to."

"Is that why you turned on Amyntor?" I asked.

The Maker remained silent for a tick. I figured I'd pushed too far and he'd stay quiet. "He failed us. He had three thousand years to fix Tehrahey and heal the Erima, but he didn't. Do you know how many lives could have been saved if not for his slow response?"

I scoffed. Did he really want to make that claim, considering how he governed Tehrahey? "How many have died during your rule?"

"I am well aware of how my people are suffering! But it was all necessary to ensure I could save them."

So far so good. We were getting information, but none of it seemed helpful. "Is Samuel still alive? I heard you talking to him."

"So you did see that." The Maker looked away. "He turned on me, so he had to go. It's better this way."

I remembered the panic on the Maker's face when it had happened, heard his scream. "It looked like an accident."

"You're a child. I wouldn't expect you to understand." He refused to talk anymore, so Andy let the Tablet slide back into the bag, and we proceeded in silence.

Chapter 36
-The Home of Tehrahey's Future-

2-12.11.12.17.15 T.S.T.
Ozmerald, Entstal
Tehrahey

After less than half a cycle, the path led around a bend, and stone steps climbed a jagged cliff face to Ozmerald. The temple loomed over us as we ascended the stairs. Once at the top, we found ourselves in a courtyard illuminated by pale blue flames bursting to life atop wooden poles. I practically jumped out of my skin at the sudden ignition. I wasn't the only one; Andy's hands latched onto my arm, and Max yelped.

On either side of the stairs, carved stone railings curved toward the temple, forming a half circle. The railings stopped at two large square towers that framed the courtyard on either side. Directly across from the top of the stairs, at the far end of the courtyard from us, rested the Temple entrance. A set of giant wooden doors, rounded at the tops to form an arch, stood between us and the inside. Above them resided a sun-shaped red window that resembled the one at the gate. Another larger carved sun rested in the center of this courtyard.

This place didn't feel right. The blue firelight gave the entire area an eerie feel. The light danced around us and caused shadows to waver. The tower walls sparkled as light bounced off the thousands of crystals embedded in the stone. At first, I thought the jewels were simply reflecting the light from the burning torches, but while studying them, I noticed the building glowed. Even in the darkness of night, I could clearly see that the tops of the towers shared the same color as Cat's eyes.

I tried to determine the source of the dark energy radiating from this place while we crept across the courtyard. Spotting Cat took a tick, but I managed to find his pale eyes watching from across the courtyard in the shadows by the door. I took a deep breath and hurried to join our guide.

As we passed the first set of fires, I noted nothing contained the flames. They simply burned freely atop large wooden posts. Approaching the second set, I noticed they were not posts at all; they were tree trunks. Each tree resided in a circular opening of dirt within the pavement. I could see the tops of their roots digging into the ground beneath them. I thought this would be comforting.

It wasn't.

What kind of person would decide to set trees on fire as a source of light? They were probably cruel, like Ms. Hess. A chill ran down my spine as a worse thought entered my mind. The lands around Ozmerald represented Tehrahey's future. Did that include these trees? Could the flames represent the approach of Relyt? Would Tehrahey burn in fire after all?

The temple doors were set into the wall, with a column carved into the stonework on either side. Intricate metal swirls branched out from the hinges and decorated the wood. A large, black metal ring hung halfway up each one just above my head.

Cat eyed me expectantly. "Open them. They can't see me. If they figure out I'm a cat, you're in trouble."

I grabbed the cool, dark metal. It resisted for just a moment before swinging outward. More blue light flickered from within.

Cat darted inside before the adults ascended the top steps.

The Maker stopped, and so did his followers. "This isn't right." His head swept back and forth, scanning the temple for something. After a while, his gaze fixed onto the four of us. "What have you done to this place?"

Cat groaned and rolled his eyes. "Ozmerald is a temple dedicated to Travelers and builds itself to suit the ideas of the Traveler currently in it!"

With caution, The Maker and his companions crossed the courtyard. "You're a Traveler?"

Cat ignored the question. "You first came here with Amyntor, so I take it you're used to something a little more Greek with golden flames? I always preferred a French gothic look myself."

The wind outside blustered and sent dust flying in rapidly changing directions as the four of us stepped inside. Blue flames glowed inside half crystal bowls mounted on the walls around us. The eerie shadows from outside were just as prominent in this rectangular room, about half the size of the CTS mess hall. Across from us stood an identical doorway that led farther inside. To our right and left, on the shorter sides of the room, stood smaller, much less intimidating doors. The same pale blue covered every surface in the room except for the wooden barriers blocking each passageway and the ground upon which we stood. It almost felt like being back in the ice valley but warmer and with more room.

My friends observed their surroundings with caution. Jason spied each entryway, probably waiting for someone to walk through them. Max watched the flames for a moment before wringing his hands together and eying the escape route behind us—if it could be called that with the adults creeping closer.

Cat headed straight for the doors opposite us, and Andy rushed to open them. As another larger but just as dark room was revealed, a horrible scent greeted us. Andy waved her hand in front of her face before clamping it over her mouth and using her thumb and pointer finger to squeeze her nose.

Max gagged and hunched over.

I mimicked Andy's action while Jason turned his head away.

"Hurray," Cat said but did not sound excited at all.

Andy's hand muffled her next words. "What is that?"

Cat answered with a single word, one I didn't want to hear. "Death."

Our group exchanged concerned glances before following him inside. We didn't like where this was going, but we couldn't turn back.

Colored flames burned atop carved crystal pillars on either side of the doors. Two more pillars ignited farther inside, then two more, and then more. Each set of braziers revealed a central aisle bordered by row after row of benches, all facing something hiding in the shadows ahead of us and the occasional great stone column that reached high to hold the vaulted ceiling far overhead.

The shadows that called this room home cowered along the sides, away from the light. There they seemed darker. The light didn't make the room feel much better than the shadows. All the crystals within the temple reflected the icy firelight in strange shapes. The patterns danced around the enormous room, making the building look alive. These did not feel like the warm, comforting orange flame burning on our candle.

At the very back of the room, crimson flames ignited atop a black shrine. Sitting upon a pedestal rested a red Tablet—the Tablet of the

Future. It didn't glow like the first two had, instead, it seemed to consume the light cast by the flames.

Cat studied the temple for a tick then flicked his tail. "That's not so bad." His voice bounced around the room for a moment before vanishing into nothingness.

He pointed with his tail down the main aisle before darting to the side to be with the shadows.

Our footsteps echoed through the emptiness and mingled with the sounds of the crackling light sources. I'd never seen a bigger room before. There were easily enough seats for every kid in the CTS, and probably most of Entstal too. As we walked, I remembered the first time I had explored the CTS. Everything had felt so big and strange, and I had no idea what laid around each corner. I hated it.

The Maker strode into the temple with a steady gait. The scent of death halted him for a moment before they kept marching on as Mr. Ethan retched behind them. The Maker's head swiveled around. "Where has your guide gone?"

"I'm still here, Roger," Cat said with a chuckle. His voice bounced around the room, making it difficult to tell where exactly it came from.

"Stop calling me that!"

The wind outside howled and lashed against the windows high on the walls.

Cylus gave his boss a wary look, and I wondered how much he knew about the man he worked for. From what I could tell, Cylus was the Maker's right-hand man. Did that mean he knew how old his ruler really was, or what he had done in the past? Or was he left in the dark like everyone else? How much of our earlier conversation had he understood?

The benches stopped near the front of the room, and an empty space rested between us and the shrine. Another sun was carved into the ground in the middle of the gap here with ancient Tehraheyian written within it.

Andy grabbed my shoulder and prevented me from going any farther. "Wait," she said.

We watched as she leaned forward to examine the writing.

"What does it say?" I asked.

"I can answer that," the Maker said. He and the others stopped a few benches back. They were still keeping their distance, but they were also closer than I was comfortable with. "Hidden in time three tablets are. One within the flow of life, protected by Death. The Island, obviously." He smirked. "Another left forgotten in isolation and fiercely guarded. Where was that one, by the way?"

For a tick, I thought I wouldn't tell him. Then I decided that sharing the information might put him in a better mood, which would be good for us. "In Glachalis, guarded by Living Snow."

He cupped an elbow with one hand and used his other to tap against his lips. "So those monsters were real. I suppose that explains why that city is so dangerous." His face grew serious. "I should have known." He cleared his throat. "The Final, for the world to see"—he gestured with his hands at the altar—"found by the old, claimed for the young."

What did the last part mean? The Maker found it, and we were here to get it, and we were younger than him. Did that mean the Stars were on our side? I hoped so.

"Reunite them in order, and *The Book of Time* shall be your reward, Destiny's son." He stopped to study us. "There's something else. From this point on, only one can proceed, or all will die."

I glanced from him to the altar in the background. The top step was just above my head. The shrine loomed over us like Ms. Hess. A wide mix of terrifying emotions flowed from it. Anger, fear, and sadness all flooded from the object and seemed to pool in my gut. The dark object with its single glaring red Tablet eye watched us, awaiting our next move.

Chapter 37
-Twenty-One-

2-12.11.12.17.15 T.S.T.
Ozmerald, Entstal
Tehrahey

The Maker stepped forward. "Those steps are cursed. No one has been able to touch the Tablet of the Future." He studied the altar. "Nothing I've done has worked."

The four of us stood in silence, our eyes stuck on the Maker. How could we get to the Tablet if the stairs were cursed?

Jason broke the silence that had fallen over our group. "Now what?"

"This is where it pays to come prepared. Step aside, sand rats." He made a shooing motion with his hands before turning to his guard. "Cylus, release the prisoner."

Cylus marched forward.

The four of us moved down the row of benches to avoid him, with Andy in the lead.

Shock crossed Mr. Ethan's face, when for a brief tick, he thought he was being set free. As he was dragged forward and he realized what his release really meant, our old teacher panicked. "No! It was an accident!" He shouted anything he could think of to change the Maker's mind. The pleas echoed through the large room.

Andy covered her ears and lowered her head.

Max scanned the room as Jason kept his gaze locked onto Cylus, and I could see the hatred burning in his eyes.

I did my best to keep an eye on the Maker.

The Maker didn't seem to be bothered by the display at all. In fact, the way the corner of his mouth twitched, I think he enjoyed it. As Cylus unbound the teacher, the Maker spoke in a cold voice. "You insulted me. Either Cylus kills you now, or you climb those steps."

Mr. Ethan looked from the Maker to Cylus to the steps. He ran his hands through his thin hair, pulling out some more in the process. His whole body sagged as he took that first step toward the Tablet. As he stepped over the carving of the sun, the lines glowed red. Tendrils of light rose from the stonework and snaked around his feet, but he either didn't notice or didn't care. He kept walking, and as he placed his foot on the first step, darkness swarmed in around him and enveloped the entire altar.

I couldn't see anything other than an occasional bright flash of red light. For several agonizingly long ticks, we could do nothing but wait. After one more flash, the darkness retreated to the shadows as quickly as it had arrived.

On the steps lay a body. It had to be Mr. Ethan, but it didn't look like him. His thin brown hair had turned white and was longer than it had been before. His limbs looked scrawnier than usual. What had happened to him?

Andy gasped and turned away.

The Maker showed no traces of sympathy or remorse as he studied the body. "What a disappointment." Then his gray eyes focused on us. "That is what happens to people who get in my way."

I had dealt with enough bullies in the CTS to recognize the threat in his words. He had no intention of letting us out of here, which didn't surprise me. It just meant we really needed to have an escape plan.

"It's your turn, Tablet Collectors." The Maker gave a small bow in our direction, and when he rose, his eyes narrowed.

I felt a bit of pride at how much he hated us for doing a better job of getting the Tablets. I glanced at Andy to see she wore the same worried expression as me. We needed to think of something, and Max's strategy of running seemed to be our best option. With my eyes, I gestured to Max and then to the shadows where Cat hid.

She thought for a moment then gave a subtle nod.

I took a deep breath and stood up straighter. "I'll try."

Andy's mouth formed a thin line, and her eyes shimmered, but she stayed quiet.

I shouldered past Max and whispered in his ear, "If things go wrong, do what you do best."

He frowned but nodded.

Jason and I locked gazes for a moment; I could see him deciding if he agreed with this. I tried to give him a look that said this wasn't up for debate. It must've worked, because he didn't argue. He just offered some words of caution. "Be careful."

I stepped toward the shrine. "I'll do my best." I ignored the smirk from the Maker and his bodyguard as they watched me from down the aisle. When I stepped over the carving of the sun, the lines glowed red again as the tendrils rose to weave around my feet. The lights circled around me and continued their mesmerizing dance across the floor.

When they showed no signs of hurting me or vanishing, I proceeded toward the altar with a gulp. I would be on my own this time. I didn't feel confident like I thought a leader should. The last two, I had help getting. Sure, all I had to do was climb some stairs this time, which seemed easy, but I knew something more accompanied this Tablet—something sinister.

Once my foot touched the altar's first step, the room darkened. I couldn't see anything beyond the steps and the Tablet of the Future. The same blue crystals that comprised the temple created the shrine as well, but little light illuminated them, making them appear black in comparison. I could just decipher my distorted reflection in each of the gems. Hundreds of little Kyles stared back at me with nervous faces.

With a deep breath, I climbed the first step. It was small, nothing too scary. The Tablet flashed red, startling me and illuminating the ground beneath the shrine for a tick. I gave the floor a second look, but darkness covered it once more. I thought I saw bones down there. I took another step and watched the ground. The Tablet flashed again. There were bones!

I froze. How many people had the Maker sent up here? My breath came in shallow gulps, and I struggled to return it to normal. They were just bones. They were dead. They couldn't harm me; whatever had killed them, that could get me, but the bones couldn't.

I hesitated before taking my next step; something felt off. Something had changed. I climbed two more steps, and the Tablet flashed with each one. The ground was farther from me than usual. I'd grown taller. Another step and another flash. I stepped again. My distorted reflections were definitely taller. What was this Tablet doing to me?

I climbed three more steps.

A strand of hair tickled my nose, and I brushed it out of my eyes, thinking nothing of it. A few more steps and my foot bumped against a black mass on the step. My heart stopped at the sight of Mr. Ethan. Shadows obscured his body, but when I focused, I could discern his silhouette. His left leg, arm, and head rested on the steps. His other side hung over the edge and dangled into the pile below. I took several breaths to try and calm myself down. It helped, kind of.

I climbed a little farther, avoiding the body with care. In my reflections, my hair lightened and dangled in front of my face. The bodies at the base of the stairs—the more recent ones—they all had long gray hair and wrinkled skin. None of them had been young when they died, though they might have started out that way.

That's when I understood; each flash of the Tablet of the Future made me older. I had to get out of here. I stepped back down. I needed to talk to the others, to figure out a better way to get to the top. The Tablet flashed again, and a few more hairs grayed in front of my eyes. I froze as panic gripped me. I couldn't go back. Turning around didn't help; my entire surroundings were comprised of inky darkness. I could see nothing but the altar and the red Tablet eye glaring at me.

I looked up to the Tablet. Almost there, eight steps to go. Thirteen steps were behind me. I didn't know if I could survive thirteen more flashes, let alone eight, but I knew which way offered more hope. I could make eight more steps. Maybe.

"Stars, watch over me."

I took another step. I had to get to the Tablet before I ended up like those at the bottom. The people who lay there had all tried and failed. That didn't give me much confidence.

Seven.

Six. Each step seemed higher, seemed harder. My breath grew ragged.

Five.

Four. My legs shook and threatened to collapse. My mind said I wouldn't make it. I ignored it and kept going.

Three.

Two. I fell to my knees. I struggled to breathe. No matter how hard I tried, I couldn't catch my breath. My body ached and shook. It wanted to stop and give in to the surrounding darkness.

My friends needed me. I needed to keep going.

I crawled up the next step. One.

My hands were wrinkled and shook violently. The unrecognizable face of a wrinkled old man stared back at me from the gems. That couldn't be me, could it?

With quivering arms and legs, I crawled to the top of the platform. The Tablet flashed once more. It felt like someone stole the air from my lungs then sat on my chest for good measure. I couldn't breathe. I reached for the pedestal where the Tablet rested, barely able to maintain my balance on three limbs. My hands shook. My legs ached. I couldn't breathe.

I stretched for all I was worth, wiggling my fingers, hoping to find the smooth crystal surface.

The Tablet of the Future flashed red.

2-12.11.12.17.15 T.S.T.
???
???

Reaching for the Tablet atop the shrine in Ozmerald was the last thing I remembered. Yet, I definitely wasn't in the Traveler's temple anymore. I found myself at K'aktun, the beach where we had discovered the Island, but that couldn't be right. Maybe I had Traveled here, but I didn't remember any sort of experience like that. By this point, I knew what it felt like to Travel. There was no pulling of the stomach through a long, seemingly never-ending tunnel. There was no slight feeling of nausea. It couldn't have been that.

By the Stars, could this be a dream? That seemed more likely. With that in mind, I examined this false landscape. A rugged, brown stone cliff fell below me and overlooked the ocean. The waters tossed and rolled in a much more violent manner than what I had witnessed here while awake. The waves surged up the beach and crashed against the stone cliffs, all but washing away the sandy shore. In the sky above, the large crimson sun glared down on Tehrahey and burned my eyes. Even the quick glance at it left colored spots in my vision. Flames erupted around the sun and seared the sky until it too glowed red.

"Welcome, Kyle of Tehrahey, the Child of Destiny," a familiar voice said. For the first time since I heard it, the voice didn't come from within my head.

A man walked out of the Erima toward me, and I recognized him. He had black hair, brown eyes, and tan skin. The same sun pattern carved in multiple places within Ozmerald was emblazoned on his forehead with red paint. He wore only deer skin pants—the man from the ice.

"Yaluk?" I looked at him, confused. I'd never actually seen him in a dream before, and he never really acknowledged me in his head. "You're here?"

He offered a small smile and placed a hand on his chest. "I am."

I scanned our surroundings. "Where is here?"

"We are in K'aktun, the Fire Cliffs."

I paid attention to the horizon where the world shimmered, but not like a mirage shimmer. This looked more like reality ceasing to exist because I couldn't see it—because this was a dream. "But not really?"

"No. You are still in Ozmerald," he answered, confirming my suspicions. "You made it to the Tablet, and so *The Book of Time* is yours. I trust you will use it well."

I had so many questions. How did I get the Book when I only got the last Tablet? Would I resume being an old man or return to my normal self? What I settled on asking first was, "How are you here? Aren't you dead?"

"I froze to death in Glachalis after hiding the Tablet of the Past. But my spirit and energy, however faint, live on with Tehrahey and the Tablets." He waved his hand in front of himself, and the Tablets materialized in the air, blue, yellow, then red. "Past, Present, and Future. By bringing them together, you made it possible for me to offer guidance when needed. When you combine them, *The Book of Time* will be yours."

If it was so simple, why talk to me? Yaluk had been helping us throughout this journey, but he never once actually talked to me. "Why are you here?"

He moved his hands behind his back. "I have a message for you. Only two outcomes exist for Tehrahey tonight. It all falls to a single choice."

I gulped. "What do I need to do? I'll do anything I can to help."

The Traveler offered a sad smile. "I know you will, but that is why the choice isn't up to you."

I blinked several times. Why tell me this if I couldn't do anything? "Then whose choice is it?"

He ignored my question. "When you return, the Maker will expect you to relinquish the Tablets." Yaluk's face grew serious. "If he tries to take them by force, the final days of Tehrahey will have arrived."

Time stopped. I struggled to inhale a simple breath.

"What is left of my power is fading, and with it, so is Tehrahey. Long before you or your friends entered this world, the Devil himself came into Tehrahey. He convinced Roger that Tehrahey belonged to him. This is why he turned against Amyntor and doomed Tehrahey."

A chill ran down my spine, yet I stood in the Erima, a place where cold did not exist. Our world really was done for.

Walking to the edge of the cliff, Yaluk wore a small frown, as if he hated what would happen to his world but, at the same time, didn't mind. "The levees of this world broke long ago. Ever since then, chaos and destruction have flooded in as its life leaked out."

I stepped closer to him, my hands rubbing one another. "Are you sure we can't do?" As much as I hated this world and many of the adults in it, the idea of leaving caused some guilt. We'd be leaving people to die. With *The Book of Time*, couldn't we fix Tehrahey?

His gaze fell onto me, and he shook his head. "Looking into the future is tricky. Once a person sees something, they can either accept what is to be or try to change it. In the end, the results are usually the same. For centuries, I have known how Tehrahey would die, and now I sense that time is upon us." His eyes grew distant as he studied the horizon and whatever lay beyond the ocean border of Tehrahey. "In less than two months, Tehrahey will experience its final day. The seas will boil," The ocean foamed and bubbled below. "The sand will turn to glass …" The dunes behind us glowed red. "And fire will rain from the heavens." The flames on the sun intensified. They ripped free from the orb and fell to the ground, scorching everything. Yaluk turned to me, a sympathetic look in his eyes. "This will be the end of Tehrahey."

All my life, I had wanted to escape Tehrahey and leave it far behind, but, in all my wildest dreams, it continued to exist. However, that wouldn't be the case. We would leave, and the world would die, and so would everyone in it. Leaving would feel like I was leaving people to their death. That didn't sit right with me.

"Don't do that to yourself," Yaluk said, interrupting my thoughts. "Tehrahey and its people were my responsibility—no one else's. My failures, not yours, caused the coming deaths." He headed into the Erima and crouched before a burning dune. He ran his hand through the remains of the golden sands of the Erima, the monster that consumed his world. He rose to his full height, the last particles of sand falling from his grasp and landing on glowing glass. The strong posture he had approached me with vanished. His shoulders slackened, and his arms hung limply at his sides. He hesitated at the edge of the burning wasteland before he glanced over his shoulder and met my gaze. "I fear this may be our last communication. I implore you to leave Tehrahey. Other worlds out there are worthy of having a Traveler to protect them. You and your friends deserve better than the dead world I left you." He faded from sight.

Alone, I studied my surroundings once more. The ocean no longer existed. Cooling dunes of glass reflected oranges and reds. Fire fell from above. Then the sun exploded, and everything burned.

Chapter 39
-The Expected Betrayal-

2-12.11.12.17.15 T.S.T.
Ozmerald, Entstal
Tehrahey

The blinding light faded, and I found myself kneeling on top of the shrine, the tip of my finger grazing the Tablet of the Future. The wrinkles on my hand faded. The dark color returned to my hair as it shrunk to its normal length. I rose to my feet, expecting my legs to shake, but they were steady. My body returned to its normal thirteen-year-old self. I studied the ruby-red tablet on the pedestal before me. It didn't radiate its own light, like the other two. The only thing that illuminated it was the dim flickering light from the fires burning at the back of the shrine. I remained fixated on the relic, and it filled me with a sense of dread that matched the feeling in my stomach as Yaluk's messages echoed through my mind. Tehrahey would die, and the Maker could not get the Tablets. With hesitation, my fingers grabbed the edges of the Tablet and removed it from its resting place. The darkness around me gave way to flickering firelight.

My climb down the steps was much easier than going up. The hardest part was avoiding the body of my teacher. Stepping off the last step, the final bits of darkness around the altar faded, as did the red tendrils of light in the stone sun carving. All the flames in the room shifted in color from an icy blue to a deeper shade. This color felt softer and warmer. The room might have felt peaceful if not for the dark looks from the adults and the wind blustering outside.

I stood perfectly still, clutching the tablet to my chest, as the Maker glared daggers at me while Cylus looked ready to throw a real one at any moment.

My friends, on the other hand, wore relieved expressions.

Just like the others, this ruby Tablet messed with my emotions. I could feel it playing with my fear and worry. I was afraid of what my future held. Oddly enough, when I studied my reflection in the large gem, I didn't look afraid. My reflection reminded me of Jason but without the exhaustion and anger.

We had the last tablet; problem was, we still had the Maker to deal with. I got the feeling he wouldn't be letting us out of here with any of the Tablets, if he'd let us leave at all. I doubted the threat of Cat or losing the Tablets to the bag would hold him off for much longer. He'd been looking for them for hundreds of years, and we had brought them all together for him. Probably should have left the other two in Glachalis. That would have been the smart thing to do. Being the leader is hard.

The large room grew still. Everyone seemed to sense the impending fight, but wanted to see who would make the first move.

I kept my gaze on Cylus. Instinct told me he would be the first to attack and that a dagger could come my way at any tick. Since I was holding a Tablet, I would be his prime target. They'd deal with Andy and the bag after me. The thought terrified and comforted me all at once.

The Maker spoke first, with a tone that suggested we should listen to him. "Thank you for your help; now hand over the Tablets."

Andy's hand tightened around the bag's strap as I shook my head. "We can't do that."

The Maker's hand stretched toward me, begging for my Tablet. "You've done well, but if you keep going down this path, you will get hurt. I will not leave the fate of Tehrahey to children."

I didn't blink as I held his gaze. "Yaluk said I can't let you take these."

His hand lowered. "Yaluk said what? Who's Yaluk?" His gaze drifted to the shadows where Cat watched with narrowed eyes.

"Yaluk is the first Traveler. He's been helping us, along with our guide."

"And why would he say that? I'm trying to save his world."

"He said if you try to take the Tablets, then Tehrahey's final days have arrived."

The Maker's shoulders stiffened as he straightened up. His mouth formed a thin line as he processed this new information.

I crept closer toward my friends. If he remained distracted long enough, I could pass off the Tablet.

"What?" The Maker's shout bounced around the cavernous room. His harsh gaze landed on me, stopping me in my tracks. "Everything I've done has been to save Tehrahey, and this is the thanks I get? Last chance. Give me those Tablets."

Taking a deep breath, I met Andy's eyes. I could see fear in them, but determination as well. It was time to end this. I rushed forward, holding out the Tablet.

Andy ripped it from my grasp and stuffed it into the bag as she ran for the shadows of the room.

The Maker roared in frustration, and Cylus aimed a knife at Andy.

Jason charged at the bodyguard with a shout that seemed to shake the whole temple. Rage and anguish filled my friend's cry as he rushed forward. The sound jarred something in my brain, and suddenly, I understood why my friend hated the Maker so much. A bald man had killed his father. Cylus was the Maker's bodyguard. He'd killed Jason's father!

The sudden assault stopped the man from throwing his knife as his attention shifted to Jason.

Jason collided with his target, but instead of staggering his opponent, the man lifted Jason and tossed him aside. He skidded down the aisle and collided with a crystal brazier. He lay there, stunned.

At the other end of the room, Andy reached the shadows where she stooped over and scooped Cat into her arms. Then nothing happened.

"Get out of here!" I shouted.

"I'm trying," Cat hissed. He jumped from her arms, the tip of his tail flicking back and forth. He disappeared and reappeared farther away. "I can't Travel anyone but myself inside Ozmerald!"

Great, if we wanted to Travel, we needed to get to the gate.

Before anyone could react, the Maker stepped into a black hole in the aisle and reappeared behind Andy. He staggered forward but managed to latch onto the bag's strap as she tried to dart away.

She shrieked and pulled on the bag, but he held on tight.

True to form, Max acted faster than me. He charged forward. "Let go of her!" He grabbed the strap and swiped up, cutting through the leather with a knife.

With the sudden release of tension, Andy fell backward. She scrambled to her feet as Max pointed his blade at the adult.

"You two really need to pick up after yourselves," he taunted. That's why he had tripped when we entered the temple grounds; he had picked up Cylus's knife!

"You two get out of here!" I shouted while running to help Jason. I trusted Max could handle things there. "Jason!"

Hearing his name seemed to shake some of the dust from him. His legs trembled as he stood, and he used the small pillar to steady himself. Despite his state, his hand shot out to stop me from coming any closer. "This is my fight, Kyle."

I stopped but didn't like the look of this. Jason knew how to fight, but he'd never faced an opponent of this size in the CTS. I also knew the last time these two had faced off, Jason ended up knocked out and on his way to the CTS.

For the first time ever, Cylus spoke. His deep and menacing voice reminded me of Jason's any time he spoke to a younger opponent. "You won't win. I've killed dozens of men."

"I know," Jason said with a groan. He raised his gaze from the floor and stared into his enemy's eyes. "One of them was my father."

Cylus chuckled.

Jason's eyes hardened and without warning, he plunged a hand into the brazier and roared as he scooped out a handful of burning coals. In less than a tick, he flung the objects into the man's face.

Cylus screamed and wiped at his face in a worthless attempt to rid himself of the pain.

Jason used this opening to launch himself forward. He lowered his shorter frame and slammed his shoulder into the man's stomach, knocking the wind out of him.

Cylus toppled onto Jason, who kept pushing despite the fact.

He forced the stunned man backward several steps before letting him fall to the floor.

Andy's voice echoed, "Max, let's go!"

My head whipped around to see Andy reaching for Max who stood stock still, staring at the Maker.

The adult smirked at my friend as the knife in his hand trembled.

Andy grabbed his other hand and dragged him away.

The Maker's shout followed the pair as they ran for the door with Cat at their heels. "You're a coward, just like him!"

"Get out of here!" Jason ordered between punches on Cylus's dazed form.

I raced up to him. "Not without you!"

Jason ignored me and resumed his assault, screaming with each blow he delivered with every limb. He would have stayed there forever if I let him.

I grabbed his shoulder and tried to pull him away, but he resisted; he just kept kicking.

"Jason, we have to go now!"

My friend didn't seem to hear me. He wanted this, had ached for an opportunity at revenge since he had arrived in the CTS, and he finally had his chance. He didn't realize that if he did this, he'd be no better than Cylus, Davy Jones, or Cizin.

"Don't be like them." I grabbed his arm and forced him to look at me.

His breath came in quick, shallow gulps. His fists were clenched at his sides. Blood oozed from the burns on his right hand. Tears spilled down his cheeks.

I understood what this meant to him. He had to convince himself that he was strong, that he could beat the man who had taken everything from him. He didn't need to be afraid anymore.

"You've proven you could do this, now let it go. Come with us." He stared at me for a tick before he tried to resume his task. I caught his arm and held his gaze. "Enough, Jason."

Jason wiped his eyes on his shoulder and nodded once. We ran down the aisle toward our friends.

I chanced a peek over my shoulder to see if the Maker would follow us.

He remained motionless as the gaze from his narrow eyes followed us down the room. The wind howling and the sound of sand scrapping against the stone walls outside grew louder with each tick.

I had a bad feeling this wasn't over.

We reached the entryway, slammed the doors closed behind us and found Andy, Max, and Cat waiting on the other side of the room. Andy chewed her lip as Cat paced in small circles. Meanwhile, Max's blank stare studied the wall separating us from the adults.

"What are you still doing here?" I asked. They were supposed to keep running toward the gate.

"There's a sandstorm outside," Cat grumbled.

Sandstorms never looked like a lot of fun from the CTS, but why would that stop them? "So?"

"If we went out there, we could get lost, and, if we did make it to the gate and left, Cat wouldn't be able to find you two without my charm." Andy was quick to explain the situation, and as usual, she had very good points.

"Fine, we'll go together. We don't have time to waste." I prepared to open the door and could hear the sand blasting against it. I surveyed my friends, ensuring they were ready to go. We didn't want to get separated.

Andy studied me, Jason nursed his hand but met my gaze with determined eyes, and Max kept eyeing the other room.

"Max, you ready?"

My friend tore his gaze off the far wall to blink at me. Something was different in his eyes that hadn't been there earlier, and I didn't like it.

"You okay? What happened back there?"

He resumed staring at the wall. "I don't want to talk about my father."

"No one said anything about him." I recognized the tone in his voice. It was the voice we all used when we were remembering our parents. What had the Maker said to him?

Max scowled, and his voice grew unsteady with each word. "My father worked for the Maker, betrayed him, and so the Maker killed my parents for it." Tears spilled from his eyes as he looked at us. "The Maker's the reason I ended up in the CTS. He sent his guards after my mother and me. He said my father was a coward, and that I am too."

"Max ..." Andy started but didn't know where to go, so I continued for her.

"You're not a coward." I stepped from the door and placed a hand on his shoulder. "You stuck with me when the leopard attacked. I know I can count on you. Don't let the Maker, of all people, convince you that you're not brave."

"What about what he did to my parents?"

"Maybe he's lying," I suggested, but Max didn't seem convinced. "If he's not, we'll make him pay, but when the time's right. Right now, we need to get out of here."

Max shut his eyes tight and took a shaky breath. "He will pay. Let's go."

I opened the door and took my first step outside. The wind raced past, doing its very best to knock me over while throwing sand in my eyes. The weather seemed determined to keep me within the temple.

Without warning, the sandstorm retreated from the courtyard. The Maker stood hunched over in the center, panting heavily. Why was he able to Travel too? Couldn't he have just gotten some of Amyntor's powers, not all of them? The Stars did seem to be on our side. Traveling affected him more than it did Cat. He already looked as bad as Cat did after taking two trips to bring all of us anywhere.

Knowing that made me feel a little better about our chances. I doubted his ability to make another jump tonight, which meant it was our chance to get away. If we could make it to the gate, we stood a chance.

Problem was, he had caused this sandstorm, and it showed no signs of disappearing anytime soon. As if to prove my point, the Maker straightened up and sent a barrage of sand at me.

The force of the blast knocked me off my feet. I landed on my butt back inside the room.

Andy used both hands and Jason used his shoulder to force the door shut.

Cat watched me as I picked myself up and dusted off the sand. "I take it you don't have good news."

"The Maker's out there. He's causing the sandstorm."

"Great." Jason slumped to the floor. "Anything else?"

I shared my observation, hoping Cat could provide some insight. "I think the Traveling is tiring him out."

Cat nodded. "I would assume so. I doubt he's had much practice."

"So, we can wait out the storm?" Andy asked.

"Unlikely. Think of the abilities to Travel and perform magic as two different muscles. He may have tired out the one; the other appears more than capable of sustaining this for a while."

"So, what do we do?"

Cat's blues eyes fixed on the bag on the floor next to her. "We'll need magic to win this."

Andy understood the meaning and opened the bag. She removed the Tablets one by one and passed them to me.

Once they were in my hands, I offered the Tablet of the Past to Jason.

He looked at me like I was crazy.

"Hold it in your burned hand," I instructed, using a tone that told him there would be no arguing this.

He obeyed, and we watched as the burns on his hand faded.

"Once you're better, we can combine the Tablets to make the book, but who gets the powers?" I asked and received varying looks of disbelief, even from Max who hadn't been paying much attention at all these last few ticks. Even Cat gave me a look that suggested I had just asked the dumbest question possible. "What?"

"You," Jason answered, looking up from his hand.

Max nodded while Andy voiced her agreement. "We wouldn't be here without you."

When we had started this journey, I had hoped maybe I'd be the one to become a Traveler, but, as we continued, that hope became smaller and smaller. In my mind, they all did far more important things than me, but while I wasn't the best at anything, I always tried to help. According to Yaluk and Mali, that was all that mattered. It seemed my friends agreed with that sentiment.

Jason handed back the Tablet of the Past, and with unsteady hands I stacked them in the order Yaluk had told me: Past on top, Present in the middle, and Future on the bottom. The Tablets grew warm and glowed brighter until we all had to turn away. When the light faded, a large leather-bound book with a red sun on the cover rested in my hands. *The Book of Time*, we found it! We actually did it.

Nervous energy radiated from my friends and echoed within me as I opened the Book. A flash of light shone from its pages and blinded me for a moment. As I blinked to get rid of the dozens of multi-colored spots, I noticed my name on the first page directly under five other names, one of which was Yaluk.

So far, I didn't feel any different. Flipping through the first few pages, I expected to find some sort of instructions on how to be a Traveler and use any of those powers. They'd be pretty helpful for getting out of this. To my dismay, nothing jumped out as saying, *This is how you be a Traveler*. Most of it looked like Yaluk had written what had happened to him on certain days. It looked way more interesting than anything in the CTS library, but I didn't exactly have time to read it from cover to cover. It was a big book, and no matter how many pages I turned, the end of the book didn't get any closer.

Andy's gaze bounced from me to the pages, which she eyed hungrily.

A thought occurred to me. I closed the Book and handed it to her.

With care, she took it from me and opened it in her lap. There was no flash of light, and her name didn't appear beneath mine.

As she browsed through the pages, I put my hands on the door. "How certain are we that I have powers now?"

Cat studied me for less than a tick. "Only you can say for sure."

I pressed my forehead against the door with a groan. That wasn't what I wanted to hear. Since I was the leader tonight, and maybe a Traveler, that meant I needed to be the one to fight. Hurray. My friends could help, sure, but I didn't want them to. The Maker had magic, and none of us had any experience with dealing with that. If I was a Traveler, only I could face that with any chance of surviving.

I pulled away from the door and turned toward my friends. "I'm going to face the Maker, alone."

The statement earned protests from my friends. Unsurprisingly, they didn't like me wanting to do this alone. I appreciated it but couldn't let them join. I explained my reasoning, and even Andy had to admit I was right. Next was the issue that two of my friends were clearly distracted. Neither Max nor Jason were focused on the fight. Both wanted payback. I didn't need someone else with a desire for revenge in this fight. It had severely hurt Jason. Luckily, we had the Tablet to fix it, but not anymore. I wouldn't chance either of them getting hurt again.

"If a moment presents itself, the two of them are going first," I said, looking at Cat while pointing at Jason and Max.

The pair didn't like this change. They tried to argue, but I shut them down. "Fighting won't fix this mess. If we want to save Tehrahey, we have to avoid that outcome."

The doors creaked and groaned behind us. The wind stopped long enough for the Maker to shout, "You can't hide in there for forever!"

I swallowed the lump in my throat. I didn't want to fight, but there was something to be gained. The angrier the Maker got, the dumber he would become. Keep them angry, keep them stupid. It worked on kids in the CTS, so why not here? I could distract him. "I'll go out and keep him preoccupied. You wait for a moment to run for the gate."

"Kick his butt for me," Max instructed.

"I'll do my best." I opened the door and stepped into the storm. Wind and sand buffeted my face as I marched forward. The flames out here had also changed to a deeper shade of blue. The flickering light filled the courtyard and stopped at the swirling wall of airborne sand surrounding the area. I couldn't see anything beyond the vortex.

To my surprise, Cat followed, matching my steps with his own tiny ones as we walked forward, and I felt grateful. I wasn't completely alone.

The Maker watched the two of us with unblinking eyes. Beads of sweat gathered on his forehead despite the wind. His ornate red robe flapped wildly, as did his hair. He looked so different than the first time I had seen him. He didn't look calm, collected, or in control. He looked like someone who had nothing to lose. I did not want to fight someone like that, but it wasn't my choice to make.

Still, I had to try to avoid this. "Last chance, let us go. We don't have to fight. We can try to save Tehrahey together."

"I made the mistake of trusting people once before. Never again!" With a roar, he sent a wall of sand hurtling toward me.

On instinct, I raised my arms to cover my face and closed my eyes, awaiting the impact. It never came. Instead, the urge to sit and rest hit me as the air grew cold and filled with the familiar sound of grains scratching against a wall. Opening my eyes, I found a wall of thick, blue ice, just like in Glachalis, stretching across the courtyard and shielding me from the attack.

The ground lurched, sending me to my knees. Cracks appeared in the temple walls as the gemstones darkened from blue to match the night sky. The sandstorm returned, closing in around us tighter than before. The blue flames of those trees flickered and sputtered, threatening to extinguish at any moment and leave us unguarded in darkness.

Panic gripped my heart as I looked to Cat. "What's happening?"

For the first time ever, Cat's voice betrayed him as he shouted over the chaos. "The temple is collapsing! It represents Tehrahey's future, and now …"

"Now, there isn't one," I finished. There was a small chance that Tehrahey could be saved, and that kept the temple standing.

Then the Maker decided to fight us, and the magic keeping the temple standing faded. This was the beginning of the end.

Chapter 40
-A Traveler is Found-

2-12.11.12.17.16 T.S.T.
Ozmerald, Entstal
Tehrahey

The sun window above the temple doors shattered, sending shards of glass flying across the courtyard. Chunks of gems and stones left gouges in the stonework where they landed. My thoughts immediately turned to my friends rushing from the structure.

"Cat, get them out of here!" I ordered.

"I can't Travel anyone but myself within the walls of Ozmerald!"

I pointed at the crumbling structure. "Everything is collapsing. I bet the magic is too."

Recognition dawned on his face. He bounded toward my friends, his tail pointing skyward as I rose to my feet.

With that ice wall up and Cat able to Travel again, I didn't have to fight; I just needed to wait for Cat to return.

From behind me, Andy's voice rose over the sound of the wind and crumbling world. "Did you do that?"

I spun on my heel. "What are you still doing here?" Her being here startled me more than seeing one of Ozmerald's towers collapse behind her.

She raised three fingers and counted them off. "One, Cat can only take two people at a time. Two, you stupidly thought I'd leave without you, and three, I'm not leaving you alone!" She said with a growl as her hair ignited, ready to fight me on this.

I didn't get a chance to answer. The wind howled, and the ice wall shattered. Bits of blue rained around us as sand lashed at our faces.

The Maker stood on the other side, his eyes narrowed in my direction. I don't think he saw me as just some dumb kid anymore. "What did you do?" he shouted, stepping past my broken barrier.

"I read the Book. There's no reason to fight anymore." I had to keep trying. I clearly had powers, but I had no idea how to use them. How could I hope to win in a fight against someone who could create sandstorms on command?

My goal had been to calm him down, but the revelation did the opposite; a gust of wind sent Andy and me to the floor.

The Maker strode closer, his hands in his hair and the veins in his neck bulging "Do you have any idea what you've done? You've doomed Tehrahey. Relyt is upon us!"

How could he blame us for his choices? Yaluk had told me the choice to save Tehrahey wasn't mine to make. He kept choosing to fight me. I did everything I could to prevent it. He refused to accept our help. That's what had led to this outcome.

"You caused this!" I said, rising to my feet. With my hand behind my back, I waved for Andy to get away while I circled the Maker. I didn't check to see if she listened. I remained fixated on my opponent.

With a snarl, he marched forward.

I took a deep breath and did the same. If he wanted a fight, I'd give him one. With practiced ease, I struck first. I slapped the Maker across the face.

His head spun.

It felt good to slap an adult, especially the Maker. His reign had let the CTS get as bad as it did. His betrayal of Amyntor had doomed Tehrahey. His orders had led to the deaths of Jason's father and Max's parents. He deserved that hit and so much more.

The strike shocked my opponent. By the time he had recovered, I delivered a blow to his gut. He toppled forward. If this was how well he fought, this would be easy. I'd been worried for nothing.

The Stars decided to put me back in my place. I went to knee his head, but a powerful gust knocked me backward. As I tried to recover, another hit my side. One more hit the back of my legs. I fell on my butt as the Maker straightened up.

"You little sandpile!" he spat, his whole face red with anger, his left cheek redder than the rest.

The wind strengthened, and sand attacked me. I squinted, trying to block the debris and not let him out of my sight. The storm worsened. I covered my eyes, and the Maker cackled. Peering under my arm showed me a terrifying sight.

The same sand lashing at me covered his body. Layer after layer piled on until he stood twice as tall as before. His head disappeared last. Two pieces of black gems stopped where his eyes should've been. The wind retreated to the walls of the vortex around us, but the sand remained in place. The Maker wore it like a massive suit of armor, as if a sand dune had risen from the Erima and came to life just to kill me.

I was in so much trouble.

The Maker's distorted voice still managed to find its way to me, despite everything covering him. "If all of Tehrahey is to die, I'll make sure you are the first."

I scrambled to my feet, trying to figure out how I could deal with something like this, especially with everything blowing into my eyes. I could barely see. Maybe I could control the wind too. I focused as hard as I could on getting the wind around me to stop moving. The gusts didn't seem to care what I thought. All this succeeded in doing was getting me backhanded by a massive fist.

My body ached as I flew and tumbled to a halt near one edge of the remaining bits of melting ice wall. Pain coursed through me. How had I created the ice? I'd really appreciate being able to do anything like that again. I'd settle for creating a ball of fire above my hand if it could save me. Would it be too much to ask for a healing spell?

The Maker lumbered closer, the ground trembling with each step.

Somehow, I forced myself to stand. My body ached in ways I hadn't thought possible. My chest felt bruised, my head spun, sand filled my mouth, and scrapes covered my arms and legs. All in all, the injuries seemed too little for getting punched by a sand dune.

Andy rushed over.

Our furry guide had returned and swayed next to her as his tail drooped. With exhaustion heavy in his voice, he offered us an escape. "I can get you both out of here right now."

Hearing this didn't fill me with relief. Instead, my gut twisted into a knot at the thought of running. I couldn't say when my heart had changed its mind, but it had. The Maker needed to be stopped. He'd hurt too many people and would continue to do so until he had *The Book of Time*. As a new Traveler, I figured that meant it was up to me to stop him once and for all.

"Just get her out of here," I said with a cough. This was my responsibility, not hers.

Stubborn as always, Andy reiterated her earlier promise. "Not leaving you."

Cat didn't make a move, seeming to take her side over mine. Figures. "I have enough left in me for one more trip. That's it. If I leave now, I'm not coming back for a long time."

The Maker loomed in the courtyard. I couldn't see his face, but I imagined that wicked smile he liked to wear hiding beneath the sand. He had us. We should run.

I looked to Andy and realized she would not leave me. We were in this together. We were the only ones with the power to stop him. "We can't run away," I said.

Cat grumbled, but his ice-blue eyes hardened.

"Any chance you could do something like that again?" Andy asked, indicating the remaining bits of ice.

I shook my head. "No idea how I did that."

Without a word, she removed *The Book of Time* from the bag. "Stall him." She pointed toward the giant sand monster as she retreated toward a large pile of rubble. "I'll find you something to stop him!"

I gave her a look of disbelief for wanting me to go up against this man. I might have been planning on doing that but hearing it said out loud sounded ridiculous. The thought that I really needed to learn how to make better plans crossed my mind as I faced the Maker once again. He still hadn't reached us, so either the Maker enjoyed taking his time with me or he couldn't move very fast in his armor.

As he approached, he raised his hand above his head, readying to bring it down on top of me.

Not wanting to get buried in less than a tick, I ran around him and headed for the other side of the battered courtyard.

His fist slammed down moments after I moved, and he barely had time to attempt to swing at me again before I was out of reach once more.

So, he couldn't move fast, even if he wanted to. I could work with that.

Taking a play from Max's fighting style, I darted around the Maker, hurling as many insults as I could come up with. As a child of the CTS, I knew a lot of insults. Rotten Pitahaya, Sun-Baked Old Man, and Fart Breath were just a few of the taunts at my disposal. Each insult angered him more than the last. Coupled with the fact he couldn't hit me, I had him furious in no time. Max would've been proud.

Things became more fun as I put my thumbs in my ears and waggled my fingers at the Maker while sticking out my tongue. I dodged out of the way of his fist, not thinking of where it would land. It crashed into the remains of a tower wall and sent debris hurtling at Andy and Cat.

She shrieked and dodged out of the way.

Our enemy straightened up, focusing on her and the Book clutched to her chest. "What do we have here?"

The blood in my veins froze at the realization that I no longer held his attention. "Sandpile, leave her alone!" I shouted, trying to get him to focus on me again.

It didn't work; he lumbered forward, and I raced ahead of him.

Too focused on protecting Andy, I didn't notice how close I got to the Maker.

He swatted me away.

My brain rattled in my head, and my body burned with new scrapes and cuts as I came skidding to a halt. The older ones continued to pulse and throb. My whole body screamed to give up and close my eyes. Then it would all be over. I heard Andy shout, and a blurry version of her crouched over me.

"You have to get up, Kyle," she begged. "By the Stars, don't you dare give up!"

"You're pushing my limits, kid. I'm not a magic user," Cat hissed from my other side. He placed a paw on my shoulder, and things cleared up.

He removed his paw too soon for my liking; everything still ached, but I found the strength to sit upright with Andy's help. With a grunt, I rose to my feet once more. I could feel my body warning me that if I took another hit, I would not be getting back up. I ignored the warnings. I had to try. I turned to the smartest person I knew. "What have you found?"

Andy picked the Book off the ground and stood beside me. "Elements are very emotional. That's probably why the Maker causes sandstorms when he gets upset." She snapped the book closed and chewed her lip. "My best guess, point your fist, think of fire and every reason why he can't win."

I swallowed and faced the Maker.

He raised a hand and clenched the fist. Trails of sands fell through his fingers. "You should have stayed out of my way." His stomping footsteps shook me to my core, but I didn't back down.

I didn't see how fire would help here, but I trusted my friend and did as she had instructed. I tried to picture fire emerging from my hand, like it had for Yaluk in my dream. I thought of avenging

Amyntor, of ridding Tehrahey of the Maker, of protecting my friends, because, if I didn't, who would? I pointed my right fist at my opponent, and it tingled and froze, yet orange flames shot out with a staggering amount of force. I steadied my arm with my left hand and kept my aim directed at the Maker. Fire lashed at him, but he didn't slow. Meanwhile, I could feel my energy fading. This wasn't easy.

"You stupid … child." The Maker panted. "Like the Erima, my armor can withstand any heat!"

His armor turned crimson, and he slowed.

I remembered the dunes of the Erima turning to glass in my vision and understood Andy's goal. Hope blossomed in me. This could work. If the desert could burn, so would his armor. At that thought, the flames intensified, and the sand glowed brighter.

A howl echoed from the molten armor.

With a breath, I stopped the fire and lowered my hand. My legs shook once then gave out. I would've fallen, if Andy hadn't caught me. Even though fire had just come from them, freezing cold sensations clawed at my knuckles. Just for a tick, I thought there were snowflakes on my skin.

The Maker's howls faded, and so did the storm. The glowing sand ceased moving and cooled to glass in the night air.

Chapter 41
-What Happens When You Fight?-

2-12.11.12.17.16 T.S.T.
Glachalis
Tehrahey

As the glow of the sand faded, we were left in darkness amongst the ruins of Ozmerald. The temple and its towers were gone, along with the burning trees of the courtyard. Nothing remained standing. In the distance, the lights of Entstal shimmered and flickered. I didn't want to stay here another tick or risk seeing exactly what had happened to the Maker in his armor.

When I turned around, I saw Andy already had Cat in her arms. "Let's get out of here," she said.

Without a word, I placed my hand on her shoulder, and the ruins of Tehrahey's future faded. We stood in a dark tunnel. Far away, a warm orange light grew as we were pulled forward. We stopped moving, and the darkness gave way. Pleasant warmth caressed my face as the crackling of the fire graced my ears. The smell of smoke and dust drifted in the calm air. My heart finally slowed, and my nerves melted away.

We were back in Glachalis.

Jason stood by the fire with arms crossed while Max paced nearby. They looked up at our appearance, and their faces relaxed.

Cat jumped from Andy's arms and headed for the bed, stating he needed to rest. As he did that, we sat around the fire while Andy and I recounted what had happened with the Maker.

"So, let me get this straight," Max said once I had finished. "You defeated the Maker by shooting fire from your hand?" He examined his own hands as if they might shoot fire as well.

"Yep," I said, popping the *p*. I studied my hand, still amazed it had managed to do that. The thought that I was a Traveler, capable of performing magic seemed so unreal.

With the story over, my shoulders slumped, and every fresh injury ached. Exhaustion weighed me down, and I could see tonight's adventure catching up with my friends as well. We needed rest. "Let's get some sleep; we'll figure things out in the morning."

There weren't any arguments, and in no time at all, we were soundly asleep. For the first time since we had started this whole adventure, no dreams haunted me. The Maker couldn't bother me anymore. On top of that, I was out of the CTS, and my future didn't seem so grim. I was a Traveler, and my dreams did their best to predict what adventures lay ahead of me.

<^>

We woke up late that morning. The sun had almost reached its halfway point as we left our home and headed down the snow-covered street to Alvis and Helina's. Under the cover of clouds, the snow used to look dark and mysterious. Today, with the great red sun glaring upon it, the snow sparkled. The blinding beauty of the white blanket covering the mountains and town hurt to look at but was impossible to ignore. I'd never seen anything like it. All that open space and nothing out there to make a sound other than a faint breeze and the dripping of water. It felt like the world, or at least Glachalis, was at peace. I found it hard to believe this would all be gone in a few months.

We kicked the snow off our boots before entering our destination. As we descended the stairs, Helina rushed over and embraced us one by one while scolding us for being late.

Alvis looked up from the meal on the grill. "I told you they were fine."

As he studied us, I became aware of how I must look. All kinds of new markings covered my body. They'd heal with time, but they probably looked pretty bad. Jason too had a few bruises on his face and knuckles from his fight with Cylus.

"Aye, now. You two weren't fightin', were you?" He pointed between Jason and me.

The two of us shared a look. "No," we lied in unison. How could they have possibly known we had left last night?

Alvis offered us a hard stare as Helina fussed over our injuries. "Let me take a look at those."

Alvis rose from his chair. "You two are friends; you can't be gettin' into fist fights with one another."

It dawned on me what he meant. They didn't know we had left; they just thought Jason and I had fought each other. We had been bickering a lot the last few days. I almost denied that we had fought then realized where that would lead. By the way the two were fussing over us, I knew they'd want an explanation of some kind. I trusted Alvis and Helina, but I didn't feel ready to tell them I had become a Traveler overnight. How could I explain it to them when I could barely explain it to myself? I'd tell them eventually, when I had a better grasp on being a Traveler.

"We didn't mean to get into a fight. We've just been annoying each other so much lately." For the time being, I'd go with what they assumed. Getting punished for fighting wouldn't be fun, but it would be easier than trying to explain recent events.

"Everyone disagrees from time to time, but that doesn't mean you should resort to fighting with one another," Helina scolded.

Jason's face scrunched in a frown. He looked about ready to argue, and I wagged my finger from where it rested by my hip. I prayed to the Stars he'd see the subtle gesture.

For once in his life, he did and sighed. "We're sorry. Things got a little out of hand last night." He wasn't lying about that. Last night did not go exactly as we had expected. He braced for our punishment and ensured to look appropriately apologetic.

"I promise it won't happen again," I added, preparing for whatever might come next.

"I'm very disappointed in you two." Helina frowned as she finished examining us and shared a look with Alvis. After a moment, she placed her hands on her hips and fixed us with a hard stare. "It better not happen again."

The order in her words was crystal clear, and we both nodded in unison.

"Now, help me finish with lunch while to the two well-behaved children get to relax. And I'm sure Alvis will find some extra work for the two of you later."

My shoulders slumped as she led us away. I could see on Jason's face he didn't like the results of our lie very much, but it had turned out better than we'd expected. For the first time in my life, getting into a fight didn't result in a beating.

Andy and Max relished their well-behaved status as they watched us work. "I tried to stop them," Andy stated with disapproval dripping from her voice but a smirk on her face, "but they never listen to me." She crossed her arms for added affect.

Max swooped in beside her and draped an arm over her shoulders with a smirk of his own. "Yeah, they never listen to us."

Andy stiffened at the contact, and Max seemed to snap back to reality and quickly put some distance between them. That was probably the most physical contact they'd ever had. The two of them tried to play it off like it had never happened, but one look at Jason told me that we wouldn't let them forget it any time soon.

Chapter 42
-Learning to Fly-

2-12.11.12.17.16 T.S.T.
Glachalis
Tehrahey

My friends and I practically inhaled our lunch while Alvis and Helina chided us for missing breakfast. If they only knew how hungry we were from taking down a horrible tyrant.

Afterward, Alvis did find some work for Jason and me to do. We spent all afternoon stacking and restacking wood. By the time we came in for dinner, we were ready to pass out. Once we finished eating, we said our goodbyes to Alvis and Helina, and the four of us headed to our house with the promise of not fighting again. While Max and Andy bounded through the snow, laughing and full of energy, Jason and I trudged. This only caused our friends to giggle more.

After a tick, their laughter stopped. That should have been our warning. The silence of the evening shattered when a snowball shot through the air and nailed Jason in the face. It exploded in a shower of frozen crystals, and he staggered backward from the unprovoked attack. Before I fully understood what had happened, a snowball collided with my chest.

"Nice shot!" Max commented as Andy jumped for joy.

The two celebrated their victory as Jason wiped away the snow on his face. The exhaustion in his eyes disappeared. He would not take this assault lying down. We knew what we had to do. My ally let out a war cry as he charged our younger enemies. The roar dissolved into laughter as the two scattered to escape him.

The chaos provided me with the perfect opportunity to stockpile an arsenal of snowballs. Each one formed faster than the last. In no time, I had an ample supply of ammo and unleashed it at Andy. My first shot hit her.

She squealed and ducked behind a house, narrowly avoiding the second.

Meanwhile, Jason struggled to hunt down Max, who barely sank into the snow as he darted around.

With Andy hiding, I launched a shot at Max's head. The projectile hit its mark and stunned my enemy long enough for Jason to tackle him. The two disappeared within the white fluff.

Andy returned for revenge, a snowball in each hand.

I dodged the first one and fired back. Snow splashed across my face as her second shot landed. A tick later, the same happened to her. We burst into laughter as we threw snowballs back and forth.

Eventually, Jason and Max entered the fray, which resulted in Andy and me forming an unspoken truce to fight against them.

The war lasted for several ticks. At some point, Alvis and Helina came to see what all the noise was about. Once they realized we were safe, they flung snowballs too. Throughout the battle, no alliances were sacred. People swapped sides at will, all in the effort of landing an easy hit on someone.

It was some of the best fun I'd ever had.

The fighting ended when we were all thoroughly drenched in snow and gasping. As we stood around, catching our breath, I couldn't think of a time when I had felt more relaxed. There were no parental guardians who could ruin it. The adults who were here had actually joined us.

As our fits of laughter waned, the cold finally hit, and we rushed to our homes, grateful for the warmth and shelter they provided. I sighed with relief while shedding my fur outfit and standing beside the fire. The warmth washed over me and seeped into my body, chasing away the cold.

Jason sat on the ground and with each tick, he leaned farther backward until he laid down. His eyes closed, and a satisfied smile resided on his face, something I couldn't remember ever seeing before.

Max tossed his coat onto the back of a chair and sat on the edge of the bed, watching the flames dance in the center of the room.

Andy stood beside me, and we communicated by bumping our shoulders from time to time, letting the other know we were still there.

Today had turned out so different than yesterday, and especially from how things had been two weeks ago. We were free of the CTS. None of us were going back. I'd never have to see Ms. Hess again or deal with her rock. Even the Maker couldn't hurt us anymore. He was trapped in glass surrounded by the collapsed ruins of Ozmerald. I wished things could have ended differently, but he didn't leave any choice. His actions had led to that outcome. He had started the fight, while I had tried to prevent it.

A yawn broke the silence of the room as Cat rose from the bed and arched his back. What was he still doing here? I figured he'd have left, since he claimed to hate Tehrahey so much. Before I could ask, he spoke up in an extra grumpy voice. "Where have you been?"

"We were with Alvis and Helina," I explained, hoping he wouldn't ruin the peacefulness that had settled over us.

He left the bed, strode across the room and jumped onto the stone ring of the fireplace. "Well, we need to leave." His statement woke everyone up.

"What do you mean we need to leave?" Andy asked.

"Yeah, I thought we were done," Max commented.

"You misunderstand; you three won't be going anywhere for now." He used his tail to point at each of my friends in turn. "Kyle and I need to head back to Time's Keep to begin his training."

I liked the idea of learning to use my new powers. I didn't want to hurt my friends like the Maker had, but I didn't want to go alone. "Why can't they come?"

"They wouldn't want to." Before I could argue that he didn't know for sure without asking them, he continued. "It's a castle trapped in permanent darkness. On top of that, they would have nothing to do there. There is more for them here in Glachalis."

I fixed him with a hard stare, my arms over my chest. "On a dying world?" My friends mirrored my concern over this plan. We were supposed to be in this together.

Cat rolled his eyes. "They'll be on your home world; they'll be fine." How typical of him, providing an answer to a problem that made no sense whatsoever.

"Why does that matter?" I asked. Yaluk had mentioned something about home worlds when speaking with Mali, but I didn't know why they were so important.

"Time flows differently across dimensions," Cat explained, "moves faster in some than others. When a Traveler leaves their home dimension, time halts until they return. They won't even know you're gone."

So that was why Yaluk never left for help. Tehrahey wasn't his home. He was afraid time would move too quickly while he was away. If he did leave, he could return and find everything he cared about had changed. I, on the other hand, was born on Tehrahey and grew up in the CTS. As much as I hated this world, it was my home. We could use that to our advantage. I could go learn to be a Traveler and find a new place for us to live before Relyt arrived. This could work, but the thought of leaving my friends still terrified me.

Cat seemed to sense all our unease. "Andy still has her charm. I can be here whenever they need me."

Knowing Cat could be here in a moment's notice helped, and I knew I wouldn't be far behind him. I would never leave my friends when they needed me, which is why I had to be sure about this plan. If there was any doubt I could come to their rescue, then I couldn't leave. "Are you sure about this?"

Cat answered in his usual, no-nonsense tone. "Yes." I was one tick away from agreeing to go with him, but then he added, "But that is no guarantee."

I scanned the room and each of my friends for any advice they might give. I don't know what I expected from them, but I valued their input. They were my family— not the one I had been born into but the one I made for myself. My friends chose to stay by my side while my mother had given me up. Maybe Helina was right that my mother had a good reason for what she did, but I still couldn't forgive her, and that was fine by me. I didn't need her.

Max rose from the bed and watched me with uncertainty. When our eyes met, he offered a half smile and a shrug.

Jason sat on the floor with his legs bent and his arms resting on his knees. He stared at the wall for a long time before giving me a simple nod.

Andy had become motionless and stared into the flickering flames. I bumped my shoulder against hers, and she managed to pull her gaze from the fire. Her lips were pressed together in a thin line, and her nose scrunched as she stared at me.

It looked like no one liked this plan, but we all silently agreed it was the best one. With Amyntor's help, I'd learn how to use my new powers and scout out a new home for us. As this realization settled over the room, no one dared say anything. Instead, we remained in silence, trying to hold onto the joy we had felt moments ago.

Jason acted first. He rose to his feet and approached me. "Don't forget us," he said, his voice a little shakier than normal.

Max joined us as well with a teasing grin. "Yeah, and don't let all that power go to your head." He poked my forehead for good measure.

I shared an awkward hug with each of them and did my best not to cry. By the Stars, fighting back tears from Ms. Hess's punishments proved to be easier than this. "I won't. I'll find us a new home and come get you as soon as I can. Goodbye, guys."

They stepped away, leaving only Andy. She stood facing me, but quietly regarded the flames to her left, not meeting my gaze for a tick. The firelight flickered across her emerald-eyes and shimmered on the forming tears. "Stay out of trouble," she said, finally acknowledging me.

I forced a grin. "You know I can't do that without you." A quiet moment followed, and I struggled to break it, but I had to. "Thank you, for sticking with me. I couldn't have beaten the Maker without you."

"Yes, and no," Andy said with a sad smile. "Give yourself some credit. You would've figured something out eventually. I just helped you avoid taking more hits. You'll do fine on your own."

I opened my mouth to argue, and she stopped me. "I'm always right." She stepped forward and hugged me. Unlike the embraces with Jason and Max, which had been light and quick, she squeezed tightly. Her hug made leaving hurt less. "Be safe," she said into my ear. "And come back soon, okay?"

"I will, I promise." We gave each other a final squeeze before parting.

Andy wiped her eyes. I did the same.

They'd be safe and happy here. They had each other, as well as Alvis and Helina. Stars willing, they wouldn't even notice I had left. They would be fine.

Meanwhile, a whole new adventure lay ahead of me, one I had to take on my own, at least for the time being. What would it be like to be a Traveler? What worlds would I see? What would it be like to perform magic as easily as breathing? There was only one way to find out. With a racing heart, I looked down at Cat. This felt like leaving the CTS for the first time but more exhilarating. Then, I'd been afraid of what the future held. I didn't know if I could face it. I knew better now; I could face the unknown and survive.

Countering all the energy I felt building within me, my guide wore a calm look in his ice-blue eyes as he stood. "The universe is waiting."

I picked him up, and the smell of the fire faded, the warmth of the room disappeared, the stones underfoot drifted away, and the world around me turned to black. The last thing I saw of Tehrahey was my friends waving goodbye.

"I'll come back," I promised the darkness. I had no idea what lay before me or whether I was ready, but whatever the future held, I'd give it my very best. That was what mattered most.

End of Book 1
-Discover Your Destiny-

Tehraheyian Reference Guide

Akna (ahk-naw) - An ancient city built on the birthplace of Tehrahey lost to the Erima desert for thousands of years. Only a handful of people know where the ruins are located.

Alvis (al-vis) - A large man with a dark hair and a beard living in Glachalis, married to Helina.

Amyntor (ay-mean-tore) - The second Traveler of Tehraheyian legend, credited with bringing a lot of modern ideas to the world.

Ananke (anna-kay) - The Greek Goddess of Fate who Amyntor often prays to in the form of written letters that are then burned.

Archipotamou (arch-ee-poe-ta-mou) - The closest city to Glachalis, built along the upper banks of the Yperoko Fiorda south of the Glachalian mountain range.

Baktun (bawk-toon) - A Tehraheyian unit for measuring time and is the fifth number from the right in their calendar system. One baktun represents twenty katun, or one hundred and forty-four thousand days. (0-1.0.0.0.0) **See Also: Tehraheyian Calendar.**

Berumada Pit (bear-oo-maw-daw pit) - A great hole in the Erima along its southern edge. Seems to be a connecting point between Tehrahey and Cat's home dimension.

Black Guards - The Maker's personal guards who protect him and anything else important to him.

By the Stars - A Tehraheyian exclamation similar to "Oh my God."

Cabrakan Spine (ka-bra-can) - A mountain range near the eastern side of Tehrahey that divides the two sides and protects the east from the sands of the Erima.

The Child Teaching System (CTS) - A Tehraheyian attempt at creating a school system influenced by Amyntor's teachings but has since been corrupted.

Ciyt (sigh-eat) - An island and city on the southeastern coast of Tehrahey that serves as a major trade hub in the region around the Bakha Bay.

Cizin (sih-zin) - The King of Tehrahey, though he only has control of the eastern side of the continent. Rules from Metnal.

Cylus (sigh-luss) - A tall, intimidating man with a bald head who serves as the Maker's head guard.

Eden (ee-den) - A city in a small mountain range in the southwest region of Tehrahey. Used to be an island before the oceans receded. Supplies most of the food in Entstal.

Entstal (ent-stall) - The western capital of Tehrahey, created by the first Maker in honor of Roger Tal and Samuel Ents. The city cannot support itself due to its location halfway up the western coastline and must import goods and water from Eden in the south and Vamvakipolis in the north.

Erima (air-ih-maw) - A great sand dune desert that spans most of the Tehraheyian continent, stopping only at the Glachalian and Cabrakan Spine mountain ranges. Nothing lives in this desert.

Glachalis (gluh-chall-liss) - The frozen city on Tehrahey's northwestern peninsula. Used to be home to dozens of people and even served as one of Amyntor's homes while on Tehrahey but is now largely abandoned due to the never-ending cold.

Hand cycle - The Tehraheyian term for an hour.

Ha'bih (haw-bih) - The raised stone road that used to follow the southern coastline from Vamvakipolis in the west to Metnal in the east. It is now abandoned to the Erima but is still intact.

Helina (hell-in-a) - A tall woman with dark hair living in Glachalis, married to Alvis.

Hess (hess) - A tall, thin woman with brown hair and gray eyes who is the Omega Guardian in the CTS. She loves to make kids cry.

In a gust - A Tehraheyian saying that means in a hurry or in a flash.

Janu (jaw-new) - A parental guardian in the CTS.

K'aktun (kack-toon) - The cliffs along a large section of the southern coast of Tehrahey. Sometimes referred to as the Fire Cliffs for the red glow that sailors have often seen in the cliff face.

Kanta (cawn-taw) - The fifth month of the year, represented by the number four on the calendar. (0-0.0.0.**4**.0) **See Also: Tehraheyian Calendar.**

Kass (cass) - A parental guardian in the CTS.

Katun (caw-toon) - A Tehraheyian unit for measuring time and is the fourth number from the right in their calendar system. One katun represents twenty years, or seven thousand and two hundred days. (0-0.0.1.0.0) **See Also: Tehraheyian Calendar.**

Kin Naltz'am (kin nalltz-am) - The Maker's palace in Entstal. It is a sandstone structure shaped like a crescent moon around a manmade pond with a large tower at the center arch of the crescent. The whole area is gated to keep people out and serves as a home for the Maker and his Black Guards.

Kirsten (keer-sten) - The daughter of Alvis and Helina.

K'ubih (coo-bih) - An old, abandoned road that used to branch from the Ha'bih to head north to Akna. Is largely lost to the Erima.

Lahna (law-naw) - A young woman with black hair and gold-colored eyes who has been working as a teacher in the CTS for seven years. Has a soft spot for Andy and her friends.

Lejos Noble (lay-hoas no-blay) - An eastern Tehrahey city built at the base of the Cabrakan Spine on the southern edge of Tehrahey. Serves as the last city before the Erima that Cizin still controls.

Long Count - This is the left most number in the Tehraheyian calendar. One long count represents fourteen baktun, or two million and sixteen thousand days. (1-0.0.0.0.0) **See Also: Tehraheyian Calendar.**

The Maker - The self-titled ruler of Tehrahey, though he only has control of the western side of Tehrahey. Has very limited control outside Entstal. The title has supposedly been passed down a familial line for centuries, though there has never been a queen of any sort.

Mali (mall-ee) - Friend and wife to Yaluk. She helped him keep Tehrahey going for as long as they could. Her body was buried in Yaluk's tomb at Akna.

May the Stars watch over you - A Tehraheyian blessing of fortune.

Megalo Dromos (meg-ah-low droe-mose) - A large stone road Amyntor built to connect Eden with Vamvakipolis.

Melinoe (mell-ee-no) - Married to Cizin and is queen of East Tehrahey.

Metnal (met-nawl) - The eastern Tehrahey capital and the largest city in the world.

Omega Guardian - The head parental guardian in the CTS. Ms. Hess currently holds the title.

Ozmerald (oz-mare-awld) - A large temple the first Traveler of Tehrahey built near where Entstal would one day be founded. The structure is adorned with crystals and the grounds morph to reflect the future of Tehrahey. The gates only open at night with moonlight. The temple itself will alter its appearance in relation to what Traveler first arrived on the grounds that night.

Parental Guardian - An adult working in the CTS who is meant to impose order amongst the students and sometimes the staff as well.

Pile of sand - A Tehraheyian insult stating someone is as worthless as sand.

Pray to the Stars - A Tehraheyian saying, often used to ask the Stars for help in a given situation.

Records class - The CTS equivalent of a history class.

Relyt (rell-ight) - A Tehraheyian belief that the world will burn in fire to be reborn again from the ashes.

Rodos (row-dose) - The largest village on the Notos-Boreas Islands. Is home to a seafaring people who largely avoid interaction with the rest of Tehrahey.

Stars - Shortly after the stars faded away, they gained a godlike status amongst Tehraheyians and were often evoked in sayings such as "by the Stars," or "may the Stars watch over you." Over the years, the belief that the Stars would return to save Tehrahey has waned away, though the sayings still remain fairly common.

Stavros (stav-rows) - A large, burly man who is the head cook within the CTS.

Tablet Hunters Prep - A CTS class meant to prepare students for searching for the tablets by teaching them very basic survival skills. This is only taught to students in their final Year of Teaching.

Taraxippus (tah-racks-ih-pus) - A large, black horse with red eyes belonging to Queen Melinoe.

Tehrahey (teh-ra-hey) - The world the Traveler Yaluk created as a haven for his people. Used to be covered in lush jungle until his disappearance, at which point it decayed and desertified.

Tehraheyian (teh-ra-hey-ian) - A person or thing from the world of Tehrahey.

Tehraheyian Calendar - The six numbers (1-2.3.4.5.6) represent different aspects of time keeping similar to the number used on Earth calendars (01-02-0003). The right most number on the Tehraheyian calendar counts the days, from 0 - 19, the next number over counts the months, 0 - 17, next is the years, 0 - 19, after that is the katun, 0 - 19, followed by the baktun, 0 - 13. The last number, separated by a hyphen, represents the long count. The date can be read out as follows: month, day baktun.katun.year of the (long count) count.

Tick - The smallest Tehraheyian unit of time. Stands for both seconds and minutes, so context is important.

Time's Keep - A small, dark stone castle built on an island on an infinitely small sea in a small, dark dimension. This is the current home of Amyntor, Luna, and Cat.

Traveler - The official title of a person or being who can teleport from place to place, or even to other worlds. They often have other magical and amazing abilities, including magic, weapons mastery, elemental control, stealth, and strategy.

Vamvakipolis (vahm-vaw-key-poll-iss) - A city built on the mouth of the Yperoko Fiorda and is known for growing many of the cotton used for clothing in Entstal.

Waklahun (wack-law-hoon) - The seventeenth month of the year, represented by the number sixteen on the calendar. (0-0.0.0.**16**.0) **See Also: Tehraheyian Calendar.**

Xic-Patan (zeek-pah-tan) - A long-forgotten city along the Ha'bih that was once on the southern coast but has since become landlocked within the Erima.

Yaluk (yaw-luke) - The first Traveler of Tehraheyian legend who is credited with the creation of Tehrahey.

Year of Teaching (YoT) - The CTS equivalent of grade levels. The Years of Teaching go from First Year of Teaching at age five to Thirteenth Year of Teaching at age seventeen. The two years before that are referred to simply First and Second Year, age three and four respectively, since there is practically no teaching at those ages.

The Traveler

The Lost Heart

Preview:

The scent of this new world hit me first. Tehrahey, the Erima, and the CTS all smelled dry and dirty. Earth didn't smell dirty. It smelled like water but different from how the ocean smelled. It was cooler, cleaner, and less salty.

I liked it.

This place proved to be darker than Time's Keep, which said something; the castle was stuck in a small dimension where night reigned permanently. Once my eyes adjusted, I found myself surrounded by trees and plants I'd never seen, with no living thing in sight.

Something creaked in the distance.

"Hello?" I called. Did I say it right? English was my second language. As a Traveler, I could learn languages quickly, but speaking anything other than Tehraheyian felt weird.

No one answered.

This was my first trip to Earth and the first time I Traveled anywhere outside of Time's Keep without Cat's help. I could return to the castle once I felt strong enough. Amyntor warned me I might feel a bit tired after the trip, which was an understatement. I felt like I'd just spent a night hiking across the Erima.

The plants here were soaked with water, the ground was muddy beneath my feet, and clouds covered the skies. Water and life filled this place. I'd been here maybe a tick, and I already agreed with Amyntor. His world had more promise than mine.

Colors burst across the world as energy streaked through the heavens. Not even a tick later, the world erupted with a loud explosion. I dropped to my knees and covered my ears as the sky continued to roar. Water fell from the clouds to drench the forest. I ran for shelter under a tree, but it offered little protection from the raging storm. What was that explosion?

The howling wind shook the trees, sending droplets crashing over me. It collected in pools before running off down the hill. In no time at all, the cold soaked through my gray uniform that had never been meant for weather like this. A part of me wanted to leave, to return to the castle and dry off, but I didn't feel up to it yet. I still felt like I'd rolled down a massive sand dune.

Even if I did feel up to it, I didn't want to leave. I'd never seen a storm before. Every few ticks, the world lit up for just a second; the source came from the clouds themselves. Ticks after the world returned to darkness, there would be an explosion, sometimes loud enough to shake the ground; sometimes, it was nothing more than a faint grumble. Once I was used to it, I found it spectacular. I couldn't take my eyes off the sky.

When I finally looked away, my breath caught in my throat. I swore something ran through the bushes, rustling leaves and squelching through the mud.

About the Author

Tyler started writing ten years ago as a way of focusing his daydreaming in high school. Since then, he has worked hard to get his ideas down on paper. When he isn't writing, he spends his time at his Arizona home building, gaming, and trying to appease his spoiled cats.

If you liked the story, please leave a review on Amazon and Goodreads! I'll give you a high five if you do!